The Journey
of Anders Sparrman

PER WÄSTBERG

The Journey
of Anders Sparrman

TRANSLATED FROM THE SWEDISH
BY TOM GEDDES

GRANTA

Granta Publications, 12 Addison Avenue, London W11 4QR

First published in Great Britain by Granta Books 2010

Originally published in Swedish as *Anders Sparrmans resa: en biografisk roman*
by Wahlström & Widstrand in 2008.

The publication of this book was supported by a grant from the
Swedish Arts Council.

A CIP catalogue record for this book is available from the British Library.

1 3 5 7 9 10 8 6 4 2

ISBN 978 1 84708 130 8

Typeset by M Rules
Printed and bound in Great Britain by
MPG Books Ltd, Bodmin, Cornwall

The Journey
of Anders Sparrman

A Note on the Novel

Dialogue excepted, all other text within quotation marks is taken from Anders Sparrman's own writings, with some modernization. In this English translation Sparrman's journal extracts are based on the 1786 and 2007 English versions mentioned below.

With the exception of one or two minor figures in the chapter on adolescence, the characters in this novel are all inspired by real persons and appear under their own names, though little is known about many of them.

No book on Sparrman himself exists, but there are some informative pages in the writings of the Swedish historians Sten Lindroth, Ronny Ambjörnsson, Sverker Sörlin and Rolf E. DuRietz. The works, letters and diaries of his friend George Forster are still being published (20 volumes, Berlin, 1958–). Four biographies have been published in East Germany, the best of which is by Klaus Harpprecht, 1987.

Anders Sparrman's Journal was published in English translation in 2007 by the IK Foundation & Company, London & Whitby. It comprises the 1786 English translation of *A Voyage to the Cape of Good Hope, Towards the Antarctic Polar Circle, and Round the World*, and a new English edition of *A Voyage around the World* translated by Eivor Cormack.

The epigraph on p. ix is taken from Johann Wolfgang von

Goethe's *Elective Affinities*, translated by R. J. Hollingdale (Penguin, 1971).

In the extract on pp.127–8 from *The Journals of Captain Cook*, selected and edited by Philip Edwards (Penguin, 1999) some punctuation and capitalization has been changed, but the original spelling retained.

The extracts from Anders Sparrman's letters on pp.205–11 are taken from volume 18: *Briefe an Forster* (1982) of the above-mentioned edition of *Georg Forsters Werke* (with minor modifications of spelling, punctuation and capitalization).

Swedish Place Names

In this translation, some place names have been rendered into English (e.g. King's Meadow), but most are left in their Swedish form, not least to aid identification on the ground; although for the sake of clarity they are occasionally expanded with a tautological generic term (e.g. the island of Resarön; Kungsträdgården Park). The main generic elements, which may occur in the indefinite or definite (in parenthesis) form are as follows: *gata(n)* street; *torg(et)* square; *bro(n)* bridge or quay; *brink(en)* hill, bank; *berg(et)* hill; *holm(en)* island; *sjö(n)* lake; *fjärd(en)* inlet; *ö(n)* island; *älv(en)* river; *gränd* alley (here sometimes translated as such).

You wanted first of all to show me your travel journals in correct sequence and in so doing to reduce to order all the papers that belong with them, and with my support and assistance to assemble out of these invaluable but muddled leaves and notebooks a whole which we and others might enjoy.

J. W. Goethe, *Elective Affinities* (1809)

Sound the depths, to ascertain where you are; observe the visible signs in the atmosphere, to ascertain what weather awaits you. But don't dive to the bottom; you will never reach it. Don't rise in an airship to the ether, that uttermost limit of the Earth; you will never reach it. Everything below is cold and dead; everything above is cold and dead. The warmth of life is only to be found on the surface of the Earth.

Adolph Törneros, *Letters* (1825)

Contents

III

POSTSCRIPT

I

Encyclopaedia Entry

Sparrman, Anders (27.2.1748–9.8.1820) physician, scientist, explorer. An apostle of the botanist Carolus Linnaeus, S. sailed as ship's doctor to the East Indies and China 1765–7. In his 1768 dissertation *Iter in Chinam* (*Voyage to China*) he described the butterflies he collected on the journey. He joined Captain James Cook's second expedition as a naturalist, published *A Voyage to the Cape of Good Hope, Towards the Antarctic Polar Circle and Round the World: But Chiefly into the Country of the Hottentots and Caffres, from the Year 1772 to 1776* (I, 1783; II:I, 1802; II:2, 1818). Member of the Swedish Academy of Sciences and curator of its Cabinet of Natural History 1777–98 (he collected a considerable proportion of its items himself). Approximately 1,300 botanical specimens from his travels are in Swedish museums.

In the 1780s and 90s S.'s interest turned to the slavery question, which had preoccupied him ever since his voyage to the Cape. In 1787 he was able to make a study *in situ* on an expedition to West Africa with the like-minded C. B. Wadström and C. A. Arrhenius, an officer and chemist. Assistant navy-surgeon in Karlskrona 1789 and succeeded Peter Johan Bergius in 1790 to the chair of Natural History and Pharmacy at the Collegium Medicum in Uppsala, where he became an assessor, or advisory member, in 1803. Physician to the poor in the Stockholm parish of Klara from 1814. This post has been regarded as evidence of his inability to establish a remunerative ancillary practice or, unlike his colleagues, to amass enough capital to live on. An alternative explanation consistent with his character could be that he was drawn to Emanuel Swedenborg, without being an orthodox Christian, wished to do good and viewed his own circumstances with some indifference. In his expeditionary accounts S. comes across to the reader as an agreeable and broadminded man. He died in poverty.

Sparrmannia is a substantial bush of the linden family, called house lime. *Sparrmannia africana* has large flowers with white petals and tightly clustered stamens, which, when gently blown on, open like the tentacles of a sea anemone.

Family Background

Anders Sparrman's paternal great-great-grandfather was Erik Rungius, rector of Sparrsätra, near the town of Enköping, who married Ingeborg Sparrman, a parson's daughter. Their children called themselves Sparrman, and the four daughters all married clergymen. Rungius would not allow those who failed to pay their dues to attend church.

In 1643 Nils, the rector's son (later to become a district judge), was denounced by his wife Sara Larsdotter for having accused her of spreading rumours that he was a thief. She was clapped in irons and hung against a wall for six hours. The rector beat her with a stick. His wife threatened to whip her naked body with a switch of thorns, and their son Nils went so far as to say that she ought to have her nose and ears cut off. The official record of the case has been lost.

His great-grandfather was Johan Sparrman (1624–90), dean of Tuna in Södermanland. He was tutor to Gustaf Adolf, son of the Swedish Chancellor, Magnus Gabriel De la Gardie, became court chaplain in Riga and succeeded his father-in-law as rector of Tuna, where he inscribed on the first page of the minute book, 'Cursed be he who loseth this book.' He commented on quarrelsome individuals in the parish and wrote the following remark on the wealthy farmer Pehr Ericsson: 'Seldom doth he come to church, and when he doth so, he falleth asleep. He is a slanderer, and disrupter of peace and order in the parish. While others do sing, he standeth as wooden as a statue, not even moving his lips. His God is his belly, which he filleth with spirits, tobacco and beer.'

Anders' grandfather Nils Sparrman (1668–1722) was rector of Ängsö on Lake Mälaren and later in Biskopskulla, west of Uppsala. The church annals record that he 'suffered the misfortune of having his right hand removed with a saw, whereupon negligence led to gangrene. But he did live a further eight years and used his left hand to write with equal proficiency. His beasts and his grain were confiscated in 1715 for arrears of tax.'

Anders' father Eric Sparrman (1706–65) took his MA at Uppsala University and was ordained in 1734, but his probationary sermon in Solna, Stockholm, 'did not please their Majesties, who advised the Cons. Collega in Uppsala accordingly by letter in 1735'. He succeeded his father-in-law Anders Högbom as rector at Lena, north of Uppsala, in 1737, and was promoted to dean at Lena in 1756 for the years during which Dean Kihlmark was held in custody. Eric was then rector of Tensta until his death in 1765. In 1736 he married Brita Högbom (1711–94), the only surviving daughter of Anders Högbom, 'an earnest, erudite and diligent man', who 'caused the church and rectory wall to be beautifully repaired'.

Eric and Brita Sparrman had eleven children. Six of them reached adulthood: Nils (1738–1809), rural dean in Skånela-Norr-sunda, between Uppsala and Stockholm; Christina (1739–92), unmarried in Stockholm; Catharina (1741–96), unmarried in Skånela; Anna Magdalena (1746–93), married Jonas Ekengren, organ-builder and chair manufacturer in Stockholm (she died a month after her husband); Anders (1748–1820), named after his brother, who died on his third birthday; Charlotta Gustava (1753–1808), unmarried in Skånela, where, like her older sister, she lived with Nils. Of the latter's children one became a clergy-man, one the town medical officer in Gävle, and his daughter Hedvig Eleonora married Axel Fahlcrantz, ornamental mason in Stockholm.

Childhood Home

Lena rectory, where Anders Sparrman spent his early years, was built in 1728 using thirteen layers of logs on stone foundations, with a roof of bark and turf, and two chimneys. A living room in the centre, two bedrooms on the east side and a kitchen on the west, plus a porch. Two attic rooms. A living-room door with a lock and key; two windows of twenty panes each; a stove and damper. The bedroom off the living room was plastered and whitewashed. The other bedroom had access from the hall. The kitchen had three windows, a stove and a bread-oven with uprights and a base-plate from the Vattholma Ironworks. The maid's room was off the kitchen and had a brick-built tiled stove.

There was a wash-house with a turf roof; a fireplace with a built-in copper boiler; a stable-door with mortise lock and key for the upper half and a latch for the lower. The grain store had twelve ceiling hooks, and a loft ladder that led to a hatch with double flaps. Adjoining the food store was the straw-thatched cattle shed with sixteen stalls. The pigsty had a roof of wooden boards, and two sheds had been constructed with timber from the rectory forest. The well was brick-built with a timber roof, shank and handle. The hen-house and privy were made from old doors. The vaulted cellar had an alcove for home-brewed beer. Nearby was a sleeping cabin, with a bookcase in its porch.

Further away from the house stood a barn with a corn store, as well as a tool shed, straw shed, cow shed, pigsty, and a shed for sheep with its own hayloft. The bath-house also contained the malt-house and drying-room, and spices and hemp were kept in its gable loft. The garden was bordered by cherry trees and an apiary with a hundred or so hives. The meadow produced forty cartloads of hay.

The rectory also owned the crofts of Kolbottnen and Hammaren, as well as two cottages for the poor and disabled.

The church at Lena stands on a ridge above the valley where the River Vendel joins the Fyris. The walls are yellow-plastered with white corners, the roof is of tarred shingles, and it was built around 1300 in a region which was converted to Christianity in the eleventh century. The weathercock is perched on a globe. The parish hall from Anders Sparrman's time is still there.

The thirteenth-century church at Tensta is situated at the point where the Uppland plain meets the northern forests of the province. It has a huge seventeenth-century wrought-iron key, which is still in use.

The ploughed land yielded fifty-three barrels of seed; the meadow sixty cartloads of feed; the apiary had two hundred hives. The incumbent was obliged to pass on to his successor everything pertaining to the rectory: cows, sheep, pigs, iron pots, pestles and mortars, plough, harrow, sledges and an iron-wheeled cart. When Tensta rectory was inspected after Eric Sparrman's death in 1765, it was so rotted by mould that it was only fit to be demolished.

Growing Up

1

Throughout his childhood the days went by as placidly as water in a peat bog. He was the apple of his parents' eye. They had high hopes of him and he felt loved by them.

He used to wait for his father to come home from church in the little blue drawing room they called the parlour, off the living room. There was hoarfrost on the windows and the bottle of communion wine had been cooled to prevent it turning sour. His father used to put sugar in it. Jesus' blood is sweet, like all human blood, as the children had often been told.

His mother was a buxom woman and had woven her dark cherry-red skirt herself. She would move soundlessly over the mats in the passageway, and suddenly be standing behind him and saying with forgiving tenderness, 'Is my little boy experimenting with things he shouldn't?' That was when he had plucked some butterflies to pieces and swapped their wings over: he wanted to create a new species that would be difficult to classify.

On the finely embroidered topsheets his parents' *S* and *H* were intertwined. The threadbare undersheets were unmarked. The maids slept on bleached flour sacks they had stitched together. The thresholds and the table rails were worn shiny and hollowed out by centuries of feet. In his mind he often returned to the rectories in Lena and Tensta, but in reality never.

He hated being sent to bed and dreamed of waking up as a

grown man. Even as a child he used to go into the forest with the farmhands, stump-grubbing and cutting birch bark. Once, he found an old rusty ploughshare by a mound of cleared stones, and the grass there had such a powerful smell of mint and wormwood that it made him sneeze.

Conversation in his childhood home was subdued, exchanges guarded. The high-collared clerical garb emphasized duty and virtue. His father liked to preach in his sonorous voice about the swamps of the soul, but he had also written a lucid instruction manual on how to turn Uppland bog into land fit for cultivation. He was a hunter too: there was no lack of grouse or capercaillie on the table on Sundays. He rode on horseback or was driven in his carriage, and regarded Nature as a tapestry, a little damp around the edges but conveniently rich in bird-life. His was a mind less affected by spiritual rigour than by a desire for knowledge.

'Even the most obstinate have to accept that they are God's creations,' he was wont to conclude.

The son would accompany his father on his journeys between two parishes. They drove in an open carriage, and on one occasion his flax-blue breeches got soaked in a cloudburst that had the horse snorting frantically. They managed to cover a sack of seedcorn they had with them, and the rain soon laid the dust as the clouds gathered low and scudded away. They saw signs of hare, beaver and lynx. The air was so translucent that the landscape seemed magnified.

His father had curly fox-red hair that went darker before later turning white. He had a freckled brow and a skin which easily burnt in the sun. He was not averse to a hot toddy or a laced coffee. In the stable by the barn door there was a stall where you could sleep off any inebriation. In his case it had happened only once: it was usually the farmhands who ended up there.

He put on his reading glasses to prepare his sermon and sent his son to hang the hymn numbers on their hooks in the church.

'My congregation have learned to sleep with their eyes open. It's a medical phenomenon.'

He himself was obdurate in his resolve to do his utmost in the eyes of God and man; so he opened his black coat to the reluctant congregation and clasped them to his bosom.

Anders noticed at an early age that, unlike many another clergyman, his father was not entirely committed to the hereafter, which he seemed to see as an extension of his lease on the Uppland farm with its rolling hills, gentle valleys and peaceful fields, and its verges so luxuriant with flowers that they might lead the way to Paradise.

His mother Brita often seemed to be immersed in dreams. She saw a meaning in everything and even read a mysterious script into the insect tracks under the bark of trees. She could feel the presence of her five lost children when the family sat in silence over the gooseberry fool, and she noticed that when rain was on the way the honeybees and bumblebees stopped buzzing.

Lovingly concerned for her youngest son, she would burst into tears when she looked into his future, and anticipated her distress at the thought of such a sensitive disposition coming into contact with the ruthlessness and calumny of the wider world.

A clergyman's daughter herself, and accustomed to the observances and conventions of the church, she mostly kept her eyes cast down in order to protect herself and avoid humiliation. She was a clergyman's wife with an unfathomable God. She sometimes bit on the sacramental wafer as if testing a coin to see if it was a forgery. The parents' feelings for one another had perhaps taken second place to their natural affection for the children.

The youngest son remembered her in a rust-coloured pleated skirt, the best one she owned, waiting for a visitor. She had been afraid of going blind for some time, and had trouble sleeping. She used to sew by the window as long as she could before darkness fell, then would light the oil lamp and put on an apron from the chest of drawers. A bunch of heather burst into flame in the stove and threw sparks up the chimney.

She opened the door to the pedlar who went from house to house with a bag of medicinal herbs, barley sugar, cinnamon sticks, soap, scented water, buttons, scissors and a necklace with an amber heart. And he did not display his wares in vain. Humbly infatuated with Anders' mother, he would always reduce his price by a *daler* or two. He flattered his beautiful and noble-minded lady – as he called her – and she blushed in confusion when thus confronted by the dark powers playing their wily games. Then came the cloud-burst, and the crafty tradesman had to be provided with lodging for the night. He was given water from the ladle that hung on the hook above the bucket. He admired the scoured copper vessels, and expressed his gratitude by going out to the woodshed and carrying in an armful of firewood for the maid.

Mother led the parish children in a long line up to the maypole. She knew most of them and called them by name. The June market was a mass of butchers' barrows, creaking farmers' carts, wagons with tar barrels hanging underneath, and the high-wheeled carriage from the Bielkes at Salsta with the flunkey's seat at the back. Horses reared up, beer tankards went the rounds, a joke or a taunt was taken amiss, some apprentices started fighting, a cudgel flew through the air. The silhouette-cutter vied for attention with two deformed calves. The entire hillside swarmed with people, like an anthill, and it was almost impossible to hear what anyone said through the general hubbub.

Hedda the maid had narrow, scornful eyes and gave him a slap from time to time; somehow or other he always managed to offend her. Skirts billowing, she swung round the bedpost in his parents' bedroom, and whispered spitefully, 'You can't help it, Anders, you're soft in the head.'

He leaned forward, grabbed her hands and dug his nails into her wrists, wanting to draw blood. But she was smooth and slippery, he lost his grip, and she always got the better of him.

She was rowing the flat-bottomed boat on the lake near the church as he let out the net. She was laughing in the twilight, and he was at first uneasy and then frightened. She splashed water over him with the blade of the oar. He dangled his hand in the lake.

'Watch out for the pike!' she warned, and he took her seriously. He could not read her expression.

She made the boat heel over so that water lapped over the sides. Bubbles rose from the muddy depths and smelt as if one of them had broken wind.

''Tis the creatures at the bottom of the lake: they feed on the fresh water down there.'

She half-bent towards him, 'If you fall in, you'll feel them between your toes, worms as thin as thread, slimy snails. They stick to you. They want to get inside you.'

'Is it the same in the big seas?'

'Much worse. Unimaginable. But don't worry – you won't ever get that far.' Defiantly, she went on, 'You think I'm just a clergyman's maid.' What else could she be? That was it. 'When your father taps the barometer, it indicates Very Dry. When I tap it, it goes to Stormy.'

'Why?'

'That's something for you to think about. Can you see the first migrating birds up there? They're flying to hot countries that neither you nor I will ever visit. They know best what I mean. But when they come back in a year's time they won't be able to explain anything at all.'

2

The spring floodwaters were abating. The bulrushes stood black and upright. The birds were celebrating their nuptials, their songs suspended somewhere between Heaven and Earth. The birch leaves were emerging, the nettles were still young enough to pose a threat. The pine trees smelt of resin and turpentine. An elk lurked behind trailing lichen and dried-up fir trees. Meadow pipit and sedge warbler competed to herald the dawn. And there were evenings when lightning ripped the skies apart and the divers glided away over the surface of the water.

Early in May, when the first yellow stars of Bethlehem came into bloom, the paths opened on to a Garden of Eden. The morning light came filtering through the foliage and slender branches, cobwebs and glistening thaw. The father encouraged his son to go out with the farmhands to set plants, break stones and drain the peat bogs and marshes for pea fields and pastures.

A few weeks after the lapwings arrived the gnats began to dance, the rivers to rise and the pike to sport. The green woodpecker called from the corner of the house and the pied flycatcher chirped in the ageing elm. Anders was often outdoors when night took over from day and they summoned him in for his porridge. He had a box of insects, and gave his sisters due warning.

He was eleven years old and entranced by all the life in the forest. He was soon up to his knees among the ferns picking bog myrtle leaves. The lake lay still beneath its pearly surface, scratched by the bream from below, and the swallows skimmed across it as if trying to pierce the membrane of the water.

His father would sit with his papers in the honeysuckle arbour. He sometimes took the children for a walk, and they listened to his memories of childhood in Biskopskulla. He had a compass, which he kept in a tin. Yet sailing on the River Fyris upstream from Uppsala was not something ever to be undertaken. Its miry banks were home to a frightening mud-brown creature, curled up on itself, quite inhuman.

His mother used to send Anders out to gather apples, windfalls from the Tree of Knowledge. The sound of the organ thundered out from the church like the roar of a river-flow vaster than any he had ever seen. He leaned against the stone wall and thought he could feel the road heaving like the deck planks on a ship. And the music coming from the church continued, regardless of who had called it forth. He could hide himself in it as it hovered just above the grass and lifted the ground to reveal a glimpse of how his future might look.

The aspen grove abounded in red German catchfly, meadow-sweet and cow wheat. The thistles were a mass of blue and grey blossom. And new souls replaced those of the dead. Seeds blowing in the wind attached themselves to the gravestones. People vanished as quickly as stars behind the moon. There were very few graves – and mostly of wood; stone was for clergymen and the fine folk from the big houses, usually under the floor of the church, near the altar.

Death came like the hasty snapping shut of a book before reaching the end. No-one can describe the most important moments in their life: birth and death. Or perhaps they are not so important, because they are always happening. He had forgotten the names of his dead brothers and sisters.

But he could see before him butter-pears covered in hoarfrost, oak-apples that gleamed red from afar, white dead-nettles flattened to the ground under the weight of the rain. They lit their fires in open hearths with the withered leaves of plum, redcurrant and apple, and the house was filled with fragrance. It put everyone in a better humour, and his father's authoritative voice pontificated: 'We must strive for a happy medium. We must talk to one another, read, repudiate the handiwork of elemental spirits. None of us has a magic wand. We must take care not to sign away our souls with a careless stroke of the pen.'

In the distance the river looped between alders and bracken. Nightjars whirred like spinning wheels, and the full moon came out, as white as a skull and portentously large.

3

Much later, at the Cape, Anders would recall the rectory kitchen where Sara the maid churned butter, made broth from calf bones, and starched the rector's cuffs. She slept under a shelf on which lay soap, medicinal and culinary herbs and roundels of crispbread on a pole; and below her was the cellar with its root vegetables, beans and apples. He remembered the whitewashed ceiling of the living room, and the box-sofa where he had sat with Lidström helping him to mend his violin. Lidström was once allowed to bring this worldly instrument into the church to play, but its notes were completely drowned out by a sudden thunderstorm, much to the amusement of the congregation.

Lidström was an indigent curate from Sigtuna who had come as the rector's chaplain and assistant. He had a humped back and a hollow chest, and the top of his head was both angular and round, like the head of a blacksmith's nail. Unmarried, he lived in a pair of cottages with his elderly housekeeper Margit, and an emaciated cow that browsed among the boulders in the overgrazed pasture. Tall hollyhocks stood on guard by the porch steps. He had an armchair and a bookcase; the windows were low and let in only moderate light. Some of the walls were covered in embossed paper with sepia-coloured stars stencilled on it. There were patches of damp on the ceiling. He used to go out to meet the post coach. He watched the farm carts trundling along the ruts in the road. But he never went anywhere himself.

He delivered his sermon about this life being a precursor to the angelic delights that would slake the thirst of the soul. The mere thought of all this wafted like a cheering breeze across the poor man's cheeks. No amount of poverty could impede the flights of his spirit. He was on intimate terms with death, since it would not separate him from anyone. He had no-one, he loved no-one, and he used to say to Anders, 'The only reason you are miserable is because you are so full of contradictions.'

Lidström listened carefully in order to comprehend the voice of God, which he then interpreted through paraphrase. He never made elevated speeches, but took his metaphors from the domestic pigs and chickens; and he would receive no visitors who were not in need of the piety and patience his heart could furnish. He was the confidant of many, since he had more time to spare than the rector. People brought their problems to him.

Strangely enough, he never complained about his situation. Some evenings he could be heard singing melodiously, while his housekeeper was busy at her tasks. Those who demanded explanations for everything assumed that a sorrow or a failure of some kind had afflicted him and made him content to live out his days in poverty and quietude.

He was a humble man and completely unlike his rector in temperament. For Eric Sparrman had an emotional nature, and when guests arrived he would rush out to embrace them with hearty exclamations about how much he had been looking forward to seeing them, and send his son to fetch a long-saved bottle of home-made cherry wine from their store. Eric Sparrman's solo singing was held in high esteem and outdid the noonday strokes of the wall clock and the invective of the crows.

In the cool morning breeze, in the company of sharp-winged swallows, Anders' father was not afraid to invoke the sun, which was still a few points to the north. Midges danced in the high blue skies, and raucous cocks crowed their morning salutations all over the district. Anders associated his father less with sermons than with farming, with the smell of new-mown hay and the distinctive trills of joyous larks.

His father began his day with a cup of coffee and a little distilled spirit (good for gout), and in the evening he would take a stoup of malt liquor. Löfberg, who made tiled stoves, had permission to dig clay in the rector's fields, and whenever a shower threatened to delay his departure in his ox-cart he would stay on for a glass of punch. Violent storms and gale-force winds sometimes interrupted his father's sermons, and then he would reproach God for not observing the Sabbath.

Eric Sparrman decided to clear some land to grow more vegetables: beetroot, carrots, spinach, butter beans and sugar peas. He wanted the rectory to be a model for the district. Spiritual sustenance was not everything. His son helped plant fruit trees on an uncultivated part of their land. Fences were erected around it and a well dug.

'Will I be able to reduce the suffering in the world?' Anders asked his father.

'No,' he replied, 'but you can study, pursue research, enlighten the ignorant. God's dominion shall be from sea even unto sea, and from the river even unto the ends of the Earth. We don't know whether He beholds us through His magnifying glass. You must simply follow your own convictions – even if you are criticized by the Dean and Chapter. Don't shy away from the cruelty of the world! No thoughts are unalloyed, think them through, but reject any that don't encourage you to find out more.'

As the days lengthened and it was warm even in the shade, the rector became increasingly sanguine and assured both his sons that he had never assumed the way of the world to be just. The intoxication of spring led him to express rather careless and inappropriate opinions on God's mercy: that he was certain his death would be his first encounter with it.

We are no more than the buzz of a fly or the bite of a gnat in the eyes of Heaven, his mother Brita attested. She had a way of reading the Bible backwards, as if looking for something which was not there at the beginning. She was watchful and protective; that was how she showed her love and concern for her two youngest children, Anders and Charlotta Gustava.

A newspaper would occasionally arrive from Uppsala with stories from a world where children were buried alive and volcanoes swallowed up entire families. And their own books included *The Life and Strange Surprising Adventures of Robinson Crusoe*, translated into Swedish three years after Anders was born. He had read it several times, but his father said, 'Read serious books! Otherwise you will never grow up.'

So he took the opportunity to ask, 'Is it a sin to play cards?' That had been one of the pastimes of the sailors on Robinson Crusoe's ship.

'Not as long as you lose.'

The dust floated up and down inside the roof windows in the gable loft against the moonlight, which cast its pale glow on the roses in the hedge outside. Making his way down the narrow attic stairs where the mice rustled, he stumbled over the old spinning wheel. He had to open the horn window of his lantern to see better. Skeins of night mist clung to the plaster on the walls and began to seep into him.

When his brothers and sisters were not watching, he would sit on the slender-legged sofa in the living room, with its blue-washed wallpaper. There, the portrait of his grandfather Nils Sparrman hung above the chest that would eventually accompany Anders on his travels. His grandfather's lips seemed to preach moderation, but his deep-set eyes were unfathomably dark. The chest contained a map of the hitherto-known world, a Latin dictionary and some trinkets of Lapp origin. It was said that the Lapps used to drive their reindeer down the Dalälven River all the way to Älvkarleby, but that was a long time ago.

4

He inhabited a realm of splendour. The great stars were his closest neighbours. Around Lady Day he heard the cries of whooper swans and cranes. Woodcocks winged their way along the edge of the forest, seemingly unconcerned that they might be shot. Between the high trunks, beneath the lofty canopy, sunbeams danced with the nymphs of the forest.

He would often go to this secret place and listen to the sounds of silence, and to the organ-like boom in the treetops. Hawthorn berries glinted on the ground, solitary beech trees wore bark like unpolished pewter, and the birch polypore a light sprinkling of enticing golden lichen. He lingered until the new moon rose in the east. He did not divulge where he had been. The rapture he felt – would he ever experience it again?

From an early age he loved the company of birds. He heard the shrill sound of the wood sandpiper's courtship song in the reeds. In the twilight hour the hobby hunted dragonflies along the flat shoreline. He found a treecreeper's nest, built of bast fibres, with five red-speckled eggs. A harsh-voiced gander had taken up residence in the stable with no fear of the horses' hooves or the inquisitive mice. And the cock was pacing up and down the yard as if aware that he would soon lose his head. One of the farmhands had shot a lynx, its claws retracted, its coat gleaming a ruddy brown, enough for two winter hats. The head of a wild boar hung in the porch. If the tusks moved on the stroke of the New Year it meant: next year it will be your turn.

'Man's uniqueness lies in his knowledge that every act has its consequences,' his father used to say.

Anders' brother Nils taught him that the history of Sweden began a few miles away from them, in Old Uppsala, where their maternal grandfather had once been assistant vicar, the home of Yngve and Agne, Adils and Ottar Vendelkråka. Anders was descended from generations of clergymen. Unlike his brother, he would break the mould.

Wearing his grey linen housecoat, his father sat down in his adjustable writing chair. Without speaking, he inscribed figures that might have represented the distance between the stars, the number of sacks of oats or debts owed to the archdiocese. His quill pen scratched, but he altered nothing in notes of meetings, accounts or lists of servants' and labourers' wages. Then he would go over to the bookcase containing the Bible and collections of sermons, abraded by years of fingernails and warm breath, the handbook of animal husbandry, a dissertation on the weather, and the publications of the Workers' Educational Association.

Also on the shelves was Haqvin Spegel's *God's Work and Rest*: eleven thousand stanzas on the creation of the world and its constant renewal with discoveries such as 'the giraffe found in Jamaica'. And there, too, was Fredric Hasselquist's *Iter Palæstinum* (*Voyage to Palestine*), published by Linnaeus. Hasselquist had inspected Rachel's mandrakes and Christ's crown of thorns, and dissected a crocodile in Egypt in whose belly he found two fish-hooks. So Job must have meant a crocodile and not a whale when he asked, 'Canst thou draw out Leviathan with an hook?' The explorer had rescued the theologians from an ancient conundrum.

His father turned and addressed Anders in uncharacteristically mild terms. 'I have stepped into a dead man's shoes: my father's. You will have your own boots made for you. Ensure that you avoid blisters and bitterness! It's probable that I shall never know who you are or what your concerns are. I shall have to get used to the idea that I may never see you again. You will be sorely missed whenever we try to identify the bird struggling in the net and are reminded that you were always right.'

Anders would come to remember the mutton with dill sauce and the baked crayfish, and the poached eggs with anchovies at the rectory. But this time of plenty was an exception. The day after Christmas Day, out went the tree that had accompanied the calf-liver pie, ginger ale, preserved pears, sweet gruel, singing and fireworks. Such liberality was beyond the means of the house.

January and February were austere months. His mother poured out one jug of skimmed milk a day for their coachman. There was soup on the table every Saturday, lumps of white bone-marrow swimming in a broth. He found it difficult to eat and sometimes nearly vomited if he chewed on pieces of fern or resin.

He would often wake with a start, as if someone had struck him. Immediately, his mother would be there, seeming to step out of the wallpaper and straight into his dream. 'You are as thin as a rake, you really must eat more.' And she told him not to be arrogant. Where he felt confidence and hope, she saw danger and destruction. He was becoming someone she no longer understood. She was already sensing that he would follow the wind and the waves, while she withdrew into the house where he had grown up. She stepped aside, as was her nature, and thought him self-centred for so stubbornly wanting to burst his bounds.

In the kitchen the fish bones were simmering down into a sort of glue in the process of being transformed into soap. His sister Anna sat in her tie-blouse, her hair in a bun at the back, practising the piano with clumsy fingers. There were seven years between his older and younger sisters, but that didn't stop them whispering, giggling and chattering to disturb him in his homework for Nils. He yearned to be somewhere else, far away.

His mother was at her narrow looking glass with its dull wooden gilding. 'I pray for you to resist all temptations. Read the hymn book. It doesn't take up much room! Remember there are higher values.'

'I know there are, but we find them in many different places.'

'If you are overcome by your urges, think about the poor creature who might give birth to a child and lose it, or see it grow up without any education, beneath everyone's contempt.'

'Your words are etched on my heart, Mother. But 'tis isolation and freedom I shall be seeking. I shall be my own companion.'

'There are no miracles, but we must strive for perfection.'

'We can expect no perfection, Mother. Our path has no end. The Earth is round, however many byways there may seem to be.'

He saw in her eyes that she feared for his precociousness and his hubris. But he knew she would not complain to his father.

'Perhaps we don't belong here,' she ventured. 'In the world of the birds, the fish and the living beasts. We are a part of something else. Oh, I'm talking nonsense. If only I could lead you back to your God . . .'

'Which god, Mother?'

'The One the desperate call to in their hour of need. The One Who holds you like a drop of water in the palm of His hand.'

5

The birds never overslept. His summer paths resounded to their cheerful songs. He carried a sack of grass and turnips to feed the animals, tipped them into the trough and stirred them well. There were still six months to go before winter feed: straw mixed with swill.

The estate was full of activity. The potato clamp was dug out to the depth of an ox and the wood store prepared for thirty cords of firewood. The farmhand burnt the brushwood on the meadow and the smoke rose straight into the sky. Their maid Sara shelled peas and sliced apples. The other maid, Hedda, brought out the jug of dark syrup and set to work making rye pancakes in pork fat in such haste that she broke a tumbler. A swallow's nest had fallen from the eaves. A smell of dung emanated from the stable where the horses were pawing the ground. They wanted to come out and dance in the heat of the sun.

But his soul was becalmed. He dreamed of lands where there were no fields and forests, but volcanoes, hot springs, sacred grottoes and hidden caverns far beneath his feet.

'Sometimes you are the first up,' said his mother, 'now you are lying in bed half the morning. What am I to make of all your whims? Here am I, scrubbing, sweeping, cleaning mushrooms. You obviously don't believe in crime and punishment.'

'As little as does the cockerel in the yard.'

'But you eat the chickens. May God spare you from heavy burdens.'

'He is His own heaviest burden!'

His mother gave a shriek, and rushed out of the room making what looked like the sign of the Cross. A butterfly fluttered in through the window. 'Look, there's one of God's miracles!' he shouted after her.

What if God were a scarecrow and the Church His disguise, a magnificent costume? This seditious conceit made his eyes water. Perhaps Christianity was just the final chapter in an age-old story. With a shiver of insight he had realized that the Earth was its own creation. Sun, winds and seasons were its engine, and they in their turn . . . yes, there was always something else beyond, as generations struggled back towards the once seen but soon incomprehensible; and as forgetfulness closed page after page of signs that were now indecipherable.

The archdiocesan inspector arrived in a barouche with a torn leather hood to visit the rector, and the clergyman's wife received him with the lively loquacity of which she was sometimes capable. He was accompanied by the surveyor, a thin craggy fellow with a shrill, effeminate voice, who held his thighs together as if in need of a piss, while they ate porridge at a table laid with a stiff waxed cloth. The rector wanted to add a few acres of extra holdings to the estate, even though he himself would never benefit from them. They leaned over the plans and sketched in the border along a stony mill road used only by the occasional ox-cart.

Their evening was accompanied by the cries of the black-throated diver and the curlew, lengthening into the echo of earlier calls. Anders was aware of dog roses and sheep droppings. He threaded the thin pike from the lake on to a stick over a slow fire, the heifers staring inquisitively at him from the edge of the reeds. The birch trees were starting to turn, and the church bell was ringing for the end of service. A farmhand was heading off the calves on the old road to the church, and another was pulling a cart of tar-kettles to lay a new roof on the forge.

He washed in a basin of rainwater as his youngest sister Charlotta Gustava played hopscotch with her skirt tucked up round her waist. A magician roamed the district forlornly waving his wand; he no longer made much impression, since he conjured away far more than he conjured up.

The hay had not yet been cut. A family of elk had trampled the crop. Tall purple thistles and sinewy marguerites covered the juniper slopes. Closer to the road stood parades of lupins and drooping bird's-foot trefoil and harebells. Snipe drummed in the distance. The scents of summer were becoming fainter. The first plums were dark blue, splashed with blobs of resin.

And the stars shone over blackening waters. A silent drizzle announced the end of summer. Crows and autumn. The willow-herb was bending beneath its lustrous tendrils. The mosquitoes were swarming around the animals' spring. The potato harvest was poor: limp tubers, as wrinkly as an old man, with wispy beards. The voles were tunnelling in the grey glacial earth. Above them the October sky loomed rose-hip red and vengeful.

6

There are very few extant diary entries from this period. What follows was probably written in Tensta in 1762 or 1763.

Minus twenty degrees. The snow has packed down solid during the mild days. Really cold out on the ice. To Aunt Brizelius in the evening. They had cooked a brace of partridge. The younger clergy children sick with measles.

Put up a capercaillie hiding in a bush. Missed a jay and a hare. The snow was a good ell deep on level ground in the forest, sometimes more than knee-high. Saw a pair of bullfinches. The wind so strong that the mills were grinding empty.

Captain Lehusen stopped by, suffering from a cough, took some quinine powder. I persuaded his pretty daughter Olivia to listen to the first merry songs of the larks. Weather execrable. Only thin ice on the lake. Two snipe rasping like iron rods grating against one another.

The sounds of spring and thaw are in the air. Below the house our River Vendel is rushing through three channels, between alders shedding their cones, and between the big rocks with a dipper hopping from one to the other. Millwheel in poor state of repair.

Found a bank of wild strawberries. Skies bright, Nature calm. Mother came home with the girls. Catharina, Christina, Anna and Charlotta were making as much noise as a wagon-load of old women. Salenius, a young theologian who had studied in Dorpat, came to see us to pay his respects to my father. My sisters all agog.

Visited my teacher from the parish school, who had moved to Vattholma. His gaze was unsteady, his arms and legs twitching, and he seemed not to be in control of his movements. What a wretched jumping-jack of a schoolteacher! But most of what I have learned has been from my father and brother Nils, teaching me at home for several years.

Father now prefers sitting with his folios to struggling to turn the empty pages of his congregation. He talks about communion with the dead.

The rectory repainted with oil and vitriol, the roof tiled. We planted another rowan tree where the old one had been struck by lightning. We salted and laid down several creels of crayfish in the cold-cellar. Summer making ready to depart.

7

Every shadow requires a source of light in order to exist. 'Devote yourself to finding the light,' his mother cautioned. 'Don't just race around aimlessly.'

He was fourteen that day. They had been living in Tensta rectory for two years and, over braised-pork stew and pears in lingonberry juice, his father remarked that he was fully aware of the fact that his son did not want to don a clergyman's mantle and promulgate the Word of God. He would be entrusted with tasks of a more secular nature. Even so, he would not be spared mankind's lamentations, which were more piercing than the tones of any flute.

The world was perverse and ungovernable, especially in the big cities. Rusty iron knives competed with daggers to maim, poison and kill. Villains would appear like vapours rising from the soil. The wingbeats of war, the harsh trumpets, the neighing of horses, infantry in rags – no-one knew what was lurking around the next corner, even between Tensta and Norrtälje. And no words of exhortation or invocation from pulpit or lectern could influence cruelty, dishonour and wickedness.

'Your future is not mine,' his father said. 'You love the earthquake more than the wheatfield. You run while your siblings stand still. But I shall not hinder you.' He raised his eyes to God, forming three creases on the nape of his neck, and continued, 'Some of you children disappeared to join the ranks of the dead. Perhaps it's your role to arrive in our midst and then go galloping off, for ever, like a restive horse we cannot hold. You've outgrown your clothes. Handed down, all of them. Altered to fit by your mother while you children were asleep.'

So the hour was approaching for him to abandon his parents in order to drink at the well of learning in Uppsala. His sisters had woven a garland of clover and cornflowers, buttercups and may-weed for the maypole, but now it was withered, and the June inflorescence of the chestnut trees had long faded. But still he dallied in the Uppland summer, where the buzzard soared through the skies and the blackcock cooed in the top of a fir tree. Then he left for ever.

The garden was in a state of silent slumber. Two ageing hens were scuffing about in the shade of the raspberry canes and would soon have to be cooked before they tasted of nothing but wood. And the last hint of honeysuckle wafted across in the dusk.

But he could hear panting from the forest, as if the trees were short of breath, and then a sound that seemed to echo their sighing. He went down a path that ended at the lake-shore, where there was a laundry jetty overgrown by reeds. Everywhere around him he could see the borders between untamed Nature and the work of man. He followed field boundaries delineated by mug-wort, tansy and yarrow. A delicate white haze rose from the ground. Where the sighing came from, he had no idea.

His mother packed pillowcases, a pair of holland sheets, a bag of biscuits.

'You will meet God on the high seas, where the whales call with His voice in the storm,' she said. 'No-one is unknown to God. You have great intelligence, but the Holy Spirit does not speak in you.'

She put bread and meat on the table, and a honey and cinnamon cake. He ate alone and his heartstrings tightened, but all he said was that they could expect a lot of snow that winter. She stood watching in her threadbare apron. Then she took the opportunity to cut off a lock of his hair as a memento, warning him, 'Don't behave like a foolish ass, running wild with the other students. Don't sit with your elbows on the table propping up your chin with your hands, and don't involve yourself with a young woman you cannot support.'

Now, again, for the last time, he had to hear about the five children who had died before they could even walk: life had flowed out of them like blood from an open wound. She had suckled them at her breast, and now they were beyond all tears and laughter. Yet they are still mine, she said, as if she herself were a deserted child. She pressed her face to Anders' cheek, because she was convinced he would never return to the rectory. His father told her to pull herself together.

At the kitchen door Anders said his farewells to the maids, Hedda and Sara. They, too, would up and leave with their bundles one day. He gazed at the churchyard, the stone gateposts, the poorhouse. The wind soughed in the trees and the birds flew noiselessly into the darkness of the forest.

He made his departure in a half-covered carriage. The potholed country road crossed the river on a bridge spanning four piles. A jackdaw flapped its wings in warning. He felt neither hungry nor replete. His spirit soared on ahead. The future was an ogre.

A farm cart which was going to Uppsala later on would bring his grandfather's oak chest, now relinquishing its place in the living room for ever. It contained the two brothers' few possessions: for Nils was also coming to Uppsala, to pursue his theological studies and to keep an eye on his brother, younger by nine years.

For his journey from Tensta to the university Anders was dressed in a dark grey school coat, with pockets for crayons and pens. From the sideboard his father had taken a sheaf of cartridge paper suitable for ink. His mother had given him a pot of mint from the kitchen garden, and a recipe for a decoction of vinegar, mustard and belladonna, which his father had tested on the nervous maids. He plucked some nettle and foxglove flowers himself from the side of the house as a remedy for shortness of breath and glandular fever. Much of the emotion in my soul will have to remain locked in for ever, he thought.

His father sat by the tiled stove with its glowing turfs of peat. The early summer, when he had put on his gloves to collect flowering sloes, was long past. In August the phosphorescent stars cascaded like tears from the planet Venus as it prepared for its transit of the sun.

Anders recalled a substantial travelling breakfast with porter and wine in jovial company, swaying in a post-chaise to Rickomberga, and floating over the waves of green grass till they met strong winds from the north-east. They had said farewell to a curate's widow, an attractive and delightful woman, who had left Uppsala without any hope of returning there. In her face he read her thoughts: 'You are too young for me, and clergymen's sons are dreary.'

Before the autumn darkness descended on the fields of potatoes and beans, and the many languages of learning opened up to him, he had meandered aimlessly in the forest. Linnaeus, Uppsala's lord and master, had been inspired with confidence in his youthful potential after hearing about him from Captain Carl Gustav Ekeberg, a neighbour of Eric Sparrman at Altomta, though seldom home from his voyages for the Swedish East India Company. It had come out in conversation that Anders could navigate by the stars, that he walked barefoot to the parish school in order not to wear out the soles of his boots, and that he sat poring over his books instead of letting his heart be stolen by any silly infatuation. He was also physically tough and good-humoured – this his father had been able to assure the famous archiater, Professor Linnaeus.

A sliver of moon adorned the blue-black slate of evening, like a comma in the flow of time. He took his leave of the pastures, of the lake with its shaggy wooded island, and of a brown-eyed, thirteen-year-old girl who was visiting his youngest sister. All this aroused in him a desire to cast himself adrift, not to comply and conform. But the only thing he could manage to write home to his mother about his journey to Uppsala was: 'Quite hilly, buckets of teeming rain, and recompense and nourishment on arrival a less than palatable bowl of soured milk.'

The veils of mist between knotty oaks aroused more exalted emotions. But the springs of the carriage were not of the best; at times it leapt about more than the horses. The coachman's bony hands reached out to light a lamp. And soon the two young men burst into song, suddenly exhilarated.

On they drove through changing forest and tortuous bends towards the city of learning. He could smell birch webcap, the acrid scent of larch bark and the smoke of burn-beating in the distance. Nature would be his life's work, and it was already an integral part of his progress, slowing and speeding him on his way.

Uppsala Years with Linnaeus

1

Anders Sparrman enrolled in the Uppland students' union and was placed under the supervision of the president and senior members. His first term comprised a revision of previous knowledge, studies of French and German, church attendance and evidence of virtuous conduct. He practised gymnastics in a former cholera hospital. He observed dissections of an itinerant beggar and of an illegitimate child that had died from natural causes, both in Professor Rudbeck's Anatomical Theatre. Physics was taught in Professor Duraeus' house, chemistry in Torbern Bergman's laboratory on Strandgatan, medicine in the University Hospital on Riddartorget. Anders Celsius' observatory was on Svartbäcksgatan, and further down the same street was the botanical garden where Linnaeus received his apostles after their expeditions out into the world, often to the beat of drums and the notes of the French horn.

Uppsala was a square, rectilinear city of two thousand inhabitants, with hop gardens, cabbage patches and tobacco plantations, and cultivated land and pasture extending right up to the houses. Little turf-roofed huts alternated with red-painted wooden houses, most of them student lodgings, along streets which were in a pitiful condition. A ferry crossed the River Fyris, drawn on a rope by an aged Polish man; a sure way of ingratiating yourself with him was to malign the Russians.

Beggars were everywhere, some with their begging-bowls, others shambling around in a world of their own. They stood unwashed beside farm troughs and city fountains, commiserating with one another on life's injustices. At night drunken apprentices arrived on the scene. Manure on the streets and squares was cleared away by peasants who were entitled to half of what they collected.

The five city gates were called Vaksala, Svartbäcken, Fjärdingen, Slottet and Kungsängen. The town ditch ran alongside the Bävern quarter. Linnaeus' garden marked the northern edge of the city. There were fifty inhabitants to every public house. The temple of learning was next to the double bell-towers of the cathedral, and educated not only the children of the nobility, but also the sons of a coppersmith and a ladies' tailor. Brawls between students and soldiers were a daily occurrence.

The school lodgings in Uppsala reeked of leather, sweat and hay. The superintendent spoke with gravity and sincerity of the boys' future being dependent on their ability to rise above the primeval ooze from which mankind had emerged. This individual, a former student who had achieved grace, was usually very restrained, but could on occasion come out of his shell and behave like the rest of them. At other times his admonitions stung more than the smacks he meted out in passing.

Nils and Anders took up lodgings with a widowed landlady in Bäver Alley, while the student house was deloused. She was responsible for the staging-post, which was more than she could cope with. Yet she refused to give up the guesthouse and blamed everything on the stable lad. She was on the point of being dismissed, since the citizens of Uppsala had complained of the long delays caused by the coach being used unlawfully for students' pleasure trips in the nearby countryside.

The student houses put on theatrical performances anywhere and everywhere. Audiences would crowd into an attic to see a play about a reprobate pedant. Students would turn somersaults in the air and stand on their heads for a coin. A failed theologian declared that the foundations of the houses on Svartbäcksgatan had been built on the rubble from Sodom, and that it had become a gambling den for the dregs of society. The clamour could be heard out in the country beyond the city boundaries, and no respectable person who valued his own skin would dare go near this seething volcano of ruffians.

Many of the students were under sixteen. They had been sent to Uppsala to be taught by eminent academics who gave private tuition in order to survive on their inadequate salaries. Most parents lived in rural areas and were unable to supervise their children. When school was over the boys were left to their own devices or in the hands of a landlady. A tutor then stood *in loco parentis*. He would usually be a more senior student or young graduate, whose friends would be other tutors, and so the pupils always had the opportunity to meet older and more established students.

Anders wore a light green waistcoat, a striped shirt underneath, breeches of blue-grey broadcloth, white woollen stockings, high boots laced up in the front like short boots, and a lined fur cap on his head.

'I hope you're not being an unruly young gentleman offering raisins to the girls, but are remaining upright and honourable,' his mother wrote. 'Make sure you're not set upon by bullies. Don't frequent loud and disreputable beer cellars, where temptations may lead to those lamentable diseases which may not manifest themselves for some goodly while.'

Anders had put Latin and Divinity behind him when he took up the study of the basic elements of the physical world. He registered for service in Nature's temple and he intended to remain within her expansive embrace. His education had been founded on outdated learning, which he would soon be in a position to refute; for instance, that water consisted of air-water and earth-water, the former comprising dew, rain, frost and snow, the latter spring water, pool water, lake water and mineral water.

From the writings of Olof Rudbeck he learned that the planets were clusters of coarser matter suspended in the more subtle ether, sometimes so close that they had an influence on one another. The universe consisted of dense vortices, with each fixed star a sun in the centre of its own vortex. Burning masses trying to escape their own flames, like comets.

Nearer to home, reading Rudbeck, Anders found the flowers of his childhood: butterwort, sundew, maianthemum, kidney vetch, golden saxifrage . . . They all had their own virtues and characteristics. He decided to become better acquainted with the flora of the earthly garden at first hand. He perused some of the oldest maps of the world in the library, each of them different. The world was in three parts: the Mediterranean, the region of the great rivers, and, in the east – which was drawn at the top and surrounded by walls – the earthly paradise. But the poles were absent, as was Africa south of the Sahara.

He read a lecture which Olof von Dalin had given at the Academy of Sciences: 'In Central Africa live a type of Moors, completely white, with hair of the same colour, as curly as wool, long ears, drooping eyelids and round eyes, the iris pink, the pupil Aurora encased in a yellow membrane through which the light penetrates . . . They are as haughty as other peoples, consider themselves to be the noblest race, for whom the world was created, and that once their time comes, they will have dominion over all.'

2

The cleaner, a colourless old woman with pallid lips and a nose disfigured by snuff, came in with her son, whose father, the night-watchman, is a substitute for his real father, one of the students. The boy showed us a bird he had trapped, but when it refused to sing we made him set it free.

The north wind had built up drifts of snow right across King's Meadow, looking like little houses. The wind was so fierce I sought shelter in the church, even though having to listen to Father B. was a high price to pay.

Duty visits on Saturday to my teachers Georgi and Steincour, who are so high and mighty and treat me like a child. You have to share a pack of Panama tobacco, smoke a pipe and play backgammon, whether young or old.

After all the trouble my brother Nils has taken with me, I have now mastered my conjugations, and Livy and Sallust. I am applying myself to my handwriting with an instructor who teaches calligraphy.

As Father wanted me to learn a craft – since one never knows what Fate has in store – I have chosen to try my hand at the lathe. But I suspect the pipe stem for my father and spindle for my mother will never be used.

A letter from Mother to say they have cleaned out the well and that she has collected a bucketful of birch sap since the snow thawed. She sent a messenger with crispbread, rye bread and a marinated beefsteak.

For some time now Nils and I have been taking our repast at an inn that offers herring rissoles on Mondays, salt cod on Tuesdays, pea soup with ham on Thursdays, herring on Saturdays. Never aught but porridge of rolled oats in the evenings.

I have taken to drinking coffee and chocolate nearly every day. They taste so much better since they were forbidden by the Estates of the Realm.

I was greatly afraid my carriage would overturn in the darkness beyond the church in the village of Danmark. The horses were fractious and impossible to control on the reins. Professor Linnaeus showed me the design for a laboratory kiln he had in mind to construct. May my soul ever enjoy the sentiments his presence inspires in me!

No letter from Peter Forsskål in Arabia. We begin to fear that he may no longer be among the living.

Unremarkable days. This city lacks completely what a little imagination, artistry and wealth might have achieved. I have met with nought but kindness from my hosts, but upright and honest people are indeed a rarity.

There are those here who eat only the tiniest biscuits in the morning, and whisper about things which are not for young ears and yet which are in the newspapers the following day. Indiscriminate gossip. They say that Carlberg is taking his coffee with the mayor's wife, as well as dallying with her sister. And while the tanner is under investigation by the district auditor for fraud, his wife is being bedded by the very county bailiff responsible for searching the house.

On my way back from the apothecary I chanced upon two fellow students to whom I had lent my history notes. A quarrel ensued, enmity arose between us, but peaceful relations were restored when I offered to treat them to lemonade and preserves in the castle gardens. Then we played billiards at Granström's, and

I dined with some amusing companions at Christian Wahlund's, with egg toddy and hunting tales afterwards. We're called milk-sops, those of us who prefer playing chess to skirmishes with the apprentices.

In the Zoological Department I dissected a crow and a beaver. Paid a visit to Gustaf Livijn in the evening, after I had fetched my clean collars and cravats. Went to the Academic Concert. After-wards we partook of a couple of glasses of toddy each. I would rather have supped with the girls.

The storks have arrived in Uppsala and wheeled carts replaced the sledges. Wrote a letter to Father about my studies, the lam-entable processions of the fellowship orders, and the tightrope dancer who strung his rope between the chimneys on Drottning-gatan. I have no real friends here, maybe nowhere.

Read Rudbeck's *Atlantica* and was surprised that at the end he declines to assert that Sweden was created thousands of years before Babylon and Troy.

In the Gustavianum, from a cabinet of curiosities taken from Nuremberg during the Thirty Years' War, I was shown the skin of the serpent which deceived Adam and Eve, and a pair of slippers worn at the marriage in Cana.

Why should I concern myself with the Day of Judgement and the Resurrection, when they are going to remain in obscurity until the end of time? And why torment myself by denying them? I do not wish to despise the incomprehensible, but neither do I wish to worship what I cannot understand. A capacity to do good and a determination to assist the unfortunate are the most important qualities, and they don't stem from belief or compulsion.

Supper with a glass of punch at Aunt Alina's. Miss Magdalena Reenstjerna and Mr Utterdahl, the schoolmaster, were there, play-ing duets at the piano. I don't play an instrument, for I would rather not play at all if I cannot play divinely. Will I ever find a lover to press to my breast?

On my way to be examined by Dr Georgi, I met Johan Gabriel

Oxenstierna. He had been chopping box-wood to be turned on the lathe, and had purchased amaryllis bulbs from Professor Linnaeus' head gardener. He is obsessed with flowers, trees and cultivation. In literary circles at Skenäs Manor, near Lake Hjälmaren down in Södermanland, his studies in Uppsala were regarded as a course in atheism. He had besought them to open their minds to the truth, and not to wallow in their featherbeds of prejudice.

On the first of May, the trumpets announced the dance on King's Meadow. Servant girls came en masse, but ladies came too, attired as maids in order to make their way through the hop gardens unrecognized. The musicians were rewarded with coins, bread and laughter. Singing and general rowdiness, and the Devil's name invoked more often than the Lord's.

During a thunderstorm (an unusual occurrence in May) I sketched a map of the road from Uppsala to Norrtälje, with a key to symbols, as an aid to preparation. Will I ever have any opportunity for distant travels? Or will I end my life as Director of the Office of Land Surveys? If only I could see fifteen years into the future!

3

Anders Sparrman called on Professor Linnaeus and found him in melancholy mood, exhausted by his work and by his wife Sara, who disliked receiving guests and made him undertake insignificant work to augment the family's already substantial means. In his dressing gown and green fur cap Linnaeus looked even more diminutive than when he was walking along, thin and stooped, but his face had a receptive and open expression. He spoke enthusiastically about learned visitors from other countries.

Anders was invited to play Sevens with him and Sara. He showed his teacher a draft essay on butterflies, a diversion from his main medical studies. Linnaeus criticized his style as turgid and many of his observations as unsubstantiated. He ought to write a monograph on the earthworm. It would teach him discipline.

A while later, standing gazing out over his herb garden, brushing some powder from his waistcoat as the maid put out buns, preserved ginger and coffee, Linnaeus addressed Sparrman in his familiar gruff voice.

'I know you are wont to stutter, but give me your response in a measured and natural voice, and only answer after you have afforded a few minutes' consideration to what I am about to propose. Would you be willing to embark on a voyage to China in two months' time? As barber-surgeon, since you have not yet taken your examinations. But actually as my botanist. Southern China is fertile and luxuriant; grapes may be unknown, but the trees are in bloom twice a year. However monstrous their animals may appear to be, the local inhabitants don't find them unappetizing. The people live in wretched conditions, but they have gunpowder and tools. They are ingenious, economical and loyal to their emperor. Much is worthy of study there.'

When the great man had finished outlining his proposition, his young student replied, 'Professor Linnaeus, if you enjoin me thus, I shall go. Then it will not appear as if I am deserting my mother and father, but leaving on your recommendation.'

'I shall write to your father forthwith. You shall not tarry in the schoolroom. Look around you, not too passively, and never indifferently. Then we shall see what becomes of you.' The master was playing with his tortoiseshell paperknife.

To whom should Anders say his farewells? Parents, brothers and sisters, the servants at the rectory . . . So far his life had lacked purpose, and now here he was suddenly hazarding it all on a voyage across oceans deeper than sound or lead could reach.

Linnaeus let him inspect the tea plants, the first to have survived the transportation from China. Carl Gustav Ekeberg had cultivated them in propagating frames on board ship, and his wife had travelled in a closed carriage from Gothenburg to Uppsala with a plant box on her lap. Students rode out to Linnaeus' cottage at Hammarby for tuition, and every Saturday Linnaeus, wearing his apparently indestructible green coat, conducted excursions into the countryside around Uppsala. He took little sleep, but relaxed in the evenings. Foreign guests were accommodated at neighbouring farms and were given some hours of instruction a day. There were Russians, Germans, Dutchmen, Norwegians and Danes.

As the youngest of the students, Anders Sparrman worked in the four gardens: the Siberian, with hardy plants; the plot with Swedish summer plants, from spiked speedwell to dittany; the fruit orchard on the south side; and, by the house itself, the vegetable patch and the beds of perennials and climbers. He weeded and thinned. Every species had to be preserved, but none permitted to dominate.

Linnaeus would open up a flower with his knife and appear to talk to it. Unmoved by the depth of the cosmos, or by the Plough, Sagittarius and Capricorn above, he investigated Creation's innermost nooks and crannies and strange secretions. Anders relished the sound of his master's voice, and hoped he would say something more to him before he advanced further into the subject that was to be his destiny.

'The garden wears its nightshirt and its thin summer shirt more or less as we do,' Linnaeus said. 'But it's an insomniac, it never sleeps.'

Sparrman was all attention.

'I suspect you are idle,' Linnaeus continued. 'But I believe you have a modicum of genius. And you are a good-natured soul, without artifice. I'll excuse you from building stone walls.'

'I have nothing against working in the rain,' Sparrman replied.

In the second week of April the crocus and the snowdrop arrived at the same time as the wagtail. Monkshood, pheasant's eye, pasqueflower and wild tulip followed in May. The fritillary flower and columbine mingled with marigold. Seeds from China and Egypt were still hiding in the soil.

4

The Uppsala meadows were marshy, with fever-inducing mists and mosquitoes that caused ague, covered in spring by floodwaters which offered a welcome to pintails and goldeneyes. The cries of waders were everywhere audible, and Uppsala men went out to shoot great snipe on King's Meadow. Anders noted the bird's delicate ribcage for further investigation.

On his way to Hammarby in August, on a short-legged steed belonging to his widowed landlady, he saw the winter rye being sown, the cornfields being harrowed and the earth levelled under the rake, while the cattle grazed on pastures where the grass had already been harvested. As he rode home, lightning flashed and the sky turned slate-grey. His horse lifted its hooves with the utmost care: the ground must have been vibrating under the lightning's assault.

In winter, relentless squalls knocked him off balance as he walked along the wet stone quay by the River Fyris and battled his way across Iceland Bridge in a headwind. The post-sleigh skidded through Fjärdingen Gate, and when there was a snowstorm the night watchman would start beating his drum and calling out well before dusk.

Despite his lambswool waistcoat and coat of oiled jute, he felt himself vulnerable, unprotected. Now and then he saw a faint, pulsating spark flickering under the ice of the Uppland lakes, like a quick-tailed eel that no-one could ever catch.

Uppsala, Anders wrote to his father at the Tensta rectory, is one of those towns where little gets done. The most important thing was to be seen, which diverted energy and concentration from more essential pursuits. Indolence and lethargy affected both pupils and teachers in the classroom. Just being in Uppsala, close to books, was sufficient. Some immersed themselves in the sustained notes of the oboe and had nothing more to say. Some concealed their secrets in prime numbers, others devoted themselves to factoring numbers. They were delving into limited numerals and needed eternity to show them the way.

The professors hopped back and forth in time and research, as if the current year were of no importance. So much knowledge was obsolete and the truth so remote that it was easier to fabricate it out of nothing. No-one had made much of an impression on him – except Linnaeus, a man so small that with his eyes fixed on the ground he was no distance at all from the realm of plants in which he found such satisfaction.

'Excellent' and 'curious' were two adjectives which Carl Linnaeus and Anders Sparrman frequently employed. 'Excellent' for what was unusual and surprising. 'Curious' for what was remarkable and almost incomprehensible. Man's transformation into grass and earth was wondrous, curious.

The supreme quality that Linnaeus cultivated in his pupil was the ability to enter into Nature's delights with open eyes, and to encounter the dipper that dives into the waterfall, the siren that sings in the sea, the mussels that consume the very rock they cling to, the polecat that defends itself with a noxious stench. Phenomena such as these filled him with reverence for the world's cornucopia. Though he did not underestimate the cruelty involved in the processes of life. Nor indeed did he attempt to shrink from anything in this world where all creatures 'tear each other limb from limb without mercy'.

During those two terms of 1764–5, Linnaeus lectured on the theory of nutrition. More than two hundred students filled the largest lecture theatre in the university, nearly half of them medical students like Anders. He described to his parents the way the professor aroused mirth when he commented on the absurdity of male and female fashions, the fragility of life, the near-death experience reported by those who are drowning. And the ageing process that begins at forty-one. He was lucky to have been born to healthy parents 'in the heat of passion'.

Linnaeus condemned luxury goods – almond cake, caviar, oysters, Tokay wine, tobacco, silk sheets and masquerades. Anders perceived – from listening to Linnaeus – that science has no sacred documents: knowledge has no Bible, but jumps from tussock to tussock, from generation to generation, along paths slippery with leaves and tracks newly forged.

Linnaeus was not interrupted when he lectured, and there was no time for questions: everything was just as he stated. Soon they would all be out of his orbit, students, pupils, epigones, high-flyers. No allowance was made for error or scruples, and everything was accomplished speedily, as it seldom was in that Uppsala so burdened by the weight of its past.

At dinner with Linnaeus, Anders met Carl Peter Thunberg, with whom he was to become better acquainted a few years later in Cape Province. From him he attempted to learn something of method and meticulous order, for Thunberg was a man not given even to letting pins lie with heads and points in opposite directions. Thunberg always seemed ready to move up to a higher school, while Anders still languished among the weeds in the playground. If Anders gestured in alarm at the black clouds gathering over the sun, Thunberg explained it impassively in terms of gradations of the barometer.

Linnaeus wrote to Eric Sparrman in Tensta that Anders was about to leap over the farm fence, and go off to explore the oceans and distant shores and islands where no-one spoke Latin or knew the Son of God. Of his own free will he was determined to venture forth into the wider world. He wanted to observe and analyse the unknown and the unseen.

Anders, in turn, noted of Linnaeus: 'Whenever he raises his eyes from the plants of the soil, he is consumed by anxiety. His spirit seems to shudder and shake at the sight of the lifeless, vast and amorphous expanses high above the plants and grasses. But when he opens a snapdragon, or lets his finger be flecked by the pollen of the orange lily, his eyes light up with the purest joy. Then he is at home with his children, in humility and wonderment.'

When Anders was on the point of departure, Archiater Linnaeus took off his apron, and washed and proffered his hand.

'Make sketches of everything in order to remember. Keep precise journals. Overlook nothing, because only later will you be able to judge what is of value and what has already been observed by others. Be a vagabond in the true meaning of the word, seeing all the beauty and profundities of the world, from its deep ravines to its droplets of resin and sap.'

So Anders Sparrman was ready for his journey to the East Indies and China. The autumn sun was pale, he was young and full of vigour. His thoughts poured out of him like spilt ink over the whole realm of Nature, but gradually came under control in the cooler air.

And as a final farewell to Linnaeus, he attended his obituary speech in honour of his friend Andreas Neander, who had been forgotten by his motherland. 'It is not sufficient to perform one's duties competently,' Linnaeus said. 'Everything depends on timing and good fortune.' Virtue and good fortune were man's two servants, the former gentle and considerate, the latter wilful and inconsistent. 'When we walk in bright sunshine, we have a double shadow that follows at our heels, however much we twist and turn, and wherever our path may lead us.'

Voyage to China

1

My father came to Uppsala to say farewell to me and to see Nils. I gripped his hands tightly. He was wearing his otter-skin cap, his black woollen stockings, and black shoes with brass buckles. We did not smile at each other; the moment was too serious for that. It was late autumn. I would miss the smell of the sun on the slushy roads of Uppsala, the sweet sense of repletion after cheesecake and bread and preserves at Mam'selle Bolling's, and the ominous jackdaws flapping over Kungsdammen Ponds.

I joined the post-packet from Skeppsbro Quay in Stockholm for Gothenburg, and sailed two weeks later at ten o'clock in the morning of the 28th of December 1765, on the *Stockholm Castle*, a full-rigged ship with a staysail between the masts and the prow. I had my own stock of lemons and medicaments. My destiny and my future were shrouded in impenetrable darkness. At times I felt very apprehensive.

The crew had been taken on in Gothenburg, one hundred and fifty men called and inspected. Ballast of pig-iron and rocks was stowed, divided between the fore and aft holds. Lead was laid on boards on top of the ballast. Eighty water casks arrived on river-boats from the city. And a couple of hundred sacks of ship's biscuits, eighty score of stockfish, forty ox-hides of ship's liquor, birchwood for the cooks, and several hundred barrels of smoked herring to be offloaded at Cadiz. Carpenters built pens for the pigs on the lower deck and cages for the hens on the 'tween deck.

We left the red warehouses of the harbour behind us, the Cliff Inn, the shipyards and a brig careened at the quay, to the reverberating thump of hammers. It was a reasonably calm day for sailing, jellyfish drifting beneath us, the wind north-westerly. But a day later the ship was rolling horribly in a high swell.

The weather deteriorated and we had to close the shutters over our windows. We could not walk about the ship, and had to cling on everywhere in fear and trembling. We reefed the mainsail and fought our way through raging seas. The topgallant and topsail were hauled down, as was the mizzen, long before the waves were halfway up the mainsail. Thank God the wind changed and the currents helped speed us on towards the distant Cape.

We were accompanied by a naval convoy as far as Cadiz, in order to avoid capture by the English, and had an escort from a Swedish frigate on past Cape Verde.

I had to employ quicksilver to treat two sailors who had amused themselves in Cadiz. They will be left with dark blotches on their cheeks, to bear witness to their exploits. All the crew and their bunks and sea chests were inspected for spoons and buckles that had gone missing from one of the supercargoes' cabins, but without result.

Captain Ekeberg, who holds my father in high esteem, showed me his many books, fine copperplate engravings of natural curiosities, and his own notes on magnetism and meteorological phenomena. He admired the chest I had inherited from my forebears, but considered it rather heavy. It has to withstand all the battering it gets when the sea gathers strength and goes on the attack, said I.

He advised me to learn to cope with unforeseen circumstances, not to try to protect myself from them. He went on to say that I could expect much travail and adversity and intense sun.

He asked for my assistance in fastening a blackened leathern strap around his tightly twisted pigtail, while jesting about the *bon viveurs* who made a pitch for any highly desirable goods as soon as they were listed by the East India Company. Our learned Captain also wrote parodies of Olaus Rudbeck's speculations that everything had originated from Scandinavia, and we composed drinking songs and funeral dirges for deceased sailors, and eulogies to the cows and hogs that had to sacrifice their lives for us. Time was a plentiful commodity in the Doldrums.

I saw a bird running on the water which looked like a starling and was in fact the oft-described storm petrel. And, sure enough, the storm came the next day, so we struck the yardarm and took in all the sails except the jib. The tackle was moaning so loudly that nobody could hear anyone else without shouting right into their ear.

After a day and a night the wind eased. We hoisted the sails and made seven miles an hour. Bunches of seaweed floated all around us. We spied a big shark as long as a man is tall, lowered a hook baited with meat and caught it, bringing it aboard with rope snares, and watching warily for its ferocious teeth, which could snap off thighs or arms like cabbage stalks. The cook was only too delighted to have it, and the Captain unlocked the brandy cupboard.

Dolphins were leaping on both sides of the ship, bouncing and rolling like skiffs, making the water foam. But our harpoons did not find their mark until nightfall.

The body of a seaman was committed to the waves. The ship's bell, its clapper bound in a cloth, gave a muffled ring. The sailors stood in line, some dressed in darker garments. The stars clustered above our wash as it enshrouded the corpse.

Will-o'-the-wisps frightened and spurred our imaginations. The beguiling moonlight conjured up mirages of non-existent lands on the horizon.

The phosphorescence on the sea discharged its restless dancing spirits, reminding us that somewhere the blood of pillage and defeat was staining the ground, and washing over the beaches. History never pauses in its unremitting march, and time casts no anchor. The world is a bottomless morass, swallowing up first the good, then the evil.

Rarely does the sea give warning of its intentions. Some men come near to choking on the salt-laden waves that break over the deck; some are given to vomiting; no-one can sleep in a storm. Once the heaving of the ocean lessens, we stow ourselves away for a few hours' sleep.

When the night is over, I see the sick awakening with stiff limbs and in mortal fear: gangrene! The sea is rising with a sound like someone climbing the side of the vessel. The deck slippery from the rain. The black waters constantly in motion. A thunderstorm lurking on the horizon, silently following the ship.

The equatorial ocean must be where the dead go, for here time and wind cease altogether, in a stillness so complete that I fear for my reason.

As barber-surgeon, I sit at the top table with the Captain. But the food gets worse and worse with every passing day. Peas, pitiful and rotten, ship's biscuits mouldy, water tasting stale.

The supercargoes – Grill, Gadd and Pike – have their own table, with their own cook, steward and servants, who are excused watch duties. There they plan the East India Company's business without interference from the officers. The most lucrative but prohibited merchandise is opium. They say the supercargo in Madras smuggled one hundred and fifty boxes to the supercargo in Macao.

The steward rules supreme over the oxhides of wine and barrels of arrack. The crew are treated to punch on Sundays at one o'clock, from an iron-studded bowl big enough to drown a soldier in. When it's blowing up a storm, the brandy bell announces extra tonic.

The Spanish sows, bought in Cadiz, farrowed: piglets with long black tails; they were slaughtered after a few weeks, already extremely fat. The boar was meaty and delicious. Our supercargo opened a few bottles of wine and passed them round.

Winds variable. Large birds, fulmars, appeared. Trumpet grass spied floating in the water: a sign that we were nearing the Cape. Lemon juice sweetened with sugar an excellent notion. One of the sick men became delirious. He sang all day and night before expiring.

2

Carl Gustav Ekeberg was one of the first to follow the exhortation of Magnus Lagerström, director of the Swedish East India Company, to collect plants and other natural curiosities wherever his ship might land. Ekeberg had an aptitude for the natural sciences and kept journals on all eleven of his voyages. He brought back a slave boy, whose freedom he had purchased, to his home at Altomta Farm in the parish of Tensta, close to the Sparrman rectory, where he also housed the collections he had not donated to Linnaeus. The slave boy was baptized in Tensta Church by Sparrman's father, and learned Swedish and the latest agricultural techniques.

In the first twenty-five years of the Swedish East India Company's business, Swedish ships sailed past Cape Colony without putting into harbour, to avoid hostilities from competitors. The Company had a monopoly on all trade beyond Cape Town. The export of iron and copper was balanced by the import of porcelain, tea, raw silk, silk cloth, rattan, rice, cinnamon, arrack and many other commodities.

Sparrman had left Sweden at a time when the Age of Liberty was entering an ignominious phase, characterized by monetary and moral inflation, and the feverish pursuit of pleasure. His heart was still a battleground of conflicting and capricious desires. He could not reconcile Linnaeus' system with Ovid's rules of love. Perhaps, he mused, one and the same inclination could never 'predominate in a person without changing over the years, and every period of life has its own'.

In Cadiz the Captain handed over a log to the local health-enforcement officers giving details of the ships they had met with and the ports they had entered. Fear of the plague was widespread. Bringing tobacco into Spain was grounds for a life sentence, so all tobacco was listed and impounded until the ship's departure. While in Cadiz they took on board jars of olive oil, wine vinegar, lemon juice against scurvy, brandy mixed with up to a third of water, six oxen, six calves, ten sheep, eight pigs and several hundred hens. Boxes of silver were locked away in the supercargoes' cabins to provide for payment in Canton. The key to the powder magazine was held by the Captain.

The *Stockholm Castle* offloaded iron at Madeira. She was too heavily laden to weather the storms round the Cape, to which it would take a month with the help of the south-east trade winds. After that they would enter the waters around Madagascar and Mauritius, which were fraught with danger. In order to defend the ship against pirates, the animal pens on deck were dismantled and the crew were trained in firearms. The ship had forty cannons to protect a cargo of bar-iron, band-iron, nails and steel, lead, white lead, quicksilver and quantities of minted copper plates.

One of the experiences Anders considered most extraordinary was the nightly rain: water struck water with a clatter like a thousand pairs of feet down a long corridor. During one such downpour in the Indian Ocean he observed a luminous creature falling with the rain and landing on a sailor's clothes. It was a millipede three inches in length. It did not look like a marine insect, and must have travelled with clouds and sea-breezes from the coast of Java. Later a few more such glow-worms dropped from the clouds on to the deck, one of them the same type of millipede, four inches long, with seventy segments and pairs of legs. It was preserved in wine vinegar.

The *Stockholm Castle* continued on her way through the islands of the East Indies and took on a pilot in Macao. The silt from the Pearl River made the channels uncertain even far out at sea. Chinese sampans accompanied the ship upriver. The customary greetings were exchanged with a salvo of eight shots answered from the shore.

The young barber-surgeon gazed up beyond the water-covered rice paddies towards hills of green woods, villages and small fortresses, high towers in lattice-work dwellings, villas and pagodas with uptilted roofs. Most of the streets in Canton were narrow, some paved with stone slabs that were continually being swept clean. Bast mats were suspended between the roofs of the houses to keep out the heat.

Shops were arranged by guilds and wares: one street for porcelain, another for silk cloth, a third for hats and caps. Craftsmen painted and varnished wood, polished glass, carved ivory, sewed and embroidered. Wild ducks, tame ducks and whole pigs hung on display, emitting a nauseating smell. Hawkers sold fish, fruit and vegetables, which they carried in baskets on a bamboo pole over their shoulders. Fortune-tellers, charlatans, nail-trimmers, tooth-extractors and barbers offered their services out in the street.

The Swedes who ran the trading settlement were forbidden to have their families with them, or to bear arms, use palanquins, employ Chinese servants or row on the river without permission. Sparrman was authorized to make an excursion with an interpreter to the island of Hainan with its gardens and temples, and to remove plants. He bought a selection of herbs, wrote a paper on the cotton cultivated in sandy soil fertilized with bone ash, and began work on his dissertation *Iter in Chinam*, which he dedicated to Captain Ekeberg.

In Canton, Sparrman had filled his medicine chest with the podded fruits of the tamarind tree for stomach complaints, quinine for venereal diseases, liquorice root, yellow wax, saltpetre, camphor, camomile flowers, linen for plaster bandages. It also contained his instruments as barber-surgeon: trepanning irons, needles, brass pestle and mortar, suction cap, cauterizing iron. He had a drawer full of sago, rice and soya for his brother and sisters, and arrack for hot punch for himself. Spices were worth their weight in gold in Stockholm, and if he put *Arabicum* or *Indicum* on the labels of the bottles, the price on the apothecary's shelves would rise tenfold.

On the return voyage he spent days on the upper deck with Captain Ekeberg, who stood with the first mate at the wheel before the mizzen mast, surrounded by a fixed brass compass, a directional compass and a binnacle compass, and with the deep-sea log within reach. The sky merged into the ocean. The *Stockholm Castle* moved languidly in the warm tailwind.

On deck were the deckhouse and cabins for the Captain and four mates, with the poopdeck at the stern. On the lower deck the main cabin, the four supercargoes' cabins, and smaller cabins for the chaplain, doctor and ship's clerk. Smoking was sanctioned only on the forecastle and upper decks. No-one was permitted to have their bedding stuffed with hay, straw or any other flammable material. It was forbidden to light candles in the cabins, with the exception of the officers, who were allowed lamps in covered lanterns.

The drinking water was purified with quicksilver, but started turning foul after Batavia and smelt of putrefaction. A sail was dropped from the mainmast into the hatch to draw in fresh air. Sea chests and hammocks were brought up on deck to air in fine weather. The ship was washed down daily inside and out when the weather was favourable, and was fumigated with juniper berries and lighted gunpowder, then sprinkled with vinegar to ward against scabies.

The seventeen-year-old barber-surgeon was himself afflicted with the swellings and inflammations he had been appointed to cure. Tinctures, mint water, parsley root and opium distillate proved of little help. He realized that he, as physician, was not immune to the ailments that his patients had so vividly described.

He kept to his cabin, where the air was suffocatingly humid. His breeches were up and down the whole time. Amid the spots of quicksilver on the mirror he saw a sight reminiscent of pale green lagoon water. When the ship crossed the Tropic of Capricorn he discovered little white worms in his mug of drinking water.

After taking on water and provisions at St Helena, they sailed into a raging nocturnal storm. It extinguished the hand lanterns and the lamps by the compasses, swirled around the sailors' feet, and a wave smashed the cabin door of the ship's clerk. The pumps creaked and groaned as they all waited for the dawn. He could hear the cattle lowing, the pigs squealing, the turkeys and geese cackling in terror. The sea swept down over the 'tween deck and into Sparrman's cabin, where the bedclothes doubled their weight and his slippers and dictionaries floated across the floor, along with his very first wig.

Rounding the Cape without running into a storm, Captain Ekeberg's chaplain opined, was as rare as leaving Cadiz without suffering the maladies of love.

When the winds had subsided they played lotto and draughts to keep up their spirits. Sunday's blessings having been dispensed from the pulpit of the apothecary chest, the iron-studded bowl was stood upon it, full of brandy. The steward distributed the creature comforts with a copper ladle.

The last and youngest of the apostles filled his grandfather's massive oak chest with seeds, fossils and plants, both living and dried, from his China voyage, all of which took their place in Linnaeus' library of flora.

In August 1767, after an absence of twenty months, Anders Sparrman returned to Uppsala to take his doctorate. He found a third of the city burnt down. He saw the new firehoses put to the test, with a jet so powerful that he thought it would pierce holes in the stone walls. Professor Linnaeus' botanical garden and house had almost met their end in the flames. So Linnaeus had begun to construct a museum out at Hammarby to which he could transfer his collections.

Anders had received a letter from his brother Nils, who had graduated in theology, telling him that their father had passed away. He had simply changed position, as it were, stepping down from the pulpit, going out into the churchyard and making himself invisible. Life had not bowed him, nor had he been frightened by its abysses, of which the grave in his own church was one of the least threatening. An osprey had soared over the fields, an unusual occurrence which people talked about long afterwards, because it arrived at the very moment the church bells began to toll for the deceased.

It was said at Eric Sparrman's funeral that he would rather have given solace to the wretched than to have predicted their damnation. No tears came to his widow's eyes when the coffin was lowered and her husband was united with those residing under the soil, who had always been more numerous than those above.

There he lay without a sound; even while alive he had not found it easy to breathe.

'They say the soul is set free in death,' Anders remarked to his learned brother, 'but in my opinion that's when it's locked up for ever.'

Once, at morning service, Anders had been told, his father had looked out across his church, with its whitewashed walls concealing Papist paintings, and had reminded his congregation of the ravages of the Russians and Cossacks along the coast, and that 'it might not be the last time they plunder our carrots and apples, harvest our winter rye and burn down our houses'.

He had given edifying sermons like no-one else in the parishes of Lena and Tensta, and like few others in the archdiocese. In the night he had heard the Almighty pray for both the stubborn and the oppressed. Wide awake – as he mostly was – he had his wife's hand in his, and his two daughters' hands on his brow, as he made his departure into the realm of the imagination.

After his death, the diocesan consistory commended Eric Sparrman for displaying 'untiring zeal for the cure of souls, and unalloyed tenderness and support for the poor and needy'. The local peasantry were praised as 'assiduous, resolute and of a happy disposition'. No-one was starving. The prospect of frugal subsistence generated a feeling of self-sufficiency and well-being. All the villagers knew each other personally, which created an equality in their everyday lives which was not at odds with order and good manners.

An obituary also noted that the rector showed his displeasure if anyone travelled through Tensta without calling upon him. Straw mattresses, furs and coats would be brought out for unexpected guests, and meat and strong beer fetched from the pantry.

But the property left by the deceased as listed in the inventory – wooden sleigh, cart, wolf net and beekeeper net, ploughs, iron bucket and pans – was not sufficient to appease the creditors.

After the death of her spouse, Brita moved in with her daughter Anna Magdalena and her husband, the organ-builder Jonas

Ekengren, in the parish of Katarina Church in Stockholm, and later went to her son Nils when he was given a living in the town of Gävle. Many years later she was dressed in a shroud of white nettle-cloth, with a silk nightcap on her head. 'Eric has waited long enough now,' she said.

Anders remembered her in a blue tunic, which was passed on to Sara the maid. The memory lingered: the flimsiest blue membrane between life and death.

Voyage to South Africa

1

Having gained his doctorate in medicine, Anders Sparrman sailed from Gothenburg on the 10th of January 1772, as before with Captain Carl Gustav Ekeberg on the *Stockholm Castle*, and once again at Linnaeus' commission.

To the north of Scotland they encountered a storm, which, he commented in his journal, 'carried away our main topsail, though it was quite new, and made of a strong cloth. The damages were reckoned to amount to several hundred rix-dollars. This ravage and destruction afforded in itself nevertheless a fine spectacle, which to me was entirely new. The long shivers of the topsail got loose and, being white, were distinctly discerned waving to and fro in a most alarming manner and, at length, totally vanished through the darkened air. At the same time the violence of the wind caused those parts of the sails which yet remained on the mast, together with the ends of the broken cordage, to beat about with the greatest violence, making such a crash withal, as for a time to drown every other noise.'

The storm compelled the ship to put in at Portsmouth for a week of repairs. These years were difficult for the town: he overheard on the harbour steps that the ports of Plymouth and Southampton had taken over. Grass grew along the docks. Coasters were being loaded with timber and salt fish, and setting sail for Cornwall and Cork.

The High Street was lined with ironmongers, sign-painters, butchers and sail-makers. The paving stones were uneven and tripped pedestrians into the gutter. Carts rattled by, spraying mud on to white silk stockings. Anders had never seen such commotion: taverns and coffee-houses, laughter and curses and the cries of street vendors. The side streets were full of women selling fruit, and men carrying meat and vegetables. Boys whipped cows and sheep down narrow sloping alleys. The Mary Rose Inn, built in 1742, was named after the ship that had sunk in the Solent. Beyond King James' Gate lay Portsmouth Point, a curved promontory enclosing the old harbour where the merchant ships docked.

Naval officers put up at the George Hotel. In the next block Anders could hear a tailor of military uniforms in furious argument with a betting agent. He examined a bust of Charles I on a pedestal, and the semaphore station on top of the Square Tower. Broad Street ran through King James' Gate and divided the respectable part of town from the pawnbrokers, coffee houses and brothels of the disreputable quarter. In one of the bawdy houses was a workshop where the teeth of the children of the poor were extracted and sold to the toothless rich.

Standing on a stool provided for public speakers, a reformist was railing against the deplorable, unhygienic conditions – complaining that elegant ladies used ivory backscratchers to rid themselves of lice instead of availing themselves of the bath-houses, that gentlemen seldom bathed more than twice a year, and that more people died from foul air, smoke and pestilence than in all the land and naval battles combined.

In hard times such as these the communal graves were left open until they were full, and the stench of rotting corpses dissuaded the clergy from administering the last rites. Sewage and toxic substances from smithies and workshops flowed straight down into the harbour basin.

Anders drank tea with white sugar, listened to the sailors bellowing on the streets and watched wreaths of mist creeping between the houses. Not everything could be explained, not even Professor Linnaeus' intentions in exposing him to such great perils. His senses reeled at the smells of tar, seaweed and dried cod. Out in the Roads vessels were drying their sails, which were beginning to smack as the wind blew up. It felt as if a fishing line out at sea were straining to haul him in.

It was the last night before sailing and he decided to follow his desires, which at that moment felt perfectly natural and understandable. It was a subconscious rebellion against the uncertainty that lay ahead of him.

He visited a prostitute on Oyster Street. Her name was Emma and she was a young widow who had learned that her boatswain husband had died of blackwater fever in Calcutta. Without any other means at her disposal, she had stayed in Portsmouth to provide for herself as well as she could.

She was not dressed gaudily, and was thin and pale, with amber hair in a bun at the nape of her neck. He thought she had the most beautiful eyes. She was alternately shy and angry, tense and relaxed. Anders had never had a woman. He had expected a debauched, dissolute night, but she lay still on her back and at her request he stroked her from the top of her head to the soles of her feet. He laid his hand tentatively on her mound of Venus, and she licked her finger and moistened his member and guided it in, her feet entwined around him.

He noted the variety of her scents, her quick movements, her steady breathing. He saw her from above as a landscape: she was his garden of delight for this one night. Her body entranced him with its valleys, meadows, dark pastures, little pink-tiled roofs.

'I'll not be here long,' she said. 'And you are a bird of passage that will never return, so we need not dissemble. I have my own Purgatory: I am full of indescribable feelings, but no joy.'

Her trunk stood in a corner of the room with a washbowl on it. She had come with the post-coach from the area of Stonehenge, where heathen rituals took place at the summer solstice. Their encounter in the room was also a ritual. He caressed her till liquid oozed from beneath her mound. When he sank into her, she mumbled something meaningless – as if she were talking in her sleep.

He rested his forehead against her shoulder in exhaustion. He felt satisfaction and release, rather than any profound emotion. He fixed her green eyes and delicate English features in his memory. He stroked her head absently with a yearning that went far beyond her. Her hair shone, her throat pulsated gently. She ran her hands slowly over his body – like a net being drawn across a sandy seabed.

He had promised himself he would pay her generously, he felt so grateful, purified, even resurrected. Was she of lowly birth? She was part of humankind, which he intended to make as much the subject of his studies as flora and fauna.

'If you marry a sailor, then you meet again in Heaven. You are going away, like all the others. You have time on your side. If you're lucky. If my young man had been a miller or a baker, I would have him here yet, and would not be in this plight. Nothing in my stars prepared me for this. I must be strong. I must grow accustomed to demeaning myself for a while. There are maids and washerwomen here aplenty and to spare, and I have nothing to sell but myself.'

He stared into her eyes and knew he would never see her again. He felt his soul lurch when he thought of how that sensation of now or never, near and far, could slide like a finger across a nautical chart. What name would one day hold him fast? Not Emma. Perhaps no name at all. He had entered her, but he was tapping on another door, in vain. He had not seen a woman clearly, even in his dreams.

'Your voyage will absorb you utterly,' Emma said. 'Destroy you or make you famous. I shall end up with my mother, who is a widow in the country.'

'You'll find a man, and have children. Maybe in about three years' time, one day when Venus is in Aries.'

'If your heart is heavy, a sea voyage can do you good. Have you the courage to give me your real name? You're a foreigner, so it will not be one I recognize.'

'Anders Sparrman, as true as I stand here.'

'I shall remember you when times are bad, and at other times, too, in my daily chores. You will see things I shall never see. You will see a pattern in Creation, but I shall never find my place in it. If I were carrying treasure, I would sink to the bottom of the sea with it, but you will learn latitude and longitude to salvage me. That's the difference between men and women.'

He was twenty-three. She was almost twenty-nine, as she had candidly told him. He wanted to ascertain her exact position, cup his hand round her elliptical head, watch her gaze travel like the moon across the sky. He had never met a woman so communicative and so vulnerable.

He was glad to have escaped the ritual of seduction as he had heard it recounted; all that was encompassed by such inane words as 'seizing' and 'conquering'. It was a chance kinship that had arisen, a compact, since their meeting was so direct and limited in time. Neither of them was leaving the other or being left, and he had done nothing she had not wished. She was a siren call from a different country, an alternative geography.

'You're a very young and temperate gentleman,' said Emma kindly. 'Take care how you sail! You are full of life, which was more than my Peter was, and I'm certain you are very clever. You will know many women, and in the end will not be able to remember them apart.'

And she continued, 'My life has no steerage way, no visible draught. There's only mud. I'm heading in a direction I cannot control.'

She had an iron pot on the stove, and in the morning she would go to the market and buy something with his money to fill it with, and no-one would reproach her for attempting to make her living in a squalid town where rain flooded the streets.

On the wall in her rented room she had but one personal possession: a pastoral scene of a cracked archway, cedar trees shading a waterfall, and a meadow with lambs and wild flowers. That had been her life before the boatswain who had married the sea.

With a smile so transitory that he wasn't sure if he had even seen it, she said, 'I only know one thing, and that is that I have lost everything. Otherwise, I'd not be here.'

He would never touch her again. They would disappear from each other's lives and die their separate deaths. He looked at her intensely for a long time, as if she had access to something of which he was ignorant.

'You are bold and outspoken at heart,' she said, 'but now you are shy and diffident, even though you are trying the best you can. But nothing is particularly special. Things are what they are and seldom more.'

The dawn cast its glow through the window, and a soft tinge of colour lit her face. It was January outside and a mist was wafting in from the English Channel. In a low voice she added, 'You have nought to fear, Sparrman. I'm not infected, and I'm older than you . . .'

Anders gave her some money and told her never to entrust her life to a higher power.

2

The *Stockholm Castle* set sail once again. The lights of the town dissolved in reflections that diminished in intensity until they vanished from view altogether. Sailing past Brittany, Cape Finisterre and the coast of Portugal, they reached Cadiz for the usual reloading. Later on they were so close to Cape Verde that they could see the baobab trees and the basalt cliffs of Cape Manuel.

On board ship Anders Sparrman was schoolteacher to the younger members of the crew: mathematics, arithmetic, astronomy. The vessel was fumigated against rats, the ballast adjusted. Every morning while they were at sea a boy piped to the foremast the men whose sores needed treatment by the doctor. Some of the crew had signed on in order to escape a worse fate on land: embezzlement, the wrong woman, alcohol or gambling debts. Their ages ranged from fifteen to forty.

They were sailing in a night as black as the mouth of the cannon which stood outside the cabin window, through sudden gusts that made the deck planks groan, in the silent absence of the moon; a darkness so impenetrable that the helmsman could see no further than the glow of the compass lantern. He could hear only the whine of the rigging and the dolphins swishing through the foam. Three months was the average length of a voyage from Gothenburg to Cape Town, and every day sailed could mean one dead seaman less.

Time was different at sea. The rim of the sun appeared over the horizon as though somebody had pressed a spring and a hatch had opened in the ocean. The hens clucked in their cages and would soon be consumed. A sailor who had stolen a cheese was whipped by the boatswain with the cat-o'-nine-tails. The sails flapped. Anders turned the sheets of his notes and thought they must have been written by someone else, someone who had not yet come aboard.

The waves rolled towards them like black lava. Flying fish streaked across their bows like evil spirits. Near the forecastle was the cabin where the doctor performed his bloody handiwork under a flickering tin lamp. The fetid atmosphere on the 'tween deck sometimes almost suffocated him. He sweated in the stench. His lips and eyelids had swollen up.

As the ship's doctor he visited the sick twice a day, at eight o'clock and four o'clock, and reported to the Captain or the mate on duty. When there was a death he made his report and the mate shared out the dead man's clothes to those in need. If anyone died in port the flag was raised at half mast and a boat brought a coffin to collect the body. At sea it would be stitched into a hammock, laid in front of the mainmast for a few hours, then cast overboard with sand or lead round its feet.

The sailors sat on benches at a rough table, with dirty socks, boots and shirts scattered about them. A meal comprised a bowl of soup, a piece of salt meat, a lump of rock-hard cheese and beer. Ship's biscuits contained, Sparrman noted, 'a surprisingly lively menagerie of insects'. Some of them could be ground to a powder to replace mustard. In the Doldrums bacon rotted and had to be cooked in alcohol. The ship's rats multiplied many times over during the course of the voyage, and the cook had to resort to flaying them and serving the scant meat fried in oil.

Carl Peter Thunberg and Anders Sparrman landed at the Cape in April 1772. Both were doctors who had put their knowledge into practice during the three-month voyage on a crew partly scraped together by unscrupulous agents, so-called soul-seekers, and who were inveigled on board by trickery or taken by force. Thunberg had sailed under Captain Rondecrantz from Kalmar on the Dutch *Schoonzigt*, and more than a third of the crew had perished on the voyage. He himself was severely affected when the cook mistakenly added white lead to the pancake batter, as he discovered when he analysed his vomit. This poisoning provided the subject of Thunberg's first academic treatise, which appeared in the *Proceedings of the Swedish Academy of Sciences* in 1773.

The watch at Lion's Head fired a cannon when the *Stockholm Castle* hove into view. A flag was hoisted on the citadel when she entered Table Bay, and the ship responded with a salute. The Dutch flag was raised on Robben Island, which all vessels had to pass. Anders could make out the inhabitants of the island: life-prisoners whose daily task was to collect seashells on the beaches and out in the cold channel, to be burnt to make lime for the East India Company's buildings.

Thunberg had planned his expedition to South Africa down to the last detail, whereas Sparrman had not given any thought at all to the matter of his upkeep. But Captain Ekeberg had sent a letter to P. J. Bergius at the Academy of Sciences: 'If a sober and stable young man, well-versed in the German, French and Latin languages, with a sound knowledge of arithmetic and geometry, had a stipend of travel money, he would be able to serve the sciences at home with collections, for which there is here an inexhaustible supply, and himself with an income of one hundred to one hundred and twenty rix-dollars in addition to perquisites and privileges.' He added that the Resident, Johannes Fredrik Kirsten, had children in need of tuition.

With a recommendation from Linnaeus and through the good offices of Captain Ekeberg, Anders Sparrman was thus appointed tutor to the family of the Resident in Simonstown at False Bay, and in the summer at their Alphen estate near Constantia.

He felt the call of Africa, he later wrote. He knew he would never have a complete overview of it or gain even an impression of the whole of its extent. On his map of Cape Province, which was to achieve fame as the first accurate representation of the coast, he named one point Cape Ekeberg, in recognition of an exceptional navigator. And in honour of the farmer and master of Altomta Farm, he named a previously undescribed tree, a Cape ash of the mahogany genus, *Ekebergia capensis*.

With the Resident at the Cape

1

This is not what I call a civilized society. Smallpox and measles are the most dangerous of maladies. When the pox appears, people flee inland. The food is overly cooked and tastes of nothing. The produce, corn and cattle of city and countryside are managed no better by the Dutch than by the Hottentots. Dutch captains wear their hats indoors, and light their pipes at the meal table, without it being considered ill-mannered.

There were a couple of sailors at the inn with bottles in their hands clasped tight by the necks, ready for a skirmish. A toothless giant made a lewd gesture with his finger. I saw no respect for Creation among those who would gladly dance on others' graves.

The town is a sleepless cauldron, where the screams of the slaves and the roars of the masters give rise to a general nervous debility, and the drunken clamour outside the recruiting office is a reminder that man, unlike animals, is totally reckless.

Cape Town is two thousand paces long and the same wide, the streets unpaved, the houses of stone, whitewashed, some painted in the green colour the Dutch favour. They are two storeys at the most, with flat tiled roofs or covered with reeds. Only the Vice-Governor's house and the Company's warehouse have three storeys. Roof beams are imported from the East Indies; straight tree trunks are rare here.

Beautiful gardens have been dug up for fruit and vegetables.

European oaks have been planted along the streets. Smoking is prohibited in the street, for risk of fire. There is one Reformed church, with two rectors, on a square with an ornamental fountain. Several batteries of guns line the shore. The mists blow in from Robben Island, though the air remains rancid with the smell of fish guts. Fungi shoot up everywhere from a fertile breeding ground. There is no shortage of water. The streams rush down from Table Mountain where the clouds gather above its high plateau, and whence the baboons come to raid the town's kitchen gardens.

A tamed guenon monkey flew at me in a fit of rage. I was obliged to break its back with a hefty blow of my stick. When I stopped to rummage for some tobacco from my tin, I happened to see scalding water spill from a pot on to a slave child. I picked up the child and carried it across to a tub of cold water. The young mother was beside herself, ripped off the cotton cloth she was wearing and wrapped it round the infant, standing there naked with a smile on her face: it was enough that the boy was alive; she was used to worse fates.

The townsfolk have the right to establish hostelries and hire out carriages to travellers. Many inns and wine cellars are appointed not so much for drinking, shouting and fighting, as for dancing, the guests encouraged to take to the floor by the musicians. No card games are permitted, and the dancing continues until a certain hour of the night, at which point everyone goes peacefully home.

Few white people are employed by a white merchant or manufacturer. One exception is the tannery, to which three Flemings deliver hides for boots, shoes, coats and saddles. Basket-makers and carpet-weavers conduct their business in the shadow of the castle. Malay slaves in yellow tunic-shirts run barefoot with pails of water on broad yokes. Shells are burnt for lime beneath heaps of twigs and branches. The sticky paste is moulded into bricks in kilns fired with heather, grass and bushes.

French ships lie in harbour alongside Danish and Portuguese, and the languages blend into a polyglot jargon that seamen and slaves comprehend, despite some disastrous misunderstandings. Officers auction goods they wish to sell, and pay five per cent to the fiscal. European goods go for twice their purchase price.

The garrison at the Cape comprises recruited adventurers from various corners of Europe. Most settlers are retired soldiers granted a piece of land on which to support themselves. They have to perform some military exercises and report for duty whenever danger threatens, either from the sea or from the unreliable natives. They despise physical labour, which is allotted to the slaves, and they increase their landholdings by extending the boundaries towards the wilderness and the wild beasts. Researchers such as Thunberg and myself are regarded as spies, for the Dutch themselves are too much occupied to devote themselves to the sciences.

There seems to be a permanent frenzy prevailing here, a convulsion of wantonness and frustration that gives rise to excesses which Calvin's God struggles in vain to curb. The slimmest and most undeveloped slave girl may be carrying children that all too closely resemble her master. The men grab at land, animals and women. Unmentionable things happen in dark corners, for here there is no history, no legacy from past generations, no roots, no respect to impose restraint on anybody.

The Company's slave barracks is the principal brothel. European soldiers and sailors can be seen visiting it every evening. At eight o'clock the Company officials lock the gates, count the slaves and turn out the Europeans. The men entertain the women slaves in the taverns of the town in exchange for their services, sometimes giving them hammocks and clothes that are better than they get from the Company stores. Even in a more permanent relationship between a male and female slave (marriage is forbidden) the men often encourage their wives to take a white lover, to provide them with some income.

What is also discreditable to the city is a gallows and a wheel and spit that the Government has erected by the fortress. The gallows itself is an unsavoury enough door to eternity, constructed by a tyranny that even in such a small town can find seven victims at a time to hang in a row.

I went into a workshop where the implements of slavery were made: whips, iron collars, branding irons, shears, tongs, a saw with teeth as sharp as a bat's, a cage in which a brutal master could lock his slave and let the tide flow in and drown him. I have heard of slaves eating soil in order to die, and being punished for it with an iron mask over their face.

There are rumours too of caves where fleeing slaves hide themselves, only to emerge at night, like beasts of prey, but no-one knows their whereabouts. The slaves can expect the most horrendous retribution, but their desire for liberty is too powerful. Those who are discovered are put on the wooden horse in Cape Town, have their fingers bitten off, joint by joint, and are sometimes flayed alive. Apart from the Hottentots, the slaves come from Madagascar, Malabar and other parts of India. As a sign of having lost their freedom, they go about barefoot and bareheaded.

The motto on the Cape Town coat of arms is 'Here Liberty is Manifest'.

I have trapped and skinned a white sand mole that was causing damage to the Resident's garden.

2

Anders Sparrman was a tutor in the Resident's house in Simonstown at False Bay from April 1772 until near the end of that year. Only with reluctance had the Resident, Johan Fredrik Kirsten, accepted this pinnacle of his career. He had arrived in the Cape garrison as a soldier thirty years before. For want of good schools, his five children, especially Jacob, Johannes and Gesina (called Geessie), who were in their teenage years, needed tuition in geography, mathematics, French, English, Nature studies and moral precepts.

The Resident, dressed in a smoke-grey coat of Canton silk besmirched with a few wine stains, instructed Anders on his duties. The latter expressed his unwillingness to teach religious doctrines. The Reformed Church would do it better, and there was already a spiritual atmosphere in the house, he had noticed. Religious knowledge was refractory in itself, and the young were often reluctant to absorb it when it was imposed upon them. But as his pupils they would not be lost souls: God would see to that.

The whitewashed walls of the kitchen bore traces of dead insects. In the garden rosemary, laurel and myrtle grew to the height of a man. The vegetable beds were green with cabbage, peas, lettuce, leeks and radishes. Yet the Resident complained, 'Can we not have a decent meat broth? No self-respecting man can swallow this.'

Another day it would be apples and onions that made him

bloated and gassy. He took his coffee black, and spilt food, which lodged in his beard. They ate from a flower-patterned dinner service of Dutch faience. At best, smoked fish or lobster from the Robben Island Sound, arrack from Batavia, sweet Constantia wine, and afterwards a pipe of tobacco on the porch steps.

Outside the hovel, where the slaves left their maize gruel to harden into cakes, evening fires and tallow candles glowed, to the sound of singing and stringed instruments.

'They're enjoying themselves, they have no concept of suffering,' said a gentleman who had come from the Reformed Church service to join them for fruit pie, cake and a tall glass of toddy.

The Resident read aloud from the Bible to emphasize the holiness of the Sabbath. His wife Johanna Catharina – with sun-bleached eyebrows and a prominent chin – wrapped herself in a shawl the colour of ox-blood.

'God preserve and defend us!' she murmured, sounding somewhat dispirited.

The wash-house, stable and kitchen were separate buildings. A low parapet ran along the front of the terrace, giving shade and shelter. Tree roots protruded from the ground, grey-barked deciduous trees bent beneath the treacherous sand-laden wind from Cape Flats. A slave shook out a quilt, which split: goose feathers drifted across the flowerbeds and over the horses, which stood tethered by a stone wall. The slave went on with his task like a sleepwalker, as if nothing were amiss.

Through a cloud of starlings Anders saw the milkmaid hobbling up from the harbour jetty, a yoke across her shoulders. She was a pretty seventeen-year-old whom the predecessor of the previous Resident had conceived with one of the female house slaves. That was why she was free, and allowed to wear shoes and stockings whenever she wished.

The Kirstens came home one evening from a party given by the Governor, Rijk Tulbagh, who had also arrived at the Cape as an ordinary soldier and progressed to become the highest in command.

They were merry in both senses of the word: it was their annual indulgence. The Resident wore a moleskin coat against the harsh south wind and sank snuffling into a camp chair. Sparrman lifted the daughter Geessie, in her dusty yellow dress, out of the carriage, its rhythmic jolting having sent her to sleep. Her hem was soiled with dirt from the road, but her shoes had silver filigree on the toe-caps. She held her hat on tight and smelt faintly of cocoa. He put his hand under the nape of her neck for the first and only time, and carried her across the raised terrace and into the house, the finest in Simonstown. He laid her on the bed.

Her father jerked up with a start and complained of black cormorants pecking the flesh from his body in his dream.

'You take a lot of notes,' he said to the tutor. 'Writing is the white shadow of conscience.'

One of the slaves muttered something in a strange, hybrid language and hurried off with a lamp in his hand to fetch wood. Jacob awoke and shouted to be heard over the waves crashing against Simonstown's newly built stone quay. Prince the dog barked in the yard. The candlestick on the Resident's desk rattled, the mahogany clock on the sideboard struck, even though it wasn't yet the full hour.

Pale brown moths singed themselves in the heat of the fire. The night air smelt of wet lime-plaster; there was a distillery along the beach to the north. The sky was as dark as the rough skin of a black radish.

The next morning the Resident's wife ground cherry stones to a powder tasting of bitter almonds, while her husband looked up references in his volumes of Dutch law. The children played in silence.

Sometimes, on a Sunday, one of the slave women would wash and put up the Resident's hair. Then he would walk out with a silver-capped cane, wearing his blue dress-uniform trimmed with gold braid, his wife beside him, her hair piled high and secured with an ivory pin. Two slaves shaded them with parasols.

3

Early in September 1772 Anders Sparrman drove from Simonstown to Cape Town in a wagon drawn by six pairs of oxen, around
bays where the waves splashed up into the cart. A slave wielded a
whip the length of a fishing rod with both hands and steered their
cart with violent lashes. Another with a whip ran in front of them
the whole way. The carter used no reins. They broke their journey
in Meusenberg, where they changed to a carriage with four pairs
of horses, which took them to Cape Town. That was where Sparrman and Carl Peter Thunberg met, spending half a day together
before going their separate ways, and only seeing each other again
many years later in Sweden.

Thunberg undertook three expeditions by ox-wagon and on
horseback, totalling five hundred miles. He described the Hottentots' soured milk as the grandmother of Norrland fermented milk
in Sweden. A buffalo killed two of his horses. He climbed Table
Mountain fifteen times during his three-year stay in the Cape. He
managed to support himself as a doctor more or less adequately,
but seldom had sufficient funds for travelling.

After the farewell dinner for Thunberg, Sparrman borrowed a
horse, but lost his way in the dark. Arriving at a farm, he was
attacked by dogs. As many as twenty slaves refused to answer his
questions, conferring among themselves instead. He understood
their reluctance: strangers harassed them, sold them, clapped

them in irons. They could so easily have robbed and murdered him, then buried him or thrown him to the wild animals. His horse, taking fright at a beast of prey, stumbled into a hole, throwing him and galloping off. Eventually, in pouring rain, he found a house willing to take him in. He was reunited with his horse the next day.

He rode to Paarl and proceeded on foot to observe 'the lilies on the ground and the daughters of the land, as well as the products of other districts'. He hired a 'tawny' guide, who carried a staff with a plant press at one end and a sack of food as counterweight at the other.

They passed the night at an impoverished elderly white woman's house, complete with earth floor and lice. Gout had made her irascible and her female slave was forced to walk about in shackles. They were given a drink of water.

'The old lady immediately quitted the fine instructions that I was about giving her with respect to diet, in order to go and look at the strange and wonderful sight that was to be seen on my hat. But what astonished her the most was to see the little animals run through the body with pins, and fastened to the brim of my hat. As my box of insects was already quite full, I was obliged to put a whole regiment of flies, other insects and dung beetles round the brim.'

He then arrived at a farm where an obliging slave restrained the dogs from savaging him and led him to 'the absent *baas*'s own bedchamber. The bed was tolerable, but the floor was made of loam, the walls bare, and the whole furniture consisted of a cracked teacanister, with a few empty bottles, and a couple of chairs. As the door would not lock, I set the chairs against it, so that in case any attempt should be made against my life I might be awakened by the noise. After this I laid myself down to sleep, with a drawn knife under my pillow. The many murders that, to my knowledge, were committed in this country, rendered this caution extremely necessary.'

He sallied forth into the green fields of this 'cape at the end of the world', often hungry but without complaint. In the district around Paarl he came to the house of a Boer farmer: 'His well-behaved daughter about twelve to fourteen years of age set on the table a fine breast of lamb, with stewed carrots for sauce, and after dinner offered me tea with so good a grace that I hardly knew which to prefer, my entertainment or my fair attendant.'

They sat in a parlour with the lamp turned down. A farmer's widow in the neighbourhood was open to admirers, the Boer suggested. Anders drank in silence, the very idea a portent of death. He would not linger here.

A female slave showed him the shallowest fording place over the next stream, while he continued his search for rare botanical specimens. 'She seemed to lay her account in receiving some amorous kind of acknowledgement, in which she could not be otherwise than disappointed, as she had the misfortune to meet with a delicate as well as weary philosopher. In the evening I arrived in good time at a farm, where the father and mother were from home; but Master Johan and Miss Susey gave me house-room notwithstanding.'

He set off the next morning, 'lively and brisk after the high treat I had had of milk. On the road we passed a cow-keeper, who was roasting a small tortoise, the flesh of which tasted like that of a chicken.' Coming to a lake, Anders undressed to a 'state of innocence, my hat and queue excepted. My skin quite parched up by the sun, served, however, to convince me that I had lost in my little paradise the dominion over the gnats and horseflies.'

He next arrived at a miller's, who ordered his slave girl to bring out some food, while he himself continued to pore over a seventeenth-century astrological almanac. Sparrman asked whether he was disturbing the gentleman. 'It's our duty to assist travellers,' was the miller's curt response.

At the house of a coloured sexton and his wife he picked some medicinal plants and gave the woman to understand, 'with very little circumlocution, that her stay in this calamitous world was likely to be of very short duration'. She was only too glad to be freed of life's misery. Even her husband was cheered, opening a bottle of wine and taking him to see the church next door. 'This temple of the Lord was, indeed, as big as one of our largest-sized hay-barns, and neatly covered with dark-coloured reeds; but without any arching or ceiling, so that the transoms and beams inside made a miserable appearance. The pulpit was too plain and slovenly.'

At another farm he watched lambs being castrated, while the ewes had to listen helplessly to their bleats of pain. He was offered brandy, tobacco and anise root roasted in ashes. The spirited old man showed him shelves of tomes on 'almost every science, all of which I could do no other than commend, as he did nothing but run between me and his bookcase, and read over the whole title-page of every book, the printer's and bookseller's name not being omitted'.

He was accommodated for the night, and 'was waked here by the horrid shrieks and cries of January and February, who were undergoing the discipline of their master's lath. Many people call their slaves, some after the months, and others after the days of the week on which they were born. The woman was goodness itself, but in a phlegmatic body. The old fellow's phraseology, as well as his library, discovered, that he was, as well as myself, a runaway student.' He had married a parson's daughter, hence the books, and, being of a choleric disposition, he had beaten several of his slaves to death.

Losing their way on the homeward journey, Sparrman and his assistant were wandering over a vast plain when 'we at length met with seven of the Company's servants or soldiers, but by no means to our advantage; for these my fellow-Christians, intoxicated with the wine which they carried about them in leathern bottles or calabashes, were at variance among themselves, as every one of them pointed out to us an almost entirely different way. Jabbering to me all at once in High Dutch, Low Dutch, Hanoverian, etc., they all endeavoured to make me believe that I should meet with rivers, mountains, deserts, and the like, if I did not steer my course right. I thanked them, and got away from them as well as I could; on which they formed a ring round my servant, and chattered to him about the road till his head was quite turned.

'Being without chart or compass, I endeavoured to direct my course by the sun, till I overtook a black heathen, who was tending sheep; and in consequence of whose sober and sensible directions I arrived at a farmhouse, the bailiff of which, a Hanoverian, welcomed me in the most friendly manner, with a hearty slap of the hand, in the African style. He entertained me with milk, and an account of the love affairs and intrigues he had when he was a soldier in England. He also gave me a scale or list, as the result of his own experience, of the constant order of precedence in love, which ought to be observed among the fair sex in Africa, as follows: first the Madagascar women, who are the blackest and handsomest; next to these the Malabars, then the Malays, after these the Hottentots, and last and worst of all, the white Dutch women.

'During the whole evening I had seen the slaves in such good humour, and so kindly and familiarly treated, that (the want of liberty excepted) they really seemed to be better off than many servants in Europe; I therefore observed to my host, that his mildness and kindness was the best pledge for their good behaviour, and the surest preservative against their attacks.

'"It may be so," replied he, "but besides that, there are always some runaway and rebel slaves wandering about, in order to plunder houses of victuals and firearms; we have likewise instances of the blacks becoming furious at night, and committing murder, more particularly on the persons of their masters; but sometimes, if they cannot get at them, on some of their comrades, or else upon themselves.

'"To avoid jealousy, quarrels and murder," the bailiff continued, "my master does not permit any female slaves to be kept here; but I, for my part, could wish it were otherwise. They are lonesome and solitary, and consequently slow and sluggish enough."

'Slaves, even under the mildest tyrant, are bereaved of the rights of Nature. The melancholy remembrance of so painful a loss is most apt to arise during the silence of the night, when it ceases to be dissipated by the bustle of the day. What wonder then, if those who have deprived these poor fellows of their liberties should sometimes be forced to sign and seal with their blood the violated rights of mankind?

'Ought not my host, gentle as he was, fear the effects of despair on twelve stout fellows forcibly taken from their native country, their kindred and their freedom – and even shut out from the commerce of the fair sex, which sweetens life?'

4

In the churchyard the youngest Kirsten now lay buried, having died from dysentery at the age of three. Butterflies fluttered purple-red around the worn stones: the souls of the dead making a return visit. The coffins lay in shallow graves just below the hardy Cape heath flora. Anders imagined their wooden lids under the ground. Roots entwined through skulls and mouths, pulling them apart and moving them away. It looked as if the dead occasionally drew breath and expanded their ribs to let in more soil.

A kite swooped down like an ill omen, perhaps having spotted something between the hard clods of earth. Then a sinister breeze came whispering through the air and the tree trunks quivered in resistance, like men trying to halt a landslide with their bare hands.

Johanna Kirsten was wearing a brown cotton skirt and embroidered bonnet. She was still weeping for her dead child, and confided to the tutor that she was gradually going blind. She could hear the swallows and storks, but could no longer see the fruit trees clearly or the bedding the slaves spread on the grass to air. She was a good-natured woman who seldom bemoaned her lot, but it grieved her not to be able to help her husband rein in a horse any more or collect the rents in the neighbourhood. And the Resident was becoming agitated about the opium dens, where sailors were waited upon by slave girls and squandered their pay to suck on a pipe.

On the walk home from the churchyard they rested under a tree that smelt of bat urine. A magnificent calm day was followed by a moonless night, and the seals were barking with the voices of the drowned. The Resident's wife was afraid of the dark; her nerves were fragile. When she thought she was alone she would sing the catchy tunes of her homeland. Despite the number of servants and their attendance on her, she would withdraw from time to time into ascetic privation – as if to escape some dreadful temptation within herself and the wild forces in the surrounding countryside.

She was anxiously aware of decay and decomposition, and suffered from the harmful miasma of the summer heat. She saw the sailors' excesses, the lecherous banquets that ended in hangovers and remorse; the chastisements meted out to slaves to keep them in their place. Occasionally, her husband would wake her with frightful screams from his nightmares. There was something calamitous about their existence in Cape Town, and she told herself that this was no life for her.

But in the morning the cocks crowed and the Antarctic terns flew down from Table Mountain. One slave was already at work planting a mulberry tree; another had a box of spongy seed potatoes; a third was on his way to gather the eggs from the hen coop; a fourth was drawing off the sweet juice from the upturned perianths of the sugar bush that he would boil into syrup.

A light wind brushed the grass, and the clatter of the counters of the Resident's board game could be heard: that was how he started his day, the game organized his thoughts as he bent over his table of cherry-tree wood. He collected geological specimens, put minerals under the magnifying glass and invited Sparrman to analyse them. There were fossilized snail shells in the sandstone, and streaks of lead and sulphur. The collection included serpentine and thunderstone, the orange bark of the hawthorn with its long white thorns, and Bushmen's needles. The Resident piled up everything without system or order, but Sparrman examined and transformed what he saw. The two men were quite dissimilar, not

only in age but also in temperament. Minerals, the actual forma-
tive elements of the Earth, were in Anders' opinion devoid of any
intrinsic or potential sensibility, but he praised those which were
translucent or reflected the light with particular clarity.

A slave was setting traps for moles and voles. The Resident's
wife reminded the children not to forget to say their prayers.
Jacob and Johannes were playing pirates and called out to their
sister, 'Man overboard!' and 'Weigh anchor!', but she simply
turned away. She was riding the smallest and most docile of the
horses, bareback but with the promise of saddle and spurs in the
months to come.

The Resident put his head in his hands, which meant he craved
the damper climes of the lowlands back home. Looking through
his onerous bills, he sighed. 'We were enticed here to secure the
happiness and future prospects of this land. Perhaps truth and
falsehood will coalesce at some point long after our own lives are
over. My wife . . . well, she's trying to find some way of using apri-
cot kernels.'

Johanna had brought with her from Holland a waistcoat of
beaver skin lined with black silk. She wore a simple pearl necklace, but in other respects she could have been a servant. Anders
accompanied her to the cellar, where she counted the jars of honey
and guava preserve, and he recorded the numbers in the house-
keeping book. She moved slowly and kept coming to a halt in the
semi-darkness.

He wondered whether she wanted something from him, or
whether what she needed was something to hope for. He tried to
imagine her fear of growing old at the Cape. But she said nothing
except to mumble figures. Her glance sufficed to indicate that the
task was complete, and he kept a pace behind her on the short
walk across the straggly grass.

When he regarded the pallid complexions of many of the
people here, despite the sun, and the Resident's drained expression, his wife's sunken cheeks and the bags under her eyes, he

thought their days were numbered, that they were heading for dissolution and oblivion, and that some indeed had but a very short time to live, though no-one spoke of it. The salt-laden westerlies made voices croak, and it was no better for the health when the direction changed to a burning north wind from the Kalahari.

After the Easter Day service he found Johanna Kirsten beside the pot of crocus bulbs. She was rubbing the back of her hand across her forehead, as if trying to wipe away a cloud of sorrow or loss. When he proffered his own hand to wish her good health, he noticed that her fingers were trembling. She responded to him with calm dignity and he could see every detail of her face as clearly as in a painting. The horses out in the yard pawed the ground impatiently, ready to be off. He thought he discerned a weariness in her eyes, which might indicate that she no longer regarded her life as being of any value. As if her soul were making ready to fly away into solitude.

Suddenly she said, half-hidden beneath her broad-brimmed hat of waxed taffeta, 'We all have our own battles to fight. Most of us never asked to come here. There is no place for genuine feelings here. Even the cows look sanctimonious. There are many who would like to stop repressing their vexation, and so lighten their burden of disappointment.'

Anders had a touch of ague and a headache, so he went out into the night air streaming down from the back of Table Mountain. A harbour store on two floors had been built near the Resident's house, with a bakery, a smithy, a cooper's workshop, a butcher's and a hospital. When the north-west wind prevented ships from anchoring in Table Bay, they resorted to the lee side – off Simonstown at False Bay, where the Resident had command of two sergeants and a company of thirty men of the watch.

Anders had been appointed to act as interpreter for the Resident whenever French vessels came into port. A trumpet blast signalled him to his post. The first mate was drunk and had seen mythical beasts wallowing in the swell off the Skeleton Coast. The captain was a strict Breton who suspected mischief and conspiracy everywhere.

'Is there any rational man here who can tell me why he's Swedish?' the mate wondered.

'No need to worry yourself about that,' Sparrman replied.

'We've put in to make our own observations,' the Captain declared. And anyway the ship needed a new pump.

'You'll find French Huguenots from Brittany and Normandy living here, especially in Franschhoek,' Sparrman informed them. But the Captain was not interested. They had themselves rowed back on board before the Resident had even arrived.

Anders Sparrman watched them go, then heard slave boys singing, softly, as if their vitality were ebbing away. Even his own energies were sapped. He had a weird dream of being crippled and an outcast, or perhaps just a lost child. He felt himself entering a darkness in which he was totally abandoned.

5

The Cape doves gleamed like black and white damask. They swooped down over the anchorage of Table Bay and the turbulent eddies where the cold northward current met the west winds. Jellyfish were drying up among the ribbons of trumpet grass. Bearded vultures, necks craned, landed noiselessly on corpses and offal. Anders thought of all the hidden regions in the vast expanses of the oceans, of all the rotting matter being swept along the bottom, of the drowned, rising and falling in the depths.

The female slaves paused for breath on the main staircase: there was still the outside to be scrubbed down. They had no time-keeper to oversee them: they worked until darkness fell or until a bell rang to call them to their evening meal. Watch fires were lit on Table Mountain and on the breakwater in the harbour. Dutch ships with their imposing sterns were anchored in the Roads. They had taller rigging to carry more sail than the Swedish East Indiamen. One of the soldiers keeping a lookout for ships from the heights and signalling their approach by hoisting a flag was also a huntsman who supplied the Resident's table with game.

In Cape Town you could purchase decoy birds and carved sticks. A freed slave had set up a shoemaker's workshop, making simple shoes of pungent leather from gnu, eland and young buffalo. A coffee-house served guava juice with arrack from Java, and beer in heavy tankards. The woman who ran it was Danish and somewhat broad in the beam. The sailors and craftsmen made passes at her, trying to fondle and squeeze her, but she responded unperturbed: 'No fingers in the food, if you please!' She kept her money high up under her skirt in a handkerchief, which she pulled open with her teeth.

Anders chanced upon a carriage-maker of Swedish origin, a stolid fellow who had missed his ship. He was quite skeletal, with knotted, sweating muscles. His only possessions were a workbench, a bed and a chest of tools. He had lost all his front teeth and was determined to struggle on until he found peace.

'Is it so important to find peace?' Anders asked.

'What would be your preference?'

'Some project of the utmost significance, even if it felt arduous beyond endurance,' replied Anders.

The carriage-maker was stiff-legged and suffering from the heat as he sawed up oak timbers to make wheels for ox-carts. He no longer made any effort to attract women, and had no wish to chase them: it was humiliating enough as things were, and he was content to take his pleasure with the occasional ewe out in the fields. After all, they were God's creatures too: submissive, anonymous. He had become quite partial to them, and there was no likelihood of a child resulting.

Sparrman installed cisterns with filters and clean sand at the Resident's house, and covered them with gauze to keep out insects, especially those considered to be the cause of stomach complaints. He had seen the sewage ditches running out into the bay: a brown and bloody mess, slaughterhouse waste floating in and out with the tide, and indolent fish swimming among kidneys, livers, the heads of calves and dogs.

'God knows who is the progenitor of so much misery,' said the Resident.

The evening meal was over and done with and they were standing in the dark hall. Sparrman bowed his head in silence: it wasn't the time or place for tactless comment. He had gradually become

Mr Kirsten's secretary. The elements of agriculture he had imbibed in Uppsala stood him in good stead, and he read verses of Virgil's *Georgics* to his master as he filled the inkwell and the sandbox.

'Many are dying at this very minute,' the Resident went on, seeming to peer towards some distant theatre of war. 'We execute people almost every day – for what would elsewhere be regarded as mere trifles. A native steals a couple of silver spoons: off to the gallows, without even a priest to direct him towards God's throne. A girl kills the child she has secretly borne: off she goes to follow him, to Heaven or to Hell.'

'And what conclusion do you draw?'

'We should be more merciful, without compromising any of the necessary discipline. If we could set the condemned to building breakwaters and chapels, or to making sails and tents, they could live under supervision, provided they behaved themselves. They would never escape the torment in their own souls, in any case. A saucepan may have a sooty and buckled bottom, but that does not imply that a good meal cannot be cooked in it, as long as it's well stirred.'

Anders was sorry there were no copies of d'Alembert's and Diderot's *Encyclopaedia* at the Cape, not a single one of the thirty-six parts. That book had opened so many windows on the world that world and book had quite simply exchanged places: there was now more world within this massive work of reference than there was outside it. At last, many of mankind's deepest mysteries had been illuminated. From his experience at Uppsala he knew that reading had lighted up new stars in the skies and brought the universe closer. But there still remained geological strata of Hell with ever higher temperatures.

The fish in the water know when it's raining, he wrote, just as we sense what we lack even though we have never experienced it. Most things disintegrate, decompose, disappear – but not the *Encyclopaedia*. Yet here in the Cape a lizard or a calf can be born with two heads, and the monstrous is perceived as of more interest than the much greater wonders of true knowledge.

The Resident's daughter was a contrary character, and usually woke up cross and defiant. She had an oval face, brown eyes, hair that clung like tendrils about her head and cheeks, and she showed off her bosom quite shamelessly. At first she used to look at him with a timid and anxious expression on her face, but had gradually come to evince an increasing irritation and distress at everything that was being imposed on her.

Anders had a vision of her growing ever stouter, marrying a kindly old merchant in Leiden and dying in childbirth. Then the poetry album would be closed for ever. But before she turned into a corpulent matron he would at least have taught her English and some French, calligraphy, drawing and European history. He had observed her slow and deliberate way of moving, putting her hand up to her face or turning her head – as if she wanted to give him plenty of time to notice her every little gesture.

He scrutinized his fourteen-year-old pupil for a moment. She took up so much more space than the modest Jacob, whose thoughts always seemed to be elsewhere. She met his eyes without embarrassment. It was the briefest of games, for he was determined not to land himself in any troublesome *amour*, impossible as it would be to bring to fruition. The world was too important to him to risk endangering his place in it through any ignominious episodes. His alibi was the temporary nature of his appointment, and she had her parents as a safety net. So he could meet the coquettish look in her eyes with the tolerant hypocrisy of a clear conscience.

Geessie's long neck was accentuated by the peach-coloured dress, which she said she had made herself and which smelt of camphorated oil, an aroma that reminded him of the rectory. But her chubby fingers were not designed for piano keys. She would rather dip them in the sugar bowl and lick them. Under the piano lid the hammers were festooned with the corpses of insects, moths and hymenoptera. They defined the tone no matter how hard she pressed the pedals.

While she was thumping and thrumming the pianoforte, her smile would change to haughty remoteness whenever she heard anyone approaching. She would half-close her eyes when Anders was teaching, but as soon as he fell silent she looked straight at him with a sort of aloof curiosity.

Sometimes she could be high-spirited, turning up in a man's hat and asking whether her tutor knew any card games or could recite some poetry. Anders managed to call to mind some lines of John Milton:

And now the Sun had stretch'd out all the hills,
And now was dropt into the Western bay;
At last he rose, and twitch'd his mantle blue:
To-morrow to fresh Woods, and Pastures new.

Jacob yawned and pretended to be dying of hunger. Johannes had walked out. Geessie clapped, but without conviction. Anders saw them as half-wild, lonely children, Geessie a dreamy and self-centred girl who had no companion of her own age to play with. He decided not to analyse her constant attempts to evade her lessons and yet to emerge on the other side as a self-assured young lady with an enigmatic smile on her face. She collected braids, fringes and brightly coloured scraps of cloth. Anders used them for stuffing her cat, and she thought it looked more life-like than before.

She was even more absent-minded than Anders.

'Repeat what I said!' he instructed. She would blush and remain silent.

He was a sober twenty-three-year-old, she a restless bird. There were stronger forces drawing him on, and he tried to convince himself that she, as a young woman, meant less to him than any of the animal species he was engaged in classifying and recording in the far-flung lands of the Cape. And it would not be long before the capricious changes of expression on her face would rigidify in the strong west wind. That was what he persuaded himself, whether he wanted to or not.

7

There was much he did not understand in the post he occupied in Simonstown. For instance, why the Resident's wife Johanna had ripped the bed curtain to pieces one morning in a rage and, according to the maid, crawled around on the floor hissing like a snake and then bursting into such shrill laughter that she sounded hysterical. He wandered into the garden, the buzz of flies in the air, and Johanna came out on to the steps for a moment, dressed all in black. She might have been a bird of prey searching for richer spoils. Her extraordinary eyes fastened on him and he felt heavy at heart.

He reminded himself that she was in her excitable late flowering, he in his all-too-fleeting youth. How deliciously degrading it would be to throw his arms about her person, associated as it was for him with the suffusing honey-like warmth of the sunlight. She beckoned him over and invited him to sample a brew she had left to ferment according to an old Dutch recipe: a sort of mead. And with that the sensual mood was broken.

Her forehead was like a pale opal and her nose a little too long. There were lines of tension around her mouth, an expression of self-restraint in her eyes, as if she were succumbing to voluptuous fancies which she was determined to deny herself.

She put some roses in a glass jug which had lost its handle. Anders noticed she was trembling. Her clothes looked like widow's weeds.

'Your shirt is very faded and worn,' she remarked in a sympathetic tone, as if it had done him an injustice.

She had brought lilac and laburnum from Europe. She grew lemon balm and mixed the leaves in her reticule with smelling salts. In the furthest part of the garden lay a mysterious glade behind a mound of rocks. Swallows skimmed overhead and sparrows were chirping.

When everywhere was swept and cleaned for the weekend, order, neatness and quiet prevailed in the house. Cabbage from Robben Island had been steeped in vinegar with green peppers. The lamb had been marinated, and pickled marrow brought out. The volumes in the little collection of books were shelved by size. Anders did not think he was going to have time to sort and dry all his plants.

He had handled harmless snakes and snared hummingbirds in nets. He had heard the helmet shrike calling with three notes, meaning 'Don't come here, there's no water.' He prepared his meagre haul and sent it by the first ship to Gothenburg.

Filled with a burning desire to pursue my researches in Nature, he wrote, I could not help harbouring resentment that in a place with such good resources my hands were tied by day, for the sake of other occupations; and the long evenings, for want of books and other necessary equipment, and especially for want of friends and lacking the company of anyone who valued studying, were wasted.

He also described sunsets so magnificent as to be overwhelming. He wanted to hold on to them the way one might hold a breath.

'If only I had someone to share them with!'

He wished he were like the lizards, whose defence lay not only in their agility but also in their lack of scent. He remembered Linnaeus describing a columbine as accurately as if he had pressed the plant to the page of the book. There was no monotony here: each discovery was a fresh beginning.

He listened to the carts trundling over the paved roads and to the wails of the people subjected to punishment that day. He watched a lady in a mauve silk hat with a silver cross at her breast walking by with her servant, her eyes self-absorbedly intent on the far distance. He saw an old woman selling tobacco and weighing it on little scales made of horn.

'Our race,' said the Resident, 'has virtues which make it incumbent upon us to settle in Africa. We know something of honour and truth, which they do not. If we could abolish slavery, these dark creatures would be happy to work for us if we simply steered them with a firm hand towards riches they themselves can hardly even imagine.'

Anders objected that the white man's lack of justice had destroyed any appeal his religion or culture might have had for the black man. Their huts had been demolished, their land stolen, the joy in life extinguished in their voices. They had nothing to fight for and nothing to hope for. Mr Kirsten replied that he was not insensible, but that Sparrman had not been living long enough in the province to understand.

'And the English are on their way, you mark my words,' he continued. 'One fine day we shall all be playing cricket. Our colony will be one great cricket pitch.' He gave a resigned smile and seemed not entirely displeased at the notion.

Then his tone of voice changed, and he said slowly and grimly, 'I have a presentiment that I shall never be free of Africa.'

8

Anders taught the Resident's children Nature studies and told them of the marvels of Creation. The power of attraction between many bodies, he said, was so great that not only did they attach to one another, but lost themselves in each other and became an entirely new body. In others the power of repulsion was so strong that they could only be held together by force. And there was a third power through which bodies could be both separated and also reconciled.

He gave them a demonstration of dispersion and affinity in chemical reactions by putting a little ground chalk in a drinking glass with vinegar. The chalk dissolved like sugar in coffee, the vinegar remained clear, and the two substances, chalk and vinegar, were chemically combined. Then he poured into the chalk solution a little sulphuric acid in the form of oil of vitriol, and the result was a precipitate caused by the oil of vitriol combining with the chalk in the vinegar to make a new solid, plaster, which sank to the bottom of the glass as a sediment. The addition of sulphuric acid made the chalk separate from the vinegar and enter into a closer alliance with the sulphuric acid than with the vinegar.

He filled a bottle with clear water and some lead acetate and introduced a zinc rod. The metal turned black, the water cloudy. Gradually more and more small glistening bodies attached themselves to the metal, increasing in density on the rod nearest the surface, where they formed a knot and from that knot a mass of branches, so that it looked like a tree of dots sparkling in the sun. It was called the Tree of Diana.

He asked Johannes, Jacob and Geessie whether they could imagine the Earth as a crystal generated in the oceans of the world. The future would determine whether the Earth had been formed from a ball of vapour or a ball of fire. There were celestial bodies the consistency of porridge and, like the spot in an egg, there was a nucleus in them which caused a vortex, turning vapour into water and water into solid matter. But all knowledge was uncertain. The only thing he was certain of was that the realm of Creation would one day be opened up to us in all its majesty.

Take the colossal planet Jupiter, he said. It seems to be a viscous orb, like our own Earth at the beginning of time. Its surface could be a sea in constant flux. And even further from us, on the rings of Saturn, protrusions have been discovered which astronomers think are hemispheres of smaller planets conjoined by the laws of gravity. The highest of these mountain masses has been calculated to have an elevation of nearly two thousand miles.

He guided them into Nature's workshop. He explained why the moon rose over the horizon so regularly, like an obedient servant. And how both emperors and midges moved with the same ease in the atmosphere, which was for the Earth what the nervous system was for the human body.

'See how everything draws its energy from the elements!' Sunlight extracts oxygen from plants, invigorating existence and imbuing all creatures with the glow of life. It gives rise to fiery spices, savage beasts, the violent passions of mankind. The air brings with it the resonance of life and liberty, exactly as a person buried in a cave hears the benevolent voices of his unknown saviours.

The grass pushes up through the stones and the pine through the cracks in the rock. Shiny beetles climb the blades of grass. The

eagle scans the valley from the tops of the pines. And the anima-
tion, fullness and abundance of our own existence arise from our
feeling for the soil, our relish for thirst-quenching water, our sense
of the spreading warmth, our auditory perception of the tremors of
the air, our ability to see all the shades of light. Everything that
comprises the body of the Earth is reproduced in exquisite detail
in our own bodies.

At the same time he recognized that human nature could not be
pinned down the way a flower is dried and pressed. He could see
that Johanna could change unpredictably, month by month, and
Geessie too, whereas the animals he had made it his business to
study seemed to have unvarying habits. Nevertheless, he found
the way of life in Simonstown static. Perhaps because Mr Kirsten
distrusted knowledge more than he craved it.

'You are passing on to my children learning from Europe that I
never had myself. Unless my memory is failing. I hope you are balancing the scientific discoveries that are undermining God's
majesty with your lessons in moral behaviour. The children pay
heed to you: they may be unruly, but they are not entirely obdurate.'

Had he ever, Anders responded in his own defence, called into
question the divine serenity of Nature, its eternal, imperceptible
movement, like that of the Earth on its axis? The tranquil stillness
of the air was proof enough that heavenly influences and earthly
forces balanced each other, and that every living creature drew
benefit from that.

9

Sparrman travelled from Stellenbosch to Cape Town in a four-seater post-coach. The post-horn was blown in every village they passed through. The coach rattled noisily along, its wheels reinforced with iron rims, which protected them from wear and tear on the stony roads. He changed horses at an inn, and visited a farm where the owner grew mulberries, figs and black grapes, and bemoaned the amount of work his woods involved. The maize field produced a good harvest, but his old-fashioned Franconian garden, with its clipped box hedges and apple trees, was hard to keep in order.

Anders bought cabbages and radishes. He caught a quail in a snare. Broiling hot sun alternated with biting wind. Heathland covered in broom, rivulets of fresh mountain water, young copses with pigeons and kites. He found a poisonous toadstool that was rumoured to aid sleep if taken in moderation. He reduced its potency by drying it on sticks. It had been a beautiful day, he wrote. But no moment was ever like the previous one. Far too much happened all too rapidly.

He wanted to travel further – into Africa. The guttural sounds of Dutch collided in his head and sounded like compost being shovelled up into one great slop-heap. He longed for the precision of Latin, and the clarity and musicality of Italian. He could hear the slaves singing their incomprehensible songs and their hoes hacking the ground.

The fireworks subsided. The carousel man collapsed in exhaustion. The riotous festivities to welcome yet another East Indiaman faded away after one person drowned and another was knifed. All that remained were the cooper's hammering and the coachman huddled up on the box in what appeared to be an everlasting sleep.

The days dried up like stale bread. To cut them would have required sharper tools than he possessed. In the Resident's house a secrecy, or amnesia, had begun to prevail, which he could not work out. Something was going on out of the range of his sight and hearing. He was tempted to make his escape, but the Resident would be able to send out a search party and confiscate his passport. He wished he had come to South Africa as an anonymous traveller with no identity, a man seeking isolation in Nature and not in need of support or sympathy, just to be left in peace.

He threaded his journal pages on a string to prevent their sticking together in the damp. He threw his energies into the piles of paper that he wanted to collate into a narrative about things which no-one else had seen or experienced. He had travelled to Africa to overcome his fears and to examine the manifestations of Nature so much more powerful than himself – according to Linnaeus the best medicine for arrogance and vanity.

One evening, free of mosquitoes, as high and still as a church before the sonorous organ booms forth, he sat alone on the verandah, with only the crickets for company. He was applying fern root to a blister, and peppering his wine to treat the colic which was afflicting him. He picked up a doll of bark fibre, which a slave girl had made for Geessie when she was little.

The sun was sinking over the sea in the west in a thick, almost opaque haze that presaged mist and sickness. He struck a light on his tinderbox. A group of people had settled down, presumably for the night, under an umbrella pine with a twisted trunk.

The vegetation was breathing gently. The nocturnal animals

were on the alert. He groped for invisible handrails. The stars shone brightly in the southern sky and over the undiscovered continent's endless polar ice. But Africa was at last becoming fully connected to what he regarded as the inhabited world.

Voyage around the World

1

On the 1st of November 1772 Captain James Cook sailed into Cape Town on his second circumnavigation of the world. Anders Sparrman was invited to join the crew of the *Resolution* to assist the Forsters as zoologist, botanist and physician.

Recently, Anders had been feeling sluggish and full of foreboding. On his own now, he knew he needed some magic formula to redeem him. He wanted for nothing. His melancholy was not tinged with homesickness. But he lacked any sense of direction, any aim that might counteract his prevailing uncertainty.

That was when the message reached him.

In the summer months when ships could anchor in Table Bay, the Resident moved to his country estate, Alphen, near Constantia on the southern side of Table Mountain. He had bought it in 1765 for his eldest son Johannes Pieter, who was then seven years old. It was one of the most beautiful houses on the peninsula, and is now a historic monument.

The commandant of the Fort in Cape Town, Hendrick von Prehm, was interested in the sciences, a friend of Sparrman and married to the Resident's eldest daughter. He brought the Forsters, father and son, to Alphen. Their host, born in Germany himself, was delighted to have two compatriots as guests. Sparrman showed them around the countryside. George Forster wrote later that this pupil of Linnaeus was an enthusiast for natural history, knowledgeable in medicine, had a heart worthy of a philosopher and was endowed with the warmest sentiments.

Sparrman was given twenty-four hours to decide. He paced up and down among the cherry, orange and lemon trees the Resident had introduced from Spain. Thrushes and flycatchers filled the air with their calls. He thought of Geessie and Jacob without any particular sense of loss, and hardly at all of the little ones, who had remained fairly untouched by his teaching.

Reinhold Forster was a forty-three-year-old clergyman from Danzig, of partly Scottish descent. He had committed Linnaeus' *Systema Naturæ* to memory, and translated Bougainville's travel accounts and Pehr Kalm's American expedition into English. He had joined the ship in Plymouth with his seventeen-year-old son George and the artist William Hodges. The father has been described as an emaciated pedant with curly red side-whiskers, easily offended, arrogant and endowed with an exceptional memory.

The Forsters even went so far, wrote Sparrman, 'in their zeal for the more accurate investigation of Nature, as to think of procuring an assistant, at no small cost to themselves, and therefore offered me my voyage gratis, with part of such natural curiosities as they might chance to collect, on condition of my assisting them with my poor abilities. I recollected that the great Linnaeus had frequently said, nothing had vexed him more in his whole life, than that, when he resided in Holland, he had not accepted the offer which had been made him of paying a visit to the Cape of Good Hope.

'If my voyage should prove unsuccessful, I was in hopes that my miseries, together with life itself, and all its train of attendant evils, would have a speedy end. Occupied by reflections of this kind, I passed the night, more restless perhaps than will be easily imagined. The next morning, by daybreak, the distraction of my thoughts carried me to my chamber window; here I fixed my eyes on the adjacent meadows, as though I meant to ask the plants and flowers that grew on them, whether I ought to part with them so hastily. They had for a long time been almost my only joy, my sole friends and companions; and now it was these only, which in a great measure prevented me from making the voyage.

'At length I came to the resolution of undertaking it; yet with a fixed determination, that if I had the good fortune to come back to the Cape, I would again occupy myself on the same spot with the most delightful of all employments, the investigation of Nature. I therefore began to get ready for my journey and sent specimens of the insects and plants I had collected to the Chevalier Linné and other lovers of the science.'

'Think of me at the South Pole, as I of you in Japan,' Carl Peter Thunberg wrote in a letter of farewell, staying on a while longer in the Cape himself.

'Let us look forward to botanizing again together, if not before, then in the Elysian Fields,' Anders replied. 'May Heaven assist your hands to your profit and pleasure. Your sincere friend, Anders Sparrman.'

The *Resolution* was a two-decked Whitby cat of four hundred and sixty-two tons, just over ninety feet long, with sixteen four-pound cannon and a crew of one hundred and twelve men, both civilian and military. The ship was the type that carried coal down the east coast of England, of shallow draught to be able to reach the river ports and with a flat keel, so as not to tip over when she stood on the bottom at ebb tide. Of four hundred colliers that plied between Newcastle and London, half were built in Whitby, where Cook arrived on foot in 1746.

It was generally assumed that some of the crew would be lost to fevers, drowning or falls from the rigging. The provisions loaded at London and Cape Town had to be sufficient to feed the men for two years. Ship's biscuits and salt meat were the only dry foods that would more or less keep – despite maggots and a certain amount of decomposition that could be ameliorated by strong spices and beer. The drinking water soon went putrid and was mostly used for mixing with rum for their grog.

Eight tons of iron ballast and coal, partly for ballast and partly for the galley, plus goods for barter, ropes, sailcloth, tar, cannon and ammunition, all encroached on the sailors' space for their hammocks. The cargo included ready-hewn timber that could be used to construct a replacement vessel in the event of shipwreck, or to explore 'the shallower rocks and shores of the new supposed continent'.

On Cook's first voyage they had observed the transit of Venus, discovered the Society Islands, sailed around New Zealand and mapped the east coast of Australia. Cook's mission now was to investigate whether 'the yet untraversed part of the southern hemisphere was made up of masses of water only, or contained some considerable land which in extent might compete with the already known continents'.

The myth of the southern continent, *Terra Australis Incognita*, was accompanied by rumours of gold, silver mines and civilized peoples. A fifth continent was deemed essential as a counterweight to Asia and the northern land masses to prevent the Earth from tilting.

Did the oceans emerge from a spring at the South Pole, since the currents flowed northwards from the Antarctic? Many thought there was a circulatory system of water inside the Earth equivalent to the flow of the blood through the human body, and that maelstroms sucked the water down to boil it pure in subterranean fires and send it back up again as fresh water from springs on land.

Anders Sparrman went aboard with his grandfather's oak chest. He was billeted in a dark cubbyhole on the extra third deck. There was a folding table where he could spread his plants, a sailcloth stool and a tin plate. The stench below deck was oppressive, but he grew accustomed to it, even when it increased in calm seas.

On the 22nd of November 1772 the sister ships *Resolution* and *Adventure* raised anchor and set a south-easterly course in a moist wind that soon thickened to fog. A frigate bird paused in flight over a patch of still water and its shadow seemed to linger on the gleaming surface.

One stormy night water came pouring in: the boatswain had left the window to his storeroom open. The men pumped for their lives. Captain Cook was convinced the ship was about to sink.

The strong wind brought storm petrels and Cape petrels, called malefices, because they were a portent of evil. They perched on the rigging, while at the same time nine albatrosses were lured into swallowing pieces of mutton skin on hooks and hauled aboard. The meat was 'tolerably edible'.

On George Forster's eighteenth birthday storms shattered glass and porcelain, bottles and chairs. The whole ship was a scene of chaos and destruction. A new sail-room forward was cleared for drying and repairing sails. When the gales had subsided the botanists started sorting their flora from the Cape.

On the 5th of December it began to snow, and the water froze on deck. Long underpants and woollen sweaters were distributed. Sailors and officers of the watch were provided with fearnought jackets and felted trousers. An iceberg floated imperceptibly towards the ship through the drift ice, two thousand feet long, over two hundred feet high.

On the 11th of December the weather turned so cold that some of the animals died, and the masts, sails and ropes were covered in a crust of ice. Severe hailstorms from the north-east forced them to heave to under a foresail to spare the pumps and avoid violent lurches. Then they saw the white, black-beaked storm petrel, which they thought to presage even larger expanses of ice.

'On the 12th of December in thick fog the voyage continued between six mountain-like masses of ice, one of which was in parts tinged snow white, in parts crystal-clear transparent, in parts with sapphire blue in between, and about two miles in circumference and sixty feet in height. Despite this height, the forceful, raging, dreadfully breaking green waves frequently submerged this iceberg in sky-high foam and froth.

'Penguins made themselves heard through their harsh music, as if tuned by the inhospitable zone, an irritating hoarse sound or screech which, in some of the travellers, awoke images of something from the abyss or its vicinity.

'From being spectators we might become like actors tossed up on the awesome stage and be ground down and wrecked from the tallest ship's mast to the smallest human bone.'

Reinhold Forster and William Wales went out in the pinnace to measure the temperature of the water. In the mist they lost contact with the ship. They fired shots into the air. The wind increased and they thought it best not to row further. They and their oarsmen lay in the bottom of the boat prepared to die – apart from Forster, who eventually heard a ship's bell nearby, and they were saved.

Christmas dinner 1772: 'In the cabin a more pleasing and warmer climate reigned today with punch, stout, port and Madeira, claret, Cape and other wines, to which the Captain and Mr Forster treated senior officers until late into the night, so that all of us regarded the ice and hazards of both that day and the voyage with a more philosophical composure than usual. All ices were missing from our desserts on the table, although we were surrounded by them, mountain-high near and far, and threatened with shipwreck that much sooner, as a number of the seamen, dazed by the vapours of a bacchanalian mist, saw either too little or too well, objects appearing double to them. Drinking themselves drunk would have been for most of them the greatest delight, and their Christmas merriment and their games consisted of fighting in the English fashion, called boxing.'

New Year's Day 1773: Icy snowstorm, water supplies almost depleted. Cook had baskets lowered to catch pieces of ice that were broken up and packed in barrels, and provided a fresher, sweeter water than that which they had brought with them from the Cape.

On the 17th of January the expedition crossed the Antarctic

Circle, for the first time in history. The maze of ice struck fear into the navigators where they stood at the wheel with two compasses secured to the deck planking. At 67° 16′ the sea was blocked by a continuous mass of ice from east to west.

'*Aurora australis*, the southern lights, had probably never since the day of Creation until now, the 17th of February 1773, appeared before the eyes of a European. The blazing and radiance of this light was bright, not really bluish. With its ever whiter colour, it was different from our *aurora borealis*, which adopts several colours, in particular of fiery and purple hues.'

It was a long time since they had seen any driftwood. The surface of the sea was dark grey, as if paved. The icebergs, blue where they rose from the sea, shaded into grey towards the top, most of them as level as Table Mountain. Others floated by like ships on their way to eternity; some, small and peaked, swayed like a truncated cathedral-spire; some had melted from below, become top-heavy and overturned.

Anders felt himself momentarily in a state of rapture, so gratified to have heard the dull growl of the icebergs and to have seen the points of light they emitted. Then he encountered one of the boatswains, his face drained white with terror, his features distorted in panic at the sight of the inexplicable phenomenon drawing them relentlessly towards it. The carpenter had laid down his saw and his chisel. Several of the crew were huddled together in the forecastle in great anxiety. Lee shores, hospitable harbours with fresh water and generous women were what they wanted.

How much they had to subject themselves to, for Captain Cook to be able to make his way over unexplored deeps, through dangerous sounds, up uncertain estuaries on this intractable globe – all the time fired by the torch of ambition and with his eyes focused on the sceptics at the Royal Geographical Society in London. Was it not sacrilegious to want to achieve so much?

2

The irregular juddering, the shifting of weight in his own body, reminded Anders when he woke that he was on board ship, not free to choose his own route or direction. An iceberg floated past them, scarcely appearing to be moving; an island without beaches, a ship without a helmsman, menacing and heavier than anything else on the waters of the Earth. From within could be heard hammer blows that grew louder with every upwind before dying away again.

The depths gurgled to the stirring of wild monsters, the clocks stopped in the Captain's cabin at the stern. Islands of ice floes broke up in the Antarctic summer – with a jangling of keys like someone going around a big house unlocking door after door. Anders Sparrman was shaking with cold and had trouble holding his pen between fingers and thumb.

The immense mountains of ice slid silently by or caused a thunder of breakers as the waves hit them, and from time to time rang out with a sound like crystal chandeliers shattering in vast palace halls. The sails flapped reluctantly when the west wind changed to north. All of this embodied both a threat and a beauty which defied description.

The penguins kept one eye on the intruders but showed no interest, for they bore no resemblance to the rapacious skuas that stabbed them from the skies, nor to the leopard seals that consumed a dozen birds a day. The penguins would stand in serried ranks for hours on end, and if anyone encroached on their trampled path they simply made a diversion. They enjoyed displaying themselves to one another. They squabbled and squawked as if they were being thrashed. Their stomachs were full of krill, for which their young hammered at them with their beaks until they got a regurgitated portion. They stretched their necks towards the heavens and the wildest lament arose from their throats.

'I saw a penguin asleep standing up, and was ill-natured enough to kick it so that it fell and rolled over several times, and then it eventually woke up,' wrote Anders Sparrman, back in Stockholm. 'I do not think that my kicking such tough birds could have caused the slightest fainting fit, which tended not to occur even after blows with the musket butt or after deep falls from rocks, but they are said to take their recreation in the form of a deep and long sleep ashore, by way of reward for their lengthy wandering about across the immeasurable fields of the sea in a state of wakefulness.

'The cry of these birds is most unpleasant, and the hoarse lament of their short sharp croaks tormented our ears even at night. I shudder when I remember how floating icebergs, cold, hunger and the screech of penguins all conjoined to make those three summers so unpleasant, when I was ploughing through the southern Atlantic and Antarctic Oceans and could no more than send a thought to the land where the song of the siskin and the nightingale alternated between night and day.'

After a morning of squalls, the sea fell back into repose and the sails slackened in the midday heat. The decks were swabbed and rinsed. Repairs were set in train, ropes strengthened, the wheel was lashed tighter. At the rail two sailors were hauling up seawater in bowls and buckets. It was an opportunity to wash underclothes and blankets free of lice.

Time stood still and made no demands, but on board ship the water was getting ever more putrid, the meat more rotten. The sea was becoming choppy, vibrations in the rigging gave warning that the calm would not last long. A venerable hump-backed whale with majestic tail fins clove the waves. There was no way they could catch this giant of the deep: harpoons would merely prick his body like needles. Sparrman had seen sharks snapping at lines and oars, but a dancing pod of cetaceans could capsize a schooner.

William Wales, the ship's astronomer, noticed that the elder Forster was managing to quarrel with everyone on board. His most frequent outburst was, 'Leave me alone! Can't you see I have much to do?' He complained that a ewe was laid outside his cabin to give birth. But despite the overpowering stench he carried on equably with his zoological studies.

His son George was obsessed by stories he had heard about the insanity that overcame people in desolate waters. If the son was a worrier who speculated on the capacity of the brain and the natural aptitudes of the individual, the father was an undisciplined scholar who loved the sound of his own voice, and was intolerant of those he saw making notes for their own journals. Anders knew from George that Reinhold Forster was determined to be the first to have his observations in print. And in this he succeeded – to the extreme annoyance of the Captain.

Dressed in his leather waterproofs, Cook arranged his instruments and periodically revised the all-too-blank chart which he kept protected in its cover of oiled jute cloth. In his cabin he had Abraham Ortelius' and Gerard Mercator's *Atlas*, a magnificent work which the Inquisition had condemned for denying God His own image of the world. Reinhold Forster had brought with him a library of a couple of hundred volumes, possibly more books than there were in the whole of Cape Colony. Anders and George jointly translated a pioneering work into English: Nils Rosén von Rosenstein's *The Diseases of Children, and their Remedies*.

'We have no dominion over the sea,' Cook said. 'It may rage when we are calm. Or we may roar like wild beasts, but the sea will always outdo us.' Anders was struck by the Captain's unruffled temperament, which evinced neither submission nor rebellion. An inner voice seemed to drive him on to further knowledge, to a more complete chart, while those who came after him would be motivated by greed, would risk their lives in their insatiable thirst for plunder, and fire cannons of shot for a morsel of pepper or gold.

Anders' feet and eyes were familiar with the worn and buckled parts of every board on the ship's decks. Despite his lambswool sweater and oilcloth coat he felt himself naked and unprotected. The icebergs ground against one another in the swell with a sputtering hiss that ended with a sigh from the depths.

Suddenly, the *Resolution* shuddered in a blast of wind that came out of nowhere and the sails bellied and expanded near enough to rip. But slackened again, and the blocks of ice could be heard grinding and splashing against the surface of the sea. Sometimes a slurping throat would open in the lee of an iceberg and a whirlpool of snowy foaming saliva would try to suck the ship down.

The sails billowed as a fair wind sprang up, pulling the heavy vessel forward like a team of oxen. And with the wind gradually changing direction, the sea threw up tumbling waves that yelped like foxes.

There was a red glow on the western horizon; to the east a mackerel sky. The days were long in the Polar region. When the sea settled down, its surface was rough and dead – a desolate province of isolation, filled with a void that compass and sextant were hard put to circumscribe.

The ice held them in its grip for what seemed like an age, and they thought they must be beyond the boundaries of the Earth. Here lay a riddle surpassing those they had been commissioned to solve, and it would have been an achievement too dearly bought to snatch away its veils. In the fading light the expanses of the ocean stretched endlessly before them.

3

At a distance the icebergs look like white bell-towers, without a clapper in their bells, just a low rumble through the clear air. The black water between them heaves like molten lava. When a shaft of moonlight reflects on the water, the surface angles stand out razor-sharp.

If we were to lose control of ourselves we would cry out to God and our mothers and fathers from the darkness. Isolation reigns supreme here, even in the forecastle and at the Captain's table. We have had no fish for a long time. We catch seals, sea-elephants, albatrosses and petrels. We drink the blood of penguins.

All the men on board have left tough lives behind them. They know nothing of Paradise. The sea is their nearest and dearest. It holds them in its embrace, its bowels will be their death.

What will become of us tomorrow? The nether portions of the icebergs are as deep as our ignorance of them. I can make out an enormous Face in the water, near the bow. The black hook of the anchor forms a shadow beneath it. I can imagine depths that even sharks cannot penetrate, and where there is no swell.

We have not set eyes on the sun for two weeks, just grey skies, grey seas. The sailors are true acrobats, at the end of a yardarm, grabbing at sails, emptying them of wind, rolling them up and tying them down, while waves and spray crash over them. Those who struggle with ropes and sail have their hands bloodied from the cold. We are at the outer limits of life on Earth.

The unnatural silence at times surrounding us increases our sense of our perilous remoteness, of a distance from the inhabited world no-one has ever experienced before, a threat from powers totally indifferent to our fate that can crush us to pulp, while the sails are motionless, and railing and hull offer only minimal protection.

The icebergs move infinitesimally, as if trapped in a magnetic field. They change their form, become a threatening haze. They have their own heavy breathing. Inside the visible ice is a harder core that does not collapse and crumble and dissolve in the water. When the sun is at its midday zenith they emit a blinding light from within their glassy walls, like fireworks, and melt-water cascades down the sheer precipices of the sides that face the sun.

I peer between the icebergs with my heart in my mouth. When the floes rub against each other, they make a noise like the bellowing of an immense herd of buffalo, and when the bergs collide, there is a roar of such awful reverberation that the sea seems to split asunder.

Here are our open tombs, here no leaves fall, and here every aspect of our life on Earth evaporates into nothingness. The waves have their ominous dirge, their dissonant voices. Here there are no supernatural mysteries, no pregnant secrets, just impenetrable depths without shape or form and a light that magnifies and reduces surface, space and distance with terrifying effect.

A ravaging wind, so lifeless that the air it conveys bears no hint of human beings. Our senses are benumbed. Though free in majestic desolation, we feel ourselves confined. If we founder, we will leave no trace. Yet we continue breathing every day, in the hope of bringing back report to our fellow-countrymen of a world that will remain as untouched as the inside of a volcano.

At times I am downhearted. The innermost essence of our

existence is not illuminated, but for ever sealed. Yet I am alive, and am part of the divine mechanism of Nature. In all humility I feel I am coming closer to the dreams and passions of mankind. I am swimming in the great cranium of the Cosmos.

As the fog thickened I sat in the caboose staring at my seaman's chest and its iron mountings and thinking that no person before us had had the frozen honour of being further south. I could smell rotting penguin meat.

In this air which produced its own shadows of mutely whirling granules of snow, in the incomprehensible monotony of these wastes, our crew seemed to be paralysed, economizing on move-ment and even respiration. Confronted by these ghostly watery shapes, the men seemed to demand a retreat from the unexplored, an order from the Captain that this was enough, if it was not already too late.

And the order came, and our vessel creaked in its eagerness to sail north, thankful not to have been reduced to splinters. We fled from the knell of those harsh waves. But almost at once I missed the emptiness.

4

From the Antarctic regions the *Resolution* continued eastwards to New Zealand. After eleven thousand nautical miles and four months on the high seas, they cast anchor in Dusky Bay. At last they had fish to boil and fry instead of the finger-thick maggots that resided in the salt meat. For Sparrman, New Zealand was a paradisiacal break from storms and ice – a table laid with roasted fowl, stews and pasties.

In the primeval forest he came to a lake, a prelapsarian wilderness. 'There reigned the deepest silence and tranquillity in the landscape. Not a breath of wind penetrated to this body of water, enclosed between high hills and large forests. Not a single fly or insect, let alone a bird, was seen or heard here.' He found a plant which he named after his scurvy-afflicted friend George, *Forsteria sedifolia*. Linnaeus was given the first specimen.

A Maori delegation ventured on board, and what astonished them most of all was the ship's cat. The chief smeared a reeking unguent on Cook's forehead and inscribed some sacred signs in it, reciting incantations as he did so. When the ship's artist William Hodges wanted to do a portrait of a Maori woman, she was so delighted that, as the greatest compliment she could pay, she smeared seal oil on the very gentleman who was so renowned for his cleanliness and fragrance.

'Having been well paid in advance for going down to the cabin, she thought she ought to give immediate satisfaction in return for the gift and do so in the manner she understood and had perhaps previously practised with our sailors,' Sparrman wrote. 'In amazement she received the instructions to sit down on a chair. Such a different request must have occurred to her as unreasonable, because initially she even offered her painter various reclining positions on the same chair. To her further amazement she was finally correctly instructed simply to remain seated on the chair, entirely inactive. Then to her own astonishment and amusement and to that of the couple of accompanying savages, she very soon saw her own likeness appear drawn in red crayon.'

Some of the officers from the *Resolution* visited the nearby Maori camp to barter for lobsters, yams, wild celery. The Maoris were attired in dog skins and bird feathers. Sparrman recorded the date: it was the 23rd of November 1773.

'They soon noticed a human head without its lower jaw, several limbs and intestines and the remains of a 16- to 18-year-old youth. The rest of him the savages confessed to having eaten. They stated that of the enemies who had died they had only been able to carry off this now maimed body, whose pierced heart had been hoisted on the prow of a canoe. They also said that they had lost some of their comrades, whose weeping widows had slashed their foreheads with shark's teeth till they bled as a manifestation of their grief. Lieutenant Pickersgill, who wished to preserve this head in *spiritus* for the Hunterian Anatomical Collection in London (where it was later placed), bartered one nail for it.

'When it was brought to the ship, two of the country's young savages caught sight of it and immediately expressed their wish to eat it. But the owner only allowed them a small piece, which he cut off with his penknife. The savage further urged to have this roasted, which was also granted, and it was roasted on the embers in the galley, despite the cook's protests.

'What is surprising in all this must surely be that among a civilized nation there had been some who did not detest the embraces of female man-eaters who, moreover, with their paint, oiling, dirt and lice, fleas and bugs ought to have appeared very disgusting, and among whose hideouts and food packs roast human flesh had sometimes been discovered. But the fire of certain unpolished and headstrong sailors was as intense as it was unclean.

'The New Zealand savage, now so degraded in body and soul, and the needy situation in which he finds himself, will probably not for centuries be able to rise to any higher degree of civilization. Yet their health, tenacity and desire for our bread and other good things might easily make young savages take up service at some colony in the area.

'I remember well having read in my childhood that their nose greeting was in use among our more northerly compatriots, the Lapps. Little did I imagine then that I myself should many times practise the same form of greeting in New Zealand. That my nose had been so very close to cannibals' teeth and that I had none-theless been brought back home to Sweden safe and sound.'

From the 13th to the 21st of December 1773 they passed 'the direct antipodes to Sweden. I was now on the spot the most distant from my native country of any on the whole globe. This astonishing distance, however, did not prevent my rapid imagination from frequently visiting my beloved countrymen and relations during this period, while my feet were in direct opposition to theirs.'

In January 1774 they crossed the Antarctic Circle for the third time.

'On the 28th of January we penetrated into the southern regions as far as we could possibly go, being, before we had got to 71 deg. 14 min., prevented by the ice from putting in execution the scheme we had fondly formed of hoisting the British flag in a sixth part of the world, or even on the southern pole itself. Since we had got as close to the ice as we dared, we began to turn the ship away from there and northwards. In order to avoid the usual noise and bustle during such a manoeuvre, I went below to my cabin to watch more calmly from its window the boundless polar ice theatre. That is how it happened, as my travel companions remarked, that I went a little further south than any of the others in the ship, because, while turning, a ship always lags a little sternwards before she can make speed under the new tack as her sails fill out.'

5

So the *Resolution* set course for warmer latitudes. They sailed without flag, and only raised the British ensign on meeting another vessel or preparing for attack. When a storm was in the offing, the bell was rung and the crew were given brandy and gin to fortify them.

Captain Cook noted that the aim of the expedition had been achieved: they had approached the South Pole from several directions and ascertained that there was no habitable land. The larger proportion of the voyage had been spent seeking something that did not exist. So truth and reality could at last replace centuries of dreams and fantasies.

The ship anchored at Tahiti, four years after Cook's previous visit. Following a skirmish with thieves and warning shots from the cannon, Cook received permission from King Ahetua to go ashore with some of his officers, the two Forsters and Anders Sparrman.

Half an hour's walk into the island they found all the people gathered, with one shoulder bared as a sign of respect. In their midst sat their king, a tall eighteen-year-old with a gentle face, dressed in white, flanked by the elders. Cook presented glass beads, nails, an axe, a mirror and a piece of fabric. The king was pleased, and any mistrust evaporated. When Reinhold Forster gave him a tassel of scarlet feathers, he exclaimed in delight. The ship carried a substantial supply of gifts: semi-precious stones, coloured glass beads, scissors, combs, dyed handkerchiefs, tinkling bells.

'Another great fault inherent in this nation,' Sparrman wrote, 'although in many of our sailors' judgement desirable and lovable, was that the greater part of the unmarried class neither considered it a crime, nor made it particularly difficult, to share and exchange intimate love relationships with the opposite sex. What a hope and what a lure for the sailor was not this, already outside the harbour seeing the hundreds of such willing girls, gentle as well as comely, and naked to the waist, surround the ship! Here he saw himself at the gate to the paradise of the goddess of love about to be invited in, yet all lovesick fire must surely have cooled off in an instant! The keel of the ship crashes on to a coral rock sending each one staggering on his legs. These naturally terrifying lunges followed one another while we were gradually driven further on to the reef, with the awesome breakers below the cabin windows threatening every moment to end this dreadful spectacle in total shipwreck.

'Once the ship was free again, I accompanied Captain Cook down to the wardroom, when, having been seen fully active and alert from beginning to end while taking command, he now broke out into a cold sweat, was limp and had stomach pains so that he could hardly stand on his legs. I persuaded him to take a well-tested Swedish remedy: that is, a really good tot of aquavit. His colic and weakness disappeared at once, and most of us hastened to gather new strength from a good meal.

'The king of Tahiti received a pair of goats and Mr Forster's shaggy gun dog. A *hoa* was ordered to carry this dog, and it may be that a special national office was established to care for the same. It also has to be said to the credit of this King that he took great care to inform himself about the usefulness of the goats, their tending and care.

'Our hot tea water was to them a wondrous preparation, as were soups, for the Tahitian nationals do not possess any cooking utensils. Butter was likewise something new to them. They called it Britannic oil or ointment, and they enjoyed it with us spread on fried and roasted slices of breadfruit.

'One consequence of the royal visit seemed to be that the indigenous fruit was sold in abundance at our marketplace, set up next to the camp or the tents, and that in the evening the ship's deck was overrun by Tahitian girls seeking night lodgings and earnings, and in such numbers, that the visitors could easily over-power the crew if they were otherwise only half as brave as amorous. A group of the Tahitian girls performed their dances at dusk, animated by someone's fluting on a pipe like a transverse flute, but which was blown through one of the nostrils. They would often join in with their own song, which, no less than half the dance itself, sometimes gave the idea that these dancers and singers were not very scrupulous about their modesty, which is the greatest asset and adornment of their sex.

'But what about the English sailor? His religion and weak philosophy will be hard put to the test and soon found wanting. Often enchanted by the sight of beauties swimming around the ship and less than half-clad girls dancing and singing on deck before their eyes, many less stable minds were confused into following local custom. They spent their small fund of nails, knives, scissors, mirrors and so on, which could have been put to better use. But what of the consequences? Well, generally remorse and frequent visits to the ship's doctor, a diet and a general low fine set by the Admiralty as a perquisite for the doctor, which is deducted from the patient's pay for each treatment of a disease which they have brought on themselves through their own sins.'

Sparrman likened Tahiti to the old European feudal system, albeit with a milder climate and a plentiful provision of food. Envy, greed and ambition seemed unknown. The freedom of the unmarried was so universal that in Cook's words it could not be called a vice, because it encompassed the whole society.

'What sensual power! What love of life!' exclaimed George Forster, who was more outspoken than Anders.

'Funding for expeditions such as ours used to be put up by the Emperor of Russia or the King of England,' William Hodges said, while cleaning his horsehair and beaver-bristle brushes. 'Now we have little money, but a lot of time. I followed in my grandfather's footsteps and took apprenticeship as a watchmaker, but I am more at home with pencil and brush.'

His charcoal flew across the paper. He balanced foreground and background and painted the sea off Tahiti so shimmeringly mother-of-pearl that it would have made a fine wallpaper in a princely bedchamber. A wash of Naples yellow and yellow ochre recreated the beach with its breaking waves and brown-hued fig-ures personifying the very sweetness of life.

The *Resolution* took on board two hundred and nine pigs and a quantity of domestic fowls. But when Cook came to step into the pinnace to return to his ship, the natives fled from him. Cook recorded what had happened in his journal.

'Mr Sparman being out alone botanizing was set upon by two men who striped him of every thing he had but his trowsers. They struck him several times with his own hanger but happily did him no harm. As soon as they had accomplished their end they made off after which a man came to him, gave him a piece of cloth to cover himself and conducted him to me. I went immidiately to Oree to complain of this outrage takeing with me the man who came back with Mr Sparman to confirm the complaint. As soon as the chief heard it he wept a lowd as did several others and after the first transports of his grief was over expostulated with the people shewing them how well I had treated them both in this and my former voyage or some thing to this purpose. He then promised to do all in his power to recover what was taken from Mr Sparman.

'I disired him to send some people for the stolen things for I saw it was to little purpose going farther, for the thieves had already got so much start of us that we might have pursued them to the very remote part of the island. Besides as I intended to sail the next day, this occasioned a loss to us by putting a stop to all manner of trade for the natives were so allarmed that none came near us but those that were about the chief. The accedent which befell Mr Sparman was first made known to us at the tradeing place by the precipitate retiring of all the people without my being able to conceive the meaning till Mr Sparman appeared. It became therefore the more necessary for me to return to *Endeavour* to restore things to their former state.

'All was now harmony and peace, the people crowded in from every part with hogs, fowls and fruit so that we presently loaded two boats, the chief himself made me a present of a large hog and some fruit, the hanger, the only thing of value Mr Sparman had lost, and part of his waistcoat was brought to us and we were told we should have the others the next day.'

Cook never saw himself as a conqueror and colonialist. More than any conquest, he loved a new point on the chart, a line between two islands, and – as he himself wrote – 'the pleasure of being the first'. Any excesses perpetrated by the seamen were punished with the whip in the presence of the wronged parties.

Wounded, but treated with his own medicaments, Anders watched the Captain standing motionless at the wheel like a contemplative saint. A few years earlier Cook had seen the transit of Venus reflected in the still waters around the Society Islands, and when the twinkling red planet was rendered invisible by daylight, the waves had begun to rise in an unexpected south wind, cold, strong and perfumed by the islands' breadfruit trees. The light had spread up the valleys, where the bee-eaters squawked to protect their eggs.

6

George Forster is the same age I was eight years ago when I set out on my voyage to China. He does not have the freedom I have, since anything significant is taken care of by his father. George does not participate in serious decisions, but is given practical work like skinning a pilot fish, cutting up a penguin before it's delivered to the cook, or tying pieces of coral into a watch chain for his father. He has close-set, almost translucent eyes, and moderates his voice to please his father.

He is a decent and well-bred young man, with a large nose, quite slim hands but less slender of body, and for the present without side-whiskers like his father's, but not really of strong enough constitution for this voyage. He is always glad to assist me, having been at first reticent and respectful, but later happy to seek my friendship. Like his loud, tyrannical father, he evinces a lively interest in my conversations with Professor Linnaeus. He plays chess with William Hodges, whereas I have declined games of whist with our astronomer.

As an observer he has few equals. His eyes seem to be wide open all day long. But he is no botanist, and I have sought to extend his insight into the northern European flora that he grew up amidst by giving him the Linnaean Latin for summer flowers, then translating them into the more amusing vernacular: night-flowering catchfly, eyebright, oxeye daisy, cat's-foot, baby's breath, marsh tea. I told him that when Linnaeus talked to the plants in Latin, they answered him in perfect Swedish.

At the railing, under a shy crescent moon, we viewed the constellations, so different from those back home, he with astonishment as I pointed them out by name, important as they were for our navigation. After that he found the nights less menacing and oppressive.

I expatiated on the fact that for every secret of Nature we track down, a new manifestation awaits us. So it's absolutely essential to remain vigilant, however monotonous the days at sea may feel, since we cannot foretell events at latitudes no-one has visited before. Every chart has errors based on rumours and fantasies. Hence the value of every single observation we make.

He said the victuals were inducing in him a heaviness of spirit and discomfort of the nerves. He considered it shameful to be so in thrall to his own appetite. He has his miserable little cabin near mine, and in a calm I can hear him tossing and turning. I have opened his door to wake him from his disturbed sleep and found him lying stretched out, yet ready to spring up like a hunting dog. He is fearful he will never see the coasts of Europe again, but I think I have inspired him with fresh hope. Maybe he believes I have some influence on the invisible scales that hold his and all our fates in the balance.

We wash in buckets up on deck. The Captain has a basin made of sailcloth. I am aware that he has become a father to George in the place of the irascible and boastful Reinhold, who is always complaining about the food and is therefore banished from the Captain's table. One evening Captain Cook was in good humour. He came out with a glass in his hand, and said to George Forster and me, 'We have had successes and setbacks, but I think posterity will recognize the advances made in our exploration of the southern hemisphere.'

I noted that he spoke in the first person plural. We were standing on the quarterdeck and he fixed his half-smile on us. I felt relaxed, not frantic and agitated as was the case when we had problems to solve, but in fact sure that everything was explicable, if not now, then in the course of time.

The Captain named islands he wanted to investigate further: Newfoundland, Kerguelen, the Comoros, the Azores and Cape Verde. He said that exploration in the future would include the sea bed all around such islands, where sunken volcanoes and plateaux would be discovered, perhaps even cities from cultures long since destroyed.

'You have much material for your journal, Dr Sparrman,' he said. 'Use it well! Dry-as-dust narratives are not the thing for the first-ever eastward circumnavigation of the globe, such as we are making. But I beseech you to delay them until I have published my own logbooks.'

That evening we ate a mess of plums, laid down with sugar in the Cape to preserve them. We allowed ourselves a splash of wine each, but no second glass. We were not off duty, but were on watch and listening to the vibrations, lurches and groans of the ship. We were like insects on a host animal, dependent on its whims and moods.

I regard Captain Cook as a most unusual person, worthy of the greatest courtesy and trust. Seldom or never is there a show of anger when he chastises the thoughtless. He exercises self-control and does not invite obsequiousness. He has a systematic mind, and although he occasionally falls sick from our wretched provender, he declares he is made of English oak, or cork oak, I cannot remember his exact metaphor. He has sense enough to dismiss things which, however important, ought not to take up his energies.

He cloaks our mortal danger in dry figures of longitude and latitude, temperature, course, wind strength and direction. His matter-of-factness and love of detail border on romanticism. He has banished dreams and opened the way to the future. When our vessel finally turned back at the barrier of ice, he remarked, 'Even negative discoveries can change the world.'

He is neatly dressed and clean-shaven, and even in a storm sports shiny polished shoes as if he were back at the naval base in Plymouth. He stands with his compasses on the chart and keeps his questions to himself. He has no favourites and maintains his distance with everyone. He is in league with the forces of history itself. He alone takes responsibility for us all.

He will not tolerate the obscenities flying through the air among the crew, nor the profane or sexual curses lambasting the failing wind, that leaves us idle and out of sorts. Yet he can accept figurative expressions like 'hawse hole' for the female orifice or 'canonicus' for the man's cocked blunderbuss. So we are able to indulge in a bit of roguery; there is no virtue to protect on board. Only when we go ashore on a friendly coast does the Captain warn us, without being too grudging or admonitory, to hold ourselves in check in the presence of young women.

Nor has anyone ever seen him in a beer cellar or whorehouse, any more than in a church or an educational institution. A man without vanity, he enjoys the company of both high and low. From collier deckhand to naval officer, he has trodden a longer path than most. But he has learned the knack of exercising discipline without harshness.

When he makes his rounds the cards are quickly shuffled together, even though he does not utter a word. He has an aquiline nose and eyes as grey as the sea. We all know that without him we would perish.

Superfluous insults or expressions of exaggerated abhorrence are not his style, nor is small talk or formal politeness. He is ready to overlook minor offences. In times of shortage a half-stoup is shared among many, a test of self-control. Monotony is his friend, or rather he does not recognize monotony, and doesn't need to while it away with rough brandy or religious devotions. Long periods in the Doldrums don't make him any the less resolute. He simply finds occupations which stand us in good stead when the sea returns to life.

'Doctor Sparrman, my medical colleague,' said the Captain, 'can you assist us in determining how this dog and this fowl can be combined in the pot to provide a good repast?'

I'm often asked questions outside my field of competence, but on board ship we all have to stretch our powers of intellect to find the requisite solutions.

On the *Resolution* my conscience is at ease. We do our best. We may possibly survive. It's too early to prepare oneself for Judgement Day.

The hours pass. We sail by day and by night. Oceans on an inhuman scale! We mortals are no more than a few scribbles on its iron-grey surface. I'm not a brave soul and have no-one to appeal to. Botanical reading. Abscess on my big toe. A clay pipe after dinner with Captain Cook, whose strict probity can be alarming.

Sailing close-hauled into a spasmodic wind, we hear the slap of block and tackle, something sliding across the deck, and sighs from the hull like those of a dying man. We hurtled down into a ravine of rushing water. So lacking were we in any form of stability that my senses threatened to desert me. To withstand the ear-splitting fury of the elements, I roared out my name, as if it belonged to another. Answer came there none.

I paced the quarterdeck on the windward side. My garments were salty from the wind and spray. The ship's bell tolled four. It was early, but I felt nauseated by the air in my wretched little cabin. I am not happy with my bunk and am going to take over a dead man's hammock. In that tiny study I have to write my notes and reports, make a cork for the inkwell, sort my medicaments and treat a sailor with an injured knee. My tincture for headaches is potent enough to induce temporary blindness; it's better to dispel the pain with brandy, which at least brings pleasing visions.

The rolling lessens under a more normal wind. Captain Cook has had oil lamps lit on deck. Thanks to his foresight we don't have to dice with death and can assess the merits of alternative routes. Exhausted sailors are not pushed beyond their limits on this sea, where we have only whales and dolphins for company. We sail from one invisible point on the chart to another – advancing into the unknown with a determination that the Captain says must never degenerate into a sacrificial rite.

We eat at separate tables, but the putrid water is the same for us all. Days as heavy as lead. I am quite clear in my own mind that my death will cause neither sorrow nor joy to anyone. Bolder explorers and more learned naturalists are already active. Cartographers will abandon the Earth for the landscape of the stars, for the inside of icebergs and volcanoes, for the undiscovered recesses of the human body.

Spotted a shark, followed by pilot fish, playful and glistening. Uncertain whether they seek the shark's protection against predators, or whether they eat the shark's excrement or leavings. On another occasion saw a battalion of silverheads, followed in turn by yellowbacks. They were the fearless grasshoppers of the oceans, that could be caught without bait. When, as at some unseen signal, they flashed their shimmering bellies in unison, the entire sea shone like a shield of polished metal.

Taking constant soundings, we grope our way between the islands. Our Captain is reluctant to admit we have encountered competent navigators among the natives. Without them we would have run aground. Without them we would not have discovered a chain of islands. They have shown us a sort of chart that makes them at home in their archipelagos. But the Captain seems not to want that noised abroad, for the sake of his own reputation.

They are the citizens of the sea. They build their canoes from hollowed-out trees, use the trunks of palm trees as crosspieces to make rafts for goods and passengers, hoist sails made of bark and leaf fibres, navigate by the stars. They are by no means inferior to us.

7

They next discovered the group of islands Captain Cook called New Caledonia. Anders Sparrman described them thus:

'The inhabitants were civil and hospitable, but poor, and spoke a language peculiar to themselves. At this place, by great good fortune, I avoided eating the liver of a poisonous fish, in company with the Captain and Messrs Forster, who were extremely ill for some days afterwards. On the 15th, for want of wind, we were near being driven on the rocks, and at night were in the most dangerous situation, being surrounded by a coral reef. That evening, when I went to bed, there was the greatest probability that I should never wake again, but at my very last gasp: however I had the good fortune to fall immediately into a sound sleep, and the next morning when I awoke, to find that I had escaped the most imminent danger that could well be imagined.'

Savage Island, the 20th of June 1774 (New Hebrides): 'Soon savages came into sight. They were shown white cloths, green branches and hailed amicably, all in vain. They were painted coal black, red and white in every conceivable nasty streaking and, with their feathered heads and grimacing postures, they seemed to me more like devils than ever any of those represented in theatres and on the walls of old country churches, despite their horns and claws. With his left hand one of these threw a large coral rock at me and hit my left forearm.'

On the island of Tanna, another of the New Hebrides, a fire-spouting volcano was spewing stones up into the sky. The natives waited cautiously, but sent out an elderly man in a small canoe, who kept throwing a coconut into the sea in front of him.

Captain Cook was rowed out to meet him. The old man was amazed at the white men's skin and clothing, and was presented with the gift of a mirror. As he paddled off to report, he constantly stared at his reflection and did not notice the ebbing tide pulling him out to sea. Only with difficulty did he resist the temptation of the mirror and get back ashore, where he was surrounded by his people, also wanting to see themselves reflected in it.

The *Resolution* warped her way between the islands, taking soundings all the while in order to reach a safe harbour without running aground, avoiding tree stumps sticking up like blackened teeth in a treacherous swamp. The crew fetched drinking water from ponds and marshes. Yams and figs were cultivated on fertile volcanic soil. Peppers and oranges grew there, and the men pounded a cactus into a flour from which they made bread, and which soon had them inebriated and tugging at each other's beards.

The inhabitants were circumcised and claimed to be cannibals. Some had frizzy hair plaited into hundreds of pigtails. The men went about naked except for a narrow girdle, fastened to which was a thick wrapping round the male member. Their weapons comprised clubs, slings, spears, and bows and arrows. They harvested honey, and they pulled wasps' nests off the roof rafters and flung them on the fire. According to George Forster they were skilled at deception, persuasion and trade, and understood 'all our signs and gestures as fast as if they had been acquainted with us for a long time'.

On one of the Tongan islands, where the people had never seen a white man before and where red parrot feathers constituted a means of payment, they were received with unfeigned friendliness. The girls, perfumed with lemon and balsam, danced for them, juggling with balls and laughing with *joie de vivre*. They kissed the travellers' hands, then clasped them to their bosoms. Here people followed their inclinations openly, whereas in Europe strict custom inhibited the warmth of the blood and the urges of the senses – according to George Forster's journal. He also noticed the bats, the flying foxes, that hung in clusters from the branches of the cassowary trees above their cemeteries. They let themselves be picked off at will, eight at a time with one shot.

With a fresh stock of bananas, yam roots, coconuts and pigs, the *Resolution* sailed on. They landed at Easter Island, found little water or food, and wondered if a catastrophe or epidemic had decimated the population. Women were few in number and each had several husbands. One young woman, George Forster wrote, serviced the whole crew, without any sign of weariness.

'On the 30th of September 1774 we were once more becalmed between the rocks, and exposed to swells and currents, and unable to find bottom with the lead at 150 fathoms. At dusk a fire-ball was seen coming with a hissing from the north, of the same visible size as the sun, but of a somewhat paler light. It soon exploded and left behind it some shining sparks, the biggest of which, oblong in shape, rushed from our field of vision, followed by a bluish flaming streak. A little later our perilous calm changed into a fresh breeze.

'During these days the ocean gratified us first with the catch of a large shark, which, despite tasting of whale train oil, made a delicious change from the ship's fare, and on another occasion with an albatross, which for us in our circumstances might well pass for a fattened goose. Further and more excellent still, we were treated to a dolphin, which was harpooned and then allowed to run out a long line, during which time it was killed with five musket shots. It proved to be a female with milk in the breasts. It was six feet long. The flesh was very dark, but provided nonetheless a delicious dinner for the whole crew. It was not the least oily, for the fat was scraped off and boiled away, after which, thanks to the cook's skilful preparation, it resembled beef.'

In Tierra del Fuego Anders Sparrman witnessed the mating of sea lions, a lengthy procedure which appeared to indicate a frigid disposition.

'These animals seemed to caress each other with their noses. But for all that, their lovemaking seemed pitiable, both in its whimpering tones and as though constantly wailing.'

In the Strait of Magellan on Christmas Eve they shot a species of wild goose, *Anas Magellanica*: seventy-six birds, which provided roast goose for the whole crew.

'At our table was served both boiled and roast goose as well as goose pie, especially on Christmas Day. Our Madeira wine was the only part of the provisions which had improved over the long voyage, and that to an excellence which may never before have been tasted in neither Tierra del Fuego nor Europe, and now crowned our Christmas celebrations.

'Having presented a portrait of the Magellan goose, I would do my own people an injustice were I not to show my compatriots a portrait of the local people, the dirtiest, most wretched and most pitiable of all human children. We had hardly imagined we would meet such naked beings in the cold here. They are of small build, yet thickset, and looked starved to emaciation. Their eyes were small, brown and without any spark; the nose flat, cheekbones protruding, chin beardless, hair smeared in whale train oil, stinking, the whole physiognomy, like the body, olive-brown and bemired with dirt. Over all they look suffering, frozen, repressed, astonished, stupid or idiotic.'

8

One day the fore-topman dived into the water to free an anchor hawser from the rudder and came up with lacerations all over his body. The coral reef was taking its revenge, but they could not work out what had wounded him so badly. He died that same evening from blood poisoning, and was sewn into his hammock. The flag was lowered, the Captain read a prayer, some soil was scattered over the corpse and it was committed to the waves. Then the wind was allowed to fill the royals.

The sails were specked with mildew. Anders Sparrman let his brown beard grow. He went on his rounds among the men who had succumbed to putrid fever, dropsy or scurvy, and made sure the drinking water was filtered of flies and woodlice. After which he sat in his cabin, an unlit pipe in his mouth and a book in his hands. On his table a quill pen in the inkwell ready for his day's notes, and on the lid of his seaman's chest a medical prescription.

All lights on board were extinguished at ten o'clock, except for those of Cook, the Forsters, Hodges and Sparrman. A different perception of time prevailed at sea in the loneliness of night. The stars showed them the way. The helmsman was replaced and went below deck. The ship kept her distance from the surf breaking on the coral reefs. In a gap between the clouds low on the horizon hung the reflective orb of Venus.

Their expedition had been called an experimental voyage. 'Therefore all the passengers who were not actually part of the crew, such as astronomers, botanists and draftsman, were also called experimental gentlemen or trialists. I remember another amusing experiment on the occasion when our sow was farrowing on board and we lost fine hogs due to the severe weather. Hardly had I mentioned that in China I had been sold sow's milk for our tea and coffee, than the Captain gave orders that the present sow be milked. But as the new milch cow had earlier behaved fractiously, nobody dared to carry out the experiment.'

The boatswain on the *Resolution* had a cat, which 'did not neglect to catch rats and carry them off to its master, who then divided the spoils, the cat getting the front end, while the hind end was cleaned, fried and seasoned for himself'. The others, having to make do with sheep that had died a natural death or sickly hens and geese, were never known to refuse a really tasty dog steak.

Captain Cook gave everyone a daily portion of sauerkraut as an antidote to scurvy, although the crew at first refused to countenance such un-British food. The ship's biscuits were full of brown weevils that revealed themselves as a cold sensation in the mouth. The biscuits were lined up on the table, and if anything crawled out of them, the cook pounded them and baked them up again in fat. Meat that had gone green was rinsed in pepper and vinegar. The salt meat, now almost three years old, was dry and shrivelled. Some of the sailors had gums swollen right over their teeth and could only take food in liquid form. As ship's doctor, Sparrman kept a journal of the crew's condition. Sometimes the stench of tobacco and rancid dripping was enough to make him retch.

'That we now had many more hardships to undergo than Byron, Wallis and Cook had suffered in their former voyages round the Earth, many of our officers, as well as of the crew, attested. The purposes intended to be answered by our voyage, particularly that of approaching as near as we could to the South Pole, required other attempts to be made, other dangers to be undergone: the remainder of the voyage consequently was almost a concatenation of dangers and hardship.

'On the 17th of March we saw land, viz., the coast of Africa. Totally ignorant, as we were, of the state of affairs in Europe, we could not, even when in sight of the harbour itself, assure ourselves that we should not be picked up by some unknown enemy, who might carry us out as prisoners perhaps to the most distant part of the East-Indies. The next day, however, we overtook a Dutch vessel, and received from her the joyful news of a general peace. Before night we saw several sails more, which seemed to be steering by the Cape, and making as fast as possible for Europe; and with no small pleasure, particularly on my part, we saw the Swedish flag flying upon two of them.

'In fact, the ocean had hitherto, during our voyage, been really too lonesome and desolate a theatre to us. Neither is it any wonder, that in so long a space of time, we came to be in some measure weary of each other's company; when, for instance, those who were used to entertain the company with tales and anecdotes were obliged to have recourse two or three times to the same stories, in order to furnish their quota in conversation.

'With pleasure and longing desire we received our letters from Europe, but not within them accounts of the loss of our dearest friends and acquaintance.'

When the *Resolution* anchored at Cape Town, on her journey from Tierra del Fuego and South Georgia to England, no-one since Columbus and Tasman had undertaken such a lengthy voyage. The town received them with great festivities, and the vessel lay at anchor in False Bay for five weeks for repair and provisioning. Only three of the crew were ill enough to be sent ashore for treatment.

Cook, the Forsters and Sparrman took up lodgings again with Christoffel Brand in Simonstown. Anders could scarcely imagine that, within a few months of being in this wretched house with its hard bunks and rough sheets, his Captain would return home to accolades and honours from his own country, and be received by the king and the Government and by his wife, who would soon fall pregnant again.

As it set sail for Britain, Sparrman went aboard with the pilot to accompany the *Resolution* for the first few miles past Robben Island, and to take his leave of his young friend George Forster, with whom he was to correspond for many years to come.

'A barren, low and sandy island where many slaves and felons had been condemned and kept in various forms of hard labour. Runaway slaves were sent there, because it was impossible to escape by swimming. Even so, they would be chained for the night to a block of stone, which by day they had to hew with hammer and chisel. They preferred the gallows; Robben Island was a slow death.'

Sparrman entrusted a gift for Linnaeus to George Forster. It was a dried specimen of the four-horned boxfish, *Ostracion*, which, when suspended from the ceiling by a slender thread, would indicate the direction of the wind as surely as a flag in the open air. George declared that he would particularly miss Dr Sparrman, who had 'shared the dangers and privations of our voyage, and whose generous heart has made him loved by all who know him'.

Cape Colony Expedition

1

After Anders Sparrman returned to the Cape on the 21st of March 1775 he spent four months preparing his expedition through the south-eastern province to what were then the limits of Dutch colonization.

He had arranged to meet Daniel Immelman in Company Park. Immelman lived with his mother and sister in a low white stucco house with a thatched roof. Anders picked his way along the pot-holed gravel streets. A woman was carrying washing on her head. Two men were securing a tarpaulin over a cart with a thick rope. He watched as foreigners' hairnets and wigs went flying down the street in the wind.

Although eight years younger than Sparrman, Immelman was a seasoned traveller who had accompanied Carl Peter Thunberg on his first expedition. He had studied surveying and knew how to draw a map. He was to assist Sparrman with his renowned map of the South African coastal regions. They took an immediate liking to each other and promised to stay together through thick and thin. There were no written agreements between them.

'We will be on our own together for a whole year,' Anders explained upon engaging Immelman. 'Sometimes it's best not to talk. But it will make life easier if we conceal nothing of significance. Let us put our cards on the table, even if we cannot know all there is to know about one another.'

'We are both risking our lives in this undertaking,' the younger man warned.

'So in practical terms we shall be equals,' Sparrman replied. 'And it will not be the first time we have run such risks.'

'Life will not be easy in the interior,' Immelman continued. 'Lack of water. Thunderstorms and beasts of prey. Our oxen sinking into sand or mud. Darkness descends swiftly. It's all too easy to get lost and never be heard of again.'

Immelman's sister Anna was prettier than any other woman Anders had seen in the town. Apart from a black silk scarf, she was simply dressed with her hair fastened back. He registered the sibling resemblance and wished that she could have come with him on the journey, observant and charming as she seemed. He did not give voice to this thought, but wrote it down later.

After the meeting with Immelman he took a carriage, one of those that appeared only at weekends. The coachman asked if he should whip up the horses to a faster pace, but Anders told him to let them take their time. He didn't mind coming back late to his lodgings. A mist hung over the town. What will be will be, he thought.

He borrowed money from a trading house at an interest rate of one-and-a-half per cent, and heard a rumour that a highly gifted naturalist had arrived in a threadbare jacket with tin buttons and brown trousers tucked into high black boots.

A letter conveyed by one of the ships brought him news from home that Lidström, the curate, had died of pneumonia. His uncle Högbom had met the same fate: Anders remembered him with milk-white hair, a nose like a strawberry, a lisping tongue which gave his speech a comically bizarre pronunciation, and a habit of snapping his jaw shut with a click. Sweden was a long way away. Anders wept an unmanly tear.

Sparrman and Immelman provided themselves with a good horse that would bear light loads, and a Galloway cob, a baggage wagon with a tilt made of sailcloth, a tub of tar for greasing, drag chains and a chain for the traces. Five pairs of oxen were needed to draw the wagon. They had cinchona bark in powder form, ammonia for insect bites. Barter goods such as tobacco, glass beads, brass tinderboxes, cloth and nails. An oak cask for keeping snakes and other animals in spirit. Rice paper for drying plants, needles for insects. Coffee, tea, chocolate, sugar and biscuits. Gunpowder, lead shot and bullets, knives. Sewing needles to win the favour of farmers' daughters who might be persuaded to assist in collecting insects. Bags for bulbs and seeds, cotton and containers for birds. Anders left his family chest in Cape Town, and Immelman procured raffia and metal boxes for them.

They started their expedition on the 25th of July 1775, travelling eastwards to Hottentots Holland's Mountain and across the Palmiet River to the Warm Baths at the foot of the Swartberg, in the botanically fecund Caledon region. Immelman sought a cure there for his weak lungs and Sparrman for the blisters on his hands, that he had contracted in the Antarctic climate.

'It was very little to the honour of the African colonists that they had neglected investigating their own country,' he wrote, 'insomuch that they would soon be obliged to apply to me and other strangers for intelligence concerning themselves and the very place of their residence.'

Immelman was a colourless man with ice-blue eyes, but a beard, when he let it grow, as dark red as a newly shelled horse chestnut. He was surprisingly resourceful, as if he had an inexhaustible breadth of experience in his leather rucksack, and he found them a way out of many an awkward situation. He was a very patient man and did not expect gratitude. Rather than just covering ground, he made a point of *dis*covering it. Even if he didn't sleep a wink all night because of buzzing insects or screaming hyenas, he still got up the next day rested and in good humour.

Anders watched the young man's lamp coming closer and then disappearing again, and knew that he was seeking their lodging for the night at a farm where no bloodthirsty dogs resided. He felt rather despondent as he waited, but was relying on his companion's proficient Afrikaans, and, sure enough, they were soon standing outside a house, and a farm slave was attending to their bearers, horses and oxen. They carried their trunk in and used it as a seat.

The farm lacked furniture apart from a few fragile chairs that would have been better thrown on the fire, where dry branches were ablaze and the smoke seeped out through broken window frames. There was a bent candle and a snuffer coated in verdigris. Mouse droppings had been swept into a heap, but were still there, an apparent indication that no-one bothered about comfort or hygiene. Complaint would have been out of place, and they had to be content with what was provided and cheer themselves up with facetious banter about how much they had to endure.

The evening was rounded off with the barking of the dogs. Outside, the larch trees resembled tattered overcoats, and the white marrows in the vegetable garden slept soundly in their beds. The farmer was an erstwhile inspector for the East India Company, good-natured, dull and oafish.

Now they were about to leave these sparsely populated regions for the unknown.

2

Daniel Immelman was not an eloquent man. He would lose his
thread, chasing after words, which threw him off course. He preferred to express himself sparingly and didactically. He went along
in silence with his eyes half-directed straight ahead, half-peering
to the side. No surprises and no ambushes for him.

He did, however, say to Anders, rather unexpectedly, 'I was
watching my father one day as he sat by the fire, which was smouldering from damp or mouldy wood, when he remarked, "This
smoke is nothing but a curse, you know." Then he put on some
sheep dung and onion tops to get the fire to take. But it hissed like
a rat and made him jump.'

'Why are you telling me this?'

'Because I'm beginning to understand that we are all alike, in
our fears and our anger and the delight we take in spreading
unpleasant rumours.'

'What kind of a man was your father?'

'He used to be very hale and hearty, but his brain was beginning
to haze over into an absent-minded vagueness, not a normal distracted air but a rambling outspokenness that no-one wanted to
hear. Yet he showed immense courage when a catastrophe presented itself: he went to the aid of some shipwrecked sailors in
False Bay and was drowned himself.'

Immelman then recounted what his father had described as his
most horrifying experience. In times of danger, after a storm, the
Big Doll would show her flat face like a disc in the sky. 'Her mouth
was open, but not a sound could be heard. The sight of the Doll

was so terrifying that everyone who saw her considered any other misfortune preferable. Because the appearance of the Doll presaged vengeance and retribution.'

Evening approached once more. They drank castor oil with a dash of brandy. The dogs were uneasy. A bond was growing between the two young men, based on kindness and trust. They shared everything during the journey, but nevertheless Immelman remained an employee and subservient, and they were never on Christian-name terms.

Immelman had a notion that a cut in the temple could deaden the nerve which gave rise to dreams: that shimmer and menace of the inner eye. But Sparrman advised against attempting to remove something which ought to be there – the imagination that gave nourishment to the reasoning brain.

'It is strange that we remember colours,' Immelman also commented, 'that they are fixed in the brain: the crimson of the horizon at dawn, the blue wing of the kingfisher, the yellow or purple of the plum, the black mournful eyes of the heron.' An observation that required no response.

Anders gazed out over the stunted forest they had traversed the day before. He had killed a bush rat and dissected it. He felt a great ennui at all this collecting and classifying, all those boxes and compartments he was expected to fill with specimens. He presumed that once back home – if he ever got that far – he would have to sit down with piles of animals, plants and stones and consign them to their neatly labelled demise in Swedish and Latin. The results of his expeditions would weary him more than the adversities of the journeys themselves.

The dung beetles consumed the ox dung during the night. When the sun went down the air resonated with their buzzing and little thuds as they hit a rock or a wall.

'You know, Immelman,' said Anders, 'the strength of women lies in their ability to weep. Have you wept in the last few years?'

'I cannot remember having done so. Although there has been plenty to weep about.'

'There you are. A woman would find something to weep about. She resists, submits, surrenders herself, becomes the other person. It's a delightful and frightening process that we men seldom undergo – to our own detriment.'

But Immelman did not reciprocate with any confidences of his own, and Anders' experience was feigned.

The sunset formed glowing red streaks on the horizon, with lighter wisps of cloud between them like clothes hung out to dry. Anders sat with his pen in his hand and could feel the closeness that had developed between him and his companion. They were still young, and on the mere basis of reports and sketch maps they had ventured into a Dutch fantasy of land and riches, rivers of drinking water, the enslavement of the black people.

'We overhauled our stock of biscuit, and found that on occasion of this great holiday, we could afford to give out two to each man,' Anders wrote on the 24th of December 1775. 'We treated ourselves with an ostrich egg, part of which was stewed in our porridge pot, and the remainder boiled up with some coffee. The third dish consisted of a piece of elk's flesh.'

On Christmas Day Immelman shot a buffalo.

'During his fall, and before he died, he bellowed in a most stupendous manner, and this death-song of his inspired every one of us with no small degree of joy, on account of the victory we had gained. So thoroughly steeled frequently is the human heart against the sufferings of the brute creation that we hastened forwards, in order to enjoy the pleasure of seeing the buffalo struggle with the pangs of death. I think it impossible ever to behold anguish, accompanied by a savage fierceness, painted in stronger colours than they were in the countenance of this buffalo.'

On New Year's Eve Sparrman and Immelman sang hymns and played cards. On the 1st of January the travellers caught sight of a beautiful white girl, dressed in summer clothes, and Sparrman was afraid his companion would forget all about his botanizing. But then her husband came into view, a sturdy Dutchman, and a leopard was lurking nearby. It was soon shot, and on its fur Sparrman found an insect worthy of note.

The Khoikhoi (a word meaning 'people') were called Hottentots by the settlers. Two of them, Adonis and Ocha, who were at the head of the party, turned up one day with their faces painted white. This was because they were about to pass a holy place. Ocha spoke of cave paintings, but they paid him little attention.

Lions roared close to their ox-wagon camp. 'A hoarse inarticulate sound, which at the same time seemed to have a hollowness in it, something like that proceeding from a speaking-trumpet. The sound is between that of a German or Italian *U* and an *O* being drawn to a great length, and seeming as if it proceeded from out of the earth, though I could not hear precisely from what quarter it came. The sound of the lion's voice does not bear the least resemblance to thunder, as M. de Buffon affirms it does.

'We could plainly perceive by our animals, when the lions were reconnoitering us at a small distance. For in that case the hounds did not dare to bark in the least, but crept quite close to the Hottentots, and our oxen and horses sighed deeply, frequently hanging back, and pulling slowly with all their might at the strong straps with which they were tied up to the wagon. They likewise laid themselves down upon the ground and stood up alternately, appearing as if they did not know what to do with themselves, and indeed, I might truly say, just as if they were in the agonies of death.'

Life here was slow, arduous, and then suddenly over. It was like a candle flame fluttering in the draught on a windowsill, a flame so fine that it sews light and dark together with an invisible seam. It was like footsteps approaching, the pace slackening until they cease altogether, though we know a figure is standing in the porch, scarcely discernible among all the coats hanging there.

3

Immelman scratched himself on some thorns. Sparrman poured a saline solution on to the wounds and bathed them with spirit, of which they had only a small supply. A grass fire in the distance: they had to change course. Immelman began to grumble.

'Pull yourself together,' said Anders.

His companion looked at him pleadingly, and he realized he had now become his protector and father figure. It had not occurred to him before.

Early in the morning Anders found his friend already up, dressed in a faded work shirt and trousers of grey sailcloth, frayed where they met the boot. All of a sudden Immelman was as unconcerned about his condition and appearance as if he were decked out in an emperor's robes. He was both pioneer and eager pupil.

Their expedition from Swellendam took an easterly route along the northern slopes of the Houtniquas Mountains. After Lange Kloof they came to the Kromme River, where storms and drought had wrought havoc. On the sandy seashore below Sitsicamma in the district of Humansdorp they encountered the bog myrtle *Myrica cerifera*, the berries of which have a waxy coating. Anders noted that candles could be moulded from it which burnt better than tallow.

He made finds at almost every step. He encouraged the local Africans to collect plants and animals with a list of prices: butterflies were paid at a halfpenny each, fine specimens of bats at sixpence, hammerkops, plovers, herons and terns, a slow-worm or an alligator, rather more. In the event, his collection was to be the largest ever sent from Africa to any country.

'Nature offers abundance but little variety,' Immelman said. 'We see lightning strike. We see fields of maize and hemp. Everything recurs.'

'We'll travel on,' Sparrman decided. 'The further away you get, the quicker the fruits of knowledge ripen.'

When the wind blew through the wild fruit trees, he thought they looked like young women with narrow shoulders, the forks in the branches their legs.

His companion secured the boxes with ox-hide straps, rolled a cigarette and stood back to admire his work. Then he began to turn querulous. When would they have enough plants collected? How could they hire new oxen? Were they masters of their situation?

Sparrman reminded him of the purpose of their journey. 'Bend down and pick up those stones dislodged by water. They indicate that rivers once flowed here, torrential rain fell for millennia, yet now it's dry. The witness of the stones. We are travelling across the pages of Creation, we are insects crawling in between the lines in the book of the Earth.'

In this way he tried to keep Immelman in a positive frame of mind, and indeed the younger man listened to reason and shook off his dejection.

Anders heard the croaking of the heron in the bluish mist over the bogs of Sitsicamma. He saw the Snowy Mountains on the far horizon, he found *Mimosa rustica*, a parasitical plant he was later to describe in the *Proceedings of the Swedish Academy of Sciences*. Agter Bruntjes-Hoogte was the northernmost and furthest point Sparrman reached, and it was also the most beautiful place on their entire journey. Again and again he wished they could be left in peace, along with Nature and the black people, who understood how to use it without destroying it.

During the expedition he drew a map of Cape Colony, which proved to be the most reliable up to that date. Distances were reckoned in hours on horseback and by ox-wagon, which was double the time of a horse. There were areas he had not visited and had therefore not drawn. And he was unsure of the deltas and estuaries of the rivers. Where did land become sea, and were there islands which became part of the coastal strip at low tide?

He sat revising the map in the evenings. Every day he put in new details, marked freshwater springs and the presence of wild animals. He showed Immelman: 'Despite all my surveying efforts, it will be a long time before South Africa's true topography is fully revealed.'

'Let us hope none of this is in vain,' Immelman replied.

If only he could carry out a similar mapping of his life . . . But his own reality was not entirely accessible, even to himself. This gave him confidence, but it also made him feel the time he had devoted to his travels had been wasted. Yet there were magnificent clear days, when the air quivered as if a single raindrop had been expanded to cover the whole landscape like a cupola.

But his dreams – of jackals, volcanic eruptions, his father's death, slaves who were hanged with a last mutual curse between victim and executioner – followed him like a shadow. Occasionally, he felt himself infected and saturated by inner visions, which hindered his observations of weasels leaping and finches flying with wings as pale yellow as goat's milk.

His maps resembled the criss-crossed broken lines on the palm of the hand, grimy with stains from the oil lamp, as crusty as scabs. When, exhausted and depressed, he tried to translate the map into reality and back again, he had the sensation of being imprisoned in a hallucination of unconfirmed names, spinning him into a cocoon.

He tried unsuccessfully to find a vantage point, a coastal horizon, as he packed bird skeletons in shavings, sun-dried to prevent mould, since he had to conserve his stock of spirit. There was still so much to be accomplished in the field of science!

Toponymical designations in Sweden were counties, parishes, villages, properties. In Cape Colony it was south of the road to Dragon's Gorge or Kruger's Ford. Nothing was precisely staked out. Place names could be corrupted and bear no relation to the material world. His map could never be an exact equivalent of these shifting realities.

4

'We shall not find any mathematical solutions for Nature's behaviour. We have embarked upon a risky undertaking in search of the complicated formula which Professor Linnaeus is no longer in a position to interpret for us, and which falls apart the moment we commit it to paper.'

Lightning bolts tore at the night sky. A shooting star, a meteor. The bearers muttered at the omen. A celestial fire, a message from the studded heavens.

'I think the qualities of temporary phenomena bestow all the more importance on our notes,' Sparrman continued, 'even if the overall pattern remains obscure. Professor Linnaeus firmly believed that everything on Earth was well on its way to being recorded, down to the last detail. But by now he is probably dead.'

'When I was growing up,' Immelman said, 'I had only one desire: not to be buried alive.'

'I have sent home insects, birds, animals. What has been their fate? Have they been washed into the sea, and will it ultimately make any difference? The more I record what we are doing, the more often I have the feeling that none of it has happened. Perhaps the world would be a better place if we all did nothing.'

Immelman's expression was so withdrawn and contemplative that he was no doubt listening to the calls of distant birds rather than paying attention to Anders' exposition. They travelled on slowly, because of the oxen, and with their noses to the ground because of the plants and insects to be recorded. They roasted termites that tasted of almonds. They fried the trunk of a young elephant and found it to be the most delicious of foods.

By Storm River, a few miles before it met the ocean, they came across ledges strewn with the bones of owls and bats. The Earth opened up in deep narrow gullies, as if to swallow its own children. Their torches and tar-sticks illuminated tunnels and chambers, and rock faces with furrowed brows and cleft chins.

They stood in fear and trembling before a terrifying sheer drop. No river flowed; no bird flew there. A couple more steps – and Nature revealed her desolate workshop. Heavy drops oozed from the cliff face. The arteries of the rocks pulsated. Pillars were crowned with bizarre capitals. Waterfalls had petrified. Walls had cracked and palaces crumbled into labyrinths. In one fissure Sparrman found the youngest rocks, loosened from their forefathers' embrace. He tapped out a chunk of quartz, semi-transparent, pearly white.

Vast halls where water had been eroding the rocks since the beginning of time, and the crystals had solidified into lifeless orchids: an internal universe. So the world comprised not only sky over savannah and ocean, but also caves and subterranean vaults concealing spaces even more mysterious.

5

Sparrman was the first zoologist to study the African rhinoceros –
and at such close quarters that he put himself in mortal danger. He
established that the rhinoceros' sunken eyes could see only indis-
tinctly, and only straight ahead. He found that its flesh tasted like
a coarser version of pork. When his bearers crept up to a sleeping
animal and put a gun to its head, he was surprised at how deeply
it slumbered.

He was also the first to find evidence that both male and
female ostriches sat on their eggs, laid on the bare earth at least
ten at a time, sometimes as many as sixteen. And he sketched
the honeyguide or bee cuckoo, that exploits both honey badgers
and man to assist it in robbing the nests of any burrowing bees it
detects. Having located a nest, it announces itself by flying
excitedly on ahead until it reaches its goal. When the nest has
been plundered by those enticed there, the honeyguide takes
what is left. Sparrman, aware of this co-operation between the
human and animal kingdoms, was the one who gave the bird its
name.

He investigated bats, with their small dog-like heads, brown
eyes and white ear-tufts. They pushed food into their cheek-
pouches with one foot. They tucked their wing membranes into
a thousand folds to make air pockets that retained the warmth. He
collected their droppings of pomegranate and passion-fruit seeds

where they lay in rows under the roof overhangs of both Boer and Khoikhoi houses.

He learned from the Khoikhoi how to boil up soap from the fat of the hippopotamus with ash and acacia resin. He watched the Khoikhoi boy who knew how much whip the oxen could tolerate; when they needed to rest and when they were at risk of slipping. He saw ague, elephantiasis, leprosy. There were no cures, no escape from these. Man was given but a short time on Earth, and it could be blown away so easily. Death was insatiable.

These places had no names. They were known to their inhabitants without needing to be named. Everyone knew where they were in the world. All but he – out amidst thorns and distant thunder crashing like splintering glass. The air was full of the sounds of insects, birds and tiny scurrying creatures. A rivulet trickled beneath heavy branches that protected it from the rays of the sun.

Anders experienced a sense of peace that he had not enjoyed for a long time. In the stillness his thoughts turned to fleeting rapture, suffering and mortality, sensuality and cruelty, the play between the sexes, the arbitrary directions of his nomadic life. Nature turned the pages of her great book and let them flick past without lingering on any one of them, so that desire soon turned into loss, independence into loneliness.

The landscape was opening up to him, but much still remained hopelessly locked away. His Swedish equilibrium would suddenly fall into a precipice or trip over a termite mound. A black man wearing a rag apron over his genitals passed by with an unintelligible greeting. Anders stood mute and riveted to the spot at the sight of this stranger bending down and touching the earth, hesitantly, as if feeling a scar. Then he disappeared again, as fast as a stick in the current.

Anders marked a plus sign on his map for settlements such as Wagendrift and Luipardskloof, and a cross where he found a pool of water, even though he guessed he would never find it there again. He saw hollow-cheeked people, limping, half-blind; then he

saw those who were better nourished, moving swiftly and grace-
fully, hopping over rocks and flying over potholes with a sure eye
for every obstacle.

He saw ragamuffins surround a rotting corpse. They were silent
and starving. Further off, a vulture with a red bib, a bloody band-
age. Why had he come to this unknown land, where the sun burnt
so fiercely? How much desolation and exhaustion could there be
in the world?

The rain from the mountains in the north scudded over in
unbridled gusts, a portent of the ague that would soon strike the
inhabitants. The clouds were galloping across the sky like wild
horses. The lead boy came to a halt, and they took shelter under
a cedar-like tree and cracked hard-boiled eggs on a stone.

Off Hermanus in October, whales were cavorting, leaping at one
another, creating a swell, breeching and singing, spouting fountains higher than those at Versailles. The females turned their
bellies uppermost and the males penetrated them with a phallus
as long as a maypole. Sparrman watched what he assumed to be
their mating rituals through his telescope.

No-one sailed this coast by night. What use were gold letters on
the stern if you were in waters two hundred metres deep between
sharp coral reefs? Fortunes vanished into yawning chasms, where
sharks and octopuses ripped the flesh off drowned sailors.

At night the air vibrated with the chirping of crickets, and above
the ocean the stars sprinkled their gunpowder over *Terra Australis*.
How much the sea had to swallow! So grey and featureless, such
resources in its depths! The constant muffled boom, a breathing
mightier than anything else on Earth.

The Southern Cross shone over the sources of unknown rivers,
over lakes that no-one had seen and mountain peaks clad in tropical snow.

The new moon was the shape of an elephant's tusk. In a few
weeks' time the full moon would come rolling over the horizon
like a billiard ball.

Anders plotted the firmament and wished the stars would lend themselves to mathematical calculation. Nothing would obey him. Over him hovered a future that didn't want to know him. In moments like these, existence seemed stifling and dark.

'We are travelling much too slowly,' he sighed. 'I wish I could be transported from one place to another like a seed picked up on the hooves of an antelope and carried off it knows not whither.'

6

He rose before dawn, sat enveloped in his dreams, imbibed the scents of the earth and the leaves in the coolest hour of the day. He saw a grass fire in the distance creeping forward like a caterpillar. He prepared the grey-headed kingfisher and the crimson-crowned weaver bird for stuffing. The ringed plover from the Swedish coast also made its way to these beaches to lay its eggs in little hollows in the sand.

At dawn, when the ground seemed to have spun its own fairy yarn and silken threads, the meadows lay before him unreal in their beauty, watered by small tributary streams. A hummingbird hovered in the air like a solidified raindrop. A shy ant-bear, an aardvark, ambled across their path. The wind shook unripe fruits from a knotty marula tree; they were used in the brewing of beer. And gentle breezes frolicked over bushes in bloom.

They were progressing at a leisurely pace across a primeval landscape to the slithering sound of rock rabbits, the calls of francolins and the grating lament of the sea eagle. The air was an imperceptible body temperature, and the midday heat troubled them less than usual. The borders of silence were far away. Purple Emperor butterflies with owls' eyes on their wings flitted around him. He had discovered that their larvae contained a palatable juice, whether eaten raw or baked in hot ashes.

The sky was golden blue, the world revealed in all its glory.

Latitude and longitude could now be measured. When the wind brushed an umbrella acacia, it produced a faint rattle like a box of nails. He straightened up and felt that he and the landscape coexisted in perfect harmony.

Immelman poured water into a tin, salted and cooked dried fish from the coast. Anders shot an African grouse, brown-striped on the upper parts, pale grey on the breast – protective colours like the flounder. He plucked it, emptied its crop of poisonous berries and roasted it beneath the white stars.

He observed that goats with light vertical stripes on their abdomen were barking like dogs, but more abruptly. That day neither he nor Immelman had travelled on foot at all. The heat was so intense that they could hardly even talk to each other. When they waded through a river, leeches stuck fast to their legs and could only be prised off with the greatest difficulty. Their bearers staunched the bloody wounds with mud from the riverbed. The wagon was offloaded on to a raft they bound together with ropes and aerial roots. In the afternoon there was a hailstorm, some of the stones as big as musket balls. Anders found every day so full of hardship and preparation that if he had not written notes, the previous day would already be wiped clean like a slate.

'The attractive thing about our Hottentots,' he said to Immelman, 'is that they worship nearly everything: the sun, the moon, the spirits of their dead ancestors, snakes, and all manner of fetishes. Near enough every single object has a covert meaning, incorporates a sign and is imbued with special powers. I understand that feeling. I too find corroboration where others would discern an abyss.'

The greatest freedom that Anders Sparrman found in South Africa came with exploration, journeys to landscapes and people of the unknown. He ignored Linnaeus' demands, his desire for fresh consignments. Nature was all around them, begging to be seen, not captured and named, nor discarded.

The veldt resembled an endless lagoon in which the rocks were overgrown sea chests. The leaves, so recently as dry as mummy-shrouds, were green, full of sap again and beginning their gentle undulations. Through the salty membrane of the eye the air quivered and the trees spread their branches. The drought had branded its mark of ownership on the grey crust of the earth. A skeleton lay scraped white like driftwood, watched over by a vulture trying to stare them out. The local inhabitants roamed far and wide in search of water.

Kites were silhouetted against the blue backcloth of the sky. The dark-grey widow bird hung its nest in a fruit tree like a speckled brown sock. The wild doves cooed nervously: *doo doo, hroo hroo*. There was a feast of aromas: the yellowed grass, spices, dusty soil, stones releasing their pent-up warmth.

The mosquitoes took up the hunt at sundown and blackish-brown hymenoptera with eyes on stalks scuttled between the rocks. Nightjars, disguised by day as tree bark, hummed like giant insects, and the night itself was a frog's chorus of flutes, squeaks, distant death roars. There was nothing that did not melt and meld together in the belly of darkness.

When Anders got up at daybreak – in the southernmost Karoo – it looked as if fresh snow had fallen. He identified prints of thrush and antelope in the white covering. But gradually he realized this snow was the launching threads of tens of thousands of spiders that had taken off in the still of the morning air. They were borne aloft by the currents that rose as the Earth was heated by the sun.

He burst into a hymn he had learned in Tensta Church, and poor Immelman woke with a start and thought he was by the sea, among crabs and squid. Sated with dreams, the young assistant emerged from his bed against the wheel of the ox-wagon and pulled a straw hat down over his brow. He resembled a secretary bird taking its first tentative steps to check that the ground would bear its weight. Anders found himself wondering whether these isolated places where they made their temporary halts would one day develop into towns with paved streets.

One of the mighty African elms had fallen across their path. It looked as if it were reclining on its elbow. The termites would soon lay it to rest. A warthog appeared and shook its head, as if it had water in its ear. Anders came upon some mushrooms that looked like honey fungus, a delicate flavour, harmless.

The bearers and ox-leaders were paid a daily wage in tobacco, and lived mostly on larvae and honey, watching out for bees and robbing every nest they found. They chopped up a roebuck, sliced the meat into strips and hung it up to dry in the sun on frames of branches. Although Anders did not find it easy to meet its solemn gaze, he extracted the eye to examine it. Then he caught a water rail, and from its stomach removed butterfly pupae, millipedes, grasshoppers, and gravel for grinding up the food.

'Observe the symmetry of Nature,' he advised Immelman. 'If you keep that in view, you can hold the confusion of life at bay.

There is a healing power in the geometry, even when the pattern is hard to distinguish. We struggle on, but order brings serenity. That is why we create gardens.'

Oblivious to the hour, they continued their conversation far into the night. They still believed that life had a lot to offer them.

8

They rode over open ground of thorn bushes and elephant grass. Anders leaned his head against the horse's mane, tied himself on to its neck with the reins and was carried in a semi-doze, blearily aware of stones and roots – like lying in the prow of a boat and watching the spray from the bows and the fronds of seaweed. In the end he no longer knew what was glinting inside his eyelids and what was sunshine and shadow in the billowing sea of grass.

Immelman, always alert, riding ahead, let his horse seek out a gully, a spring, a pool. Their mounts were slow and steady, easily able to bear the weight of men with rucksacks and weapons. The wind coughed, whined and sang – he was gradually learning its language. He was on the lookout for trees that had taken root in abandoned termite mounds, where there would be good soil and water.

Anders roused himself. He shot a gazelle. It stumbled, fell, staggered to its feet again, made a few bounds and let out a cry of pain in two tones, one louder, the other subdued and almost consoling. They roasted the meat on branches laid across stones; the Khoikhoi ate it raw.

They encountered two farmers who had hacked the tusks off an elephant and dried the meat in the sun for their slaves, leaving the rest of the carcass for the hyenas. Their weapons were discarded Swedish muskets, too heavy to fire without using the ramrod as support. The ball was cast from tin and lead; if it were lead alone it would flatten when it struck the massive beast's hide.

The yoke of oxen foundered in soft sand and the shaft broke, but was soon lashed together again. The oxen felt their way across the river over the slippery stones beneath and sank in mud up to their gaskins. They were being pushed hard and attracted swarms of horseflies. The bearers unharnessed them at night, made a fire, and gathered close as protection against hyenas. One of them was an insolent rogue who cheated Sparrman and was sent home to his village.

Anders sat down on a sloping flintstone bank to make notes in accordance with his master's precepts: 'Remember that what you do not record from distant places does not exist.'

If he held a firefly, a pyrophorus of the click-beetle family, over the paper, he could just make out what he was writing. If he put seven or eight fireflies in a glass he could see the letters in the green luminescence tolerably well. By day the beetles were kept in a small box and fed with sugar and marrow and so continued to glow.

The varieties of life, and what appeared to be Nature's minor divergences, were occasionally wearisome but mostly fascinating. He extended the boundaries on his map and refined his barometer, thermometer and compass. He measured more accurate distances, reduced the number of miscalculations. He opened the zinc case of the chronometer and put it to his ear: at first he thought he could hear it ticking, but realized he was listening to his own pulse as he pressed the glass against his ear. The chronometer had, in fact, stopped. He did not wind it up, but shut the lid and felt relieved: the sun gave the approximate hour, and he was indifferent to what day it was.

During the night Immelman was stricken with stomach cramps. The dogs were barking, the oxen stamping in their sleep, and the full moon set its red seal on the horizon. They decided to postpone their departure and sang each other to sleep, Anders with a

Swedish folk song and a hymn, Immelman with a not dissimilar Flemish tune that modulated into a prolonged appeal to the ruler of the heavens.

Anders Sparrman had turned twenty-eight and regarded himself as free of pride and self-indulgence. He wore no uniform or distinctive dress. Did liberty thrive where tyranny was silent and obedience not enforced? An itinerant life, but not as a fugitive, was much superior to glittering honours. Better by far than broader prospects were the fine details that emerged in the morning light.

He had no woman waiting for him. Self-discipline had become part of his nature since the voyage with Captain Cook. When his urges became too overpowering, he spattered his seed on thistles and ferns in the darkness. He wanted to carry on navigating over the map of the world; a dowry and procreation were not for him. If he were to die, no-one would grieve for him but his brother and sisters and George Forster.

Loneliness did not dishearten him. Nor was he averse to staying in the houses of strangers. He tried to combine his need for independence with a respect for others. He noticed he was occasionally tempted to be ingratiating and compliant to smooth over social friction. It was the attitude of the teacher, rather than the rich man's son brought up with piano lessons and polite conversation in foreign languages.

When he sank into the apathy that others call melancholy he was always able to lift himself out of it and feel a new surge of energy, as could happen when he examined a rhinoceros stomach for ingested food, salt content and the survival of maggots. In anatomy he had studied the human eye, but when he dissected the eyeball of a python he saw not the least similarity. What do we look like through the eye of a reptile? he wondered. The natives imagined the Milky Way as a soupy liquid stirred up by a turtle swimming along the bottom of the heavens.

Ants, as yellow as if they had just crawled out of their eggs, attacked his stock of eviscerated birds and boxes of insects. Larder beetles of the genus *Dermestidae* were devouring his collections. He sprayed his specimens with spirit they kept for medicinal purposes, but in many instances it was too late. He had boxes divided into compartments: sawdust and rice husks for larvae, blotting paper for butterflies, cotton for fragile cicadas and orthopterans. Specimens caught while mating were treated with special care and packed with a note that they had been taken together.

The earth split open and exposed unnamed roots. He felt that all the facts he thought he knew were shifting under his feet. Something spectral, voracious and intractable was welling up beneath the objective reality.

9

'Strength and energy are what we need!' Sparrman exhorted. 'And we still have it! We'll get out of here alive, with our barometer, our insect needles and our trappers' tools intact! We may be as poor as philosophers, but as scientists we'll get our teeth into this land, and after our expedition it will never be the same again.'

Reinvigorated by this lecture, Immelman rose, threw off the aches and pains of the night, washed, and in the shimmering sun – with itching beards and uncut hair – they packed what they needed, first and foremost Sparrman's valuable writing paper.

Nature in the Cape interior was not the same tableau as the semi-wild countryside of his Uppland home. Hills and cliffs cast black shadows over heaths of thorns and umbrella acacia. Lofty mountain ranges marked the horizon at some immeasurable distance. The wind passed through the grey leaves of sporadic fig trees and blew down heavy fruits smelling of milk. All time was one and he himself out of sight of the world. He would later express his amazement that a landscape could so completely obsess him.

This was a country where everything was dictated by necessity and no-one willingly spent many hours within four walls. The colonists believed they were making history, but became demoralized by bitterness at the pitiful results. Without a church as a protective shell they appealed direct to the Lord for victory,

prosperity and more rain. Matters of the spirit became less important than a pair of woollen stockings. Many people had thus
developed a gloomy disposition and seemed never to have
danced for pure joy like the young Khoikhoi.

Then Sparrman was afflicted with ague and the fever took hold
of his body with fiery caresses under his skin. At the same time it
felt as if someone were stroking his very marrow with a cold iron.
Uncontrollable dreams and unseemly images exhausted him. He
told Immelman he had seen an elephant sink down on its knees
trumpeting violently, its hide sagging in great folds – as if trying on
far too large a pair of trousers. A woman appeared from behind it
wearing nothing but a string of animal teeth round her neck, as
was the custom. Perhaps she had come to help him satisfy all his
physical cravings.

And with pins of fever pricking his skin he saw before his very
eyes the Resident's daughter sitting in False Bay, bathed in a scent
of white gardenia. He remembered her mother miserably padding
over the stone floor in an ankle-length skirt, her full bosom bound
tightly inside her taffeta blouse; which in turn led his thoughts to
Cape Town shops with their crinkly oranges and new season's red
onions, and further off the windowless asylum with its inner courtyard where the insane and the wrongfully imprisoned cast up their
screams like spears to the heavens.

Immelman kept telling him he was delirious. Anders himself
imagined he was grasping the dark-mottled egg of a nighthawk
and hurling it into the wind, which never ceased its murmurings
in the chieftains' grass.

10

Soon they were riding over a flat landscape and on through two ravines overgrown with twisted willow trees the height of a man. When Anders gave his horse free rein he found it knew the direction of the coast.

Spotting a wisp of smoke against the sky, they came to a low house from which emerged a short, grizzled white man with an enormous dog. He was covered in blood and nodded wryly towards a bucket: he had just slaughtered a pig. He was about to melt the fat down to lard, and it had to be done without delay. Stinging nettles bordered the old man's land, which he fertilized with mussel shells. One of his hens was being attacked by an amethyst starling, plucking her downy feathers to line its nest.

'People like him say a bullet is too good for a Hottentot or a Bushman,' Sparrman said. 'I believe we should not mistreat God's creatures, even if they seem immoral or incomprehensible to us. We must not regard them as lost souls, nor see them as alien bodies. Why should so many be crippled because we have plundered their land? Neither they nor we know how extensive that land is. But we know, having travelled so far and so indefatigably, that there is enough for all of us.'

'You wrong nobody and forget any wrong done to you,' said Immelman. 'I have to admire you. You look at the old women with care and compassion, with their desiccated buttocks and wrinkled skin. You seem able to find a meaning in everything, and through their eyes see a world which is not ours.'

'We think they take life as it comes, without rules or guidelines. We see vacillation and dissolution in their society – but they distinguish betwixt right and wrong just as much as we do. They know everything has to have order if it's to be good. When they slaughter their slim-shanked black hogs, sew up their moleskins or make a net, they know what they are doing. But they know far more than that.'

'They smear themselves with kidney fat and sheep-tail grease and have a foul smell, but you tolerate it better than I do, even though I have lived here all my life. The women's genitals stink, and we cannot comprehend how anyone can want to go near them. But they themselves pay it no heed.'

'Our savages also seem indifferent to something else,' Sparrman asserted. 'Attaining eternal salvation. They are content to float as spirits over their homeland for a while, then dissolve into a cosmic breath. I have to regard that as a less primitive concept than our own.

'They are surprised at us,' he continued. 'We make such brief stops, whereas they come to a halt and set up a village. They gorge themselves on all the food they can find. They fill their calabashes. Then they look no further and sow neither corn nor cabbage. But we move on. They see us disappearing from view. Yet our presence remains with them. Everything is altered for them once we have been here.'

'I have begun to understand how they express goodness, cunning and cruelty and all the other things needed to live in the part of Creation which is theirs,' Immelman said. 'Yet I see such manifest disorder among them. Maybe all people sometimes have their heads in the clouds, and sometimes their noses under a tree root. And nobody understands what the intention was at the very beginning.'

Thus they speculated when it was too dark to make their notes of the day's observations. They were at Krysna, near the sea, on one of those chilly nights when they put stones in the fire, dug them out with a spade and laid them as a wall round themselves to keep warm.

'For them there is no such thing as time,' Immelman went on. 'They move spasmodically with the seasons. Making haste and lacking time are concepts they don't have. You are somewhat like them in that respect. You can sleep anywhere and eat anything: you must have been born under a lucky star.'

'I think it shines over me only in the southern hemisphere.'

Immelman had snared a coot. Well-versed in the art of listening intuitively, he asked, 'Why are we driving ourselves to breaking point? Why are we so keen to achieve the uttermost?'

'With our senses we take in Nature as a whole,' Anders replied, without conviction. 'Then we divide it up, dissect it, classify it – to enable me to see Uppsala again with my honour intact.'

11

From Anders Sparrman's account of his journey through South Africa in 1775–6:

'There are no inns established in the inland part of this country, so that everyone is obliged to travel with their own horses and carriages, as well as their own provision. Sometimes we made our bed under the wagon, where, being under cover, we were somewhat sheltered indeed from the rain and the dew; but on the other hand, had rather too near and not quite so agreeable neighbours in our oxen, which were tied up to the wheels and poles, and also to the rails of the wagon, and were so skittish and unruly that we could only venture to creep among the gentlest of them.

'When we had the opportunity of taking a night's lodging at a peasant's house we were for the most part rather worse lodged. In most places the house consisted of two rooms only, the floors of which were of earth or loam. The interior one of these was used for a bedchamber for the Boer himself, with his wife and children. The Hottentots of either sex, young and old, who were in the Boers' service, always chose to sleep in the chimney. A host of fleas and other inconveniences, to which we were by this means subjected, made us frequently rather choose to sleep in the open air.

'We overtook several farmers who were come into this neighbourhood for the purpose of hunting. I could not help smiling at these good rustics viewing us so narrowly from head to foot. They found me with a beard which had not been touched since the end of the preceding month, without a stock, and with my waistcoat open at the breast, my hat flapped, my hair braided into a twist, my side-curls hanging down strait and fluttering in the air; a fine thin linen coat, with a white ground variegated with blood, dabs of gunpowder, and spots of dirt and grease of all kinds; but at the same time decorated with fine gilt buttons, a third part of which were fallen off, and a great many of the remainder dangled about loose. My breeches, for the sake of coolness, were turned up at the knees, in the manner in which they are frequently worn by the Boers of this country; and after the same guise, and for a similar reason, my stockings, which were woollen, were gartered below my knees, at the same time that they hung down loose about my ankles; while my feet were set off with Hottentot shoes, made to draw up with strings.

'Mr Immelman, who, in fact, was a handsome young fellow, with large dark eyebrows and a fine head of hair, at this time wore a beard five weeks old, which was now beginning to curl in a very conspicuous manner. He figured on horseback in a long night-gown, with a white nightcap, large wide boots, and was just at that time without stockings, in order to keep his legs the cooler.

'As to our beards, we had both of us in a merry mood, formed a resolution not to touch a hair of them either with razors or scissors, till we should either get into company again with the Christian lasses, or should have an opportunity of dissecting a hippopotamus. Added to this, we wished to try how a long beard would become our juvenile years. "It is a present made to us by Nature," said we to each other, "let us keep it by way of experiment. This ornamental excrescence may possibly prevent colds, eruptions in the face, and the toothache in cold nights; at least it is probable, that in this climate it serves to defend the face from the scorching rays of the sun; and who can tell, what respect and consideration it may acquire us from the beardless tribes we are likely to meet with in the course of our expedition."

'Each guest must bring his knife with him, and for forks they frequently make use of their fingers. The most wealthy farmer here is considered as being well dressed in a jacket of home-made cloth, breeches of undressed leather, a striped waistcoat, a cotton handkerchief about his neck, a coarse calico shirt, Hottentot field shoes, or else leathern shoes, with brass buckles. A plain close cap, and a coarse cotton gown, virtue and good housewifery, are looked upon by the fair sex as sufficient ornaments of their persons; a flirting disposition, coquetry and paint, would have very little effect in making conquests of young men, brought up in so hardy a manner. In short, here, if anywhere in the world, one may lead an innocent, virtuous, and happy life.

'Tortoises could always be seen crawling among the bushes on the savannah, and the daughters of the house had collected some to eat. I sneaked into the kitchen and found the girls mercilessly putting a live tortoise, its legs kicking, on the glowing coals to roast till it cracked in the heat. The eggs, in considerable numbers, consisting solely of yolk, were a favourite delicacy. The slaves pulled up bulbs of white, yellow and blue irises, eaten stewed in milk, and both tasty and nourishing.

'It was here I saw for the first time in my life, one of the animals called quaggas by the Hottentots and colonists. It is a species of wild horse, very like the zebra; the difference consisting in this, that the quagga has shorter ears, and that it has no stripes on its legs, loins, or any of its hind parts. There can be no doubt but that quaggas or zebras, properly tamed and broke in, would, in many respects, be of greater service to the colonists than horses: as, in the first place, they are more easily procured here; and next, being used to the harsh dry pasture, which chiefly abounds in Africa, they seem to be intended by nature for this country. The quagga that I saw here at this time was in such good condition, and so plump about the back and loins, as, I believe, in that point, not to be equalled by any horse.

'The capture of slaves from among the Boshies-men is effected in the following manner. Several farmers, that are in want of servants, join together, and take a journey to that part of the country where the Boshies-men live. The farmers will venture on a dark night to set upon them with six or eight people, which they contrive to do by previously stationing themselves at some distance round about the kraal. They then give the alarm by firing a gun or two. By this means there is such a consternation spread over the whole body of these savages, that it is only the most bold and intelligent among them, who have the courage to break through the circle and steal off. These the captors are glad enough to get rid of at so easy a rate; those that are stupid, timorous, and struck with amazement, and who, in consequence of this stupor, allow themselves to be taken and carried into bondage, answering their purpose much better.

'They are, however, at first, treated by gentle methods; that is, the victors intermix the fairest promises with their threats, and endeavour, if possible, to shoot some of the larger kinds of game for their prisoners. Such agreeable baits, together with a little tobacco, soon induce them to go with a tolerable degree of cheerfulness to the colonist's place of abode. There these luxurious feasts of meat and fat are exchanged for more moderate portions of buttermilk, frumenty and hasty-pudding.

'When one of these poor devils runs away from his service, or, more properly, bondage, he never takes with him anything that does not belong to him. This is an instance of moderation in the savages towards their tyrants, which is praised and admired by the colonists themselves. Free from many wants and desires, that torment the rest of mankind, they are little addicted to thieving, if we except brandy, victuals and tobacco.

'The slave business, that violent outrage against the natural rights of mankind, which is always in itself a crime, and leads to all manner of misdemeanours and wickedness, is exercised by the colonists with a cruelty towards the nation of Boshies-men, which merits the abhorrence of everyone.

'Not only is the capture of the Hottentots considered by them merely as a party of pleasure, but in cold blood they destroy the bands which Nature has knit between husband and wife, and between parents and their children. Not content with having torn an unhappy woman from the embraces of her husband, her only protection and comfort, they endeavour all they can, and that chiefly at night, to deprive her likewise of her infants; for it has been observed that the mothers can seldom persuade themselves to flee from their tender offspring.

'At Apies River I saw an old Boshies-man with his wife, who, I was informed by farmer P. Vereira, had, a few months before, reigned over above a hundred Boshies-men; but they were now translated by the farmer from this royal or rather patriarchal dignity to that of being shepherds to a few hundreds of sheep. It is possible that this ancient couple, in consequence of their good sense and experience in life, might actually find a greater and more substantial bliss in being placed at the head of a flock of sheep than when they were on their throne surrounded by their subjects. Yet still it is a deed that cries to Heaven for vengeance, to bereave a whole community of its head and governor for the sake of some advantage and utility accruing thereby to a flock of sheep.

'About noon we went to pay a visit to the community of Hottentots assembled on this spot, who received us very friendly, and invited us to drink some of their sack-milk; which, I believe, nobody could have tasted that had not been as thirsty and at the same time as curious as we. We saw then our greasy (though possibly happy) hostess open a leathern bag that would hold about six gallons, and which was made of an undressed calf's-skin taken off entire, with the hairy side turned inwards, and at the same time lade some milk out of it with a wooden ladle, which the dirtiest kitchen wench in Sweden would have been perfectly ashamed of. The taste of it resembled that of a syllabub. By way of acknowledgement we gave our hosts a roll of tobacco about six inches long, which they seemed to consider as a very magnificent present.

'Notwithstanding the respect I bear to the more delicate part of my readers, the singularity of the fact prevents me from passing over in this place those parts of the body, which our more scrupulous, but less natural manners will not allow me to describe in any other way than by a periphrase, or by means of Latin terms or other uncouth and to most readers unintelligible denominations and expedients. But those who affect this kind of reserve must pardon me, if I cannot wrap up matters with the nicety their modesty requires.

'I think it my duty to show how much the world has been misled, and the Hottentot nation been misrepresented; inasmuch as the Hottentot women have been described, with respect to their sexual parts, monsters by nature; and it has been supposed that the men are made such by a barbarous custom. It has been thought that these latter were, at the age of ten years, by a kind of castration, deprived of one of those organs, which Nature gives to every male, as being absolutely necessary for the propagation of his species; and that the former, i.e., the women, have before their privy parts a natural veil or covering, a circumstance unheard of in the females of any other part of the globe. The women have no parts uncommon to the rest of their sex; but the clitoris and *nymphae* are in general pretty much elongated, a peculiarity which undoubtedly has got footing in this nation, in consequence of the relaxation necessarily produced by the method they have of besmearing their bodies, their slothfulness, and the warmth of the climate.

'The Gonaquas of the eastern Cape cover with a little cap, or case, made of the skin of an animal, the extremities only of what modesty should teach them to conceal entirely. In Cafferland one does not infrequently see even grown-up girls without any covering whatsoever; and in certain dances it constitutes part of the solemnity for the youths of both sexes to make such oblations to love in the presence of everyone, as by the laws of decency and of civilized nations are always consummated in private, and considered as sacred to the married state alone. The unmarried, in the very middle of the dance, withdraw to a private place in couples successively and at different intervals, without having any occasion to blush when they return again to the company. Any young woman who after such dance shall prove pregnant shall be put to death, together with her paramour, unless, which indeed is generally the case, the oldest people in the clan mitigate the punishment, by commuting it into a perpetual union, ordering them besides to forfeit an ox or a cow to feast the whole community with.

'I paid a visit to a European, who had settled in Houtniquas. He was a good lively handsome fellow, about the middle age and, I believe, of good extraction. He had served under several different potentates in Europe, and had showed them all a fair pair of heels. He gave me the history of a great many singular adventures of his, but the most singular of them all was (what I was eyewitness to myself) that two years before he had married an ugly sooty Mulatto, the daughter of a Negress. She had been the mistress of another farmer who was dead, and by whom she had two bastards. These I saw at that time likewise in the house, grown up and unbaptized.

'But what seemed to me the most singular circumstance in the whole affair was that this must have been absolutely a love-match; for though he had got a few cattle with his dingy spouse, yet the house, which he likewise had with her, was certainly not a palace. It was a miserable cottage; the walls were made of reeds tied together and supported by a few upright chumps of wood, interspersed with some rough boards, such as are generally used for fences. In the inner room the man's wife lay ill of a putrid fever. The outer apartment had a peephole at one end of it, and a small broken window at the other; not to speak of several other apertures, which occasioned a draught of air that delivered my friend and me from all apprehensions of danger from the contagion of the putrid fever, but at the same time prevented us from keeping a lamp lit.

'Unexpectedly, we came upon an impoverished farmer who with his wife and children had settled in the bush to feed and propagate their tiny herd of cattle. And these poor people were no less surprised at our arrival and fearful of being reported to the Government for being beyond the prohibited border. They only had one hut made of woven leaves for the whole family and a little one beside it as a kitchen.

'We were served sweet milk, but within minutes the bowl turned black under the swarm of flies which set upon it and soon filled the whole hut, so that we could not open our mouths to speak. We hurried back out to our wagon, lit our fires and spent the whole night listening to the howls of the wolves and the cruel roars of the lions.

'I have known some colonists, not only in the heat of their passion, but even deliberately and in cold blood, undertake themselves the low office (fit only for the executioner) of not only flaying, for a trifling neglect, both the backs and limbs of their slaves by a peculiar slow lingering method, but likewise, outdoing the very tigers in cruelty, throwing pepper and salt over the wounds.

'Many a time, especially in the mornings and evenings, have I seen in various places unhappy slaves, who, with the most dismal cries and lamentations, were suffering the immoderately severe punishments inflicted on them by their masters; during which they are used, as I was informed, to beg not so much for mercy, as for a draught of water; but as long as their blood was still inflamed with the pain and torture it was said that great care must be taken to avoid allowing them the refreshment of drink of any kind; as experience had shown that in that case they would die in the space of a few hours, and sometimes the very instant after they had drunk it.

'The same thing is said to happen to those who are impaled alive, after having been broken upon the wheel, or even without having previously suffered this punishment. This operation is performed by thrusting up the spike along the backbone and the vertebra of the neck, between the skin and cuticle, in such a manner, that the delinquent is brought into a sitting posture. In this horrid situation, however, they are said to be capable of supporting life for several days, as long as there comes no rain; as in that case, the humidity will occasion their sores to mortify, and consequently put an end to their suffering in a few hours.'

12

Before the time of Sparrman's arrival, the Khoikhoi had begun slaughtering their cattle so that the animals would not fall into the white man's hands, and themselves fled to less rainy regions. A Khoikhoi chief confided to Sparrman that they were forced to flee on an almost daily basis from Europeans who wanted their pasture. They put up resistance, stealing their cattle back and acquiring stocks of guns and ammunition. They could not comprehend the Boers' desire for expansion. Everyone was allocated a space on Earth by a higher power. There was no need for anyone to be hounded through forest and veldt, but these white men were sweeping them away like so many leaves.

In Sparrman's eyes the Khoikhoi lived a satisfying life. As soon as they had brought their herds in they milked them to the accompaniment of singing and dancing.

'We seldom saw such happiness and contentment as seemed to be indicated by this festive custom in a handful of people totally uncultivated, and subsisting in their original savage state in the midst of a perfect desert. We were received by them with a friendly simplicity and homely freedom, which, however, by no means lessened them in our thoughts as men. Besides the pleasures which these daily dances may be supposed to afford them, they have at their greater festivals the more delightful enjoyment of voluptuous love, which, at those times, the youth of both sexes, by their laws, have full opportunity given them to pursue.'

They watched a goat being flayed, its skin stretched and scraped to be turned into a rucksack or a drink container. The eyes were buried in order not to be a means of reproach. Everything else – feet and testicles, tail fat and neck – was grilled over a fire.

An old man was groaning with a leg wound that might easily become gangrenous. Sparrman, the former surgeon, was entreated and offered gifts, but he could make no promises of a long life to anyone. And what was long? What was time for them?

Pastures were being burnt off. Flames leapt from tuft to tuft, ravaging the soil and fertilizing it for new growth. The tamarind trees burst into cascades of fire and spewed out the embers in a display of pyrotechnics. Their dry trunks erupted in explosions. Granite rocks were denuded of their lichen.

The village fell silent. The men bedded their women and were jabbed in the side to make them roll over and sleep, and a wail of angry resignation was borne across to the guest hut, cleaned ready for the traveller, who lay with red-hot skin and ears pricked, wearing a linseed poultice for an incipient glandular inflammation, while his companion Immelman snored like a baboon.

Anders opened his notebook, but could not see to write. They had eaten with the village elders and added their own spices to the food. The chief wore a blue cloak with a bloodstone round his neck as a symbol of his reputation as a warrior.

'I have six wives, and I am faithful to them all.'

Anders had shot a crocodile, whose skin was smothered in leeches. They had crushed the ballast stones they had found in the reptile's stomach and given them to the chief as grit, which he swallowed to increase his manly strength. He presented them with two dead butterflies, both very large, with violet wings and black spots. He understood what his guests were looking for and was rewarded with some pretty-coloured seeds.

To keep the Khoikhoi in check, Sparrman would occasionally

pretend to be a magician. He showed the inhabitants of one kraal the sensitivity of a compass needle, and let them vainly try to grasp balls of quicksilver in a basin, then picked them up himself with invisible talc on his fingers. He showed them his beetles and winged termites speared on pins, and they were astonished that he hadn't eaten them.

The mud huts of the village cracked in the drought, were sealed again by rain, or beaten down by storms. The settlement changed constantly, like a body shifting position in sleep. When vermin made the huts uninhabitable, they moved on. They stored their water in bags made from antelopes' stomachs, with a capacity of two gallons and carried on a yoke across the shoulders, or in containers made from rhinoceros bladders.

Sparrman brought back all kinds of vessels, as well as bows and arrows. Their bows were fashioned from the grevia bush and could shoot arrows a hundred yards or more. Among the Bushmen he found iron arrowheads, which remained stuck fast in their quarry while the shaft fell off. The animal could not dislodge the arrowhead by rubbing against a tree, nor pull it out with its teeth. The feather-light tip was dipped in a poison from the larva of a beetle whose sting could kill a kudu or a giraffe, animals that weighed hundreds of pounds.

Sparrman never described the Khoikhoi or the Bushmen as semi-human or as sexual curiosities. He saw them as happy and contented, cunning and quick. He empathized with the natives, whereas his friend Carl Peter Thunberg gave his blessing to European expansion, and thanked his Creator for allowing him to be born in Sweden and not in 'the countries of Africa without worship of God, without government, without science and morals'.

Sparrman rejected the fantasies of other travellers. 'Prodigies and uncommon appearances, about which I have frequently been asked by many, who have been brought to entertain these conceits by perusing the descriptions of others, are not to be found in my journal. Cyclops, Syrens, Troglodytes, and the like imaginary beings, have almost entirely disappeared in this enlightened age. Otherwise, in fact, the public would have reason to doubt of my own veracity.'

Of the Khoikhoi he wrote: 'They eat everything that does not eat them. They drink the fat of the river-horses. Snakes and lizards are boiled thoroughly and eaten with much smacking of the lips. I saw a piece of crocodile floating in a pot with a squirrel skin shrunken by the heat.

'In the kraals, Death's visiting list is so long that no-one has time to familiarize himself with it. The eldest son bends over his father, breathes in his last sigh and carries his soul on as a blessing. The dead inhabit the living, they are in the fire and the water and the light, in all that laments, sings and flows. The dead want to make themselves known. They want children to play with.

'Death is a slow process, just like birth, first squeezing out of the mother's loins, then being initiated and becoming aware of one's destiny. So they have no numbers for time, no names for days.

'Lightning strikes conceal the unborn children who want to take the world by surprise. But they have to become seeds and take root and come up into the daylight if they are not to remain moon-children, transparent, when they show their faces over the edge of the world.'

He exchanged examples of the Khoikhois' language with his friend Carl Peter Thunberg. According to Thunberg, they lacked words for 'cooking pot', 'bowl' and 'tobacco', but Sparrman lists them, as well as the words for 'penis', 'glans' and 'vagina'.

The Khoikhoi made a sheath for the male organ out of a piece of grey fur from the back of the Cape fox, and fastened it with a thong around the hips. They appeared to be blacker than they were, because they smeared themselves with grease and cow-dung as protection against the heat and the cold. They blended a foul-smelling plant into the grease, bucku or pulchella, the stench of which was difficult to tolerate for those not accustomed to it.

'Young Immelman has shared all my adversities,' Anders confided to Thunberg. 'I have sometimes wished it had been his pretty sister Anna.'

The Bushmen's small triangular faces were wily and intelligent. When Anders had an attack of fever they gave him herbs finely chopped in goat dung, and a sulphurous mud mixed with the crushed bones of swallows. They had knowledge the earth had given them.

One evening in early 1776 the two travellers pitched camp for the night and lit fires. The ground was very uneven, with patches of rough grass. A group of Xhosa men living on the other side of the Van Stade River came running over to partake of their rolled tobacco. They were agriculturalists and pastoralists, and also smelted iron. They were tall, dressed in calfskins and armed with spears. Their cows were healthy, in Sparrman's opinion, because their owners played and chatted with them. The travellers were given milk in watertight woven baskets, but had to filter it through a linen cloth.

Some of the Xhosa wore leopard skins as a sign of valour. Others bore a fox brush tied to a stick to wipe off sweat. Sparrman rewarded them for their services with little mirrors brought from Cape Town. They turned them over and over to see whether the same picture would reappear.

'So far we have managed to get by,' Sparrman wrote. To Immelman he said, 'One can want for almost everything and still be happy. That is what these people have taught me. They enjoy life, even without passes and permits.'

'I understand now what I have not felt able to express openly in Cape Town: that this land is inexhaustible and would swallow us up if we didn't keep our eyes open,' Immelman replied. 'It possesses us. We can never conquer it.'

13

The Boers had strangely complacent ideas about their land. They imagined that people in Europe were starving, although they themselves were serving travellers gritty bread and stringy mutton.

Anders Sparrman was amazed that the dwellings of such self-righteous people had earth floors. He considered the Trek Boers unkempt, surly and ignorant of the outside world. They were at the mercy of storms, pregnancy, leopards and bandits. They seemed to be living at the furthest limits of civilization. Though at least the smell of freshly baked bread was like a peace signal.

The Boer grew or made nearly everything he needed and bought only a few necessities from Cape Town. He regarded other people as pests coming to impose taxes or duty, and even objected to the sight of smoke from the chimneys of neighbouring farms. He wanted to get his slaves for nothing, erect a gallows to hang them on, and dispense with emperor, king or governor altogether. The more affluent among them would hire a peripatetic tutor who had been in the service of the East India Company. The children of the poorest Boers grew up largely illiterate.

A typical Boer table offered a selection of sun-dried strips of meat, dry biscuits, guava and a few swigs of precious water. Goats' kidneys and sheep's cheese were the principal nourishment. The Boers also made a thick quince marmalade. They added crushed red hawthorn berries, floury and tasteless, to their soup. Large pumpkins were hollowed out to form calabashes.

The wife had never heard of rice powder or perfume, nor the custom of pinning a flower in her hair. The man's beard danced half a yard in front of him. His left eyebrow was higher than the right, giving him an expression of distrustful surprise. His index finger was set in the shape of a link of chain. Fleas hopped all over their mattresses and there was a stench of burnt bedbugs.

But outside, under the heavens, the sheep were bleating. The farm was woken to prayer and work by the tolling of the farm bell. The farmer read from the Old Testament – the New Testament was for feebler temperaments. Their hymns could be heard through the open doors, so unmelodic that the birds fled their nests and branches. Then a taciturn start to their daily toil: any pleasure was held in abeyance while they cleared the land. They had broken out of a hundred years of darkness to meet yet another darkness: the blacks, whom they had not taken into account.

Sparrman enquired of a farmer, Jan Prinzloo, whether he could find it in himself to shoot a Khoikhoi or a Kaffir without compunction.

'They have to learn that we are superior, even though we are few in number,' came the reply. 'We have brains and weapons. Some Kaffirs stole my sheep. They fired a poisoned arrow at my slaves. I had a family seized and asked them to point out the guilty men. They refused. I stood them up and shot them. I told them that was rough justice.'

Anders asked whether he enjoyed being so ruthless. Prinzloo shook his head, but the severity of a judgemental God had become integral to his temperament.

The farmer, Izaak Lourens, asked the visitors to take a pair of elephant tusks to Cape Town to pay off a debt for him. Lourens had the supercilious lips of a camel and his eyes had sunk into their sockets as if they could not bear to see all that was forbidden, sinful and perverse. His tongue resembled a dusty communion wafer, and his movements were ponderous.

He pointed out the fields where the slaves were digging ditches and spreading manure. He offered the travellers female slaves for the night. If any of them fell pregnant, the number of his slaves would be increased, so they were encouraged to go ahead and enjoy themselves. A slave girl paused for a moment in the outhouse to which Anders was shown. She did not smile, but had a questioning expression on her face. He knew he could do whatever he liked with her. He had his freedom, she her role of a young woman who had to acquiesce in everything.

The anxiety that consumed all Izaak Lourens' energy concealed a friendly soul within. He stamped his foot expressively: he had come here two decades ago from the Netherlands, 'because of compass error', as he put it. By way of farewell he muttered this advice: 'If you get dysentery, shove a cork up your backside!'

Sparrman and Immelman arrived at a farm in Swellendam, which some slaves were minding on behalf of a carpenter called Didericus, who had just been killed in a gunpowder explosion. The slaves offered them soup and porridge with some eagerness when they heard that Sweden was against slavery. The two men were able to change oxen and horses. They slept on a floor stained with cow dung and blood. They purchased a whip for one of the Khoikhoi who drove the ox-team.

They travelled on from kraal to kraal, the colonists' farms scattered between them. Sparrman shot black partridge; Immelman bought cockerels. A swarm of locusts swept past them. An old woman stood at her door with an osier basket and bucket, managing to look simultaneously both shrewd and mentally retarded. Was she black or white? They fetched some firewood and mushrooms for her.

One evening they came upon a drunken man yelling and cursing. He burst into an obscene drinking song to the tune of a Calvinist hymn.

He was striking out with a stick in all directions and, catching sight of Anders, cried, 'And you can have a bullet through the heart!'

'You reek like a dead rat,' Sparrman retorted. It pleased him to be able to use such expressions in Afrikaans.

The farmer flailed about in a blind rage, but didn't land a single blow. He shouted and swore he would kill himself if he didn't avenge such insults. Anders hid behind a rock. The rain began to fall steadily, and he withdrew into the forest. He could still hear the farmer's invective about the death of God and against women who had their faces down below.

Hendrik Kannemeyer was suspicious by nature, and not easy to talk to. He wore puttees and a red leather waistcoat. As he hung a brown cow-hide out to dry, he pulled at his straggling beard. He was convinced the moon was moving away and would return with its paler, rougher side towards the Earth, scoured like the bottom of a well-worn saucepan. They slept outdoors, with the wind freshening and the oxen restless. 'We were ill received,' Sparrman wrote, 'regarded as poison merchants and magicians, since we had snakes and parts of animal intestines in *spiritus vini*, for which they can conceive of no other use than magic.'

In April 1776 Sparrman and Immelman stayed with a widow at Nana River. Her husband had had his throat cut by his own slaves. She had been on her way home from Cape Town and would have met with the same fate had she not been warned. Their thirteen-year-old son had fled. There were no woods around the farm so he had hidden in the river under the boughs of a tree. The slaves searched for him, even dragging branches through the water; but he escaped to a neighbouring farm. Sparrman thought it might be tactless to ask the widow about the cause of the atrocity; he assumed it was the farmer's cruelty.

They found lodging in a splendid farm belonging to Johannes, a well-built man with rosy cheeks, who wore creaking hide boots of foreign manufacture. Yet he was a lone settler without a wife.

His pigs were quarrelling out on the hillside, a couple of lambs were asleep by the kitchen stove, and a slave was roasting chickens on a spit.

Anders carried a leather purse in which he kept a watch chain and a few coins to pay his way. And some bags of seeds, which he thought might be useful as presents. But the farmer refused such gifts, and asked instead whether Anders had a military rank and knew anything about fortification techniques. Johannes opened his one and only book, a calf-bound family Bible, to show them the summary of his family history on the blank pages at the back.

Sparrman and Immelman drove their oxen along a well-worn animal track and were brought to a halt by a farmer calling to them in gutteral Dutch. Gin and the wind had polished his face a sunset red and creased it like a guenon monkey's. He was on outpost duty, watching for wild beasts, natives and the treacherous hordes that abounded in this life.

He had trained his dog to bite Khoikhoi. His seven-year-old daughter, with her long dark hair, stared at the strangers and was sent out into the kitchen. There was no sign of his wife. He gave a nod heavenwards: 'Our Creator is not Lord of His Earth.'

This land was impossible to conquer: hailstorms, desert droughts, lions and hyenas. And slaves so lazy that they died in their sleep.

'Never praise them. Then they pack up and leave. They think their work is done. The cocks are just as useless here, and the hens.'

This Boer, prematurely aged and with drooping eyelids, had measured the skull of an old Bushman and found it smaller than a three-year-old child's. That said everything. He had kept the cranium to use as a fruit bowl, and offered it to the slaves just to see them recoil in horror. He showed Anders a feathered arrow, tipped with poison and intended for him. He killed what he needed with a double-barrelled shotgun. He took his guests to a ravine stinking of animals that had been unable to clamber out.

Their skeletons lay one on top of the other. Grey-leafed thorn bushes rendered the hillside impenetrable.

The travellers were served boiled red cabbage and peppered meat. Pots and pans rattled, knives carved and the cauldron simmered. The firewood, the washstand, the sooty ceiling – all this was of secondary importance to the earth the farmer burnt, cleared, extended, even though he knew the next generation would take it for granted, and the third would leave for the city, far removed from sheep and oxen.

From his bed, the first iron bedstead Anders had seen, he heard the family conversing in some ancient dialect. Were they planning to murder him and throw him in the ravine, to be discovered when it was dug out some time in the next century? His beard felt limp, his body listless. Clay pipe in hand, the farmer had subjected him to a piercing stare of inspection, with no hint of warmth. Did he suspect him of being a spy, despite having seen his papers from the Resident? Could a rebel Boer, 'to avoid any misunderstanding', go so far as to silence those whose peaceful demeanour he mistook, and whose mania for collecting he interpreted as a cover for some more malicious purpose?

Sparrman kept his musket under the blanket.

The farmer's wife was pregnant and thought she could feel the child quivering with sobs in her womb. In the morning she was rocking back and forth in a cane chair looking ashen, and confided to her husband that she had been woken by Sparrman standing at the foot of her bed, gazing at her. Her husband shook his head, apparently unperturbed by either love or curiosity.

'I cannot get used to being old and fat so soon,' she said. 'I wish God could manage things better.'

'What you need is a firm hand,' her husband replied. 'And at six o'clock in the morning you are prettiest when you are silent.'

'I come from a family where they know how to knot a bow tie. You don't understand anything.'

The farmer had rheumaticky knees and walked with jerky steps

like a stork. He was pleased they shared the same forename –
Andries and Anders – and he asked for help with a letter to the
Governor. He offered in exchange some turtle's blood that he had
dried into little scales and carried as a remedy whenever he travelled away from the farm.

'Now at last the rain and flying ants are coming,' he said.

Andries' horses, oxen, cows, sheep and goats were watched over
by slaves and driven home at dusk. The animals slept in the open
overnight, each species separated by mud walls. The settlers' hard
work, combined with the mild climate, had produced peas and
asparagus, peaches and apples. But grapes, cherries and nuts didn't
thrive there.

Every ox-plough required three slaves, a sheep farmer at least
six. Those who were incompetent were sold or exchanged. The
farmers – Sparrman noted – had more land, cattle and assistance
than they needed, but lacked good tools. There was a shortage of
metal, and a sharp ploughshare of the Swedish type cost six times
more than their own. Here was a possible export market for
Sweden.

Slaves were made to attend public punishments as a warning.
But a slave punished for rebellion was in the eyes of his fellow-
slaves a martyr for a just cause and for defiance of the prevailing
order.

'Such of their fellow-slaves as have had the courage to take away
the lives of their respective tyrants, and prefer death and tortures
to basely grovelling and crawling any longer upon the earth in an
opprobrious state of bondage, are examples worthy of imitation,
and at least deserve to be venerated, pitied, and even revenged.'

A runaway slave was desperate and frequently armed. Out in the
countryside hunger and wild beasts compelled him to stay close to
the settlers, who had every reason to fear his vengeance. The camp
fires of slaves on Table Mountain could sometimes be seen from
Cape Town. But slave rebellions were infrequent. There were considerable distances between farms and slaves found it difficult to

make contact. They came from varied backgrounds and lacked a common language that was not also understood by the whites.

A manual that Sparrman had acquired in Cape Town prescribed corporal punishment using split bamboo sticks, followed by the application of salt water to the wounds. In the case of females condemned to death, their faces were to be branded until unrecognizable. Refractory slaves could be tied back-to-back and put out to sea on a raft, to perish from thirst or be consumed by the waves or sharks.

Sparrman noted: 'A young man and woman who were slaves at the Cape, and were passionately fond of each other, solicited their master, in conformity to the established custom, for his consent to their being united in wedlock, though all in vain, as from some whim or caprice he was absolutely induced to forbid it. The consequence was, that the lover was seized with a singular fit of despair; and having first plunged a dagger into the heart of the object of his dearest wishes, immediately afterwards put an end to his own life. But how many hundred instances, not less dreadful than these, might be produced to this purpose!'

In this land, people live to enrich themselves, Sparrman wrote, and to repress those who were here first. A judge freed a Dutchman who had bound a slave to a bench and drained his blood. A farmer threw a slave to the crocodiles and forced his servant girl to witness it.

'This is not the Garden of Eden. The masses, the thousands of slaves, will one day rise up.'

Someone told him of a punishment that had been inflicted outside the castle in Cape Town.

'The soldiers laughed, but the children were silent.'

Those words remained with him like an undying echo.

In 1778, two years after Sparrman's visit, Governor von Plettenberg reported that all of the independent Khoikhoi villages in Cape Colony had been eradicated. The Hottentots who had not managed to flee inland had become servants or slaves.

Of all the early explorers of South Africa, Anders Sparrman was the only one who spoke not merely about the slaves, but also with the slaves.

He summarized his position thus: 'My desire is for a country where no-one makes unlawful use of power, where justice prevails, poverty decreases year by year, and the earth produces many harvests. Yet there can be no true amity until the country is ruled by its own inhabitants.'

14

They were back in Cape Town on the 15th of April 1776. Immelman's mother was delighted that her son had once again emerged from the wilderness unscathed. His sister, embracing him, looked so boldly at Anders that he imagined it to be a sign of mutual understanding. The mother shook his hand in gratitude as he took his leave, still uncertain whether anything significant had occurred.

The mountain plateau of the peninsula stood out in profile against a sea that foamed turquoise and white. After dusk, sheet lightning lit up the eastern sky. Watching the rain pouring down over the sea and stopping before it reached the thirsty land, Anders reminded his friend how much in life is wasted and comes to nought.

He visited his old place of employment in Simonstown. It was many years since he had eaten ox-steak with apples in the Resident's house. He smelt the muddy tang of seaweed, fishing nets and high tide along False Bay, and found Christoffel Brand's guesthouse badly ravaged by the salt winds. His thoughts turned to the wild narcissi in the garden, and the peacock Mr Kirsten had succeeded in bringing from Europe and had endeavoured to mate with the long-necked guinea fowl.

Johanna had grown darker and stouter. Geessie had been sent to the family in Holland to improve her future chances. The Resident's face had become more lined and as sallow as gravestone marble; his nose was heavily veined and his knuckles were deeply embedded in his fleshy hands.

'There are no glimmers of light here,' he told Anders. 'We blindfold one another. Everyone is seeking his own advantage. I cross the street whenever I see these disgruntled creatures. But most harm is done by those who travel around the country administering justice unbidden to the helpless, without possessing the requisite wisdom.'

Sparrman – who was no longer the Resident's employee and could therefore express himself without prevarication – said that liberty and co-operation were not incompatible with the necessary development and order. The old fantasies and improbable maps were being replaced by realistic factual surveys, and that was what one should rely on.

'Until our European virtues are generally accepted,' the Resident replied, 'we risk any tractability being mistaken for weakness. Only our intelligence and weaponry, and our demands that the laws be adhered to, can compensate for our numerical disadvantage. One has to be able to thread a needle in the dark. Even in this colony, with its disagreeable customs, we have to recognize our task. Hymn-singing, cinchona bark and leeches are not guaranteed to produce a work ethic. The natives have to be disciplined. A peaceable disposition in the individual is as useful to us as a silent regimental band. Unfortunately, my fine young tutor, most of the blessings of our civilization stem from compulsion. If we were to give the native our own freedom, he would experience it as a heavy burden. Freedom means nothing more to him than not having to work.'

A slave was repairing the broken steps. The parrot in its cage screeched so indelicately that the Resident lost his self-control, picked up a knife and cut off its head. Its green wings gave one final flutter.

'You can eat it!' he goaded the slave.

*

'No-one knows how our lives will end, if indeed they have even begun,' Daniel Immelman said.

'We must go our separate ways,' Anders replied. 'You will stay here. I shall have occasion to think of you, and often.'

'If you die before me, I shall not know about it.'

'You will feel it. Like a breath of air.'

They exchanged a few letters. Some years later Immelman described a rebellion in Cape Province. He had married immediately after his return, and in the course of time acquired thirteen children. In an unfinished memoir, now in the Cape Town Municipal Archive, he wrote:

'It was not evident from Dr Sparrman's demeanour, conversation or appearance that he frequently went without sleep or rest. Sharing trials and tribulations with him was easy, and the hours passed swiftly in his company. He was a source of help and support for everyone. He had the advantage of a natural harmony of bearing, tone and speech. He was neither opinionated nor dissembling, but rather cheerful and positive and well-disposed towards life.'

On another occasion Sparrman wrote of his companion: 'Lacking the foundation of a good education, but by virtue of a keen intellect and good memory, he assimilated knowledge on his own account. He had the skills of carpenter, turner, carver: blocks for rigging, shroud beetles, mast trucks. When I saw him first, he had a felt hat on his head of the coarsest type, decorated with a blue cotton ribbon. He had grown up outside Cape Town, near a place where counterfeiters, ivory smugglers and other unfortunates were flogged.

'Yet travelling funds can safely be entrusted to him. He is as sharp as he is honest, and able to live among people of any nation. He was a stranger I soon came to feel I had known since childhood. I kept a respectful distance, so as not to exploit the brotherly affinity that grew up between us. He had a searching gaze and did not know how limited his future horizons would be. He seemed to me untroubled by dark moods.'

Once again Sparrman sailed with Captain Carl Gustav Ekeberg of the Swedish East India Company. He had a feeling that nothing would ever compare with the vast territory he was leaving behind. He did not imagine he would see it again. He came to regard his reports as a kind of inventory.

He landed in Gothenburg in August 1776, quite debilitated after his gruelling eight months in South Africa. By then his seeds had dried, his plants been pasted on to royal paper, his birds and insects, living trees and bulbs packed in variously sized boxes.

The crew included two baboons that one of the sailors had purchased. They broke free and swung through the rigging from rope to rope. They hid at the tops of the masts until hunger drove them down on pillaging raids. They signed off in Gothenburg.

Sparrman discarded a few of the snails, corals and fossils that had been damaged on the voyage. In some instances the spirit had evaporated or leaked out and left the fish more rotten than preserved. So often Nature's rarities were not treated with sufficient care, rendering them useless for detailed study.

He took with him to Stockholm a bushbuck, an anteater, the foetus of a gazelle, a green woodpecker and a long-tailed cuckoo, whose stomach contents of insects he had catalogued. He covered them in arsenic, packed them in naphthalene camphor and loaded his finds on to a wagon to accompany his carriage.

The larger animals, salted in sealed containers, were conveyed by galleass up the coast. On his inventory were a lion, a long-haired bear, a kudu calf, the stuffed foal of a wild striped horse (the soon-to-be-extinct quagga), and a rhinoceros' skull and penis 'of singular shape'.

When he held the quartz crystal from Storm River up to the light, he thought he could discern an initial letter inside it – like the thinnest of cotton threads embroidered on a sheet. He had brought Africa home with him.

II

Letters to George Forster

The only exclusively personal letters from Anders Sparrman that have survived are those written in English to George Forster. He dispatched the first letter from Caledon, east of Cape Town, after Forster had continued to England on the *Resolution*.

'Just now on my journey to the Caffres I write you this, being obliged by a severe gale of South-East with heavy rains, to lay the helm of my "oxenwaggon" in lee. Six months (if otherwise I and my oxen can hold it out), expecting at my return to the Cape to be feasted by a letter from you or to find you there yourself setting out on some such other wild scheme as we many a time have been pregnant with on board the *Resolution*. I myself, as you find by this, have been brought to bed with one of mine; pray now for your friend that it don't miscarry.'

The years sailing with Captain Cook had created a bond between them, these two scientists and 'compatriots of the Republic of Letters', as Sparrman called them. All the time Anders was staying in Cape Town he was afflicted with 'Dutch indolence' and lacked any urge to explore, even though he furnished George with scandalous gossip. He admonished George for having left his 'Plum-pudding and her sisters' without bidding them farewell, although he had consoled them with the thought that they had probably been mentioned in Forster's *Journals* and were thus immortalized.

He followed his friend's fortunes with eager curiosity. 'Pray how do you intend further to dispose of your genius? Do you go to Oxford to study Physic? Have you let your *vena poëtica* bleed yet in favour of the press and the public? Are not the girls three times more pretty in St Helena than at the Cape?'

From Dover, where his Swedish ship put in, Anders wrote that he had seriously considered spending a further year in South Africa. After all, no-one had missed him while he was away among the heathens. He had been the first to haul a manatee from the deep and study it, and he had examined lions and pythons. He had left his horse and oxen and other possessions to be sold in Cape Town.

'I believe the Dutch are all sheep, thieves and rogues at the Cape. The rascals murder Hottentot children in a bloody cruel manner; but I think Providence will not suffer long to see innocence so huddled.'

Sparrman had used abbreviations to write his account of the expedition, and it would take some time before it was ready for publication.

'What do you think the booksellers would pay for a little history of my travels?' he asked Forster.

He proposed an exchange with George: Lapland plants in return for his duplicated specimens from the South Seas. He suspected that Captain Cook or his servant had stolen a box of valuable garments from Tahiti and requested the address of Mrs Cook.

Anders praised the new king, Gustav III. 'Was not Sweden so poor a country, he would make very soon a paradise of it.' Yet he doubted whether the king would give him an appointment which would provide him with a living.

He was pleased that Forster had published a book showing that Linnaeus was not the only one to have advanced the understanding of botany.

Linnaeus was extremely jealous of younger colleagues, even of his kind-hearted son, who became his successor. The old man, reverting to childishness, wanted science to die with him. He had attached his name to more plants than anyone before him, but he could no longer identify them. He had observed his Creator's work with acuity, and at the end there was still one manifestation of his genius conspicuous to those around him: his rapture at the wonders of Nature.

Anders had been welcomed back by Linnaeus, who was hobbling around his room semi-paralysed by a stroke, and lamenting the fact that he could not take the South Sea plants with him to the world to which his soul had already departed. It was by then a long time since Linnaeus had been in the local village church at Danmark, where his dog used to howl whenever the sermon went on too long.

The future fate of the Linnaeus collections remained uncertain. It would be deplorable if they passed to Joseph Banks or Daniel Solander in London, who seemed all too keen to hear news of the great man's death.

In his five years of expeditions Sparrman had never received a penny from the public purse – in stark contrast to Solander. Yet he was ready to travel to the moon with George Forster, though to begin with they decided to concentrate on the unexplored North Atlantic. Anders would be responsible for anatomy, mineralogy and flora, especially cryptogams; George for geography, astronomy and zoology.

'I also have nor the pride, nor the talents ever to cut the figures of a learned man, but if my health is tolerable and nobody knocks me hard on the head, I may turn a very great traveller and be useful, and yet more useful than an archbishop. As for money, we would always get by work. Such clever fellows as we, would not be wanting such trifles.'

Sparrman's next letters to George Forster were sent from the Lövsta foundry estate, where he spent lengthy periods as a guest of the entomologist and industrialist Charles De Geer.

'How does the American war go on? I hope its disaster will not reach you, but very indirect. In Sweden we live peaceably. Take a wife with 4 or 5000 pounds and you will live in great style in the southern provinces of Sweden; here it is too cold.' But, he added, he had no intention himself of marrying – the idea was even more remote than the South Pole.

Anders was offered a post by Joseph Banks in London, which he declined for financial reasons. He had his doctor's practice in Stockholm, and under the new regulations was also a practising midwife. He was simultaneously studying mineralogy under Professor Torbern Bergman (who had invented a process for man-ufacturing artificial mineral water), and anatomy under Professor Adolf Murray, both of them without peer in England, according to Sparrman. He was also personal physician to the De Geer family at Lövsta, which gave him a secure base – with board and lodging and access to the best natural sciences library in Sweden.

'I will let the world know as soon as I can where I have been in the South Seas and what I have done among the Hottentots,' he told George. 'But I have not hurried with it, not having an incli-nation to overwork myself. I wish you now with all my heart less work and better rewards than you hitherto have got. I would advise you now to strengthen yourself with artificial Seltser with more fixed air than in the natural. You may drink artificial Pyrmonter to fortify the stomach, but its iron causes a little giddiness during the cure. You cannot fail, it appears, of gaining some thousands by your journal. Cook's work got 6000 pounds sterling. What does Mr Hodges say about your observations? – his shaping or creating beard on those who never had any?'

On the 12th of September 1777 Sparrman wrote to George from Lövsta.

'My ever dearest Friend, I write of the behaviour of the Hotten-tots, taking care to show several capital lies of Kolbe and others of their own making. I describe the districts round about the Cape, the government, magistrates, etc., very shortly, seasoned perhaps with little ill-natured truths, mentioning all that can explain the character of the Dutch, the wild beasts, their hunting, the anatomy of some animals as rhinoceros, manatees, antelopes, etc. In the Swedish language I hope my style will be pleasing and flowing, a little humorous and interesting. Few medical observations. A short description of my insects.'

After a stay in Norway, Anders wrote from Stockholm in the summer of 1779 to George Forster in Kassel that he had to make use of the small hours for his correspondence, after he had finished with his patients.

'Poor myself, it is a treasure to me, to be now and then able to share my little pittance with a mother of about seventy, and four sisters. My brother, I hope, soon will be able to do more for them, as he is going to receive a curacy, to which I flatter myself of having been able to forward his endeavours. Tho' he himself as a clergy-man is a man of great talents and eloquence in the pulpit, he however wanted much more recommendations and interests, which together with money is the very soul of this damned body of a political world.

'My pension of the Academy as Keeper of their Museum is 70 ducats and two chambers for my own use. Some stupid boobies think me too good a naturalist to be a good physician at the same time. As yet I have no prospect of marrying, tho' I am persuaded that even a tolerable wife would not add a little to my happiness, but I dread devilishly being caught on those damned fishing hooks of Xantippes, as I should think but to swallow a fine bait. I truly feel the most perfect and sincerest friendship for you . . .'

On the 5th of September he wrote again to Kassel: 'Many a time I have thought of you, and cordially would have hugged you in my arms, if I had had you so near. I feel the sweets of friendship by only remembering your name. As for friendship and learning I am pretty near of the same sentiments as yourself. I am not at all anxious about distinguishing myself with many publications, nor to heap up a stock of knowledge of books and things that might surprise the studying world and encumber my own brains without improving the soul or its residence the heart.

'I would not willingly cultivate any branch of learning at the total expense of my health and enjoyments of society. However, I will not fail to work in the line as you call it, but not for the futility of fame, but for my bread, my friends and my fellow-beings. Though if I rightly examine my heart, I shall not wholly dislike it if I reap some fame and honour by it.

'I am not without a number of cares and troubles, both for myself and others, nor without wants, necessities and imaginary ones. Nevertheless, I am in some measure easy and in that respect always willingly submit to the pleasure of the Supreme Being, who most graciously and surprisingly allowed me to pass happily through and round about the world escaping innumerable eminent dangers, and has given me, I acknowledge, a better situation of life than I deserve and ventured to hope, when I first set out with both hands quite empty.

'But in respect to my countrymen, by God, I do not think quite so modestly in regard to them. Not that I am by any means inflamed with self-conceit, I pretend only that the pittance of my salary is far from being equal to the really very great hardships I have gone through, for the sake of science. A little more support certainly would have enabled me to serve society and science a great deal more, in alleviating my circumstances now inferior to several of my former fellow-students, who only have walked on the old beaten road at their leisure without any material exertions.

'It is not their fault, that they have been more fortunate. Please Heaven that we may not want honesty and virtue tho' gold should fail. As for me, I want a book on my bookcase more than bread and clothing for my body – for in books I borrow from others and read them almost with the same improvement, as I cannot afford to purchase hardly any. But the other necessaries of life I could, nor would not have a heart to borrow, tho' it is now rather the fashion in this poor country.

'I am not in a hurry to make my little talents together with my imperfections appear in public. After my Cape journal I will publish some hundred new Cape insects, printed cheap and clever enough, with their natural colours. As I am about to lodge an engraver and draughtsman in one of my rooms, to do this, if I meet with encouragements. Afterwards I will publish birds, plants and animals, which now have taken up much time to arrange.

'The South Sea ships ought at this time to arrive at England. I received early the shocking news of the death of Captain Cook. You may thank God that you happened to be at variance with him in England, otherwise you might have been prevailed on to go another voyage with him, and you might then have also had a knock on your head. We are not always able to reason and to act, when we are put to the proof, as we do reasoning over a bottle.'

The Cabinet of Natural History

1

The first few years after his return home were very successful ones for Anders Sparrman. Other disciples of Linnaeus had come back from their travels in a state of lost innocence, after everything they had collected had succumbed to fire, theft or shipwreck. He gave talks about his adventures and showed his collections. Those six years of travel provided him with capital for life, and he would draw on it over and over again, eating into it until nothing remained.

Carl Peter Thunberg, experienced and coolly rational, was more adaptable than Sparrman. They kept in contact all their lives. Just before his death, Anders wrote to his oldest friend that his own life resembled an envelope that someone else had sealed, and in reply to Thunberg's New Year greeting he expressed his own good wishes to him, 'both in this world and out in the blissful spheres beyond the grave where we shall gather flowers more perfect and more beautiful than on the savannahs of Africa'.

At a meeting of the Swedish Academy of Sciences in February 1777, in the presence of Gustav III, Anders Sparrman was elected to membership. The president, Baron Sparre, announced that the Academy, with 'warm regard', wished to award a stipend for several years 'to support Dr Sparrman, who has recently returned from a protracted voyage to Caput Bonae Spei (The Cape of Good Hope), the South Seas and round the Antarctic Circle, during which he has made a large collection of all kinds of natural curiosities and observations, which he has brought back with him, and he now requires time to order and describe them, but has otherwise no means by which to maintain himself.'

Sparrman was introduced to the king, during which conversation His Majesty burst into a regal laugh, ending on a descant cheep like a whinchat's. According to the minutes of the meeting, Sparrman showed them 'curiosities brought home from the Southern world, consisting partly of naturalia, partly of weapons, domestic articles, ornaments, et cetera, such as are used by peoples of distant lands and islands, in all of which His Majesty took much gracious delight'.

He was permitted 'to furnish His Majesty's table with a dried sea-cow's tongue two feet and eight inches in length', which appealed to the king's love of the theatrical and the unconventional. Referring to Linnaeus' view that the Earth is a museum for the work of the Creator, Sparrman argued that dedicated rooms were needed to display the many wonders of the wider world – to put them, as it were, on the public stage.

So Sparrman received two thousand four hundred *daler* to write up descriptions of the specimens and take care of the Academy's still rather insignificant natural history collections. He very soon felt constrained to sell his insect collection for a thousand *riksdaler* to Gustaf von Paykull of Vallox-Säby.

In 1778 the Academy of Sciences purchased Lefebure House on Stora Nygatan (now Number 30) and Anders Sparrman was made the curator of what would later become the National Museum. He was charged with showing Nature's remarkable products and achievements to 'the young who are desirous of learning, and to inquisitive citizens' – but to only a limited number of people at any one time. For more knowledgeable persons, appointments could be made by arrangement. Two rooms adjacent to the museum were allocated to the curator as living accommodation.

Gustav III was not very interested in natural curiosities and handed over part of his own collections in the Palace of Drottning-holm to the reluctant curator at Stora Nygatan, who put it aside, finding most of it to be lacking in scientific value. It included, according to the catalogue, 'two children joined at the abdomen, in a glass jar, deformed births of blackamoors in their cauls, a sheep with two heads, a human heart in a glass case'.

Sparrman dealt severely with objects acquired before his time that bore witness more to over-enthusiastic wishful thinking than to science. There was the 'skull of a unicorn bearing an inscription, in a round box', the teeth of a manatee, a very large fungus, a dried human foot, and the horsehair worm, Gordius, known as the Evil Bite. He was wary of visiting apothecaries trying to buy wolves' teeth, dried mice, the heel bones of hares or whales' penises as treatment for dysentery.

Count Bonde of Säfstaholm had donated the thumb of a mum-mified water nymph, bitten off by a '*monstro marino* in a lake in the county of Småland'. Sparrman was inclined to give the thumb to a child to play with, but it would not have been wise to insult the Count, so it remained in the collections throughout Sparrman's life. However, he did throw a giant gallstone – a real mineral that had stopped growing – on to the anatomical compost heap.

He was thirty when he laid down the gavel in 1778 after a period as chairman of the Academy of Sciences. He felt himself to be more experienced than most of his peers in Sweden, and hoped to be able to sail around the world once again to extend Swedish colonization. In one speech, he excused himself for not having acquired the art of oratory, since for five years overseas he had 'had to babble the unknown phrases of Indians and savages'.

He thanked the Academy for its support for one who had 'returned from the Antarctic Circle to his beloved Scandinavia', and announced that he and his colleagues had introduced more than two hundred and fifty useful plants to Sweden.

'What is Peruvian gold compared to Peruvian bark, quinine?' he asked. 'Many thousands have the latter to thank for their health and life, while the former has caused the death of many millions and confounded even more.

'We have long been able to estimate the size of the planets and their paths, and make our judgements about their inhabitants. We have determined and drawn the heights and valleys of the moon. And yet we have left some third of our own planet un-navigated and unknown. Now, at last, various lands and peoples have been discovered and, what is of no less significance, our latest voyage around the world has proved that the great Southern Continent of our imaginations has to be discounted. This has freed certain philosophers from their labours of reckoning the dimensions of mountains and lands at the South Pole, with which they wished to balance the North Pole. Their genius, liberated from this concern, may now be more happily and usefully applied to other areas of investigation.

'I want to assure you that I will exert the utmost diligence in caring for and maintaining the collections I have had the opportunity of amassing on my travels. I need not stress the invaluable utility of such collections. One may not only satisfy one's curiosity and see the whole of Nature in a single glance, or observe the peculiarities of far-flung lands in a single place, but those desirous of learning may also, without trouble or expense, enjoy the fruits of others' expeditions, undertaken with great hardship and often at severe risk to life and limb. Few would deny that to hear the descriptions of others is very different from seeing and investigating for oneself.'

He took charge of the entomologist Charles De Geer's natural history collection from the Lövsta foundry in Uppland. It was not extensive, but it included 'a young sea-horse, a piece of elephant hide as thick as a thumb, and one of its tusks weighing 100 pounds, the head of a Babyrusa pig, Tahitian woven cloths, lizards, snakes . . .'

Sparrman had a network of collectors and agents, but seldom the means to purchase anything.

'A goodly part of my income is devoted to paying off the debts of my dear old mother, now seventy-four, who impoverished herself by providing an education for her children,' he complained to one of his patrons, Clas Alströmer, some years later. 'Full many a time, my lord, would I have endured the suffering of seeing our whole family ruined before my very eyes, had I not kept us above water with my hard work as a physician. But to achieve that I have been compelled to spend my time as surgeon to the common people – time I could have used to better advantage on the study of natural history.'

In a paper for the Gothenburg Scientific Society, Sparrman took up a phenomenon denied by the great French naturalist the Comte de Buffon: double currents in the sea. That is, deep currents that flow in the opposite direction to surface currents.

In the *Proceedings of the Academy of Sciences* he also investigated maggots 'expelled from a human being'. His example was Pierre Giljam, a blacksmith from the Lövsta foundry who was close to fainting from the pain in his abdomen. After a decoction of brandy, garlic and a purgative the blacksmith released thousands of tiny maggots. They were of a hitherto unknown kind, so Sparrman reared one until it metamorphosed into a particular species of fly. He analysed for the Academy how 'fly maggots or fly larvae insinuate themselves into the living human gut'.

2

I survey the market on Blasieholmen like someone who does not reside in Stockholm. You can buy advertisement sheets, razors, masks, trinkets, and leave a variety of items to be sold on commission. All along the quay on Skeppsbron the rigging of schooners is groaning and the topsails of cutters are slapping as they dry in the breeze. People throng about the ferry steps waiting to cross to Djurgården Park. You can take a hamper over to the gun battery on Kastellholmen in a flat-bottomed boat rowed by a ferrywoman. When Thunberg comes to visit we shall climb up to Mosebacke Terrace and eat cutlets and soured cream in the arbour.

As a stranger in the city I am astonished at the lavish apparel on the streets: servant girls with silken shawls, shop assistants with silver buckles on their shoes. Anyone who is well-attired can gain admittance to Humlegården Park, to the Swedish Academy's formal meetings at the Exchange, and to the royal masked balls. Dr Lemmel, my colleague from Berlin, is surprised that ordinary citizens dress as elegantly as the nobility, and that lowly officials squander a third of their salary on their hair and their wigs. Yet he can find not a single bookshop where he might purchase a reliable map of the city.

I have dusted down my tailcoat and donned my ruffled shirt and cravat. I was invited to give a talk on my travels at the English

Tavern on Riddarhustorg. I avoid the cheaper eating houses like those in Lutternsgränd, where even women take part in dubious games of forfeits, and weaving-apprentices mingle with clerks to eat sausages and macaroni and sup weak beer, the water being often unfit to drink.

At midsummer the artillerymen, dragoons and other soldiers pitch camp in the fields of Ladugårdsgärdet, with shooting practice and military exercises. There are uniforms in every conceivable hue, and white tents and silken flags. On Midsummer Day itself, every company erected a maypole decked out in wreaths and the king's monogram, and the Royal Kitchen provided bread, herring and aquavit, tobacco and clay pipes.

I am regarded by some as unsociable, even disagreeable, because I neither play the lottery nor let myself be tempted into a game of La Belle, which puts one man's money into the pockets of another. I have seen Commercial Counsellor Printzensköld embezzle a whole city street. Our daily newspaper *Dagligt Allehanda* inveighs against wives and children being turned into beggars, and addicted householders losing all their property to their servants. But the king is in the process of issuing new decrees against gaming and gambling in taverns and coffee houses, and he orders the flogging of any boys playing at dice in the vicinity of the Royal Palace.

Despite the rumours of my reserved disposition, I have been invited to join the Freemasons. I have refused, but on the other hand I have accepted membership of the Order of Arla Coldinu, which is open to sea captains and younger officials. The uniform of the Order is a brown jacket with buttons of lignum vitae, brown breeches with red bands at the knee, a red band round the brim of the hat, and a pale blue waistcoat.

We made an excursion by boat to the island of Lilla Essingen, where, on a site advised by Bleumortier the taverner, and assisted by Dagenaer the builder, we constructed a round tower with a gun emplacement. The flag of our Order was raised on the new redoubt, which was named Carthago. To cries of *Vivat Carthago*, cannon were fired, according to instruction. A silver cross bearing the Coldinu insignia was placed in a recess, which was then covered with stone and mortar. We sailed back to Riddarholmen on the evening breeze, and all agreed that these innocent pleasures would not offend the eye of the Omniscient.

Hasselgren the merchant, Malmgren the accountant, Flodin, the porcelain painter from Rörstrand, the apothecary Lars Collin from Järntorget, engineer Joseph Forssell, the engraver Jonas Fägersten, and Erling the leather-merchant, all to a man proved themselves to be hopeless at the art of sailing. And what I had learned on board the *Resolution* I was not able to put into practice until we were rubbing against the quayside.

Much easier to reach was Master Anders on Kungsholmen, whose fresh salted herring has a fine reputation, and whose Curff – an intestine filled with rice, raisins and chopped liver – took my mind back to the Cape. His aquavit was forty-nine per cent. I avoid hostelries where the glasses are knocked over and the barmaid spends all evening mopping up spills.

Then came news that the townspeople's festivities, in honour of the newly christened crown prince, had resulted in a hundred being crushed to death. Some had their guts kicked into their throats, and mothers had foetuses kicked out of their wombs. A watchman told them not to trample on the dead. That inspired them to call for new glasses and raise a cheer for the corpses. A drunken mob is beyond all control.

In order to deal with these vagrants, we are now only permitted to change employment or abode on the 1st of April and the 1st of October. Householders must register the names of those to whom they let rooms. All travellers have to report their presence, and their names and lodgings in the city are published in the newspaper. Vagabonds are sentenced to war service. Measures have even been taken against stray dogs, which the executioner's assistant rounds up, culls and disposes of.

I have been told that police superintendent Liljensparre and the Duke, both in disguise, called on Mamselle Arfvidson, the fortune-teller, who shrieked at her caged owl, eagle owl and raven, 'Stop, you cursed sinners!' Whereupon, the visitors hastily withdrew, assuming the imprecation intended for them.

There is a stink of something rotten in the streets: it is the universal distrust, which is a strain on the nerves. Who is following whom? Who is hiding his agitation in a silence that even Liljensparre, with his purple flaring nostrils and pointed ears, cannot eavesdrop on? Taking his manuscript to the printer on Malmtorgsgatan, Major Pehr af Lund was threatened, bribed, shadowed. Then, when he received a little gratuity from Schröderheim, he gave up, less tenacious than his iconoclastic friend Thorild. Whatever am I doing in this city?

3

Sparrman went down to the Karelian fur trader in Stadsgården, where the rumble of carts was accompanied by shouting in German and Russian. He watched the fishing boats coming in under rust-brown sails to dock at Kastellholmen and Nybron. The smell of tar and red lead wafted across the quays and berths, signalling departure. He was wearing black breeches, a simple neckerchief and a grey-green waistcoat.

On Mälartorget dung lay everywhere, and the wooden piles were rotting from drain-water and urine. The buff-coloured facades of the houses were coarse-textured under their glaze of sunlight. On Järntorget only milk was sold, on Munkbron vegetables, on Kornhamnstorg wares of every kind. Second-hand shoes were for sale, heaped up, worn and twisted, bearing the impression of the heels and toes of the dead. The buckles had been removed, the scuffs remained. The trader was kneading the leather, stiffened by rain and sweat.

Carrying water and firewood was heavy work and, in common with most of the houses in the old town, he lacked a kitchen. He ate a cold meal at his desk or in one of the eating houses. Those he patronized were run by widows or unmarried women, as were most of the four hundred establishments offering food and home-brewed drinks. He never visited those which catered for 'the better classes'.

Stockholm was a city of disappointments. A glass of aquavit and boiled whitefish in a tavern, society balls in the reception rooms of the Exchange that required as detailed a preparation as a battle campaign. From his Cabinet he could see clouds being funnelled into the gap between the Cathedral and the German Church. When he walked down to Skeppsbron in the early morning, the cupola of Katarina Church just caught a gleam of sunlight.

Dr Lemmel was surprised at the silence in Stockholm. Apart from the noise of the carts, there was no general hubbub. The inhabitants looked dutiful and dull. Thieves and assailants were well known and seldom escaped. The major cause of crime was the consumption of spirits. Fines were imposed assiduously: no pails of stinking water to be emptied into the street, no naked lights in the street, no running over the ice from Munkbron to Södermalm, no cows to be left on the street, and no smoking out of doors.

Night was the liveliest time: gunshots, the clamour of dogs and goats that had escaped, the cries of the nightwatchmen. The fire brigade used their traps to intervene in brawls and against disturbers of the peace. These consisted of a pole with a horseshoe at the tip, which was closed by springs to fasten around the miscreant's neck, arm or leg.

Anders walked along Drottninggatan with the German zoologist, whose pinched face was as pale as a death mask and whose eyes were as fixed as a statue's. In Petissan's yard the cocks, with yellowing bibs, were fast asleep and the hens had nestled down on their eggs. Soot hung in the air, wood burnt in the stoves. A policeman rattled his sabre, and blew his nose to rid himself of the smell of horse piss. In the graveyard of Johannes Church dogs were digging up the bones of the poor. A fence had been erected that year in an attempt to keep cattle and domestic animals away, but it was as hard to disperse ravens and herons as it was the stench of corpses.

Dr Lemmel was travelling further north, first to visit Thunberg in Uppsala and then to study rodents, in particular the beaver. Anders took him to inspect the school of writing and arithmetic on Kindstugatan, and a school for young ladies in the Klara district. He was struck by the fact that even orphanage children were taught to read, write and count. Sparrman pointed out that learning the catechism would be meaningless if only a few people could read the Bible. Yet his guest regarded Stockholm as a city of idlers, where the master of the house sat from lunchtime till ten in the evening in coffee house, tavern or club reading newspapers, discussing politics, smoking a pipe and dining.

Anders himself sometimes used to go for walks through the city, which was no bigger than would take an hour and a half from one toll gate to another on the opposite side. On Gamla Kungsholmsbrogatan there were turf-roofed timber cottages interspersed with tobacco warehouses, fields and willow bushes. The sewage ditches were close-boarded. Smoke rose from Bergsund's iron foundry. It was just like Cape Town.

He went to visit his sister Anna Ekengren at Tjärhovet on Södermalm. She had grown into a sturdy woman in a blue bodice, brown apron and white cap. But her face was still so smooth and soft that what she most resembled was a glass of milk. Her husband had his carpenter's workshop in the yard at the back. There were screeching windmills all around the house, reminiscent of a farm in Lena transported to Stockholm.

Anna sat plucking a capercaillie when Anders arrived. A basket of eggs stood nearby and hens were scuttling about the yard. She showed him, the doctor, her collection of remedies and bandages for wounds. Her neighbours made good use of the medical knowledge she had picked up.

His mother, Brita, lived with her daughter. She had deteriorated, and spent her time sitting in the grandmother's room staring at the floor as if tracking something with her eyes, perhaps the serpent of the passing years. Her hands had become as sallow and thin as a communion wafer. She tried to hide her own frailty by commenting on that of others, but forgot to take off her slippers when going to Mass in Katarina Church, which she thought full of voices raised in needless exhortation to spiritual struggle.

She still mourned her husband, Eric. 'He had no secrets from God or man.'

'Then he must have been a numbskull,' Anna surprisingly interjected.

'No more do I . . .' Anders began.

'What you are up to is something no-one can understand,' his sister cut him short.

The gap between mother and son had increased. Just as he worried about her, so she worried about him – that he went too far, yet could have gone further if he had been more adaptable, that he lacked a sense of propriety. Brita's opinion of her son's character was still the same: obstinate, inflexible and rather lazy.

The king himself used to take walks in the streets, dressed simply in a plain topcoat. When Sparrman raised his hat, the king doffed his and continued at the same swift pace. He had recently laid the foundation stone for the new bridge, Norrbro, which replaced the dilapidated Slaktarhusbron and would finally provide a fitting complement to the creamy yellow and white Tessin Palace.

In 1779 the king attended a public meeting of the Academy of Sciences in the new reception hall on Stora Nygatan. The Council of State were present, as was the ambassador of Tripoli with his interpreter and a considerable number of the nobility. The king remarked on the fact that the curator was four decades younger than his recently deceased master in Uppsala. He enquired about Sparrman's account of his travels, and the latter replied that he was describing what he had seen in Africa without fear of embarrassment or offence, and was almost up to the final phase of the expedition.

For a year or two Sparrman was invited to receptions at the palace, to soirées at the Exchange, and to meet Elis Schröderheim and others from the Council of State. Some wanted to learn unusual facts about the world, others demanded to hear his amazing adventures; in both respects Sparrman could only mumble his responses.

'On no account come to Sweden!' Sparrman advised Daniel Solander in London. 'There's nothing but grit, detritus and manure for your garden. Gustaf Adolfs Torg is like a muddy field. Sophia Albertina's palace is still not finished. The tobacco fumes in the dreary coffee houses are suffocating, and the loud commotion from the backgammon tables is unbearable. The inhabitants of Stockholm are tiresome patriots who have no desire to exchange the Baltic for the South Seas. They lack any comprehension of the beautiful or the magnificent.'

Roaming the uneven streets of Stockholm, he tried to keep his gaze fixed on the moving clouds – what intrinsic power in those celestial ships! They were reflected in the immeasurable depths of the sea. They moved like the archangel's wings beneath the grimy vaulted ceiling of Tensta Church. And he could see in his mind's eye his father leaning over the side of the pulpit as if it were the prow of a ship, battling against the tempest of the Lord with wildly flailing arms, and imbuing himself with the mighty words of the Bible to steer his congregation on a straight and narrow course between breakers and submerged rocks. Eric Sparrman knew exactly how to lower and raise his voice between the solemn whisper and the thunderous roar, and it left none of the women unmoved.

Anders wondered whether Stockholm was sapping his zest for life and his voracious recognition of the beauty of existence. For on his homecoming to the old world his energies had begun to wane. Africa remained inside him like mosquito bites, like the ensuing fits of shivering fever, like South Georgia's perpetual west wind.

4

The reproaches increased, at first with hints and mutterings, then more overtly. Some of his colleagues had nothing but scorn and condemnation for him as an administrator and manager. He himself was weary of the perpetual arguments in committees and working parties, the bureaucratic jargon, power battles disguised by polite hypocrisy, and minutes of meetings that expunged any ideas which didn't toe the official line. So fond were his fellow countrymen of all kinds of formalities, laws, regulations and entrance examinations that in their spare time they created orders with insignia and medals, with dissertations and competitions, with amateurishly composed poems on friendship and virtue.

He felt himself to be severely restricted in Stockholm, where the very streets were cluttered with prohibitions. If you were a participant in the dance that encompassed Court and Academy and Science, every step was prescribed and any false move punished with humiliation. He strove for simplicity after eradicating everything irrelevant and freeing himself from unnecessary burdens, conjuring up forgotten landscapes, and rediscovering his lost world in the faint lullaby tinkling from the music box.

Conrad Quensel, nineteen years his junior, had been Carl Peter Thunberg's assistant in Uppsala. He had undertaken an expedition to Lapland financed by Gustaf von Paykull, identified the Scandinavian hedgehog-bombycid, and published a guide to moths. He regarded himself quite early on as Sparrman's successor. To precipitate the latter's dismissal he wrote a memorandum describing dusty cupboards and specimens drying out in containers arranged unsystematically by size.

Quensel believed Sparrman was mismanaging the museum, including the objects he himself had donated. Clas Fredrik Hornstedt, who catalogued the collection twelve years later, counted one hundred and thirty-six snakes, sixty-four lizards, one hundred and seventy jars of fish, and fifty dried or stuffed fish. The birds had been transferred to Gustaf von Carlson at Mälby, a permanent secretary in the government service who already owned the largest collection of birds in Sweden. The Academy, aware of Sparrman's lack of interest, had followed Peter Jonas Bergius' proposal in this respect. And Professor Olof af Acrel had recommended that the Academy pass its stuffed mammals to the foundry owner Adolf Ulrik Grill at Söderfors. The latter had constructed a building for his varnished fish, and his museum included hippopotami, lions and leopards as well as such rarities as the Cape blaubok, which became extinct in 1797.

Quensel maintained that Sparrman had ignored the instruction to put the cabinets into proper order. 'The mineral cabinets should be positioned along the walls to prevent excess weight resting on the beams of the building. The cupboards containing insects or amphibians and fish *in spiritu vini* should be arranged symmetrically. The smaller cabinets with glass doors, for corals, sertularians and other lithophytes, should be so arranged as to make the best effect both aesthetically and for the convenience of the visitor. The curator should have the birds and quadrupeds dusted if they are not protected under glass from moths, and also put them out in the fresh air several times in summer, and warm them by the fire, to rid them of any moth infestation that may be apparent.'

'The identification of the natural history specimens by their correct name, genus and species has required many hundreds of animals to be removed from their *spiritus* and handled numerous times,' Sparrman wrote in his defence. 'For example, to count the fin bones and gill slits of the fish, and the *scuta* and *squamae* of more than one hundred and fifty snakes; as well as to make comparisons with drawings and descriptions, in order not to perpetrate errors that might render the collections misleading rather than instructive to the Royal Academy.

'Through particular friendships, correspondence and the exchange of duplicate specimens, I have considered it my obligation to augment the collection at no cost to the Academy. In this respect Director Suther has donated to the Academy a cedarwood cabinet of birds and beautiful butterflies, for which I know him to have paid more than sixty ducats to an officer from Surinam.

'With the same zeal for the embellishment and incrementation of the natural history collection, I have donated many rare items to the Royal Academy from my own collections, transported at considerable trouble and expense from the South Seas, the Cape of Good Hope and the Kaffirs, some of which items are in no other collection in Europe.

'While I have been present no-one has ever been refused permission to view the Royal Academy's natural history collections. On occasion, of course, I have felt it my duty to deter young men who wished to oblige their young ladies, of doubtful reputation, whom they proposed should see foetuses and the like.'

Some of the members of the Academy conducted themselves correctly; some were cowardly, others negative. Sparrman made enemies easily. Wargentin and Bergman remained his friends; others broke off contact.

'The path is short from larder to privy, where Quensel sits with a falsified provenance, plucking the feathers off a bird, a really unusual bird, which he doesn't like, the popinjay.'

Conrad Quensel, officious and plump from his over-consumption of baked pancakes, lied about Sparrman's life in Africa and about animals he claimed had been reassembled into new species after being killed. Of course, he himself had no foibles or idio-syncratic opinions, the good Conrad. In contrast to Sparrman, so stubborn and unreasonable, he regarded himself as spotless, unblemished.

Anders was incensed at the timorous and ingratiating men around him, and despised himself for not having seen through them from the outset. He felt like a soiled fork that had been left in von Carlson's creamed mushrooms – had so much russula and cep ever been consumed as in the dining room at Mälby? He sometimes imagined he had been transformed into a myselium, and envisaged himself turning up as an ink-cap toadstool in his friend's summer house.

'I must avoid pomposity and bad tobacco,' he admonished himself. 'I have become a figure of fun who is never appropriately dressed for the season. These dreadful guided tours I have to give, three days a week, year in, year out! What is in the minds of these whippersnappers, dragging their betrothed along to study animal foetuses swilling about in spirit as if still in the womb? They want to frighten them with horrific sights so that their wombs close up in cramp. They tell their women they are no more than vessels for deformed monsters that might end up with me, opening hours 10 a.m. to 1 p.m.

'How I despise myself, shambling around these two rooms on a June day uttering platitudes, or even sometimes, when I lose patience, outright untruths, fabricating shameful nonsense that my audience swallow with their mouths hanging open. What I want is more seriousness and rigour, and to be enlivened by a more exalted music.'

5

Nothing improves us so much as the study of natural history, Conrad Quensel proclaimed. Zoology and astronomy have a moral dimension, reminding us of our insignificance in the universe, and our greatness in our leaps of reason across the vast expanses of the mind.

The irresponsible and the bombastic accused Sparrman of indolence, dishonesty and financial incompetence. He was indignant at the criticism of his methods of stewardship. He had his desiderata lists and orders ready for books on the natural sciences, but was denied funds to buy them from Stockholm's leading booksellers, Gjörwell, Ulff & Fyrberg. They sold *'livres philosophiques'* as provocative as any of those arousing works that one might, according to Rousseau, read with one hand.

Quensel's crumpled coat was cut from dark-blue cloth, his face, still that of a younger man, a contrast in pink. He walked, Sparrman said, bent forward like the figurehead of a galleon, oblivious to the waves rushing by or the worms devouring it.

'Dr Quensel!' Sparrman called out. 'I have submitted an account of my activities, but you have classified my work as secret. When do you intend to find time to authorize my travel expenses?'

The ever-persistent Quensel continued to write to the Academy about the deteriorating state of the Cabinet of Natural History. Boxes of carelessly packed specimens lay about chaotically in cupboards and on the floor, and the smell was like a stagnant moat. On a plinth stood a bust of the donor Charles De Geer of Lövsta together with 'an otter from the South Seas almost entirely consumed by moths'.

Sparrman rejected the reports and was suspicious of the presence of duplicitous, unapproved minutes on the files. He sought to combat as best he could this meticulous cataloguer, who was also writing texts for J. W. Palmstruch's *Swedish Botany* and *Swedish Zoology*.

Alternative methods of removing Sparrman were explored. At the suggestion of Gustaf Philip Creutz, he was offered the job of secretary and personal assistant to the Governor of Saint Barthélemy. He would also serve as physician to the colony's eighteen hundred Swedes. The island grew cotton, potatoes, turnips; other goods were imported from North America. Only the Governor had a horse. Everyone else climbed the hills with the goats. The Swedish women did not work and regarded it as beneath their dignity even to pick up something they had dropped, calling instead for a slave to do so. This much he had heard from Commercial Counsellor Planck, who oversaw the office expenses for the authorities on Saint Barthélemy. He had gratefully accepted specimens for the Academy of Sciences from Samuel Fahlberg, chief surveyor on the island. But, despite several attempts to persuade and flatter him, Sparrman rejected the offer.

Quensel stepped out of the storeroom and sat down in front of him, spreading his knees and speaking in a monotone, as if reeling off mathematical formulae.

'Your power of observation is well attested. Yet I see no sign of it here in the Academy. You do not share your knowledge with colleagues or the public. You are capable of giving answers to everything, even the price of cotton seed, for instance. But for a long time now you have been what one might call economical with information.'

Sparrman was on his way to the palace when Quensel turned up again, wearing a silk coat and foppish, pointed shoes. He drew himself up to his full height, unashamedly self-satisfied, narrowed his eyes and pursed his lips. Sparrman forestalled him.

'If Captain Cook had ordered you to climb the ladder in that outfit, you would have stepped into eternal oblivion.'

Quensel expressed his disdain for such pleasantries with a smile.

'Strange things have been happening here. It may be chance. It may be natural phenomena. Items have disappeared. Insects have invaded. Pots have been broken. Am I to draw the conclusion that your melancholy has brought on inertia, and that melancholy does not befit a scholar with his sights on the future?'

'My dearly respected Sir Spy, you are poking your nose in here to check up on me.'

Quensel's lips twitched. 'I have duplicate keys to all the rooms. As, indeed, has proved necessary. When I think of what I've had to tidy up after you, I feel like a relic of the Babylonian captivity.'

'I am much better aware than you, my dear inquisitor, of who I am and what my abilities are.'

He stood up, his heart pounding, clutching the edge of the desk. He steered Quensel out of the room and locked the door.

He consulted his pocket watch. There were different times: one time was static and had not aged, and that was what he had lived with during his voyages and his sojourn in South Africa, where his ox-wagon had ventured just a few miles into virgin terrain.

That time was his friend and no day then had been in vain. Clear visibility alternated with mists around the mountains. That was what it was like on Earth, far removed from the Academy's collections on Stora Nygatan. Sparrman stood to one side in order to be in unison with the trees and their thoughts, with the lakes, which found their own level, with the rootstocks of his life, which found no soil here in which to grow.

Passers-by noticed him from the street outside. He could be

seen wandering to and fro in his nightshirt, a book in one hand and a lamp in the other. He seemed to be talking to himself, swinging the lamp so that shadows flitted across the room like bats, from a wall of specimens to a wall of bound books and the *Proceedings of the Academy*.

When Quensel developed an incessant cough from all the dust, he blamed Sparrman.

'Go to sea!' Sparrman replied. 'The air would do you good, and not just your lungs.'

Thus had the tone of their exchanges degenerated. Yet he realized he had become impossible and that he had alternating bursts of methodicalness and excitability.

While walking in Karlbergs Park one day, Quensel dropped dead from a haemorrhage.

Sparrman reapplied for the post from which he had been dismissed, but it was given to Olof Swartz, the botanist who had travelled to America. That was several years later.

6

On occasion, I would encourage our zealous friend Quensel with blandishments, which he lapped up rapturously. I praised his reports in deliberately poor Swedish and, unmusical pedant that he is, he took my words at face value. Guile, egotism and the vanity of others had been his enemies – and now, he added, we have to deal with Gustaf von Carlson as permanent secretary. His gloomy laugh indicated that he recognized himself in every stiff-necked schemer.

In Quensel's eyes I am no more than so much garbage. He would love to put me under supervision, and replace me with a more suitable and competent person. He is so full of spite that he asked me whether my (in his eyes) weak constitution had not been a hindrance on my voyages. And he found my journals, in proportion to their length, a little thin, or scientifically insignificant.

When I formulated some comment on his hardships in Lapland, he was annoyed that I had not leavened my phraseology more delicately. He is an untravelled windbag who cultivates his jealousy and endeavours to restrict the natural sciences in any way he can, and under any pretext. Oh, if only I could rid myself of these annoyances and vexations – but principally my own small-mindedness!

I am an upstart in the world, once the beloved disciple of my master, now a poverty-stricken failure fretting over the successes of the carefree nobility. I took pleasure in sacrificing myself for Linnaeus' learned cause. For that, I ignored every kind of discomfort and opportunity for advancement. 'A brave man does not let a voyage like this slip through his fingers,' he said. 'You are assiduous and have an enquiring mind, and you can withstand extremes of climate.' Before my departure he allowed me free access to his herbarium and other collections.

I investigated the phosphorescence that illuminates the waves at night. Even with a powerful microscope I could not find a single form of life. I filtered seawater through linen cloth and blotting paper folded in four. I examined the residual sediment with the minutest attention. There was a momentary spark, but with neither body nor life. Yet the water that had passed through the paper had ceased to glow, no matter how much the glass was agitated. I filled a bottle with unfiltered seawater, and every time I shook the bottle a glow spread out to the sides.

Life seems to me to have become a similar will-o'-the-wisp – no, a maze leading towards a less than edifying end. My literary ability is slight, my production but slender, and the stimulus I receive does not come from my distrustful environment.

My adverse reception by the public, and the ingratitude and snares of my superiors, have led to a despair which leaves me defenceless against calumny. These odious insinuations! These smirking backbiters! All these bureaucrats of the intellect who have taken over Stockholm! They say of Director Edelcrantz, whose new steam mill so disfigures Kungsholmen, that he built his house just to have ease of access to the Opera and the Royal Dramatic Theatre. His delusions are well known, but I have kept my own books according to the rules and have not deserved being subjected to a special audit.

I have proposed that the specimens in the city's natural history collections might usefully be exchanged for fresh examples, since natural phenomena remain essentially the same. But eye-witness accounts, their interpretation of experiences, are an irreplaceable source. Some of my contemporaries have a limited and distorted view of achievements that fundamentally they envy. Perhaps it will be left to a younger generation to profit from the labours of their predecessors.

The Earth's wildernesses, countryside and cultivated fields, Nature's treasure house that leads us to discoveries which benefit our daily life – that is what I have tried to give a lucid and reliable reflection of in my writings. My travels in provinces of the world chosen by Linnaeus, my insights into different ways of life, my observations on how the borders between the realms of Nature and culture are as incorrectly drawn as harmfully restricting – will it ever be understood as anything but entertainment?

The richness and sublimity of Nature, which I have examined in all its forms and manifestations, seem only to flicker as a background shadow or phantasm for those who take their pleasure in the amusements on Mosebacke. There they wallow in triviality and can discern neither truth nor beauty. The Arctic oceans and the great Voltaire would affright them in equal measure.

7

In the autumn of 1783 it was finally ready: *A Voyage to the Cape of Good Hope, towards the Antarctic Polar Circle, and round the World: But Chiefly into the Country of the Hottentots and Caffres, from the Year 1772 to 1776.*

Sparrman dedicated the book to Gustaf III: 'Returned to the shelter of these felicitous shores, where our Sovereign's wise provision, under the torch of the Sciences and the Arts, guides present and future generations to further refinement and well-being, I cannot but look back with horror and pity at the eternal ice of the Antarctic regions, and at the darkness and desolation which I also found shared by the other four parts of the world.'

In a Foreword he craved his readers' indulgence. 'My style is sometimes so unhappy in point of expression that I have frequently been displeased with it myself. All my writing for these many years past has consisted chiefly in short notes and memorandums, expressed sometimes in one language and sometimes in another, and sometimes in many languages blended together. From one, whom a restless spirit of curiosity has enticed from his native country, to follow the calls of destiny all round the globe, and more particularly through the land of the Hottentots and the wild and desert regions of Africa, from such a man accounts are expected of a most entertaining and wonderful import.'

He apologized for other imperfections and ascribed them to

having travelled without funds and without further support. 'The whole of the sum that I took out with me to bear my travelling expenses was about twenty-five rix-dollars, and what, by dint of economy, I had made myself master of by the time I got home, amounted to somewhat more than double that sum. Thus so far was I from being able to purchase collections, or to obtain at my ease, and with money only, opportunities of enlarging the sphere of my knowledge, that I even could not possibly arrive at them without great trouble and danger. In this case, I have been obliged to content myself with what fortune has thrown in my way, as I may say, gratis.'

A Voyage to the Cape of Good Hope was published in German translation and with a foreword by George Forster the very next year. Anders sent Forster, who had begun to experiment with inventions, a report of an aerostatic globe made of white taffeta with blue borders embellished with gold stars. It was sent floating up into the air, and from it was suspended a basket on which were painted a sun and flying dragons. In the basket was the Academy of Sciences' cat, which ran off when the balloon landed on the island of Värmdö in the Stockholm archipelago. Anyone finding the cat was requested to return it to the Academy office for a handsome reward.

On Sparrman's first voyage to the Cape, when he was still a youth, Captain Ekeberg had asked him how he would describe himself. He had replied: not easily offended, cheerful, frank and truth-loving, carefree and sympathetic. But, in fact, those were the very qualities he in some degree lacked and hardly dared attribute to himself. Nevertheless, if any of those epithets were to adorn his gravestone, he would be content. He was not to know that he was to have neither stone nor inscription.

His life had proved to be enigmatic and occasionally beautiful. But much of it had been an emigration, an escape – from childhood, from his studies, from parents and teachers. He recalled certain images: his mother suddenly in the grip of deepest depression and slashing her wrist with a sharp piece of glass, the blood gushing out – just an accident, she had assured them. A sign that all was not well.

He had seen the manifold variety of the Earth, and yet only a small part of it. His brain was on fire from having seen so much more than the majority of people, and yet he was aware that he had missed the most remarkable things that his successors would find and study. He had collected specimens in order to make further scientific advances, not to rest on his laurels, and certainly not to put on a show of his finds for the uneducated. And although he was a collector, he did not know how to collect himself. The natural scientist was more apprehensive when it came to digging in the soil of his own psyche.

Over the years, however, he often wondered about magnetic fields and the nervous systems that ran through and between human beings, connecting them with all organic matter, with everything that grew, rotted, infected, and with the invisible attributes which expressed themselves in anxiety and pessimism, in joint pain and heavy muscles.

In a clouded mirror he saw a pale, ghostly creature with scrawny arms and narrow chest. He wanted to unearth a different person from his inner strata, a sparkling, capering man about town. But he had slipped on many a deck, and one ankle had never fully mended.

He changed his quill pen for another and wrote in minuscule to save paper. He stared at his bloodless, white fingers and felt a lump of despair in his throat. Then, all of a sudden, he could smell quite clearly the scent of the grass around the well at the rectory in Tensta, luxuriant from spilt water.

He remained there at his desk with its inkwell and sandbox, holding his quill, as if sitting for a portrait painter hidden behind a screen. He was wearing a newly starched shirt and pearl-grey stockings with black shoes. The dry, chalky summer air had been drained of its heat and for a moment he felt some solace. The breeze was finding its way in between the rattling windowpanes.

Very soon autumn had arrived. The hovels were damp again; stinging nettles had grown tall around the privy. Signs displaying angels, suns or bunches of grapes announced the presence of taverns. He went into one for a bowl of bean soup thickened with cream and oil, with bread to dunk.

In the evening – when the moon rose in a blood-red sky and the early stars glittered like silver thimbles – he would visit his nephews and nieces on Södermalm and tell them tales of Africa.

8

To George Forster, 1783:

I am writing this as I sit beneath a portrait of Linnaeus, at a pine table inlaid with a panel of slate. The door to the Cabinet is open, though a sensible man would have cause to bolt the door from the inside against supplicants and informers who come powdered and perfumed with rose-water to bring gossip and slander. It is at this table that I received – and am now answering – your cry for help from the depths of your soul:

'How weak and wretched is man! The vices of lust drive all that is good out of the body. Is this the century of enlightenment? Goethe was 35 before he saw a woman naked, in Geneva. I am nearly thirty . . .'

Unlike me, you were not tutored by Linnaeus, who spoke more often of the lusts of the senses than of the weakness of the flesh. You write that every friendship and love humiliates you. Your sister has encouraged you to believe that powerful emotions don't become the tender fabric of the female soul and body. I rather doubt whether she – or indeed you or I – really knows anything about it.

I myself feel kinship with very few, but that lack gives me all the more opportunity to discover a wider world. I am no longer a circumnavigator. I am content to reinvigorate my life with summer walks, when I descend from my pedagogical tower and enjoy more limited pleasures. I don't wish to feel dependent and servile. I breathe most freely in the shade that private life affords.

I can perceive all too clearly the baseness of others, which is the common ground of their kind of friendship. A young man whose scholarship I admired accuses me of inadequate knowledge, then goes on with shameful pretension to promote himself by taking on burdens that did not previously exist, and lying and flattering his way to advantages disguised as obligations, while, in his exquis-itely refined conversation, persuading the like-minded that deceit is irony and infamy merely the jocularity of the *beau monde*.

They make wild judgements about incidents in my personal life, then they concoct defamations about my public life which I parry with derision and composure. For if I let these tyrannical pedants have their way, they will push me into a corner, and force me to witness their triumphant public display of the sum of their barbaric ignorance.

Is there any element of high-mindedness, open-heartedness or nobility among these so-called wits? They cloak injustice in bom-bast. They find amusement in any peccadillo, but close their eyes to every achievement, even the most modest. They trot around on their high heels, and think themselves lofty intellectuals and scin-tillating geniuses. But they are mere gadflies, whose buzzing ceases by the day's end.

Quensel – let me name the man – has complained that I left my hat on the desk as a fraudulent indication of my presence while I took a stroll along Munkbron. He has made it clear that what I would be best at, in his opinion, is carrying a bucket of water from the well at Järntorget. So who am I? An unmarried academic who has ridden hundreds of miles through Cape Colony, and has been all too long poring over drawers of insects.

When did I last derive any joy from serving my country? History leaves misleading trails to lure us to a different scene of action, where we raise monuments to those to whom we owe no gratitude. Yet I have adapted myself to the state of the nation, to its colonists' worthlessness and stupidity. I have no demonic urge to court misfortune, but neither do I harbour any desire to be insulted by pettiness, gain favours under false pretences, or seek reconciliation merely for the sake of appearances.

Africa was not easy to understand, nor would it be easy to live with in the long term. But ever since I left, I have felt as if I were being swept along by the current, helpless, indecisive, not knowing whither I am bound.

We are borne along by time. Time acts for us and against us, simultaneously, like the ebb and flow of the same body of water.

Oh, you who followed your father along the Volga when you were only ten years old, and out on to the Kirghiz Steppe; you who at thirteen translated a travel account from Russian to English; you who learned the Polynesian tongues faster than any of us, and so never regarded any creature as a barbarian; you who found human beings of more interest than flora and fauna, and who, when it came to excesses in Tahiti, saw that the same instincts rule everywhere in this world, and that the costumes of different peoples are mere externals; you who now, at twenty-five, with your book of our expedition, have introduced a new epoch in the history of travel writing – how I miss our conversations, how I miss a confidant, whose ear is attuned to the stories throbbing within me that so seldom find an outlet!

Chance or fate brought us together. Was it compulsion that separated us? The world disgusted us, you and me, for several years at sea, when we listened to the growl and thunder of the icebergs and could take nought for granted. Neither life nor death could dazzle us then. Fare thee well, my dearest friend!

9

As the day draws to a close, on the 27th of May 1786, I must note down what has been diverting our city for the last twenty-four hours – it will be like getting my eyes in training again for the expedition I might undertake to the Slave Coast of Africa next year.

Ten degrees, sporadic hailstorms. Ships departing from Skeppsbron to Rotterdam, Dublin, Lisbon and Bordeaux. A score of travellers have been registered with the police: mining engineers, lieutenants, merchants. A smallpox vaccination clinic for the children of the poor has been opened in the house of Hesse, the brewer, in Maria Brunns Alley. The chattels of a retired Major of Dragoons went under the hammer in the tavern on Liljeholmen, and a consignment of Moselle wine, a single-seat sprung carriage decorated with swans' necks, and some newly invented electrical instruments were disposed of in the Castenhof. Nordström's bookshop on Riddarhustorg has a dissertation on the advantages of mothers suckling their infants at their own breast.

Ladies lacking carriage, servant and fine clothes complain in the newspapers that they are deprived of the right not to be molested. 'We hardly dare go out even at noon. Men take liberties with us, as if we were notorious for the most immoral way of life.'

A steady youth who is familiar with Italian bookkeeping,

French and Dutch, writes well and has good character references, is taken on by one of the shops, to wit, Holmberg's bookshop. A doctor from Stralsund is advertising in *Dagligt Allehanda* to increase women's fertility with alkaline water and saltpetre-rich air, and argues the case for Jews and Geats being the same people. Other newspapers print reports from Constantinople, Algiers and starving Finland.

The costermonger's stall by the Opera is selling Lübeck smoked goose, and the Dragon on Slottsbacken has Winbär's, Spanish, bitter and English beer. Reported lost or stolen: one gold-topped rattan cane, one pair of goatskin breeches and one white apron – all lost near Karlbergs Gate. A hen has got loose from Number 60 Drottninggatan and is being sought among the cooking pots on Norrmalm.

A comedy, *The Soothsayer*, is playing at the Opera. His Majesty is holding court at seven o'clock in the evening, followed by a public banquet. Our worthy Finance Minister complains about the extravagance: 'We are situated in a backwater of Europe,' he says, 'and yet in this little corner we have the grandest pretensions and the most frivolous tastes for changing fashions in dress, furnishings and all that pertains to the pleasures of life.'

Likewise, he has warned of the intrigues of the Russian minister, Markov, who has been offering hospitality to the nobility during the entire year of this parliament. Paykull, Gyllensvan and Gedda were reported as having received their letters of invitation from a footman wearing an old grey cloak over his uniform and a remarkable wide-brimmed slouch-hat pulled down low over his forehead. Karl Fredrik Reddevig, violinist in the Royal Opera House orchestra, has been named as Markov's spy.

I have been invited to a meeting of the Harmonious Society in the Rosenadler House. It has been set up by Baron Carl Göran Silfverhielm to promote animal magnetism. The Baron, a relation of Swedenborg, has attended Anton Mesmer's seances in Paris and learned the theory, and possibly practice, of somnambulism. Despite my interest in the subject, I refuse to associate with the modish ladies, officials, diplomats and self-exalted doctors who now flock to Mynttorget. I went there and paid a visit to Joseph Mazza's trinket shop instead, where he sold me a barometer.

10

To George Forster, 1787:

I was pleased to have tidings of your 33rd birthday in Göttingen. I received them shortly before my departure to France and the Slave Coast of Africa – on business dear to both our hearts, but which must remain secret for a while yet.

You have suffered injustices which have brought about a cooling of your ardour. I recognize myself in your situation. We seem all too often to fall into the hands of teachers of false doctrines, tricksters and malcontents. But you must not let it prey on your mind that your South Sea voyage on behalf of the Empress of Russia had to give way to her Turkish campaign.

I'm very grateful for your volume on Captain Cook. Even here in Sweden it has been described as a high point in German prose. I am amused that some idealist has proposed you to be ruler of a colony of German writers on a South Sea island! Of course, people have no inclination to read about feelings and morality, but rather about savages and animals, with a little about wind and weather. Those days on board when neither anchorage nor landing united us with others, and when we were compelled to live in close proximity, like the most deprived of workers, are not so interesting for them.

I am sorry you had to sell your exotic rarities to discharge your family's debts. I was rather surprised to hear you had allied yourself to the occultism of the Rosicrucian Order in Kassel, even though I have been drawn to such phenomena myself. Perhaps you were tempted by the alchemy, but your friend and neighbour Georg Christoph Lichtenberg has long warned you about these lavish experiments. I am glad you have now broken free of your alchemical captivation. Though I am aware that the unknown can frequently appear to bear the stamp of reality.

I congratulate you on your liberation from a different captivity: your six years as professor in Vilnius, Poland, where you seem to have survived the brutality, luxury and despotism you encountered. I would like to hear more about the visit to Kassel by Sir William Hamilton from Naples and his wife Emma. I know your prince has assembled some numbers of African elephants and pygmies, the latter not capable of withstanding our climate, yet on dissection found to be identical to Europeans.

Your father has translated both Pehr Osbeck and Carl Gustav Ekeberg, in very quick succession. And you are corresponding with Herder and Humboldt, and with Goethe, whom you have found less pious than reputed. I have neglected to cultivate the great and the good of my time, and am vexed with myself for not having brought on a successor, as Thunberg has. I have not fulfilled the task Linnaeus set me.

An adventure acquires its meaning when it is followed by another. And every piece of knowledge which does not lead to new questions, dies out. I am aware that I am no longer in demand. There are murmurings behind my back that I am treating my memoirs the way one prunes old fruit trees. Maybe so. Trees recover, bear sporadic fruit – that is all.

I am re-reading my notes on ravens and spotted woodpeckers, the crafty bee-eaters and other impostors of the natural world. To what purpose? Are my notebooks worth more than the Inquisition's rightly forgotten lists of the victims of false accusations and their howls of protest? Beneath my observations lies a sediment of time ebbing away.

My challenge has been to rein in a restive heart. I have had enough of dissembling and frivolity.

I have been carrying your letter around in my breast pocket for a long while now. It's noticeable that we have grown older and begun to speak with pauses between our words. But let that not make you forget to address yourself again at some point to him who remains ever your most faithful friend, Anders Sparrman.

Summer Days at Mälby

1

Gustaf von Carlson, five years older than Sparrman, was the nation's Receiver of Bribes. In formal terms he was Permanent Secretary at the War Office and President of the Court of Appeal. According to one highly placed colleague, he never considered a promotion without demanding a thousand *daler*. He had made the selling or barter of official posts his principal occupation. All positions could be bought and sold, not least the clergy. He took two hundred *riksdaler* from every regiment to keep their affairs off the record. He invited people whom he particularly liked to his estate at Mälby, near Gnesta in the province of Södermanland. In the summer they constituted quite a little court.

The *Swedish Biographical Dictionary* was later to describe Gustaf von Carlson, Gustaf Philip Creutz and Johan Gabriel Oxenstierna as a triumvirate of 'tea-party companions' with mystical and artistic interests and a jargon unintelligible to outsiders. Von Carlson's wealth allowed him to create a haven for an aesthetically refined life of leisure based on a cult of friendship and subjective appreciation of Nature. From a garden in the French style, adjoining the Italianate mansion, one could walk out into the wilds of an English park, where the winding paths allowed the beauty of lake shore and undulating terrain to be seen at its best. Thus the *Biographical Dictionary*.

For von Carlson the park was a philosophical concept, with

fresh vistas and unexpected twists and turns giving both poetic variety and examples of Nature's own unmistakeable idiom. It provided the setting for open-air theatre, with changes of scene according to mood.

Von Carlson's principal interest was ornithology. He had constructed an aviary for wild birds on an island in the lake, and in a building which stood apart from the house he kept an invaluable collection of stuffed birds from all over the world. Many of these had been entrusted to him by the Academy of Sciences before Sparrman's voyage to Africa in 1787. Von Carlson had commissioned coloured illustrations of the rarer specimens and these adorned the walls of an entire room.

The first hundred of them were published (at von Carlson's expense) under the title *Museum Carlsonianum*, with descriptive text by Anders Sparrman and illustrations by Jonas Carl Linnerhielm, in four instalments, 1786–9. The work was never completed. Sparrman's text breaks off in the middle of the description of a golden oriole.

In his second volume of prints, *Swedish Ornithology* (1806–16), in eleven parts with sixty-eight hand-coloured plates, Anders Sparrman described a black coot as an entirely new species. In fact, the stuffed specimen was a decorative bird assembled as a joke for von Carlson's Christmas table: a black coot to which the taxidermist had attached the wings of a ptarmigan.

It marked the end of Sparrman's career as an ornithologist.

The neoclassical architect Carl August Ehrensvärd had sketched for von Carlson a Lapp tent, a cairn of rune stones and a gigantic truncated pillar, but these were rejected. Nevertheless, his full-scale wooden replica of the Temple of Hephaistos in Athens was constructed at Mälby. It was thirty-three metres long, and filled with statues and plaster busts modelled on classical originals which Ehrensvärd had brought back from Italy and sold to von Carlson. Ehrensvärd prided himself on its being the first complete reconstruction of a classical temple in Europe, each of its long sides adorned with thirteen Doric columns. But this replica temple was not built for the snowy north and fell into decay, the architect lamenting that Sweden had only 'newspaper-men, apothecaries and privy councillors: the cold does them no harm, and they are the only superfluity of which we can boast'.

Johan Gabriel Oxenstierna dedicated his great poem *The Harvests* to von Carlson. When the winter snow was suitable for travelling, Oxenstierna tempted von Carlson to Stockholm in their own bird-language. 'Beloved Crow! Come and peck at the hempseed of friendship in the cage of my breast! The beat of your wings echoes in my heart the moment you fly over Liljeholmen Gate.' The letter was signed 'Magpie'.

'The air was redolent with the mingled fragrance of mown meadows, drying hay and blossoming lime trees,' Oxenstierna wrote from his friend's estate at Mälby. 'The full moon shone through the still leaves, unruffled by any breeze. The delicate blend of warmth and coolness enhanced the sensual pleasure of existence. A delicious repose reigned over all, seemingly constituted to soothe all the troubles of the mind. I found it bliss to be alive, and was for a moment perfectly happy just to be in that state, surrounded by an air as mild as Paradise, a sky as clear as wisdom, and a lake as tranquil as an innocent heart.'

The separate building housed nearly a thousand birds in eight hundred and forty-four glass-fronted cases standing floor to ceiling with one or two birds in each, so tight together that they covered every inch of wall. There were two grey-painted tables, four basket chairs and five metal lamp-brackets. Anders Sparrman spent many weeks there over several summers, drawing and describing.

It was difficult to get good originals for the illustrations. He reproduced twelve species from New Zealand and the Society Islands. Some of the specimens in the Cabinet of Natural History were 'so badly stuffed that I cannot conceive the natural form – a heap of moth-eaten feathers profits me little'.

Sparrman's sentimental, romantic language was not to the taste of the objective, factual Linnaeans. He described migratory flocks landing in the tops of oaks or cedars and being reunited with exultant melody in praise of both their own lovemaking and 'an omnipotent and all-embracing Supreme Love'.

2

On good days at Mälby I read Abraham Hülphers on Eric and Valdemar, the sons of Magnus Ladulås, who were starved to death in Nyköping Castle. I hear my friends' amiable merrymaking. The garden paths have been raked, the butter churned, stockings darned by the kitchen-maid.

There is never any lack of beverages, music and festive lighting at Mälby. Dutch herring, crayfish pies and almond cake, glazed sweetmeats, punch and tea, saffron buns, baskets of confectionery are always on offer. Honey flows freely from straining-bags. Freshly brewed mead is on tap from the cask.

We drove in a closed carriage, new-painted with von Carlson's monogram, behind two chestnut Öland horses. We took cold ham, brawn, bread pudding, aquavit, Rhine wine and coffee. The cool of the morning dissipated, a brief shower laid the dust on the road, and we returned in an open carriage and gave our swift, but now wearied, horses their evening reward of bread.

What joyous revels! What delightful lack of restraint I met with! Gustaf von Carlson, in garb as green as one of his own copses, as ruddy-cheeked as his rose hedge, was ready for an evening snack and drink. So we were sent out to pick some jugs of gooseberries, which we ate with sweet wine. We settled down companionably. The clouds had dispersed and the evening sky was an unusual soft green, like the young leaves of the linden trees. The hills were covered with oak, aspen and thick hazel, with meandering paths and shady arbours out of reach of the sun.

We talked of our ancestors who were brought back to life in our veins, and of the unknown or inexplicable causes of human behaviour. About the number of wretched and pitiful creatures who live out their existence beneath the song of the nightingale. Like a wick that cannot stand upright in its wax, people enter our lives, cast their radiance upon us, then fade away into darkness.

We did not shirk from touching on the most sensitive questions. Ehrensvärd and von Carlson were both shareholders in the West India Company. From the matter of the trade winds obliging Swedish frigates to waste so much time beating to windward to reach Saint Barthélemy, we moved on to the proposal that none but the inhabitants of that island should be able to participate in the slave trade. Von Carlson was behind the royal decree that had been communicated to the Governor of our newly acquired island, which declared the slave trade 'a necessary factor in the island's cultivation and the extension of the plantations'.

I retorted disputatiously that I was reliably informed that Swedish brigs and schooners brought hundreds of slaves purchased in Angola and Senegal to the island. They were sold on the slave market in Gustavia, and transported to other islands after the Swedes had exacted customs duties and import taxes. Some were set free if they had comported themselves satisfactorily, but were impaled on a stake if they tried to escape or took up arms.

When it comes to trade in human beings, I am unyielding. Can we not understand that others yearn for freedom just as we do? I reminded my companions of the veils of mists that clouded our sympathy, especially at a distance that ought to give us clear vision. The light that our Creator invested in us ought to enable us to imagine those living in far-off lands, above whom the same birds sing as for us. How would we like to see our own whitened skeletons entwined in rapacious roots far away from our native soil?

We calmed down afterwards, brought out chess boards and flutes.

One evening we went out on the lake spearing fish, and caught a few pike. We cast nets and took a hundred or so bream and perch. The reeds parted for the boat and immediately closed again behind us, as if we had never passed through.

The corn was gathered in. The tobacco harvesting was rounded off with brandy and pastries for the farmhands, and speeches from von Carlson and Mr Isberg, the steward. Oxenstierna played the flute. Away from the trifling pursuits of vanity, I experienced it as wholesome entertainment, a satisfying feast for the senses.

The shadows of the trees lengthen in the setting sun. A crash in the old elms and the pigeons fly up in alarm. The rain fumbles and whispers in the fading briars. A peasant woman with a feverish countenance requested help for her daughter, and I as a physician was constrained to hasten to her and administer whatever I had with me: a decoction of peppermint and mallow root, which sent her into a restorative sleep.

An aroma of manure and fermentation rises from the damp night fields. We have partaken of soup, discussed agricultural reforms, and gossiped about married men who have got their maid-servants with child and set them up in a cottage nearby.

The landscape here is like the stage of a theatre, with the birds as a backdrop. The ruin that has never been anything but a ruin, demonstrates the passage of time. Von Carlson is enchanted with the production and the stage properties. The very skies above his estate seem to have been applied with paint, in broad strokes of pink, blue and ash-grey wash. The crofter's fishing rod is as slender as if done in pencil, and the swallows are mere dots against the clouds. The hills roll away to the horizon as on a tapestry, topped with some delicately silhouetted mill vanes. Even the dark narrow passages and the barred windows of the cellars look as if they are specially designed to lend interest to the scene. But no trapdoors, thank goodness, only a sequence of tableaux and a controlled voluptuousness at just the right remove from the burdens of office.

His joy in this theatre of perfection deserts Gustaf the minute he returns to Stockholm. There he feigns a distracted deafness, which is calculating, exacting and merciless. His eyes are cold. He can be insulting beyond the bounds of social acceptability, but more often than not displays the coolness of a lawyer in his demands for concessions and covert gifts.

In the country he walks with long strides, whistling popular songs, and is full of rousing energy. He loves his collection of birds in all their splendour, and bewails the fact that neither he nor others can keep them free of dust and insects. His impassive report on the affairs of state takes on a different tone when he comes to Ehrensvärd's attempt to create a fragment of Ancient Greece in the heart of Södermanland.

How much we are all in accord that the park and lakes at Mälby inspire a sharpness and agility of thought, a gaiety of soul and a natural quality of friendship!

3

I have been given quarters in one of the wings, on the first floor, in a room starkly silent and so unreal in its snowy whiteness that it seems to portend a world doomed to self-destruction. I generally keep myself to myself, with my writing, with my rule and compasses, eyeball to eyeball with a bloodshot staring eagle owl, which I am drawing life-sized.

How often our host and his guests sit in dreamy reflection, undisturbed by one another, over a pipe and a Seltzer water; some candid, others more cautious when they converse. Here at Mälby they are not scheming, not subservient; they are congenial without resort to hypocrisy. Even in tranquillity they are models of elegance and truth – not an easy combination.

Yet I shall never entirely understand Gustaf von Carlson. Externally, with becoming modesty, dressed in the shabbiest brown frock coat or simply an open white shirt. A friendly countenance masking a thirst for power. His real character, to me, an almost unexplored, deepest Africa.

For my friends, if not for me, writing is a way of being, a personal expression, and nothing to joke about. They often hide their pen and paper, and look for hidden patterns in everything. Yet they won't hesitate to complete a poem in a moment of ecstasy, even though our host may have already summoned us to a carriage ride, or a woodcock hunt, or to dinner.

Ehrensvärd is the worst behaved, and the most talented. He would bankrupt himself for a well-aimed epigram, and he says things that are enough to spoil a man's sleep. His interjections are like flashes of lightning, and strike a spark in all of us. He is a lovable rogue. He is not tempted by conciliation or compromise. He searches for the exposed nerve in himself and others, and regards us with a look that probes to the very depths. His pen is constantly scratching away, his writing materials always to hand, and then there one is, committed to paper and unrecognizable only in one's own eyes. For him there is no such concept as the creative struggle; he is close to the beatific fount of fluency.

Oxenstierna is charmingly carefree, not beguiled by the fineries of the world, and prefers to curl up in front of the stove. In Stockholm, in his opinion, we lead spectral lives, behind blank windows which don't exist at all within the house, though from without they appear to conceal secret rooms. It is a life which is not a genuine life – just as blank windows screen a view which once existed and could have afforded us pleasure.

He is quiet and unassuming, and approves the ideas of his friends. He is at repose in his lyrical recollections, circling a few memories like swifts round a tower, finding tranquillity there. He somehow embodies a hint of transience and the most cursory reflection of eternity.

Although liberally endowed with titles, he is financially hopeless and administratively inept. He despises the intrigues of the Court and the affectation he is forced to be part of. He is much more at home with Hesiod and Virgil, and happiest with games and theatre. At Mälby he is the aspen leaf that trembles at the slightest breath of sensibility. The Skenäs estate of his youth is some miles west, and for this gentle and dreamy spirit, von Carlson's Mälby has become Arcadia.

Creutz, whom I have only glimpsed here occasionally, has a musical nature. How enigmatically he eavesdrops on the score of others' conversations! His poetic skills were fully developed even before his body, and the purest harmonies are still present in the old man. Although he is a poet, his guiding principle is order, and subordination for him, as for Ehrensvärd, is an alien concept.

A morning glow of clarity suffuses his features, unblurred by his later renown. His patience is tried only by the hesitant and imprecise. He is a statesman, completely unselfconscious, but has avoided the temptation to make everyday life uniform and rigid. Although his wings could have carried him further than they have, he is still borne up by purity and strength.

There is nothing spartan or fettered about either of them, nor overburdened. They themselves hold back, in order to give the fullest freedom to Nature, myth and music. But they don't seek the lonely summits.

They have my admiration. In their presence I appear weak-willed, trapped in childlike wonder and a flickering candle of memories. They laugh uproariously. They play like demons, and if they fall off their horses, it happens where the verge is in the softest bloom, whereas fate tips me into a ditch full of water. Perhaps the difference is mainly that they have resources wanting in me; they have the means to live a life quite unlike mine. Seldom does it induce melancholy in me, since I have my own self-respect, but there have been times when I would gladly have changed places with them.

It's rarely a consolation to know that death comes to us all. Along with the bee and the noctuid, we are heading towards decomposition and oblivion. If only we learned the precious gift of appreciation while we can still see and breathe, rather than acquiring it as a belated reward at the moment when, helpless or in anguish, we are finally eliminated.

But if we are absorbed into some greater entity, it may be in company with the swift and the petrel. And perhaps the scent of autumn apples and fire in the dry grass will follow us to the end.

4

When Gustav von Carlson died in 1801 he was revealed to be deeply in debt and the estate was declared bankrupt. The bird collection was valued at a thousand *riksdaler*, the price of a hundred bulls in good condition. The courts awarded the Academy of Sciences (where Conrad Quensel had succeeded Sparrman) the return of the birds they had deposited with him. Von Carlson's personal collection went to auction: a hundred birds were purchased by the Academy, one hundred and eighty-five by Carl Peter Thunberg in Uppsala, and the remainder by Gustaf von Paykull and Adolf Grill for their private museums. In 1830 all the birds were reunited in the new Natural History Museum in Stockholm.

Gustaf von Carlson was buried in Solna churchyard in Stockholm, and was transferred some years later to the park at Mälby – in accordance with his will, which had only then come to light. Johan Gabriel Oxenstierna was present and wrote to his wife of his irreparable loss: 'At the tidings of his death my soul felt eighty years old.'

Gold and Slaves

1

August Nordenskjöld's interests – apart from Swedenborg and Africa – lay in mineralogy. He wrote his dissertation on the qualities of tin. Born in Finland, he was also an alchemist, obsessed by the determination to produce gold from base metals in such quantities as to render it worthless, and thus bring down the monetary system.

He summarized his findings in 1787 in a treatise on 'the only true alchemical process'. He ended it, confident of success, 'Off you go, little paper, around the world, and destroy the tyranny of money, so that gold, silver and precious stones shall once for all cease to be the idols and tyrants of the world!'

The alchemical production of gold for Gustav III of Sweden was carried out at Drottningholm Palace near Stockholm – in a laboratory 'in the forest, miles from anywhere. We are not allowed out of the grounds, but are immured like nuns.' In his contract Nordenskjöld undertook 'on the holiest and sincerest oath and in breach thereof subject to eternal damnation' to hand over his manuscripts on completion of the work, not to reveal his methods and not to leave the workshop except in the evenings, 'dressed in peasant clothes with hair hanging loose and a long beard'.

This dreamer at the alchemical furnace believed in a loving Providence and was certain of his calling. He went by the name of Granberg the Enameller. Should his experiments prove successful, the king had promised to set up hospitals, grain stores and warehouses and generally to help improve the economy of Finland. As soon as Nordenskjöld had produced the *Lapis philosophorum*, he had permission to 'travel from his place of work direct to Africa, there to spend his days in the service of His Royal Majesty and the Swedish Crown'.

August Nordenskjöld's brother Ulrik had published a dissertation some years earlier about Sweden's potential benefits from the Gold Coast, where the sand was so rich that when it was strewn over the floor of a European's house 'a negress can sometimes wash out gold dust worth 1 to 1½ *riksdaler* a day'.

This dissertation persuaded Gustav III to authorize forty families to emigrate to West Africa with the right to organize their own administration, enact their own laws and create a society independent of both Europe and Sweden.

The project never came to fruition.

But in 1787 the king financed a covert reconnaissance expedition to that region of Africa. Nordenskjöld was not permitted to join it, because of his alchemical responsibilities. The members of the expedition were Anders Sparrman, Carl Bernhard Wadström and Carl Axel Arrhenius.

Officially, Sparrman was granted leave of absence from the Academy of Sciences to take the waters at an unspecified location.

Arrhenius was a chemist and mineralogist who, during his period of service with the Vaxholm garrison, had found a heavy black stone in Ytterby feldspar mine on the island of Resarön, containing the mineral named yttrium. A greater number of basic elements were found in that mine than anywhere else in the world.

Wadström, who described himself as a mechanic and humanitarian, was a scientist and philanthropist. In the portrait of him by Carl Fredric von Breda he is wearing an open-necked white shirt with an untied ruff and striped silk waistcoat. He is teaching an African boy, a map of Africa spread out over the table under a book by Emanuel Swedenborg. In the background is a thatched hut in the shade of a palm tree. The youth is a slave whose freedom Wadström has purchased, the son of a chieftain on the peninsula where Monrovia, the capital of Liberia, stands today.

The three friends met in Copenhagen and travelled to Paris, where the ambassador's wife, Madame de Staël, displayed her sparkling wit and boundless ambition. 'She will certainly make her mark as an author one day, and so ensure her immortality.'

The Swedish Consul in Le Havre, Jacques Chauvel, a ship's chandler by profession, arranged berths for them on a French vessel 'adapted for the transportation of negroes' and destined for Senegal.

The Swedish state had long coveted a part-ownership of the French mines in Senegal. A colony in West Africa would have the added advantage of completing a triangular route with Saint Barthélemy and Sweden. The Swedish West India Company shipped several thousand slaves from Africa to the slave markets on Saint Barthélemy and sent them on at prices beneficial to Swedish merchants.

From the island of Goree off Dakar, Sparrman and Wadström undertook expeditions south along the coast. Anders wrote of monitoring the king's pulse in Jaol and prescribing a medicine for 'His Majesty's brandy-corroded gut; and may I never see a more absolute monarch, for he can sell even his own children and prime minister.' The scientific findings were slim. Sparrman's sole publication on West Africa was an article on a new bird species from Sierra Leone: *Bucco atroflavus*.

As Sparrman was a physician, with the rank of professor, he was taken to visit the sick. The white crew members were dying of malaria, the origin of which no-one understood. Another prevalent malady was caused by the Guinea worm, which entered the intestines and emerged from muscles, toes and testicles. The average length of the worms was eighteen inches, which could be pulled out half an inch a day. The patients were bled, bathed in stagnant pools, given a nutritious snail soup to drink and developed eye infections from lack of hygiene. Rose water and lavender alleviated the stench that by all accounts even caused silver cutlery to tarnish.

The officers were insistent on keeping their tricorn hats, gold epaulettes and ceremonial swords, but the intensity of the tropical heat was doubled by the clothes they wore, and many drowned in their heavy uniforms when they were rowed through the surf to their ship. The living appropriated the trousers, nightcaps and shoes of the dead.

While Sparrman never wrote a proper report, Wadström published his *Observations on the Slave Trade, and a Description of some Part of the Coast of Guinea* in 1789, followed by *An Essay on Colonization*, in the hope of advancing a project which would offer employment rather than slavery to the Africans. Free trade, tolerance and inventiveness would advance understanding between peoples. Wadström was surprised that the fertile soil of Africa had not attracted Europeans other than slave traders.

He described the slaves of the interior screaming in terror when they saw the sea for the first time, believing the breaking surf to be fearsome beasts and in their frenzy preferring the hippopotamus-hide whip. Transportation into the unknown led to attempts to choke themselves on their chains, and, although the whip drove them out to the canoes, they prostrated themselves on the beach and clung to the soil of Africa to the very last.

When they were flogged to test their lungs, Sparrman could hear them howling to show they were in good health and so avoid being thrown to the sharks. They were made to lift weights to prove the strength that would condemn them to life imprisonment rather than death. Children were wrenched from their mothers' backs and tossed into the breakers, because they would have taken up too much room in the hold. Three years after landing, a third of the Africans on the sugar plantations had perished from disease, ill-treatment or grief. The Caribbean was a slaughterhouse.

Before transportation across the ocean, both the men and the women had their heads shaved and their bodies rubbed down with palm oil, so that buyers would find it more difficult to judge their age. Any who looked over thirty-five were rejected. As soon as a price was agreed they were branded, so that the white man could distinguish between them.

When the slaves were lined up naked on deck, the sailors ripped off any rings or adornments and hurled them into the water. They wore fetishes – a parrot's beak, a crocodile's tooth – to make them invisible to lions or to protect them from evil spirits. But nothing in the world was effective against the white man. They had been separated from their families, from their homeland and its gods. They lay more tightly packed than corpses in a coffin, fifteen inches being allowed for men, twelve inches for women. Every morning the living would be found lying next to the dead.

The ships left the coast of Africa at night while the slaves were asleep, so that they would not see the palm trees and the beach for the last time and try to take their own lives in despair. The sharks followed the ships for thousands of miles. Gonorrhea soon spread among the shackled, causing blindness. When one of the vessels reached Guadeloupe, everyone on board was blind, the crew as well as the slaves, all except the helmsman.

Mental illness – depression and apathy – was common among the first generation of slaves who had known only the security of their African villages. Their actions became more and more mechanical, their eyes increasingly empty, until they simply lay down and died.

2

Sparrman, Wadström and Arrhenius sailed to the Portuguese trading post of Ziguinchor, using it as a base in their search for a suitable location for a Swedish colony. The three Swedes undertook a boat journey up the Casamance River, with an African guide and eight sailors. They met an armed sloop, from which they could hear cries of distress from shackled victims. Wadström wanted to attack it, but the others advised against it: they were at a considerable disadvantage.

They soon caught sight of another vessel, and hid in the undergrowth by the bank. Sparrman stayed in the boat, Wadström and Arrhenius crept forward, with an interpreter and four oarsmen. They heard the laments of young voices. Parents were being abducted before the very eyes of their children, explained the interpreter.

According to A. W. Möller's *The Life of Carl Bernhard Wadström* (1862), Wadström pulled his pistol from his belt and yelled, 'To their aid, though there be thousands against us!'

'In front of a native hut a crowd of armed negroes encircled a smaller group, shouting and gesticulating wildly. One negro, his hands tied behind his back, probably the father of the family, was being whipped and hauled away, struggling in vain to break loose and help his people. The mother, a well-built young woman, stood surrounded by three boys, trying to clasp the whimpering children in her arms to say goodbye. The youngest was clinging to her legs, the other two, with pleas and looks that would have moved stones, suffering incessant lashes from their assailants, had their arms round their mother's neck.

'Wadström fired his pistol and shouted in Swedish, "Let him go, you brute!"

'Sparrman and the sailors then appeared on the scene and the kidnappers took flight. The liberated family embraced one another in tears and begged to be slaves to the Swedes. Great was their elation when Wadström gave them to understand that they were welcome to join them, but as equals, as friends and brothers.'

After a hundred years of the slave trade, Sparrman realized, the slave routes had penetrated further and further into the area of Africa where Swedenborg had postulated the lost Garden of Eden. Powerful chieftains were tempted by the wares the whites had to offer, and in exchange bartered slaves of their own and other tribes. And the more cruelly they treated their own, the more excuse there was for the Europeans to venture implacably on.

Sparrman watched the buyers inspecting the newly arrived slaves, drawing back the boys' foreskins and parting the girls' labia to look for signs of venereal disease, amid enough ribald laughter and provocative comments to rival a horse auction. Below the office, where Arab merchants conducted business with European shippers, was the weighing room, where the men's muscles were examined and the women's breasts and thighs measured. The male slaves were fed so as to weigh ideally 11¾ stone. Any who fell sick were taken down a corridor that led to a gate over the sea. Any who voiced objection were likely to have their lips sealed with a safety pin.

In contrast to the Cape, the Equatorial belt had a suffocating atmosphere, as heavy as an animal's breath and saturated with pestilential vapours. The aerial roots at the tangled edges of the mangrove delta looked like bent organ pipes. Sparrman observed how they intertwined and seemed to be taking over the whole environment. They were exposed at low tide and formed a spreading cyme of bow-shaped flying buttresses many feet high.

The mangrove forests, those pile-dwellings of Nature, belonged neither to the land nor to the water, but to some intermediate material between firm and floating, a fifth element of mud. The latticework of roots trapped the ooze and silt that would otherwise have been washed away by the tide. So the mud floor was constantly rising and increasing in solidity.

Sparrman imagined he could hear the innocents praying for mercy through the whole course of world history. Not even in the Cape had he experienced the icy determination and unbridled cruelty that seemed to take possession of both hunters and traders. The essence of Africa had been shipped away, with no concept of any shared humanity.

He was seized by a cramp that he tried in vain to release. Empathy without action is hard to live with. Wherever he turned he met a callous lack of feeling. A trader from Liverpool defended the transportations thus: 'Since Africans are the most lecherous of beings, can we not infer that the screams they utter when they are parted from their wives emanate from their fear that they will be unable to satisfy their lusts in the country for which they are bound?'

Sparrman had purchased for the Academy of Sciences Christian Oldendorp's *Reliable Report on the Negroes of the Guinea Coast* (Uppsala, 1784). 'The chains of the blacks are forged by greed and luxury,' Oldendorp writes. 'Sugar, which is indispensable only for the sensual pleasure of Europeans, costs millions of negroes their freedom and lives.'

The slaves knew they had to fight for their liberty. It would never be given to them. It was a door that had to be forced open if it were not to remain locked for ever. Swedenborg's land of happy spiritual beings – was this where people fled in the hope of escaping the native traders? Flight was the language of freedom. Brothers and sisters held hands and sang in order not to get lost in the darkness. They dragged mats and calabashes behind them and hoped the spirits would show them the way into the unknown. They staked their lives on putting the slave-hunters on the wrong track. They realized they had to start afresh and that they would never regain what had been stolen from them. They had to give themselves new names in places where no-one would ever be able to reach them.

Like Swedenborg, Sparrman dreamed of a different kind of autonomy, where the stateless and persecuted could grow and blossom.

'Why,' he wrote, 'do so many of us walk inviolate through this inferno that burns and lacerates me, as if I myself were one of those from the depths of Africa? Are we not ruled by any instinct other than greed?'

The blacks were regarded as lacking history, culture and religion. There was thus no imperative for the merchants of death to show them any consideration. Africa had become a continent of graves without bodies.

3

In the same year that Sparrman and Wadström were in Senegal, the very first colonists stepped ashore in Sierra Leone, a mixed company of criminals and prostitutes transported there by a British government intent on ridding itself of anti-social elements. Adam Afzelius, Carl Bernhard Wadström, August Nordenskjöld, his two brothers and some other Swedenborgians, were granted plots of land in 'The Province of Freedom'.

Swedenborg had asserted that the early Christians had over-wintered in the interior of Africa. Sparrman was doubtful about the existence of this Utopia. He did, however, sympathize with Nordenskjöld's attempts to break the omnipotence of world capitalism through alchemy. But the Swedes were prevented from pushing on to the New Jerusalem, because the slave traders blocked the rivers to any who were not part of their cartel.

Sparrman was never a Swedenborgian and did not join the Harmonious Society or the Exegetical and Philanthropic Society. Swedenborg's idea of Heaven was a petit-bourgeois artisan's dream, with additional aspects of scholarship and spiritual entertainment. It had workshops, a comprehensive administration, magnificent libraries, instruction in all subjects and all the arts. Angels were exemplary family members, who combined work with intelligent conversation. No-one was happily unemployed, because work itself was happiness. Sparrman refrained from comment on these visions of the future.

August Nordenskjöld, with the benefit of a gratuity from the king of Sweden, had departed for England in 1789, convinced that he had discovered a method of purifying 'the philosophical eggshell or the curious membrane surrounding gold'. In London he met Carl Bernhard Wadström, who had come back with Sparrman from Senegal. The two Swedenborgians issued a public invitation to a settlement on the coast of Africa under British protection. It would be a society where political power was based on work, and marriage on love, not pecuniary advantage.

Nordenskjöld continued to Paris, and on the 14th of July he was dancing on the ruins of the Bastille. He tried to interest Gustav III in the island of Fernando Po, which Spain was anxious to exchange, and which could thus be purchased cheaply and colonized.

At the beginning of 1792 he landed at Freetown in Sierra Leone, and expressed his outrage in a report on 'six slave-trading posts on Îles de Los, with neither river nor tiniest creek where the slave traders did not have their creatures and their horrors. There is no doubt whatsoever that quite good-quality diamonds may be found in this country.'

The botanist Adam Afzelius advised him against travelling into the interior during the rainy season. But cost what it may, Nordenskjöld wanted to confirm Swedenborg's assertion that an enlightened tribe was hidden away on the Upper Niger. According to Sparrman, Nordenskjöld was a stranger to reality, who was more excited by laboratory flasks and round pots than females of similar shape. One of Nordenskjöld's first letters from Sierra Leone described it as a paradise. Of all the 'uncivilized nations on the planet', he said, these negroes were the best, and more virtuous than the whites. His hopes and dreams had found a firm foothold here.

Nordenskjöld's expedition into the interior of Sierra Leone was, in fact, to cost him his life. In a draft letter from Sousse he wrote that he was longing to reach the mountainous country a few days' journey to the north, where the people were 'innocent and charming'. Fever put an end to his notes, and he died on his return to Freetown in December 1792. His belongings were sold off at auction; the inventory still survives.

At his deathbed stood Linnaeus' disciple Adam Afzelius, who dreamed of becoming a world-renowned explorer. He had revisited Sierra Leone in 1792, on the recommendation of Joseph Banks, to cultivate useful plants, an export industry that might counteract the slave trade. He collected plants and seeds for Banks and for Carl Peter Thunberg in Uppsala. He, too, wrote of the progression of the slave traders through the villages, recognizable by their striped shirts and black neckerchiefs.

Afzelius had left Sweden because he was tired of its pedantic disputes and academic constraints, and he wrote from London in terms reminiscent of Sparrman's: 'Away from all the madmen, I can now plough my own furrow, free and independent.'

Nevertheless, he ensured that through his works he would be remembered by others. Afzelius' natural history notes and botanical collections made him famous throughout Europe. He returned to London in 1796, then received the call to a professorship in Uppsala, and died seventeen years after his friend Anders Sparrman.

4

Long before that, Sparrman and Wadström had sailed from Senegal to Europe and appeared before a committee of the Privy Council in London – on the initiative of Thomas Clarkson, who, together with William Wilberforce, was leading the campaign against the slave trade. Clarkson introduced Sparrman as a man of noble character, trusted by his king and with no ulterior motives in his testimony.

'His information on the subject is extensive. He has noted facts as they appeared before him, and can produce his journal written in French.'

Sparrman made his plea to that part of the British public that was enlightened and well-disposed, proclaiming that the evil in the world stemmed from mankind not using its freedom and intellect wisely. The year before his stay in West Africa (1786) the British alone had transported forty-two thousand slaves on one hundred and thirty ships. These people had been abandoned by the universe, forgotten by Heaven.

'We dare not recognize ourselves in them, and cannot see our reflection in them: there but for the Grace of God go we.'

Anders Sparrman testified to his and Wadström's discovery that the slave traders provided themselves with poison to rid themselves of slaves if they ran low on food or suspected they would not recoup their cost on arrival. Then they would claim insurance for any that were missing. Many a woman went on hunger strike after being raped, and would then be subjected to torture: red-hot coals applied to her lips, molten lead poured over her, thumbscrews, whips. She would be force-fed and made to dance to display her muscles. If nothing succeeded and a woman lost her sale value, she was declared to have died from incurable melancholy.

'Slaves with any physical defect have their throats cut rather than causing the inconvenience of having to be shipped back,' Sparrman told his audience. 'When a pregnant negress gives birth on the way to the coast, the baby is flung into the bushes, because a nursing mother with sagging breasts and a scrawny appearance cannot readily be sold. One of the most frequent ways of putting a delinquent to death is to tie him naked to a pole set up near a bees' nest and let him end his days with a thousand stings.'

The British committee sent Sparrman to Gustav III to prevail upon the enlightened monarch of a great seafaring nation to forbid this human trafficking. The king authorized Sparrman to reply that he was unfortunate enough to rule over Saint Barthélemy, which was populated not only by Normans and Bretons, but also by African slaves, whose grim lot he deplored. Not long afterwards the Swedish slave trade came to an end.

Wadström testified to the parliamentary committee that the Europeans' methods included fomenting war among the natives, encouraging the local tribal chieftains to sell their subjects, and commandeering the human wares by guile. The negroes were, in Wadström's opinion, peaceable, friendly and by no means inferior to white men in intelligence. They had an aptitude for trade and industry and would cultivate their land productively, were it not for the slave trade monopolizing their thoughts.

'They would be of more service to Europe as a free people.'

Sparrman summed up on a note of optimism: 'The testimony supplied by Wadström and myself to a committee of the Upper House has significantly furthered the cause of humanity through the uncovering and revelation of cruelty in the slave trade . . .'

He stayed in London for several months. He wrote a letter to the naturalist Thomas Pennant in June 1788 in which he said that he was leaving England for good. He had been tempted to settle there, he admitted, but it was too late for him to start afresh, and make the friends and connections necessary for him to practise medicine.

He was forty when he returned to Sweden. In his remaining thirty-two years he would undertake no more foreign travel.

Typhus in Karlskrona

1

In the Revolution year of 1789, the *Stockholms Posten* newspaper reported that Professor Anders Sparrman, as emissary for the king, had sailed to Karlskrona on board an Åbo schooner to recommend to the county governor some as yet untested antidotes to an epidemic.

The survivors of the Swedish naval battle with Russia had sailed home from Sveaborg in Finland with sick men on board. The crews, debilitated by their privations, had been stricken by typhus, also known as putrid fever, a strain accompanied by jaundice, blood in the urine and boils all over the body.

The Admiralty physician Arvid Faxe in Karlskrona had published a book on health at sea, all about prophylactic medicine, since it was well known that the majority of deaths at sea resulted from disease. But smoking the ship with juniper twigs and sulphur, and swilling her down with vinegar, proved ineffectual. Nothing was known about bacteria carried by lice and vermin, and little about the importance of hand-washing.

Sparrman's advice was that the entire town of Karlskrona, at that time the second in the land and no more than a century old, should be disinfected. Hundreds of people had retched themselves to death in the paroxysms of fever, and one essential task was to ensure proper burial for everyone.

'The deceased have not all been adequately interred. Some

have been laid to rest above ground, or under the lightest sprinkling of soil, so that half the coffin is exposed, and the unhealthy
vapours of decaying corpses are swirling about the town.'

The infection spread to the shipyard workers, then to the garrison in the fortress and soon into the civilian population of the
town. The new sloop and longboat shed on Stumholmen was
brought into service as an isolation hospital. A marquee was
erected in front of the Admiralty Church to serve as a temporary
hospital, despite the protests of the parish. Corpses were piled one
atop the other to await the thawing of the soil. The county governor, Mr Raab, had 'suitable deep graves dug' outside the town, 'so
that the dead in the service of the Crown could be buried without
delay'.

'Death was inscribed on every fifth sickbed,' wrote Faxe, who
was responsible for more than six thousand patients in the
summer of 1789 on the island of Tjurkö. It was an encampment
of ninety tents made of sailcloth, with neither groundsheets nor
drainage. But the extreme cold forced the removal of the afflicted
to the Strübings' house and three decommissioned naval ships.
The cabin boys' school, the carpentry workshop, boathouses and
arsenals were all requisitioned. When even private houses proved
insufficient in number, the convalescents were sent home. Those
who had just sufficient strength to crawl into a carriage spread the
Karlskrona epidemic throughout the region.

The College of Surgeons was in urgent need of hundreds of
practitioners. Since there were no more to be found in the entire
country, request was made to Denmark and Germany. Of two hundred and twenty doctors and surgeons, all but six fell victim to the
outbreak. Ten thousand navy personnel died – as many as the
whole permanent population of the town. Civilian deaths
amounted to five hundred at most.

The hospital administrator, Johan Bernt Kleman, campaigned
for starving orphans to be cared for in foster homes, with appropriate remuneration. All he could do for many was pay for their

burial. Even the bourgeoisie were obliged to seek help from hospital funds when they could not afford to bury their wives and children. More than one anonymous maid gave birth on the streets of the town, and was discovered in a wretched condition, the infant dead in her arms.

In October 1789 Duke Kárl ordered the fleet to the Gulf of Finland. But the prevalence of sickness on board rendered the ships incapable of manoeuvre. After a week at sea they returned and were promptly demobilized. Gustav III then dispatched his equerry Adolph Munck to Karlskrona, receiving from him a report on the causes of the epidemic that was identical to Sparrman's.

2

Our Royal Commission has discovered unexplained losses at our Naval Station, and inspected the premises of the Admiralty Apothecary, Friedrich Brasch. His potions and medicaments were found wanting, his quinine ineffectual, his assistants to speak bad Swedish.

The fleet is in port, the crews unemployed. The labouring classes would appear to be engaged with no other business than the musket and the brandy glass. Many fail to turn up for work, and the low wages are leading to crime. Thefts are occurring: tobacco, a pig, a tin chamber pot, whatever people come across. Medicine chests are empty, the stocks of oats are exhausted and several thousand hammocks have been requisitioned for the burial of the dead.

The value of possessions is decreasing, the cost of essentials rising. Even people of rank are no longer hesitating to pawn rings or silver spoons and jugs. A captain has had to leave his uniform coat, his civilian coat, a topcoat and twelve ounces of gilded silver as a pledge for his meals.

Some of the sick are in their own apparel, some in the uniform of the Crown, and some in hospital garb. Much of the clothing is stiff with grime. An afflicted man is often put in the same bed and sheets as a deceased patient, who has been removed only minutes before. The hospital cleaners sleep in the same rooms as the patients, and themselves increase the pestilence in the air from their own exhalations, and from all the cleaning equipment, food and so on that they bring into the sickroom. The medicine cupboards are also there, and when the bottles and boxes are left open, the contents lose their efficacy and are contaminated by dust.

Hospitals have been set up adjacent to pigsties and stinking ponds. Some beds have no straw. Excrement lies finger-deep on the floor and in beds. The paucity of doctors is increasing the torment of the sick, and they are resorting to unnatural means to slake their thirst.

The main square is nigh impassable on account of all the stones, hens and turkeys. None but malefactors and stray dogs risk the slippery slopes in winter. Unlawful filth mounts up on the streets. The nights are disturbed by intolerable commotion. Citizens in their nightcaps shoot any pigs that have escaped and have yet to be recaptured by their owners. The fire brigade rounds up inebriates as they stagger out of the taverns.

From all the fortune-telling with cards, singing in taverns and clubs, carousing over the punchbowl, it is hard to believe that the trumpets of death have sounded for a healthy populace. People drink aquavit with their morning tea and imbibe another at noon. After a meal of fat lamb and dumplings at three o'clock, they settle down to a game of cards in front of the stove, and are ready for more aquavit in the evening.

I have given talks about my travels to the boys in the grammar school, seventy-two in number, and have provided them with advice on matters of health. In my temporary practice I am in competition with Nathan the corn-remover and Assur the horse-doctor, who sells cures for red hair and has some skills in dentistry.

I have visited Johan Törnström in the woodwork shop where ships' figureheads are carved, and the ropeyard, next to which timber enough for six vessels has been stacked, and also the model room with a wooden portico similar to the Pantheon in Rome, where models of ships and machines are kept, for the study of their construction.

I was very pleased to meet Lord High Admiral Carl August Ehrensvärd again, and was invited to dinner with his wife Kickan, Admiral Fredrik Henrik af Chapman and others. After which, to the theatre to see the comedy *The Landowner's Maid*, indifferently performed with the exception of Miss Wahrlund, the leading actress of the town, who had a well-modulated voice and a slender figure, with beautiful white shoulders.

Ehrensvärd complained about the king's vacillation, the incompetence of the nobility, the destitution of the people and the general disorder in Karlskrona. He did not intend to lie at anchor in the manner of a night-soil barge, but felt obliged to resort to tyrannical intervention himself to put wheels in motion. He could see roguery and dilettantism in the high command, and had from the outset warned the king against engaging in wars of conquest with an inadequate fleet. The result was that he had stayed at home with his scant garrison, and the command had been given to Duke Karl.

He explained how we were hanging on by the flimsiest of threads. There would soon be a conflagration, which would terminate for all of us in the Black Pit. And he declared he had been persuaded by Baron Reuterholm and Borgenstierna, the Chamberlain, to spend a night in the churchyard of St Johannes, long considered to be the most haunted in Stockholm. This Freemasons' prank resembled a theatrical farce. Ehrensvärd believed God had chosen to speak to us through Nature, so that we would not need to chase after revelations.

Reuterholm had then taken Oxenstierna to the same churchyard, whereupon lights had flitted over the graves, a headless figure stood in the church doorway, and a white creature, as big as a calf, had leapt from a gap in the churchyard wall and run off so fast it had kicked up sparks.

We moved on from Ehrensvärd's to Jonas Krook, the merchant, in his stone house on Landbrogatan, where we played cards until supper was served at the tables, and later partook of broken eggs as we continued into the night. I heard there that my friend and colleague Admiralty physician Lars Hjortzberg had fallen victim to the epidemic.

I assisted at an amputation of a syphilitic captain that we performed on the kitchen table in his house. Brasch provided us with plaster bandages, compresses, powder, mixtures and wound tinctures, all for a price of four *riksdaler*.

As chance would have it, I came upon two men in the hospital in the most wretched plight. They recognized me from the voyage to China. They had aged and were riddled with syphilis. A salve of mercury had no effect and their rotting bodies gave off an unbearable stench. One had got by as a brass polisher, the other as a cook. We spoke of the trials of life at sea, but they were as nothing to the torments they had since endured.

I have tended the sick time and time again without, God be praised, catching any malady myself. I now have an overview, and can say that nothing conforms to our expectations. We have no idea how to handle this epidemic. My professorial expertise offers no recipe for dealing with people in indescribable torment, screaming for water from huts which no-one dare enter.

There was never such sickness in Africa, nor such misery – except among the most severely chastised slaves. In this inferno even a Royal Commissioner is tempted to give up. Our fleet is unable to sail, and my grief is profound.

3

In 1795 Sparrman returned to Karlskrona to pursue scientific research. He carried his hazel stick with its light springy action, employing it to lift the previous year's fallen leaves and expose roots, snake skins, mouse tracks and the nests of insects.

He was the first to study and draw the green toad (*Bufo viridis*). He found one in a pile of stones by the Artillery Building, where a blackberry bush had taken root. He discovered that the Karlskrona frog spawned in seawater and that it had a white, unspotted belly. It did not emit 'the stinking odour or extrusion of slime and corrosive fluids, or have flashing eyes when threatened by animals, as reported by Count Lacépède in his *Natural History*.'

The town has changed since the fire of 1790, Sparrman noted in his journal. Stone buildings have been constructed: a hospital, terraces of houses, schools. Quays have been paved. As in Cape Town, taverns and coffee houses are closed at seven o'clock in the evening. Apprentices and farmhands who tarry after closing time are mercilessly pressed into service as soldiers. Stadig's restaurant on Skeppsbron Quay is a centre for political discussions, games of dice and the reading of newspapers: *Stockholms Posten*, *Göteborgs Allehanda* and the *Carlskrona Veckoblad* with its Supplement.

I pay eight *skilling* a day for a room with white boarded walls, including heating, cleaning and light in the evenings, at Grön-beck's on Prinsgatan. I have a sofa with cushions of stuffed hair, and sleep on blue-striped linen. I eat bread and syrup. Fresh water is always in short supply, being transported across from the mainland every day.

The grocery shops are well stocked with snuff and mustard, olives and walnuts, sieved rye flour, toilet water for the ladies. Elers, the mayor, has had paths laid for walks, and a pavilion for refreshments where Rothe's Park adjoins the marsh that goes under the name of Neptune's Square.

The girls are pretty, and readily approachable, if sometimes a little affected. In the house I visited they were clean, unpretentious and polite. One girl was neatly dressed on what she had earned in various ways. She was very pleased with my ducat, and I stayed on longer. We drank tea together. She came from the islands, and was going to cease her present occupation to become an assistant to the town midwife.

I attended the gathering hosted by Mr Bruneri, the merchant. There were performances by an Italian actor and singer, and an acrobat from Stralsund, and two dogs performed simple jigs on their hind legs. On Sundays masquerades are held at nine of the evening, and none may enter the hall without a mask, nor may it be removed. Women dance with abandon, whirling around until they lose their breath and fall exhausted to the floor.

There I met Lieutenant Daniel Wilhelm Padenheim, a headmaster's son from Söderköping, who had been sixteen years in the service of the Dutch. He was rescued from a vessel bound for South America when it was shipwrecked off Cornwall. Destitute, he set off on foot for London and entered the service of the Sierra Leone Company. He was given a military command, and a building on Wadström's map of Freetown is called Padenheim Fort. He showed me a drawing of his redoubt, shot all to pieces.

A French fleet had attacked the liberated slaves in Sierra Leone and spared only nine of the eighty white inhabitants, who had sacrificed themselves in the cause of enlightenment and freedom. Fort Padenheim was laid waste. He himself escaped. The Swedish

Ambassador in Paris, Baron Staël, made representations to the French Foreign Minister, Talleyrand, in the name of the Swedish government, the rights of peoples and common humanity.

Padenheim's objective turn of mind made him, for me, an optical instrument that dispersed the fog over the Slave Coast. He had recently returned to Sweden and declared himself content to have been appointed quartermaster in Karlskrona. It suited him to seclude himself in this little bastion. He had hung up his threadbare officer's cap and relinquished his command. In the evenings he was translating a book about the internal structure of the Earth and the causes of earthquakes.

Africa had sucked the marrow out of him. Its heat had shrivelled his skin and his mind. All the freedom and brazen behaviour at the Equator was actually a fateful constraint. 'You only have one life,' he had reminded himself in Sierra Leone. In Karlskrona he had put that life behind him.

Distant memories and more recent events intermingled in his conversation. Padenheim had never been at a loss as to what to do with himself, not since he had abandoned his position as clerk at Tanto sugar factory near Stockholm. He had never had any inclination, like others of his kind, to seek a career in the navy, farming, diplomacy or the Church. His family was the lowest-ranking nobility it was possible to imagine. He had moved around here and there, under the influence of gravity, fortuity and his own desire never to subject himself to any ruler.

He thought his posting to the Swedish naval base was his first experience of being in a peaceful haven, and he had had a premonition that reassured him about the future. Why should he worry about the loss of rank? In the stores office he could forget the haughty woman who had left him with these words: 'I do not intend to spend my whole life parading up and down the walls of this miserable fortress.' Padenheim told me he had gladly given her lifelong leave of absence.

He had come to accept the fact that his entire existence had in most respects been neither useful nor successful. He had no function even worthy of criticism. Therein lay his moral: he had no desire to go back and change anything; even all that he had left undone had now been done. Ignoble and shameless charlatans just brought a smile to his lips, the inept no longer vexed him. And there would be no more obsequiousness.

So Padenheim became his own master, though in a very minor way. Thus, unlike me, he has not allowed himself to be ridiculed and humiliated. He said that if you let your suppressed anger get the better of you here on this damp coast, you would soon find yourself suffering an attack of gout. Life was like his map of Sierra Leone: Padenheim's name endured, but both the fort and he himself had fallen.

His moustache was so luxuriant that it seemed to grow out of his nostrils. He had never worn a wig. We were of an age, and found much to converse about. Neither of us had heard from our energetic Swedenborgian friend Wadström for quite some time. But we felt the warmth of Goree and Batavia diminishing, and invigorated ourselves with tincture of wormwood. Padenheim exhaled a defiant puff of breath, as if to drive out his memories.

We also had in common the fact that we had returned from the shores of death. Padenheim had escaped typhoid fever and dysentery, and felt he could now afford to be less sparing of his remaining energies and resources. Life meant being constantly alert to death, so nothing should be wasted – we were in agreement on that.

We met again the following day at his habitual eating place, to drink Karlskrona heavy beer and enjoy the local buckling with its roe, on bread with salt butter. The town has gone through hard times, though Padenheim had seen worse things in West Africa. He recalled a moment around four o'clock in the afternoon, in the most searing heat, when the silence was absolute and you could feel death drawing the air out of your lungs.

It was strange to hear that the lieutenant was one of the last three to see our friend August Nordenskjöld, lying delirious in his hut after having looked all too deeply into the Province of Freedom, whose diamonds will be its downfall, as he himself prophesied.

I felt altogether exhausted when we parted, but nevertheless enriched, even happy. I went straight away back to my room, in order to absorb this meeting into my own recollections.

Swimming in punch is, of course, more pleasant than swimming in blood, and Dutch cheese is easier to eat than ship's biscuits with maggots. But receptions and harlequinades have never been to my taste, any more than visits to governors, or games of cards around a miserable flickering oil lamp, or the inner circle of a mutual admiration society.

I have clearly become as enraged by people as a bull. I am aware that a contented mind is the best defence of one's health, and that I have all too infrequently been able to count my blessings in that respect. I am not the jolliest of fellows, seldom in good humour, and out of tune with the pastimes others most enjoy.

I ride over my days in a rickety carriage, as it were, and frequently stick in viscous mud. My sloth turns to impotence in the unruly weather of the capital. I lock myself in an oyster shell of enforced idleness, in order not to provoke my academic colleagues to insidious pinpricks and sermons so empty of content that only birdsong revives my sense of hearing.

Even so, I am not entirely downhearted, but actually quite serene. I can breathe more freely here in Karlskrona. I stride out better. I can see the islands out at sea against the horizon and feel the southerly breeze from Pomerania and Poland.

There are twenty-five ships of the line moored side by side along Skeppsbron Quay, with their bowsprits pointing seawards. They form a single platform to walk across, a stretch of one thousand six hundred feet. There are galleasses that can carry twenty tons: they take timber to Rostock, Hull and Marstrand, iron to Genoa and Ostend, and Öland stone to Libau and St Petersburg.

I went aboard one of them, and felt deep inside a burning desire to cut the mooring rope.

Letters and Diary 1793–4

1

To George Forster, 1793:

I trust these words will reach you in Mainz in due course. I have heard from others that you have been travelling in Europe with Alexander von Humboldt, and that you married a German novelist who has lately abandoned you for another, taking your daughters with her. Thus are we freed from our responsibilities, whether we will it or no.

So, you write that you have dreamed your way through all Utopias, and that they have slipped through your fingers, even love in the end. That is the difference between us: my only Utopia was the abolition of the slave trade.

I share your concern for Europe, now being agitated by the hand of a giant. Even my country here in the north can feel the dangerous tremors. The world is tumbling around in man's febrile dreams, alternately light and dark. The future, you say, rests with Asia, which Russia is in the process of colonizing, and with the liberated United States of America.

Like you, my friend, I believe the laws of society cause more suffering and evil than those of Nature. Man is the most selfish of creatures, and his basic instinct is to appropriate all land and all the necessaries of life, depriving others in the process.

During my expedition in the Cape I saw a small group parcelling up the land among themselves, to the detriment of those

who had no laws of ownership or inheritance, and thus were effec-
tively born without land. The craving for riches is as blinding as
physical lust. We construct our existence on the basis of prejudice
and delusion, and raise ourselves by oppressing others into misery
and want. How can we demand high-mindedness and compassion
from those who are without hope?

You and I, my noble friend, have seen people who are more bes-
tial than the very beasts, even among those who have contributed
to the greatness of the world. We have described species whose
territory we have invaded, whether fortuitously or deliberately, and
if only briefly. We have found life supporting life in totally unexpected conjunctions, implanting in Nature what our eyes interpret
as beauty.

You thought you saw the light of reason from revolutionary
Paris, our new Rome, casting its radiance over the whole of Europe. Now you are witnessing the courts of the Revolution, which
put the Spanish Inquisition in the shade. You have followed the
tumbrils carrying the dead along the rue Saint-Honoré, and were
present at the execution of Charlotte Corday. Her undaunted love
of freedom and the Republic makes a Swedish zoologist feel but
a paltry creature.

Humanity, Mother Earth, even the very sunlight is being
desecrated. Love's kingdom of liberty and equality is not being
transformed into reality, you understand – despite your having con-
versed with Thomas Paine and Mary Wollstonecraft in Paris,
names we have heard even up here.

'It is a great misfortune that my enthusiasm has died,' you write.
'Who will understand me now? My soul is maimed, my power of
imagination burnt out, my vitality sluggish and purposeless.'

The birches are coming into blossom here, the wood anemones
should appear by Whitsun, and I do not wish to hear you describe
yourself as burnt out. If you put on your round, gold-framed spec-
tacles, the world will be illuminated once again! Let us remember
how untroubled we were when we sailed away into the unknown,

just to fill the sea charts with new islands and countries, undiscovered flora and fauna. Without a second's hesitation, we made
our forays ashore, and left all the decisions and navigation to
Captain Cook. Contrary to all predictions, we came safely back
home, although you, even more than I, contrived to lose yourself
in these once-familiar towns.

Oh, my sorrowful, pale and distant friend, here too it has
become fashionable to weep. There are plenty of aching hearts.
Yet no-one has swooned from an excess of knowledge, though
perhaps from excessive erudition. I myself have still not enjoyed
any of those outpourings of feeling that are said to be comparable
to Nature's own.

I have devoted more time to the precarious health of others
than to my own position. I think I am doing some good, and being
not at all niggardly, but I am in debt for three thousand *riksdaler*,
and have pawned my gold-topped rattan cane and a goblet with filigree work, the latter awarded at the presentation of my thesis,
where, as you know, honours were conferred in my absence.

I have lost most of the advantages I enjoyed when I took up this
post. In these unwelcome circumstances, I am trying to keep my
head clear in order not to burden you with my passing heaviness
of heart and outbursts of emotion. Perhaps we cannot express what
we really are.

With our friendship as a landmark, I sail on among the haphaz-
ard skerries of which our kingdom is formed. I wish you all
prosperity, and beseech you not to leave me in ignorance of your
own course.

2

I admire our impudent Thorild, who encourages inexperienced youth to express itself freely and to despise politics. In his essay for this year, he advocates love as the basis for marriage, and opines that a love match is most likely between those of disparate characters.

We must hope the forum for lectures and discussion recently instituted by some of the student commoners, in the spirit of Thorild, does not lead to gangs of farmhands being sent out to thrash them, while the officers of the law turn a blind eye. For Duke Karl is so dull-witted that only nocturnal ecstasy can rouse him – poor Hedvig Charlotta! And Reuterholm is unsusceptible to jokes. He is a vengeful fantasist and devoid of friends in his tower of vanity. I am too insignificant to be the victim of his spiteful intentions and malevolent inquisitiveness about everyone's ulterior motives.

There are many who benefit from sinecures and titles. Weak and calculating, discontented and not especially scrupulous in their dealings with others, they would have been more effective in subordinate positions. As it is, they ensure they have a hold on one another, so that no-one becomes top dog.

I dreamed that I was sorting through a bureau crammed full of illegible papers. It determined me to destroy my own papers very carefully. It's not enough to seal them. Unproven accusations, sentimental confessions, polite denials, disconsolate comments, all entrusted to me on oath of discretion – into the fire with them! Only my travel journals and my reports to the Academy of Sciences shall remain. Let everything personal vanish and rot, like my corpse.

I have had a notion of saving something for posterity. There is much to explain, while much will be lost with the passage of time, just as if I had buried something of value in the soil and set a stake there, long overgrown and no more to be found.

I transformed my life into a travel adventure. When I settled down in Stockholm at the age of thirty I was regarded as an elderly man with the best of his life behind him. Not even in the deepest Karoo have I felt so lonely. Not much has happened in my life, except a worsening financial situation. I am not one of those favoured souls of great refinement and lively mind, who can combine clarity of judgement with calm reflection.

Through the two spy-glasses of memory and imagination, I can make out my distant friends, now deceased, united in peaceful harmony, in places about which I have no information. Is there a moment of happiness in a garden when the clear afternoon light has banished world-weariness, gloom and unworthy exaltation? Is a broad field of vision more disturbing than a narrow one? He who has felt the icebergs closing in around his ship like prison walls on the most featureless of oceans is allowed to ask such questions.

Not all of our sailors on the *Resolution* knew how to read and write, but they could interpret the language of the waves, the phraseology of the winds and the exclamations of the birds. How many here at home do not prefer the reproduction to the reality, and a circuit of their room to a circumnavigation of the world? For them, a moth-eaten zebra hide and a stuffed eagle-owl surpass Nature's living creatures. To my mind, they are already living their own legacy, surrounded by decomposing family secrets.

The shooting stars of the southern hemisphere have left but the faintest reflections inside my head. Have I really seen their sparks exploding from the firmament and streaking through space? How does one know where one has been? Shall I ask Anders Åkerman, the globe-maker in Uppsala, whence he draws his talent for navigating between the heavenly constellations and the oceanic archipelagos, all from the confines of his workshop?

Thoughts and feelings shift to other latitudes. There are breaches in my inner fortifications. I suddenly feel no sense of responsibility. Nothing is my fault, nothing any longer due to my merit. This brings with it a freedom, even if it's one I have no idea how to utilize.

The days pass in empty ceremony. They are like ink that will not adhere to the paper. When my soul yearns to rise to higher spheres I am nought but an ox harnessed to the shafts and hauling my wagon in exchange for meagre fodder, my urges pulling like a rope from my ears to my privy parts.

I cannot remember any experiences of deep love, no passion of such strength that it overpowers the senses and forces the soul into a dilemma. I remember some mortifying clumsiness, a passing ferment, a voracity quickly sated, the fleeting arrogance of lust. I remember curtains being drawn across, and a darkness where only my skin had eyes.

I regard history as a series of reports whose purpose is not clear until they are read and discussed afterwards and decoded. Only if history is written down does it cease coiling around itself and become intelligible – like a messenger panting out his account, his gasps for breath punctuating the events and imbuing them with a sense of actuality.

I glimpsed the light of the sea in our well at an early stage of my life. The single element which has not been arbitrary in my subsequent course has been my travels: Africa, the Antarctic, the South Seas. Everything since then could have had a different outcome. At times of weariness one can catch a glimmer of the man one is not and has not become. One begs him to stay, but then he is gone.

I write as was my custom in the Cape: only when night falls, in the glow of the fireflies. Shades of blue linger inside me and gradually darken to the black of ink.

III

Meeting Lotta

1

'Something marvellous has happened to me,' he wrote later. 'Perhaps it was a day when anything might happen: it was certainly a day unlike any other.'

Spring had arrived, and early summer. Anders Sparrman felt that by now nothing could surprise him any more. He had hoisted his astonishment to the topmast of the *Resolution* and it had been two steps ahead of him on the tracks of the Western Cape. In Stockholm there was no scope for his wonder and amazement. So much seemed like dust and ashes in this kingdom of stuffed people and flayed animals.

Across the street from him in Schönfeldts Alley, in the house of the seamstress Augusta Broberg, he had often caught sight of her assistant or apprentice through the window. He had watched her movements as she reached for the scissors hanging from her apron, or used the measure and chalk, or rolled up off-cuts into a ball. He could see her running her fingers through the box of buttons of bone and horn and tin, and imagined the rattle he could not hear. He saw her unrolling a bale of cloth or fitting a sheeny fabric on a mannequin. He could not perceive the colours clearly, even though the two women worked close to the window to maximize the daylight.

When he screwed up his eyes he could see from her lips and gestures that she was talking to Augusta, who was straightening a piece of tissue, obviously a paper pattern for a gown for one of the ladies of the city, and they were examining it together. She seemed industrious and always to be working at the same steady pace, which made it harder for him to make out her features. He waited for her to open a window, so that he could see her more distinctly, but she never did. Perhaps there was a window giving on to the yard at the rear, or perhaps they didn't need any ventilation.

Then for a while there was no sign of her. Her absence was puzzling – his glimpses of her had cheered him, without conscious admission of the cause. He learned at the grocer's shop on the corner of Stora Nygatan that the seamstress had suddenly died and that the young woman, who was her god-daughter, had been making the funeral arrangements. Would she be coming back? It was unlikely, but as far as they knew she lived with others in a house on Gamla Kungsholmsbrogata.

Sparrman sauntered in that direction one Sunday, when the restless crowds were heading from Rödbotorget to Kungsträdgården Park and anything could happen. But then he stopped himself. Did he know what he was doing? He wasn't sure.

He sensed an alien presence within him, whether because of her he could not tell. He felt a stranger to himself and to everything around him in the town. Ripples flowed through him like sails flapping in a capricious wind. Lady Luck was alternately caressing him and dealing him blows. His mind was vacant rather than calculating, and it did not seek any explanation from the new being who had taken him over and was steering him towards her abode, regardless of the consequences.

When he arrived at a wooden shack with badly puttied window frames, and a child outside trying to tether a dog to the door handle, he came to a halt and had no idea what to do next. He was afflicted by a feeling of such paralysing unreality that he turned about – before there was time for anything to happen – and made his way back to the house in the Old Town which was both home and workplace.

Some while later – and this was the marvellous day – Charlotta Hedvig Fries, eventually to be called Lotta, came into his life in a way he occasionally found difficult to remember.

He emerged from his bedroom one morning with a sudden desire to examine the speculum of the African kingfisher. Sometimes the Cabinet of Natural History was a wilderness of glades and thickets, sometimes a cramped domain that required a magnifying glass. Between the cases his eyes registered all the things he had still not done.

And there he found her, dusting the glass cases, and he had a vague recollection of having seen her before, perhaps at one of the market stalls. He asked in surprise how she came to be working on the premises where he was still master, however circumscribed his role. She replied that the caretaker was suffering severely from gout and melancholia, and had asked her to perform some of his duties for a small wage.

'He is incompetent,' Anders protested, 'and better paid than I am.'

'I dare say he is,' she said.

She finished sweeping the floor and then went into his bedroom, pulled off the bedclothes, shook them out and remade the bed. She moved first slowly, then more quickly, in an inexplicable rhythm, as if coming up against invisible obstacles with her broom, rags and pail. Every so often she came to a standstill, as if she were conducting a house search and had to consider the evidence she had unearthed.

He was annoyed that he had allowed himself to be accommodated in two tiny rooms. Admittedly, they had painted the walls, and he had put up some of his drawings of tools and animals from the Cape, but it was not very impressive. Had he become so indifferent that he was willing to tolerate absolutely anything? Now she, this strange apparition, was witness to it all, and in the next instant he was asking her name and where she came from.

She already knew his name, but little more, despite whatever gossip the caretaker may have imparted, and he added diffidently that there was no more insignificant a person on the whole street. He nearly said no-one more ignored and unvisited, but he had promised himself he would try to cure his self-pity, as well as the bronchial catarrh that had been troubling him lately.

She told him her name and that she had been in Stockholm for a few years. She looked both worldly-wise and yet much younger than he was. And before he had plucked up the courage to enquire, she said she had worked as a seamstress in the house directly opposite. That was what he had suspected, yet had not been quite sure. But he would not reveal that he had watched her and thought about her without her knowledge.

Or had she spotted him across the street? No, she hadn't. There had always been so much to do, and especially since Miss Augusta . . . yes, her heart had simply stopped. And she had had to do all the cleaning and carrying and moving, as he may have noticed; the two corner windows almost met and it had occurred to her that in a certain light it was easy to see in.

Her hair was a reddish-brown colour. She was breathing heavily. They looked at each other as if from a distance, but they saw. She pointed silently at a corpse on the floor, wrapped in grey cloth: a bat from New Caledonia, the only mammal on the islands before the arrival of the Europeans. Anders nodded.

She put it in the dustpan. 'How did you feel when you caught that?' she asked.

'Utter delight.'

'And now?'

'The same as then.'

And as he would later admit, this episode filled him with joy. The animal was now for him nothing more than a squashed plum. He had dissected it and knew where he would place it in the great book of zoology. But who was this person who cleaned so busily, with a striped cloth around her head and a pair of strangely woven slippers on her feet?

'Why do you display things that are normally hidden – brains, hearts, stomachs, foetuses?' she asked.

'Science is all about what is hidden. About seeing what we haven't learned to see.'

'But we know about it.'

'Do we?'

The specimen cabinet with its many drawers of butterflies, flies, beetles, dragonflies, hymenoptera – dust even made its way in there, particles that caused destruction and disintegration.

'Do you think all this will still be here in two hundred years' time?' he asked.

'Something tells me that most of what you took such pains to bring back will still be here,' she replied with conviction.

'Maybe a few garbled notes that no-one can read. Paper lasts longer than peacock feathers.'

She responded with a cautious smile, almost maternal despite her youth. Leaning on her broom, she said, 'I heard you talking to yourself.'

'I was reading a manuscript aloud.'

'Just don't waste paper! Write on both sides!'

'Have you a good head for reading?'

'I don't think so. But I can spell my way through your difficult labels.'

'What is your opinion of it all, then?'

'That you've taken those birds and animals away from the forests and seas that were their homes. The gleam in their eyes is extinguished. Never again will they prepare themselves for fight or flight.'

'I am weary of them,' he admitted. 'I took pleasure in studying them in their habitat. Now they stand here just to satisfy the curiosity of the ignorant.'

Days passed. Sparrman was in a peculiar state of mind that

made him laugh out loud and heave deep sighs. He wandered back and forth in the Cabinet hunting for traces of her. He felt miserable, yet from time to time imbued with confidence.

Every morning when she came in to work they exchanged a few remarks and glances, as if trying each other out – that was how it seemed to him. He longed for her, he was worried about what might happen to her out there in the city, but he could hardly admit it, even to himself. Everything was suddenly so delicate, topsy-turvy, significant.

At what point should he tell her he thought he detected a kindred spirit? Not yet. He was afraid his thirst for knowledge might snap the delicate thread that binds two people. He didn't want her to slip through his fingers, but nor was he ready for her in the flesh. Not yet.

He prided himself on being perceptive, but he was also worried about his talent for causing misunderstanding. He may have been quick and forthright in the Cape, but back in Stockholm he was more often peevish and slow, neither a social asset nor a charmer of the opposite sex. His desire for success had diminished, his sense of justice increased. He had developed an incisive awareness of his colleagues' power games, but was equally conscious of his own lack of persistence. He had the propensity of the indolent towards the sporadic, ephemeral and fragmentary.

He felt a need to confide in her, this almost unknown woman, to share with her this view of himself and make her see the man he was. He had languished for so many years in various degrees of loneliness. He was attracted to everything new and undiscovered, but he was not good at formulating it. He felt downgraded to a mere copyist, to ornithological artist, who made a living from undertaking tasks that anyone could accomplish.

He suffered from not being a magnanimous character; he reviled when he should praise. He ought to be kinder and more encouraging. He sometimes felt in the grip of an unaccountable coldness, which even he found a strain. He wanted to tell her this, but it was still too soon for such intimacy. And he wanted to add: I can see in you something ingenuous beneath the surface which I recognize: maybe that is the root of our affinity.

He had had some notions about the improvement of human nature and well-being, but in Sweden no less than on the Slave Coast he had become depressed and wanted only to flee, without knowing where. Here, ideas were valued lower than fleeting happiness. People were satisfied with empty words and an hour's pleasure, and with the falsehoods they accumulated without seeing them for what they were.

In material terms he was content. Money and objects were mere external adornments of the spirit. His mother, now reunited with his father beneath the soil of Tensta, had been given much of his salary as a token of gratitude for his good upbringing, and for their support of his studies. He didn't think she ever realized how much he had striven for her. A civil servant could get through life on sheer incompetence; for a professor like him it was harder – they were keen to oust him and so gave him responsibility for areas others steered clear of, such as surgery and pharmacy. With shame and some surprise, he recognized that he was not adept at either time-consuming intrigues or serious research.

It was not long before she was involved in his concerns.

'Quensel passed me on Tyska brinken. He lowered his scabrous eyelids to avoid confronting the object of his abhorrence – like a frog that hops from pool to pool for fear of dry land. What he sees in me are arrogant spasms of impotence; in himself he sees active virtue rewarded.'

Anders was elated to the point of anguish, and his heart was beating so strangely that he thought it was someone knocking at the door. He would feel happy for no particular reason, but, thinking about it, he realized it stemmed from an inner vision of Lotta – like a harbinger of fine weather. He really wanted to take her somewhere where nobody knew them.

He plucked up courage and said, 'I am not one to beat about the bush, so I'll just say that I think we could come to like one another . . .'

'You make me feel very shy when you say that,' replied Charlotta Fries, whom he had not yet started calling Lotta.

'We may both have suffered at the hands of life, perhaps been blessed a few times, but we won't delve into what we have been deprived of. Let us simply hope we can bring each other contentment and understanding. But we'll remain, as it were, one another's guests.'

'Guests?' Lotta exclaimed. 'No, not if there's a heart that is ready and willing . . . I can't find the words for what I want to say.' She averted her eyes and he realized she was trying to hold back tears. Her voice became weak and listless. 'You are a great man. I am a very ordinary person.'

'Some might see it like that. We are two creatures that nobody cares about. One day I will read you some poems by Bengt Lidner. Then you will have reason to weep. He was briefly in Cape Town the year I left. He was frenetically talkative, good fellow that he was, his heart pounding fit to burst in his eagerness to devour everything in his path. Which is why he died, though he was almost nine years my junior.'

The next day Lotta arranged some flowers on the tiled stove and showed him a profile of herself, made by a one-eyed silhouettist.

'It may be rather presumptuous of me to bring it,' she said apologetically. He called it pretty and amusing, but in fact it could have been a portrait of anybody.

Having now been in her company several times, he began to imagine, to his own amazement, that he felt younger again, almost as he was with his friends Forster and Immelman in the years when they were conquering the world. He remembered how much they had laughed together, and now it was happening again. Time, which had been racing past him, had slowed down once more and was telling him to savour each day as a gift.

He walked the three streets to Munkbron and bought some radishes. He put them in slightly salted water to stop them discolouring. He invited her to share them with him. It was still early summer, but where they sat in the Cabinet of Natural History it was scarcely perceptible through the window on to Stora Nygatan. He pointed to one of the glass cases.

'You can see a ray there, flat, stiff, black. What you can't see is the way it lashes the seabed with its long tail and vanishes in a cloud of sand.'

2

Like a wave scouring the sand from the seabed. He wanted to protect himself, but could not. The grains of sand lodged in his flesh.

Was this the crashing surf that was called passion? He did not regret the times he had made love to girls he had paid for the pleasure. He thought he understood them, their false smiles and half-contempt, their fleeting tenderness and motherliness. But this was something quite different.

He confessed to Lotta that he had never had any intention of committing himself to a woman, neither one who was strong enough to slaughter a pig, nor one who fainted on the nearest sofa from a surfeit of poetry and tight corsetry. He had stubbornly resisted all advice on how to find his future happiness.

And now, in a flash, here was Lotta, completely unperturbed by the difference in years between them.

'I want to go with you to Hammarby and see whether Professor Linnaeus' fir hedge has grown to the height of a man yet.'

Later she asked, 'Do you ever feel as if part of your soul belonged to a world utterly different from this?'

'Yes,' he replied, 'and that is why I dare come out into the open with you.'

He showed her a dozen simple plates brought home from Canton wrapped in cloth. A serrated dark-blue border, no gold rim, round a lightly embossed grey-white surface, a willow wreath in the centre encircling the letters *A S*, which could have stood for *Ars et Scientia*. And he made her the gift of a fan depicting the eruption of Vesuvius in 1785.

Sparrman was as attentive to Lotta as he had previously been only to the least-studied creatures in the Cape, whether rhinoceroses or hemiptera. And she responded by immersing herself in him like water, and coming up with something happy and undiscovered in him that otherwise would have been lost.

But she did not like his rooms and collections on Stora Nygatan. Foetuses floated in spirit, lizards followed her with their basilisk stares, snakes entwined themselves about one another in jars. The rheumy-eyed caretaker on the ground floor, who had been the inadvertent cause of their meeting, gaped at her as if she were a spectre.

There was no question of staying much longer in the Academy's premises anyway. Anders was formally dismissed as curator the day before his forty-ninth birthday, a day on which a man happened to be swallowing stones at the Glorious Peace Tavern, while his tame siskin performed tricks. Conrad Quensel had emerged victorious from the protracted battle. An empty room in the Academy continued to bear Sparrman's name for a while. On the floor a bast mat from Hermanus and the skin of a grass snake. It had housed him and his 'investigations' for many years.

'Quensel is a fossil!' he roared.

'Stop grumbling!' said Lotta with a laugh.

'What you can hear,' he retorted, 'is the feeble squeak of a bat flitting around a lamp without singeing its wings. For Quensel and Palmstruch I was an insect crawling up the wall and spoiling the perfection of the world.'

He could see a veil of sadness in Lotta's eyes, because she could do nothing to help him. He was moved by her childlike voice. He kissed her, and she tasted of fresh spring water. Even disappointment contains a self-healing drug, he thought to himself.

'I never imagined,' said Lotta, 'that I would be courted by a professor and man of science.'

'Nor I that I would have a young woman named Fries as helpmeet.'

Then he asked whether she would like to be his maidservant,
or housekeeper, or whatever she preferred to call herself.

From that day on their intimacy increased, tentatively but unreservedly. A dark thread ran through his life. Perhaps it passed
through an empty space which he filled with Lotta, because he
himself did not quite exist. On several occasions when wandering
through the hustle and bustle of Stockholm, he had consciously
readjusted his gaze to pick out people who were not mummies or
wooden figures from the Office for Widows and Orphans or the
Board of Health.

But he never fully succeeded, and when he thought he was
holding out his hands towards Lotta they were still lying in his lap.
Her silence settled in him. He was aware of her features softening
and blurring in the dim light and of himself standing before the
unknown, which was nevertheless the only true reality.

Then his hand was touching hers, which was warm, in contrast
to his own, cold but gentle, letting her know he wished her well.
They said nothing for a moment, until he asked, 'Are you afraid of
my thoughts, or your own?' She was afraid of both, though even
more afraid of the human race.

They went to look at accommodation on Kungsholmen, in a district south-west of the Karolinska Institute on Kaplansbacken. But
it was too close to a rope works, a stocking mill with clattering
looms, and a tavern from which a drunken clamour echoed over
the tobacco fields. It was neither city nor country.

As it was summer, Lotta filled a basket with buttered bread, a
nicely rounded crayfish pie, cucumber from Västerås and cheese
from Arboga. They walked from the Old Town along the southern
shore of Lake Mälaren to the floating bridge across to Långholmen.
Up on the cliffs of the island, within sight of hares cavorting and a

squirrel playing peekaboo on a tree trunk, Lotta undid the basket. There was not another soul anywhere near them, and the open waters of the lake sparkled between the oak and lime trees.

She must have thought he had lost his mind, because he started talking about anything and everything, about love and scurvy, about fish and Swedenborg's multitude of angels. Words poured out of him and flowed in her direction, but how much she heard or understood was another matter. The misty summer dusk enclosed them in its scent of clover and lady's bedstraw.

Anders: 'We live in a Creation that is only partially discovered. Land and water are still changing places, extraordinary transformations are occurring, but we don't notice them.'

Lotta: 'You talk about a lot of things I've never heard of. I didn't know anything about what you've been involved in, except the names of Professor Linnaeus and King Gustav III. What you call the spirit of the times is not something I've been aware of at all. But I know I want to walk safely along the street without anyone asking me 'How are you, my little lady?' Not because I'm afraid, but because I want to be left in peace.'

She had not travelled and read as he had, and did not know the fundamentals of botany or the science of animals. She had picked lingonberries and crowberries. She could make an omelette with edible mushrooms. She could ease pain and dress wounds.

'I didn't grow up in a rectory with a soup tureen and napkin rings like you, but as a weed on a crown lease. I came from invisible people: soldiers, blacksmiths, pewter workers. My mother was a maid on a farm in Sorunda, then she made sweets, and was well known for the strong glue she produced to mend pots and jugs. All she wanted was for her glue to be considered the best. She was frugal and obedient, self-sufficient, and that was how it should be. You went to school. I am just grateful I can read and count a little. I am limited by the life I was given, but you have plucked your opportunities out of the air. I washed in a rusty bucket and couldn't abide my own body, since it wouldn't take me anywhere.'

He asked circumspectly about her previous relationships. 'I'm used to being on my own,' was all she responded. 'No-one has ever waited for me with his heart in his mouth.'

He in turn assured her, 'In my service you can be yourself. Unless I suddenly act with impropriety . . .'

'You smile so nicely, but there is always something piercing in your eyes.'

'Because I want to know you inside out, and I can tell it will take time.'

He had persuaded her by then to call him Anders instead of Dr Sparrman.

'Andreas,' she said, as if she had found a compromise.

'No, not Andreas. That was my dead brother, whom I had to replace.'

Lotta told him about an oil lamp that nearly burnt out; a hand that held her tight and pulled her through the darkness; someone who dragged her with him wherever he went. It was her brother, four years older, strong and as tall as a hop-pole. She felt like an orphan without him. He was her love and support. He was handsome and serious. They used to go berry-picking, and he was showing her how to jump from tussock to tussock in a bog when he took a false step and was sucked in. She couldn't believe her eyes. He flailed his arms, in silence, as if he could not comprehend what was happening to him.

'No-one heard me screaming except for him, and I think I'm screaming still. I was nigh on sinking myself. I was ten years old and had no strength. I ran through forest and over moor, in the wrong direction at first, and finally found my way home. My mother was on the porch steps, wondering what the fuss was about. Then she too was screaming and running. My father had only recently died.

'I showed the men the way, and they found traces of my brother and put down branches and tree trunks and hauled him out. He had been swallowed and trapped by mud and roots. There was such grief, and I felt scorned and discredited, because I was the last one to see him, and there was nought I could do. I loved him. Despite my youth, it was possible to harbour such a love.'

Anders took her in his arms. 'I never saw my brother. Some saw him in me. We draw our nourishment from the hours and days of others, Lotta, or else we would just be white shoots, cut off before we reached the light.'

Then he kissed her again and again, so that she had to gasp for air in order to speak, and they carried on kissing for a long time, searchingly, untiringly. The crab-apple trees had dropped their blossoms and were forming green fruits. The wind changed direction and carried a faint odour of refuse. They could hear hammering from Bergsund's engineering works and the cocks crowing on the foredeck of a barge out in the bay.

Lotta's father had been a tailor and suffered from migraines, so her most vivid memories of him were at the stove massaging his head through a dog-skin hood. He heated bricks in the oven and put them beneath his feet, while pouring warm swigs from the decanter down his throat. He moved little and sewed less and less as the pain in his eyes grew worse. His double chins chafed each other. He had swelled up with dropsy, and very soon died.

'How many times I wished my mother had suffocated me when I was born! I should never have lived: I was put aside with pneumonia, and yet I revived, smaller and more delicate than most infants. I would exhaust you if I told you about everything I've suffered. The days are gone when I would call upon God to soothe my soul and preserve my sanity. I've feared falling into vice and at times have not known what would become of me. But even in my hours of greatest need I was never a streetwalker. I've always managed to get by on my own.'

'I'm not easily shockable,' he said. 'I feel as if we've always known one another, and yet everything is also new for us, both having wandered the world's stony, muddy, slippery paths, each in our own direction.'

When Lotta was ten her mother also died, of consumption. She was sent in turn to her maternal grandmother and a great-aunt on her father's side. Then she was fostered in a quarrelsome but prosperous home where the husband slipped a coin in the pocket of her dress, sat her on his lap and made strange movements, from which she managed to extricate herself.

'You pinch hard, but you'll end up in the gutter,' her foster-father warned the twelve-year-old. 'If you'd only be nice to me, you wouldn't have to ruin your eyesight with all this needlework.'

She was also treated badly by Litander, a factory owner who came back from Lübeck and forced himself upon her. She freed herself from the clutches of that living skeleton, only to give birth at the age of seventeen to a baby boy in the Pro Patria Society maternity hospital. Under the terms of the king's new edict she did not have to reveal the father's name. But she did so anyway and was thrown out. The child was sent to foster-parents in the province of Närke, where it died.

Lotta wanted to take leave of life herself then. But instead she made her way to the capital, found a job serving in a tavern on Malmtorgsgatan and learned how to weave baskets. One summer she worked as a waitress at an inn on Djurgården Meadows.

'I had a lot of love in me, but I was taken advantage of, stuffed full of abusive language, and soon had no room left for dreams.'

So their memories were about as different as it was possible to be. Lotta's experiences were mostly things she sought to forget. Where he said 'I remember' she would say 'I've forgotten.' He stepped into her loneliness and brought light to her face.

He took the oars from her and let her rest and gaze down at the clear seabed, to the floating strands of algae behind her, the shifting shadows of the rocks and the pale underwater berries that would never ripen. There lay her old life, a sunken archipelago she could now turn her back on. He had regained the strength he had on board the *Resolution*, and he was steering. But now his boat was Lotta.

3

They found somewhere to live on Skomakargatan, at Number 5, and without waiting for any formal appointment Anders Sparrman began practising as physician to the poor in the parish of Klara. He still had a seat and voice as an advisory member of the Collegium Medicum, and later, when he left his Chair of Natural History in 1803, he was allowed to retain a salary on the establishment in this former role, even when the Board of Medicine was dissolved and became the Board of Health.

At first, Anders and Lotta had separate rooms, then they shared a bedroom, keeping the other room, with its higher windows and better light, for work and reading. The bells of the German Church rang out high above them, a tower of sea-blue music from Lübeck. Horses' hooves clattered irregularly on the slope below – just like the sound of wreckage washing up in uneven breakers against the rocks on the shore of False Bay.

They had moved Anders' household goods from his official residence on Stora Nygatan, followed by Lotta's few possessions from her rented room. He had gone back to return the keys to the caretaker's wife, who immediately handed them on to a barber's apprentice. Then he had walked down to Klara Strandgata and on past the tanneries spewing out their offensive fumes.

Proceeding further west on Kungsholmen he had caught sight of a garden with twisted pear trees, and phlox and marigolds, where a child was hanging by its knees from a swing. A postman blew his horn and Anders felt his heart expand with a sudden feeling of liberty. A girl unlatched the gate of a goat pen and curtsied, even though he had nothing to give her. A young woman poured a bowl of water over a cat and threw herring guts round the corner of the house. Old editions of *Stockholms Posten* were jammed into the gaps between the red-painted timbers of a rustic outhouse.

So the city crowds had very soon been left behind. Perhaps he was making his way to Ulvsunda Lake and Solna Forest; perhaps in his mind to Jakobsdaal and Odenstrom in the Western Cape. In his mood of loss and relief the paths merged, and he wished he could share the moment with Lotta.

Most people carry with them an aura from another life, which is half-secret and not spoken of. He thought of caves where bats and nightjars sought shelter, and of the almost horizontal rain scudding over the sea and weighing down the sails.

Love lay within him like water in the body, like a memory of the world's oceans. Lotta had received him with an openness that was not just sensual. She could have kept him shut out from her soul, but she had chosen not to be afraid, she had nothing to lose, not even him. She was a woman who could live without expectations. She saw him as he was, quite famous yet ignored by those who could tell the difference between the rope that raised the curtain and the one that let it fall.

He tried to liberate her from guilt and despair. He wanted to see her soar in dance. Her body was light but her heart was heavy. Solitariness was her great strength. She had no ties. She was an abandoned child who was able to surrender herself.

'I am going to enter into you, Anders, and so escape my past,' she told him. 'I don't want any memories. Yours will be enough. I will be content with them.'

Sparrman was a learned man. Lotta was ignorant in many spheres, and not particularly concerned about it. He appointed himself her instructor. She was thrilled by everything she was taught, but still remained essentially the same. To her, knowledge involved voluptuousness, caresses, a closeness that made her quiver. One day she surprised him by suddenly bursting out, 'How can we help but rely on somebody we love?'

Her boots were soaked through from the rain, as was the hem of her dress. Her plaited hair exposed the creamy whiteness of her neck. He breathed in the smell of her woollen cloak. He watched her drying her hands on her apron: how accustomed they were to stirring the tub of soured milk, kneading dough, lifting a full kettle from the fire. He had sailed around the world, seen people working, fighting, making love. But with Lotta something seemed to be starting that he had never experienced. He felt as if he had never possessed another woman before her.

Her eyes were so full of adoration that he did not feel intruded upon, only amazed to see into a soul so full of goodwill towards him, her eyes filled with tears at the thought that his life would not last long enough for her to accompany him to the grave. One night she turned gently towards him and pulled up the coarse cloth of her nightdress. He saw her in the flickering candlelight, exposed and strong, of slim figure and serene gaze.

He laid his hand on her intimate parts. 'You may be too tired to take in what I am saying, but I know you more profoundly than you think. I've been invisible by your side for a long time. I can't explain my feelings for you. Were there words for them, they would dazzle us.'

She had a way of appearing and disappearing that he could not fathom. She would glide around, barefoot and soundless. He loved her slender throat and prominent collarbones, her hair that she could put up in a bun in five swift movements. The higher truths cast no shadow over her everyday life. She accepted his plans and projects, his tribulations and desires were hers, their weather was one and the same.

'We will have to endure all the tittle-tattle,' said Anders. 'I am too eminent, you are too young.'

'I've had to contend with so much I didn't like that I've grown as old as you.'

'I'll bury my head in your neck and then I'll be as invisible as I was under the cold night sky in the Karoo, and if you cover my ears with your hands I won't hear the hyenas barking.'

Love was a demanding word. Its weight and responsibilities burdened him, only then to float upwards again like a most remarkable butterfly. But he had still not spoken the word. Yet with all the other words at his disposal he averred a love for Lotta which from the outside appeared deplorable, irrational and incomprehensible. He was aware of that from the glances of his former colleagues, which he treated with indifference. But when he sank to the level of physician to the poor, some regarded it as a sacrifice on Lotta's part that she stayed with him.

In the eyes of the world she was his housekeeper, assistant and the woman who kept his life in order. For him she was none of those things now. She was no mere halt on his journey, she was his most important undertaking, and she reached parts of him he could not even reach himself. Lotta said that when he was away she tried to remember his face as a landscape, and very particularly. Africa had etched the first tracks in it. She had to familiarize herself with that continent, even though she would never go there.

He told her about the traces of life and death in sand and moss, about cranes' feet and ravens' claws being sold on the market, and taking off his shoes at the Cape of Good Hope to feel between his toes the sand at the end of Africa.

Africa and Lotta – without them he would have found it difficult to breathe. With Daniel Immelman in the Cape, with George Forster at sea in his youth, and now in his old age with Lotta in Stockholm, he had been able to step outside his normal life and enter the existence of another person, without hidden shadows. Lotta was his unruly travelling companion.

'You look at me as if I were transparent,' she would complain.

'I'm a physician,' he replied. 'I see the tissues in your breasts, and the food you have eaten passing through your bowels. I have dissected plants, animals and humans. I can look into your lungs, your ovaries . . . I've learned to see beneath the surface, and I can never free myself from my captivation.'

'I'm studying too,' said Lotta.

'You're studying?'

'I'm studying you, in a different way. You're not boastful, arrogant and unfeeling like other men. You notice when I've been weeping, but you don't ask the cause. I only hope you don't think my heart is attached to another's, or not attached enough to yours.'

They explored one another almost as if they suspected each might be a figment of the other's imagination.

And so Lotta, the woman who had come into his Cabinet of Natural History and on into his life, took off her clothes, even her petticoat, with no hint of shyness, and stood before him. 'Now I am just me.' She cast a steady gaze upon him, but that gaze was also directed at herself.

Every morning on waking, he kissed her forehead, neck and both breasts in a tender ritual which sometimes aroused her desire to be conjoined with him at once. They could not believe that any other citizens of licentious Stockholm were behaving like this. She received him as a shallow beach receives a swimmer.

4

She wept when he finally admitted he loved her. He had said it in many other ways, of course, but the word itself had not been easy to express. He had never said it to anyone in his life. Now it was there as an affirmation whose depth she could not sound, she was swept along in a warm current of air. Her heart beat against his hand as it lay on her breast. But her eyes were steady and unafraid.

'I shall never leave you. I want to die with you.'

He tried to keep his fearful happiness in check, and even to push it away as something unbidden and unmerited, but that was only a ruse to trick it into increasing its presence.

He had met Charlotta Fries at a point in his life when he believed almost everything had come to an end and was behind him. What had been spontaneous activities, experiments and research, had narrowed to a single corridor where the doors were all too easily recognizable, and chance was an unwelcome visitor. Then, miraculously, he had lost his footing and fallen head over heels in love.

Much of his life up to then seemed to him as sterile as a parched lake-bed. He was afraid he would not be able to find his way back to the glowing windows of his past where he belonged – not in his childhood, not in adult life but in the interlude, the intermezzo, when he was borne on the vessels of others, content with his clear vision and smooth pen, his collections and his poverty. What ensued was frost and fog, mould and moths.

There was an order behind all secrets, a secret behind all order. He was not in the weave of the fabric, he was outside it, and had been since the beginning, except when he was one of the scientists on the *Resolution*. Now he wanted to skip away from time, break through it, shatter watch face and compass.

Anders concentrated his gaze on Lotta, as if she might evoke a place he had visited, a name he had forgotten, a memory that had slipped his mind. It was like peeling the bark from a tree trunk and seeing the script of the grubs. The interpretation was denied him. Or did the bark conceal nothing?

So much was still left unexpressed. He groped his way forward over her hills and dales. He followed the line of her chin and the rim of her ear, as if struggling over the wind-eroded stone blocks around Knysna. At moments when desire, from an unidentifiable source, was taking them beyond sense and reason, they instilled in one another discretion and confidence. To think they were setting themselves so shamelessly above custom and the law of the land and the sacred vows of the church!

His lust built up in her, slowly but surely. He lay still inside her until he felt her gentle contractions and saw her stomach muscles rise into a little ridge. Then he pushed higher up into her and lifted her body towards his own. When they had tremblingly found release and she was resting her head on his arm, he told himself that this was no transient folly, it was something inexorable, the force of which struck him dumb. Lotta's daily presence gave way to something unfamiliar, which united them in a new way. Lust had its own unseemly will, it was an advance guard sent out into the unknown, going ahead of them, reconnoitring and discovering what they themselves had not yet seen.

'I've always kept myself to myself,' Lotta said, her face at once both childlike and solemn. 'Now I feel gay and mischievous. My skirts are billowing in your breeze. I sparkle under your radiance. I want to be all you will ever need. Hold me tight, hold me hard!'

They no longer knew who said what. 'You are my happiness, my every joy.' 'Never have I been so close to anyone in body and soul, in soul and body.' Thus they danced around each other.

It is extraordinary how a new person can be caressed into existence. He submerged himself into something atavistic that they had in common, and within that darkness the real compact was made.

5

Their thoughts and conversations ranged this way and that, as if they were in a rudderless boat, clinging to one another, letting go, sinking and rising to the surface unexpectedly elsewhere. Whether morning or night, light or dark, they moved around each other, inside one another, with no awareness that the hours were doing the same.

He broke through the barriers into her real self – or the self she had become through his efforts. Their love was undeserved: it came to them without their understanding how or why. All they knew was that they had to hold on to it.

It was not for her qualities that he loved Lotta, and she loved him for something he could not clearly perceive. They chose one another – not for their merits, but through a simultaneous desperation.

It was totally unanticipated, the craving and the passion and the closeness they felt before every touch. He became familiar with her movements when she lay down beside him, her breath against his neck. He had never experienced a closeness like this, even as a child. And the thin white scar above her buttock filled him with a special tenderness.

She ran her hands over his body without the slightest haste. Desire freed them. Everything was permitted. Words were coined for collarbone and hollow of neck, for her curly bush and angular knees. She caused his heart to race, and then he felt the rhythm slow down in the security she instilled in him.

'What a relief to find you!' he murmured. He burrowed his nose in her armpit. She found it sensuous being kissed there.

Lotta smiled at him with her grey-blue eyes that never wavered from his. With every part of their bodies they melted into each other, and her little trills of pleasure roused his lust to meet hers, even if he lacked the energy to consummate it as often as she.

He sucked on her earlobe and whispered in her ear, his vocal cords fading. He blew softly into her private parts, the pale skin glistened, the grass wafted aside and his kisses tasted her delicate salt. His tongue flicked over her flesh, quick and greedy, gentle and careful. They melted into one another with defenceless courage – as if inching along a precipice and keeping their eyes on the rock face. She gave him the feeling that life still had another card to play.

He had been to the uttermost limits of the world, but now thanks to her also to the innermost heart of emotion. He rested in her. They were boats bobbing on calm waters.

'Look at me,' he said, and they stared into each other, so close that they could see only one eye at a time. This divided gaze was filled with a desire that fired all his limbs, and united them with her body and whole being. He felt his seed surging into her, so powerfully that they both gave a little shriek, but their eyes went on looking and looking: it was their souls they saw and their bodies that responded.

'You are pushing me to the point of insanity,' he said, embarrassed by his own sensuality. She stretched out beside him, and even when his member was slack she pushed it into herself with a smile, folded herself around him, and, once inside her, he expanded again in blissful voluptuousness. Their love was wild and reverent, and he was plunging into depths that once would have frightened him. He felt her face should never be obliterated. He wanted to restore it, as one fills in the outlines of a drawing.

How could they ever have had anything else in their lives? Every action, however banal, took on significance. He leaned over her face in wonder, as if on the trail of an undeciphered alphabet. His love did not belong with his life at sea, nor with his zoology. He clenched his fists in a gesture of self-defence. There was a streak of superiority in her, which threatened to annihilate him. At the same time his affection leapt right out into the night.

It seemed to him he had put his fate into the hands of a foreign embassy, without the necessary papers to prove his identity. Navigable waters between him and Lotta, all around them the world shut off. They circled one another, insects blinded by the light, intoxicated by the heat, so close that they were totally inaccessible to each other.

Never had he felt so much love and confusion. 'I've made many mistakes in my life,' he said, 'but loving you is not one of them.'

'I am nobody special,' she replied. 'You know my weaknesses, all my nooks and crannies, my very thoughts. I'm giving you everything I have, because I've never felt myself loved before.'

They tried to throw a harness around one another and capture whatever they had not yet experienced – until the strength of their devotion set them free. He licked her lips, putting a seal on their love from within. His tongue twirled around her nipples, he kissed her feet and slid up her legs to her belly with its tiny creases following the birth, the child that died like so many others.

He sometimes detected the deepest melancholy in her eyes, as if the whole of life were a poisonous thorn. But when she looked at him, room after room seemed to open inside him. And she wanted him then to be willing to know her completely, whatever the cost, to bear to hear even the very worst. Feelings could have an obverse, and even if he were hiding himself there, she would find him.

He sought out secret niches in her body – just as he used to seek well-honed phrases for his expedition notes to describe what he thought he had experienced. He beat upon a soundless drum within her. Come further in, come into the unbleached light. They were now united in most things, although there were thresholds they could not see. But these posed no threat.

Love could not be created and produced to order – any more than could gold in Nordenskjöld's pots and mortars. It turned up here and there, a precipitate, a glint. It took time to learn what was sediment and what was mere dross on the surface.

There were new surfaces, inner paths. And a sudden chill in October when the rose hips wrinkled like fingertips and the leaves fell off the trees like the pages of a book when the glue has cracked. They would never be gathered again and read.

Physician to the Poor

From the end of the 1790s the former circumnavigator earned his living partly as physician to the poor in Klara. After the fires of the 1750s, the houses were built of stone. They had tiled roofs and were plastered with a mixture of vitriol of iron, acid and lime. The new ochre-coloured facades made the streets lighter. It was a method recently invented by Sahlberg, an apothecary, one of Sparrman's colleagues in the Academy of Sciences. Otherwise, everything was as it had always been: the courtyards housed privies, distilleries, wash-houses, stables, woodsheds, workshops.

The local population included numerous elderly stonemasons, block-and-tackle makers, sailmakers, but also bookkeepers, printers, and servant girls temporarily without a position or a legal right to a home, and therefore obliged to earn money as best they could. There were men who worked in the harbour part-time and also helped out as coffin-bearers or night-soil collectors, or got by as unregistered traders. Young people migrated into Stockholm in order to survive and to comply with the work requirement for the unemployed. Everybody of working age and without funds had to have employment, except married women.

One in ten inhabitants of the district was signed on as poor and in need of assistance. Only two capital cities in Europe had a higher mortality rate than Stockholm. Forty per cent of infants died. The Orphanage sent two hundred children a year out to the countryside; one in four died within a short period.

Sparrman proposed in a report that Klara Reach and the channel off Rörstrand and Karlberg should be dredged; that there should be designated sites for piling up the ice from the streets; and that the tipping of filth on the ice should be prohibited. There were good-quality wells on Brunkebergstorg, Hötorget and the corner of Regeringsgatan and Jakobsgatan, with moderate levels of salt, saltpetre, lime and manganese. The others needed to be cleaned out.

Public hygiene regulations became stricter from about 1800. The Old Town was swept – under contract – every weekday during the summer. No-one was permitted to empty rubbish or excrement on to the streets. The brooms started sweeping from early dawn. Central areas had to be clean by eight o'clock in the morning; in the suburbs, householders themselves were responsible.

Anders wore the plain black surtout of the paupers' doctor, with a fleece lining and boots with brown cuffs. He carried a leather case of instruments for bloodletting. Klara was his Swedish Hottentot village. As he went from one hovel to another, he felt oddly at home in the all-consuming impotence afflicting the households. He saw this world with several pairs of eyes, with no confidence or assurance, with no fear for all he had lost and for losses yet to come.

He was surprised at how seldom he was subjected to altercations and disrespect or bitterness and rancour from those whom life had treated so shamefully.

'I can feel an affection for these hard-pressed and sore-tried people who have grown up with suffering and have no control over their lives,' he remarked to Lotta. 'These poor souls live on the threshold of death, where all the noise and commotion of the city have faded into a weary background rumble.'

He showed Lotta what the inscription said on the poor box outside Danviken lunatic asylum:

Here thou seest an image of the world, where he who is the least deranged is wise. If all madness were to warrant equal treatment, then the learned man's library, the rake's ballroom, the lady's boudoir, the rich man's strongroom, would be a madhouse. Overweening ambition and unhappy love have produced these inmates. Look upon them, O reader, and know thyself!

In Klara Sparrman encountered life from birth to autopsy. With his mineral magnet he transmitted celestial *fluidum* to the cobbler with dog-bite scars, and to the blacksmith suffering from burns, whose forehead glowed like the door of a tiled stove. He interpreted animal magnetism as a stream of spiritual energy, which might heal people of maladies as yet untreatable. He often prescribed a twenty-four-hour fast to rid the body of the heavier metals.

He delved as deep as he could into the new theories. According to one rumour, he had inscriptions beneath a seal in code, mirrors that emitted rays of undetermined strength, and electrical power stored in lead plates. He was captivated by the pineal gland, that motor for all corporeal functions, regulating daily rhythm and co-ordinating the mental activity of the brain with the mechanics of the body. Descartes considered this small gland to be the seat of the soul, since it was only to be found in humans.

August Nordenskjöld's colleague C. F. Bergklint described Anders Sparrman as Stockholm's greatest mesmerist. But, as Bergklint pointed out to Nordenskjöld shortly before the latter's death, Sparrman was not a Swedenborgian, and 'it is just as well, for his intellectual abilities don't inspire any great respect'.

As physician to the poor, Sparrman proved that Conrad Quensel had been wrong to suppose that work fatigued him. Nor was he averse to rash experimentation, at least in a good cause; he had demonstrated that in his articles. To conduct research into hidden mysteries was quite different from being seduced by false theories, hallucinations and leaps of the imagination.

The post of physician to the poor was his personal flight from fossilization and from the risk of himself becoming one of the stuffed animals he was appointed to look after for the Academy of Sciences. He really wanted to effect cures, and knew that one day in the future science would be able to save those who at present had no chance. But he could hardly say to his patients, 'If only you had been born a hundred and fifty years hence, you would have lived, because by then there will be medicines for everything but death itself.' Nevertheless, a degree of deception and dissimulation did them good. A glimmer of life could be aroused in strangely expressionless eyes. Something in the afflicted would begin to struggle towards the light.

He saw a fourteen-year-old girl, thin and emaciated with consumption, her shoulders hunched, as if to disguise her breasts. Her mother had already given her up for dead. He peered into her mouth: her tongue was grey, her saliva viscous. She looked old, life flitting through her towards its end. His medical bag stood on the kitchen table; indoors was as damp as outside. The pallid girl lying in the bed reminded him of lost happiness, something primeval, which she was returning to with ever shallower breaths. He caught a glimpse of the wild loneliness in her eyes and could not bring himself to say: 'Your time has come.'

A woman grasped his hands respectfully and besought him, in tears, to come to her mother, who had taken to her bed and was in a confused state.

'I was brought up the old-fashioned way,' she said. 'I'm not asking for charity but for your knowledge, which I'll pay for as best I can.' But after those calmly considered words she clutched at him again and cried, 'I don't want her to die! She's all I've got!' The old lady's sole possessions, apart from the frock she was wearing in bed, were a shawl that had seen better days and a pair of brogue boots with the heels worn down on one side.

An elderly man called Sven Persson had letters to the king strewn all over his table, not one of them ever sent. He had written several versions of his will; it kept him going; as did teasing his neighbours with riddles and challenging them to a game of fox and geese, or dice. His ribs were like barrel hoops. Outside in the courtyard the butcher could be heard splitting marrowbones with a chopper and shovelling bones and hides into a jute sack.

The old man had not been washed and deloused for a long time; his limbs were weak, and he mostly lay dozing. He would wake up suddenly and address those present by bizarrely incorrect names, as if he were somewhere completely different. And when he finally died, it was with mouth closed and lips pursed, as if he were ashamed of his teeth or wanted to suppress an inexplicable urge to laugh. It was a phenomenon Anders had not witnessed before.

Once he found himself sitting with his hand on the brow of a dying woman, the dust motes dancing in the thin shaft of light from the window, the gruel dried up in the pan, the air rancid and stale. She was extremely weak, and whispered that she had felt perfectly comfortable in a dream of a summer in Heaven, with no demons.

'May God take me unto Himself!' she exclaimed by way of greeting from her humble abode, with only a water butt, washbowl and broom for company.

Sparrman sought to express himself reassuringly in a low voice, to instil hope with a few unfamiliar words and phrases, without actually giving a precise diagnosis. If the right medicine did not exist, rapture must do instead. It would probably delay death a little. He did not know for sure. But he did know that the truth left them no escape. Although he might, perhaps, be mistaken. Perhaps he had always been mistaken.

He became habituated to the sound of groans in semi-darkness, people directing him towards some poor creature on the point of expiry, while running hither and thither with lamps and boiling water. They were ravaged by anxiety, objects of contempt for others, fearful of their fate. Many in Klara simply wasted away in their putrid fluids. In cramped rooms, in malodorous proximity to the sick, he perceived the intangible that he wanted to communicate to them, but could not reveal even to himself.

Sitting in silence, he held an old lady's hand in an unspoken sympathy which moved her to tears, and when he prepared her for the fact that she could not count on many more days on Earth, she nodded contentedly and whispered in his ear that she was loved by a husband now far away. She said it with the passion of affirming a lover, with a hint of the inexpressible in her voice. Anders could imagine he was seeing his own mother, her strict and parsimonious figure, which always seemed to adopt a dismissive posture towards anything unfamiliar or desirable that was lacking in her life.

The cobbler's widow with a peony-red silk ribbon and a hem-stitched handkerchief; the son with a long mute handshake; the cobbler himself laid out in his shabby tailcoat surrounded by flickering candles. He was soon removed from the house. Twelve boys from the church school shrilly performing the funeral dirge, conducted by the undertaker, who took his *douceur* in a sealed package that the widow pushed into his hands. Then a lively and riotous wake supper in a local tavern.

So many confessions he had to listen to, blue with cold, while breathing in the deathbed fetor of gangrene and waning life. He opened the low windows and let in some fresh air. The flies woke up. The dogs barked in the alley. A blacksmith hammered nails. The straw of a double bed rustled. He heard a weak, rasping cough.

A gentleman who had been dismissed as instructor at the Russian Empire's physical training establishment in St Petersburg refused to stay at home, sitting in The Grapes with the local glazier, ordering spirits from the bar. Jovial and aggressive, he pontificated to the entire tavern. He had sung second bass in the student choir in Uppsala. He was agile in body, inflexible in temperament, the quintessential Russian. The curate sat down by the chimneysweep, whom he was about to marry to a house painter's young widow, in lieu of the vicar, who considered it beneath him. The gentleman from St Petersburg ordered yet another toddy, and with expansive gestures offered around a caraway cheese.

Anders Sparrman began to recognize Klara characters: a female piano teacher who had once been a ballet dancer, a garrulous lady watercolourist, a whore called Buttercup who danced at the country inn out at Ålkistan. The fiddle solo by Samuel the beggar could be heard emanating from the snowdrift in Klara churchyard. On Hötorget peasant farmers in their freshly laundered caps milled about in front of their derisively whinnying horses.

The children were unkempt and streaked with dirt. It was distressingly evident how many of them were completely at the mercy of poverty and unable to help themselves. Did he dare ascribe to the world a fortuitous beauty, as when fingers hit keys at random – sometimes a tune emerges, sometimes discord? Do we have to shut our eyes to manage a smile?

A stooped old man approached him by Klara Reach. He had been digging for bait on the muddy foreshore and had put the worms in a jar tied to his booted leg. He could see Anders was a doctor, and showed him a burn on the back of his hand that wouldn't heal.

'I'll give you some unguent to put on it,' said Dr Sparrman, taking out a tin of zinc ointment from his medical bag. 'It will do you good. It will cool it.' He felt the rough skin and caught the smell of infection.

The old man's face lit up: 'So long as it's not extreme unction.'

Anders' intention was to give people a ray of hope. The injustice of those in power and the perfidy of the mean-spirited was so clear to him when he heard people invoke a being that he himself, a fourth generation priest's son, had no faith in. He had seen black slaves denied entry to the kingdom of God, since the inhabitants of Paradise couldn't possibly be black. Unloved, unwanted, deformed by adversity and want of recourse to the law, with no expectation of generosity or friendship, they spent the whole of their brief existence under the whip.

Just as he had once pleaded for the liberation of the slaves, so now he petitioned the city magistrate to improve conditions for the less fortunate, those who in the hospital records were registered as labourers of the lower classes. The most common causes of death among them were consumption, ardent fever, stitch and stings, and ague. Children died of smallpox, disease of the lungs, whooping cough, and poisoning. The Seraphim Hospital was full of cases of venereal disease.

In the newspapers he saw announcements of East India Company ships unloading in Gothenburg and sailing on via Kalmar to Stockholm with olive oil, Bayonne ham, cheeses, tea and coffee. And he remembered himself as a young surgeon on the voyage to China amputating the finger of a sailor who had caught it in the tackle. The finger was thrown overboard – maybe it even ended up in the stomach of a shark. The sailor had fainted, but came to when Anders rubbed citric acid on his lips. He consoled the man by pointing out that at least he hadn't lost an appendage lower down his body.

He saw some boys from the elementary school catch a rat and nail it to the privy wall. Their fathers swigged anisette down at the tavern, and scraped out a dish of lung-hash. It reeked of dripping and burnt grain-sausage. The bugs were lured out of the walls to spend the night under fresh broad-bean leaves, so that the whole lot could be exterminated in the morning with vinegar essence.

The poor, with a certificate from the priest, were allowed to present themselves at the apothecary's at the sign of the Owl on Drottninggatan at nine o'clock every morning, for advice and prescriptions from the physicians appointed by the Royal College of Medicine. In 1801 soup kitchens for the poor were set up in Klara parish: they served barley groats, celery leaves, beer, and potatoes with chopped herring and cubes of bread.

Anders gave consultations and collected his medicines at the apothecary's. He had retained his title and was treated respectfully and graciously. There was a smell of spices and tar in the air, and something more unusual: chlorine and sulphur. Even sweetmeats and a selection of groceries were sold there. He was given a discount on the apothecary's prices, and some blue and white handkerchiefs were thrown in to use as bandages.

So much to deal with! How many clammy palms had he taken in his? But his treatments failed: leeches, laxatives, hypnotic reassurance in musty rooms where people lay delirious in blood-soaked bandages. He prescribed gruel boiled with strong beer, mare's or goat's milk for tuberculosis; lily of the valley flowers with half a stoup of French wine for headache or sunstroke; for dysentery, *medicamenta opiata* – discreetly, and not entered on the patient's record.

The magic current that flowed through the world seldom found its mark. How he hoped for a formula that would work both backwards and forwards in time! What he needed was the elixir of life, the coveted tonic for which the sick, the fallen and the confused would have paid any price.

He was their sanctuary and their refuge. They regarded him as indispensable. Even so, many God-fearing and serious minded people put more faith in the stars, and thought their health and life were regulated by the relative positions of the planets. Anders warned against quacks, cheats, spellmongers and all those who prescribed unique ointments and infallible, universal remedies.

Stockholm in winter was a very different city from the summer, with a different way of life. Water froze in the wells and had to be melted with glowing iron rods, smoke rose from the chimneys, birch and pine burnt in the stoves. When the snow arrived the noise of carts and carriages ceased and only sleigh bells rang out. Water barrows slid along the alleys. People crossed the ice of the lake and the sea on both sides of Stockholm on kick-sledges, shortening the distances between the various parts of the city and its islands.

You had to go to the post office on Lilla Nygatan to check on a noticeboard whether you had mail. Sometimes it was so dark inside that you had to hire a stump of candle from an old pastry-seller. Lanterns and torches hung at intervals of fifteen paces. House-owners were required to keep them lit from nightfall until one in the morning. Herring-oil lamps gave only enough illumi-nation to show the way, and if you dropped anything your sole hope of finding it was through an advertisement in the newspaper.

The heat of summer brought the crowds out on to the streets. Animals grazed in Klara churchyard and caused devastation; grass and weeds flourished in their dung. A sectarian muttered his incantations among the gravestones.

Anders was afraid of infection and mopped the sweat from his brow with a vinegar compress. Hymn-singing could be heard from Klara School, and a caterwauling from the Freemasons' children's home on Malmtorgsgatan, that sounded like the wailing of the deaf and dumb. Injustice degraded the poor. They sang to the glory of God in church, but remained victims of an inimical fate they had no chance of bargaining with.

From the bell tower of Klara Church the treble bell rang out with a sound rather like the distant voice of a young girl. The church walls were decorated with epitaphs of the nobility and priesthood, with symbols for chivalry, fidelity and piety. And above the row of sepulchres in the churchyard were inscriptions to those who had been virtuous and noble in life, to the endless river of time and to the wanderer who stays his steps in vain.

Then the rank scent of autumn wafted through the streets and the jackdaws gathered on the heavy branches around the church.

He imagined every house ready to explode with frenzied questions, yet what issued forth was just impotent horror at the inexorable calamities that overwhelmed ordinary human beings.

Lotta washed his clothes out frequently, in spring water at home or on Rödbotorget, where the current was swift and the water cleaner, in an effort to remove all traces of Anders' visits to the sick and infectious, whose breath lingered in his hair and soiled his neckbands. It was not without risk that he went so boldly and resolutely into the houses of the doomed, even if he did bring home payment in bread, calf's liver or marrowbones. She hung the laundry out to dry in the courtyard, and on the backs of chairs and the edge of the washtub.

Klara was a world in itself. Anders only had to go out on Norrbro to see a complete contrast: self-centred gentlemen with smiles on their faces, ladies elegantly attired, the gleam of uniforms, a multitude of carriages. On the north side of the churchyard was the poorhouse for fifty unfortunates, and another nearby housed a hundred inmates, mostly old women. Many of them had served as nursemaids in the new stone-built districts on Norrmalm, or as cooks in some grandiose dwelling on Drottninggatan, where the husband complained about the food because the wife had not authorized an adequate purchase of eggs and butter. They had stood in dark kitchens and kept the ovens burning, and when they became frailer those without families had no option but the poorhouse.

As physician to the poor Anders Sparrman came to witness all the hardships of daily life. He walked home in the falling snow in leaky shoes. His own financial situation was his constant private anxiety, gnawing away at his joy in life. And the year was sinking towards winter.

'I spent too long on plants and animals,' he said to Lotta one evening. 'Now it's time for human beings.'

Soon he had made an appearance in every house in the parish. The suffering of others instilled no fear in him; he had seen too much of it. He tried to identify the warning signs in the heavy, sickly-sweet atmosphere: was it cholera, putrid fever, measles?

His spirits revived in Klara, where everything was tangible. He moved around in his internal exile with the lightest of baggage. His colleagues in the Academy were shocked into silence. All his knowledge was devoted to Klara parish. And what he in turn received from Lotta was impossible to evaluate.

The Botany of Love

1

The summer was still young. Brimstone butterflies were dancing. One Sunday Anders Sparrman lifted his nose from his engravings of exotic animals and took a walk with Lotta in the newly laid-out Bellevue Park. It had only just been opened to the public – although not for games or smoking tobacco. A stream tumbled down from the high cliffs on the Roslagen side and the sound of bleating sheep could be heard from the Haga shore.

Peasants' carts, full of pigs grunting contentedly, were queuing outside the city gate. The Customs officer brandished his stick at the crowd to remind them of his authority. And cowbells rang across the water, maybe from as far away as Tivoli Point, the spacious and airy park that Mr Piper, the architect, had been working on. Harebells, columbines and wild delphiniums were growing along the side of the road, three shades of blue amidst the green.

Here, on the edge of the populous city and its suffocating atmosphere, Anders and Lotta found a private spot between the alder trees which cast their lofty shade over the shore. There was a marshy scent of meadowsweet. The sun shone tremulously from the west over Frösunda. The trees drank in the afternoon light and leaned down over the water.

Anders took out pen and brush, ink and paper from his case. Sketching the landscape, the mirror-smooth surface of the bay and the smiling meadows on the other side, revived memories of the Cape and its veldt, where the southern hemisphere's equivalents to campion and daisies grew.

Then he handed Lotta the paper and pen, and while she sketched willow trunks reflected in the water, he lay back and watched her shoulders and neck tautly concentrating.

'The warmth of the day lifted the dew from the earth,' he wrote later. 'Nature was one great fragrant blossom. Larks and thrushes and the whole enchanting pack of forest idlers were rejoicing. But we would soon have to return to the odours of the city's victuals, the stench of the human menagerie, and seeking out a breath of fresh air we would be treated instead to the racket of the post-horse peasants.'

He danced a little jig with Lotta, and she held up her skirt as they cavorted merrily before dropping down on the grass. He wanted to make her life more enjoyable. He didn't want her just to be tending the fire, scraping turnips, frying pike, mending his breeches or sewing a silver thread into the collar of his discarded official coat. At an early stage in their relationship he had forbidden her to serve him his meals without sitting down opposite him herself and eating the same.

She sensed when he preferred to be left in peace or eat in silence. But she was often taken aback when he burst out laughing for no particular reason, or when he took out his chamois-leather notebook.

'Writing is like working as an archaeologist,' he said. 'Digging down and down, turning stones and clods of earth, scanning from side to side in case a find is lurking there.' He would sometimes draw a seal's head or a beaver's tail in the margin.

Love was a door of deep perception into the unknown. She had never had a life of her own. She had always lived the lives of others.

'Things are so wonderful between us,' she said. 'But why do you avert your gaze, Anders?'

'The better to see you.'

'We still know so little about one another that we might easily be tempted to lie,' said Lotta. 'But don't, I beg of you!'

'I know that everything you've said is true. Your face is beautiful when you have the confidence to keep your eyes on me. Then you come so close that I can't see anything.'

'I'm so afraid of losing your love before you have given it utterly.'

One cold night they lay intertwined, changing position in a shared rhythm, the sheets as rumpled as her pubic hair, and her clothes strewn about their feet. He remained motionless inside her, but she pressed him even further in and gave a low moan. He felt overwhelmed. He had had such lengthy periods of abstinence in his life. He could only hope the smouldering glow in the stove would leap into flame again from the charred embers.

She had a serene and patient temperament, but occasionally he saw her tremble with rage, and then he would take her in his arms and lay her down on the mattress with himself on top of her, and she would relax beneath him and say, 'My desire is incomprehensible and without shame. But every day I feel I'm not enough for you.'

He didn't know himself what was happening. It was something significant, momentous, like when he was entrusted with the church key in Tensta and weighed it in his hand. Time seemed to expand of its own volition. What an immense distance he had travelled to come this far.

Perhaps the value of life was these very states of resolute impetuosity, of ruthlessness and openness, each element balancing the other. The process filled him with exhilaration and sorrow in such a potent combination that he imagined everything must have been a dream, since his body was scarcely able to harbour such powerful emotions.

Her beauty made him ache inside. She was not even aware of it herself. He did not want to be free of this fragile, strong person, as he lay in her embrace and her hands rested on his head. His body felt warm and light, as if she had taken all he had to give.

It seemed to him his life had been lived in reverse. First came his adventures on the oceans and savannahs in an unpredictable and bewildering world. Then came the long years becalmed, until he encountered the mysterious love that could have befallen him in his youth, but which had waited until he had completed much of his life. Had he restrained his feelings in the early days, had he been on his guard for fear of the painful fickleness of emotion?

This cannot last, he told himself in one of his attempts to explain away some irrational joy that every so often felt beyond his comprehension, however much he strove to put it into words, sometimes poring over the poetry of Bengt Lidner to find a kindred spirit whose rapture was unassailable.

He had other things to think about, of course, and did so. He did not neglect his patients, who with good reason were solely concerned with their bodies and vitality. He entered houses of mourning and dens of iniquity with inadequate knowledge but the best of intentions, to help those who sought to conceal their distress and misfortune by counting themselves just one of the many to be dealt a blow by fate.

When the working day was over he would hasten back to Lotta, as if overtaking himself, and he was reminded that for so many years after his return to Sweden he had not had a home to share with anyone. But the place itself was not important: what mattered was Lotta's voice and gestures and laughter when she listened to his inimitable blend of seriousness and comedy.

He was amazed at how long love had bided its time. Perhaps it had been waiting in the wings, but he had not seen it. For suddenly everything had happened so fast. He had noticed Lotta's responsiveness without her having to put it into words.

'Neither of us has been truly in love,' he said. 'Now it seems the moment has come.'

2

Off-duty, Anders wore coarse woollen, reddish-brown breeches and black stockings. When the king had paid a visit to the Academy of Sciences, with a dinner to follow, Anders had attended in brown tailcoat, pale-striped waistcoat and yellow breeches. Lotta wanted to hear all about such occasions, but he said he avoided gentlemen in silk stockings who strutted around making clever pronouncements about nothing. His usual apparel was shirt-sleeves with an open waistcoat, and he had not replaced his patched overcoat in years.

Lotta dressed in a blue bodice, with a cream-coloured, thin neckerchief and a white bonnet with a blue ribbon. She also had a white skirt with a black rosette at the small of the back, a striped grey and blue jacket, and an apron she wore over a red skirt. Anders had presented her with a tea-caddy and sugar bowl, which she kept on a shelf with a bundle of sulphur sticks. He was always full of admiration for her dark eyebrows, good teeth and clear skin, and her auburn hair fastened at the nape of her neck.

Lotta would light the tiled stove at six o'clock and heat up the oat gruel. He watched her sitting on an upturned tub, scrubbing the soles of her feet with soapy water in a bowl. An iron pot stood on the stove. She inserted a glowing wedge in the smoothing iron and looked for the whisk to flick water over some of the laundry from the basket.

She put on the table whatever she had bought from the peasants on Riddarholm Quay and the fishmonger on Kornhamnstorg. She told him what they had said and where they came from: Färentuna, Svartsjö, Adelsö . . . Their boats with the square sails were waiting for the wind. They wanted to sail back that afternoon. She knew Anders did not mind what he ate; after all, he had even brought back from his travels a smoked hippopotamus tongue for the royal table. She herself had never been able to afford a decent spread.

As a seamstress, she had managed to acquire several clients – like Eva Stina Rådberg, Sofia Jernberg, Ulrika Tryselius – probably because she was industrious and friendly to everybody. It was a strain on her eyes, but it brought in money. She sat by the window, and the sound of the bells of St Gertrude's Church and the Cathedral met at the ridge of the roof.

They would sit side by side, with their backs to the fire, looking out of the dark windows. He put his hand on her knee and stroked it covertly, as if they were not alone. He kept his hand there even when he turned away. She leaned her face against his shoulder. They sat in silence.

'Everything has a beginning and an end,' he said after a while.

She replied, 'But between the beginning and the end there is something else that we can share if you want to.'

'Yes, indeed there is, but it stops, against our will. If we were born fifty years hence and met when we were twenty-five in, say, 1875, what would our lives be like then?'

'We'll be dead by then, Anders, and no-one knows where we'll be. But you will still be remembered, not I. You've torn your cuff: I'll mend it for you.'

'We shall disappear into the murky depths that we sounded off Tierra del Fuego. No-one will ever build a Tower of Babel as high as the depth of that ocean grave.'

'I've got used to you,' Lotta went on, 'used to the smell of your life. To your black woodpecker and linnet that I like, and to the skins of animals that I wouldn't have believed existed. I'm getting some clean sheets out of the cupboard. Then I'll wash your dejection away.'

It was so strange that with Anders she felt full of initiative, not awkward, shy or superfluous. She summoned all her courage to sustain the radiance that emanated from the man she loved. And he could see how her experience and her childlike disposition united to make her the person she was. He would wait for her smile, which was slow to appear, but when it did he found joy in its unconditional warmth.

Ants had made their way up through the gaps in the floor and she threw herself upon them with bucket and brush. She was the cleanest person he had ever encountered. Fine mesh curtains hung at the windows. She had painted bunches of rowanberries on the plain wallpaper. On a drinks table that could be folded away she had laid out bread, a piece of smoked sheep's tongue and salt salmon.

They drank coffee by the green-tiled stove, and Lotta told him about someone who had been kicked by a horse on Munkbron and fallen into the water and drowned. A pair of pewter candlesticks, a mirror, a sideboard, two spindle-back chairs with green and white cotton covers. In the drawing room a sofa and a birch table, where Lotta had laid her needlework frame and her case of needles and sewing implements. On top of the chamber-pot cupboard stood the shaving mirror he had bought second-hand. Those were the furnishings of their three rooms.

In April the icicles started tinkling down on the cobbles. The melt water trickled out on to the pavements from the courtyards and soon there was a steady murmur from the gutters like the buzz of human voices. Immediately after reveille from the artillery barracks, the first baker's cart crossed Nybron on its way to the Royal Guard at the Palace. The windmills on Skvalberget were turning at full tilt. Horses were stamping their hooves outside the warehouses along Skeppsbron Quay.

'You have studied the internal convolutions of the human body, the skeleton of the albatross, the contents of the sea-lion's stomach. You have dispatched birds to the Academy of Sciences and plants to Linnaeus. I haven't done anything. I've never had the chance. Have you ever seen a mermaid?'

'Only manatees. And the wicked fairies of St Elmo's fire that vanished when we sailed nearer.'

She sang to him: '*Freut euch des Lebens, weil noch das Lämpchen glüht.*' She knew it by heart, but didn't understand the words until he translated them for her, though he questioned their real meaning.

She filled the iron and pressed collars, hems and seams. He admired the sure, firm movements of her arms. All the passion of their life together was rekindled.

When she was asleep her breathing was deeper; a different body seemed to be taking care of her. Her upturned face was completely still, as if becalmed. But every morning they were up and off at dawn to continue their voyage.

3

'Waking up on Judgement Day is not something I'm looking forward to,' said Anders. 'We are a letter that Birth sends to Death. We have to hope the handwriting is not illegible.'

After some thought he continued, 'Is it truly the business of religion to constrain the passions? That is what the priests believe and the authorities hope. Religion dries up the wellsprings of our blood. If I were younger and stronger, and fired more often by the flame of life you ignite in me, I would overcome that indolence you sometimes experience, when you sit trimming your nails with the kitchen knife. The practical sciences and public education are still imperfect. But we can catch glimpses of the sun through our cloud of unknowing. Darkness is passive, light is the active day-labourer. In the next century our country will become unrecognizable.'

'I may not be the best of cooks, though I can produce two dishes every evening, and I'm not talkative like you,' said Lotta. 'We have linen on our bed and wood in our hearth, we have our health and we are alive. But we are short of money – and time for a life of our own. You are heedlessly generous. You never hesitate to do good without any expectation of reward – not even in Heaven, since you don't subject yourself to the laws of our Lord.'

'I am awaiting the arrival of a new order. But we shall not be here to see it. Nor shall we see the discovery of new forms of magnetism, nor the interplay of particles, nor the radiation of rocks.

What is invisible in our lifetime will only become visible when the detritus can be cleared away, but there is no short cut, no grace, no mercy.

'Advancing knowledge does not arouse the same sensual delight as resides in your skin, Lotta. But I have never merely dallied on the surface, whether of the body, of water, or of the Earth. The bubbles of the lungs and the moist labyrinths of the brain, the molluscs and algae, the treasures of the mineral kingdom, the roots of all vegetation – all lie beneath the surface.'

'No-one knows what kind of person is concealed inside the outer sheath of the body,' Lotta said.

'If you throw a chip of tile, or a ring, into the water, you see it spiral to the bottom, the tile more slowly because it has no hole in the centre, but neither of them sinks straight down.'

'You are the tile, I am the ring,' Lotta said. 'And we live in evil times. What is the point of our presence here on Earth?'

'On the coast of Guinea I heard the birds singing divinely, right above the auction of female slaves, whose bodily orifices had been violated, and whose children had been kicked into the sea. The equation did not balance. Its sum was an impenetrable darkness. The globe seemed to me then to be Swedenborg's black egg: eternally rotting matter.'

He held Lotta in his arms, and said, 'Death was at our heels when we sailed. Death was with us among the crew. But Love never signed on. Though it disguised itself in blithe carnality on some of the islands. There was no opportunity for love on my travels.'

He told her about George Forster. 'He was my best friend before I met you, my dearest, and he died before our time, in a Paris garret, impoverished and alone, at the age of forty.' He explained how Forster had been alternately singled out as a traitor, excused as a dreamer and recognized as a pioneer of Romanticism – only then to be shovelled into a nameless grave with others who, like himself, were first adherents of the Revolution and then its victims.

Anders felt that Forster – by his premature death – had robbed him of the chance of their continued correspondence. He had letters for him that he had never sent, and now could not remember where they were.

And when Lotta asked about icebergs and Africa, he replied, 'The southern continent does not exist. We know that now. But the continent of Africa is so extensive and unknown that we are only familiar with the coastal strips and some two hundred miles into the interior. All the rest exists, but we remain in ignorance of it.'

4

It was the season when the warm August rain drifted in over Stockholm and prolonged the green foliage of the trees. They were eating salt herring and roast cockerel at the inn at Nackanäs. They had been taken there in a two-seater chaise with two docile horses and had paid twelve *daler* to the coachman, who had driven them so competently. They had passed removal carts and wagons loaded with wood and sacks of flour: Södermalm was a district in constant motion.

Lotta's boots creaked on leaves and gravel. She was wearing a blue woollen dress, from which she had removed the lining for the summer. The evening smells reminded Anders of a childhood which may never have existed: the warm lake, willow and alder with their roots in the mud attracting sticklebacks and roach, crayfish steaming in flower-patterned dishes. Out on this little point of the lake at Sicklasjön the clatter of trays, the peep of coots and the sight of divers skimming over from Dammtorpssjön all made him sigh to Lotta: 'Life could begin afresh here.'

He laughed, not bitterly but in wonderment, and Lotta gazed at him, her eyes unwaveringly full of love. Her lips moved softly; sometimes he was so overwhelmed by her expression that he barely absorbed what she said. But the water instilled in him a feeling of peace, reminding him of the tranquil sea between the Society Islands and New Caledonia, a gentle passage which he had endeavoured to describe so objectively that no-one would question his veracity.

A bottle-green float, marking a net beyond the reeds, bobbed on the light swell from a boat being rowed out from the shore by two chimney sweeps with powerful strokes of the oars. Then the water was once again as silky smooth as a millpond, and a shoal of carp flashed among the stones. He recalled being out in a rowing boat as a child with Hedda the maid, who had talked and laughed with such odd superiority.

'If we fall sick, we'll have to find consolation in rice soup,' said Lotta.

The inn's clientele were poor people, many from the local area; but Sparrman and Lotta, having arrived by carriage, were waited on, though they were not dressed as gentlefolk. Lotta had, however, fastened her plaits together with a fine silver thread. It made her face at once childlike and severe, and more naked. Her hair was pulled tight across the top of her head, and she sat very erect.

He had been waiting for an August evening like this. He saw the delicate skin under Lotta's eyes dark with fatigue, but her hair was radiant in the glow of an oil lamp. Her hands tugged nervously at the folds of her dress. Her shoulders ached after a long day.

Their understanding of one another was still not complete, but it didn't matter, since they knew more about each other than they would ever be able to put into words. And one thing was certain: she would outlive him by many years. She would die without any sense of loss, as she had said many a time; and she had no real plan for her life.

'I'm still here and yet have already gone,' she said, 'like the grebe that just dived under the mallards out there. We can't see it any more.'

'I haven't much to give you,' he said. 'We should have met in Cape Town in 1771. The fact that you weren't born then need not have prevented us. I've looked through your sketches. I've seen the results of your needlework. You have time on your side to be something. I haven't. I take off people's soiled clothes. I let blood and rub in sulphur ointment, and persuade them to swallow decoctions I learned to make from Rosén.'

And so they exchanged life stories. Necessity had imposed much upon them, but chance had played a large part in their happiness, although it was by no means chance that Lotta only wanted to be with him. She found other people intrusive, inconsiderate and malicious, and they had made her wish her burdensome life were over.

He elucidated for her various phenomena in the natural sciences that were just being discovered. He could not afford to purchase his own copy of the *Encyclopaedia*, but consulted it in the Academy and had copied out pages he translated to her as he read. He thought she looked tired, but she said she enjoyed his explanations of how everything had a purpose – if one accepts the utility of chaos and Nature's inexplicable decay. There was a beauty and precision in everything that could be seen as designed, a flow and a dissolution – most obvious in fungi, which had the shortest life cycle.

He explained difficult words to her, let them melt on his tongue to be savoured like oysters; words such as 'educational reform' and 'municipal customs office', names such as Novaya Zemlya and Monomotapa. But he added that these unusual expressions were mostly scholarly diversions, which she needn't worry about. That made her more confident. They were no more peculiar than the butterflies he had catalogued, or the long, dark-blue skirt she kept clean and ironed. And he said the greatly admired Diderot probably believed that with his alphabetical arrangement of knowledge he could get to the bottom of the obscurest elements of life.

Lotta smiled happily. 'My head is starting to spin. And it's getting late.'

He apologized. 'Ah yes, we're not in the lecture theatre now. I forgot myself.'

'I would like a place in the innermost recesses of your soul,' said Lotta. 'I have no desire for other company. And now let's drink a glass of the red wine I've never tasted. What a beautiful evening. See, the light is fading. Shall we wait for nightfall or go back to the city now?'

'We can pay off the coachman and get another in the morning. There's a curtained alcove here in a gable-room in the attic. When we wake up we can order milk with bread to dip in it. We still have a lot we haven't talked about. And nobody will ask after us in town: they've lost interest in us. Nackanäs is a respectable inn, where no-one regards you as dishonest, or fleeing from justice, or otherwise out of the ordinary.'

There was a basin and ewer in the room, but she had to dry her feet on the hem of her dress. They were surrounded by the scent of Finnish birch from the wood fire in the kitchen. A fox was yelping on the other side of the lake and a dog barked a response. She slipped into his embrace, composed and serious.

'I'm not afraid of dying,' she said, 'not in the least, though I'm still young. I've never felt the need to cling to life.'

'I'm holding you so tight that your ribs could crack at any minute,' Anders murmured. 'And this is life, not death. I'm thrusting into you as I shall never thrust into a woman again. You are enfolding me. My desire goes deep. I can last in you for hours. It's not like it was when I was younger.'

She smiled and her eyes were suddenly as bright and opaque as the first snow. A drowsy wasp buzzed against a window pane that was only two palms high.

'I think you must be able to see me there in the darkness,' Lotta said. 'You're staring straight into it.'

'I'm using your eyes. Then my vision is clear. I was once a natural scientist, now I'm a healer and a magnetist. Though I haven't been able to capture the spark from the fire of electricity. But I have moved closer to human feelings.'

'Closer to love,' said Lotta. 'I can feel you in the tiniest capillaries of my blood. I'm breaking through a membrane, through every restraint . . .'

'Can so much felicity lead to a happy ending? If only I could rid myself of such apprehensions!'

'Have no fear!' Lotta replied. 'I'm resurrected in your love. I'm trying to forget the pain and injury I suffered, all that befell me, even though I was no different then from now. I watch you poring over your books, cutting the uncut pages so eagerly. I can sew the tapes and buttons on your coat. I can keep everything clean and tidy. And I have a soul that longs to fly to you.'

'Remember, equality and fraternity are the guiding principles of our relationship,' Anders said. 'We have abolished the notions of slavery and servant, just as I would like to abolish them all over the world. You have my well-being at heart, and maybe you are the only one who does.'

'And it's only with you that I feel at ease,' Lotta replied. 'I'm your maidservant, but you have kissed my hand and knelt before me. We are who we are.'

They were in agreement that the varieties of love were so manifold that a comprehensive botany was needed. Yet Lotta thought, without any arrogance, that her love encompassed the whole system of flora, rather than being restricted to any single plant. Otherwise, she seemed not to take Creation too seriously, and he liked that.

5

In late October the trembling leaves were losing their hold on the branches. The trees looked as if they were planted in bowls of mist. The skies were lowering. The darkness was increasing its grip on the walls of the houses. A rain-laden wind blew in gentle flurries along the quays and made off up the neighbouring streets. The feeble gleam of the sun suggested the Earth was no longer clamouring for its attention.

Winter arrived early, and was protracted and severe. Some people rode by sleigh across to the Åland Islands, where the farmers ground acorns into flour. Riddarfjärden was frozen over, but by the tanneries the ice was dark-hued from the water gushing up from below. Anders recalled the sharp-edged ice floes near the southern Polar Circle, their rattle rising into the air like a thousand nails being shaken in an empty bucket.

On his way back from Klara he collected Lotta from the quay at Rödbotorget, where she was scrubbing the bedsheets with potash and rinsing them clean in the side-channel by the swirling waters of the main current. As soon as she got home, she washed off the chill with coal-tar soap and ladled water over herself vigorously in the tub. It cascaded from her as fresh as a spring.

To keep out the draught from the staircase on Skomakargatan, Anders set to work repairing the threshold. Lotta was drawing a pattern on rustling tissue paper, and had tacked up some sleeves and attached them to the shoulders. That day's finished work was hanging over the back of a chair, so she stood on a stool and cleaned one of the windows, moistening the putty which had begun to dry out.

She made some Java coffee that was seldom more than pale brown, baked a loaf with a crisp crust and browsed through *Stockholms Posten*. The potatoes had frozen. They made oat gruel instead. In London, on his voyage back from Senegal, Anders had bought a piece of taffeta, in a blue and brown stripe, as a present for someone in the future. Lotta had made a frock from it, which she had hardly worn.

She had spread fir twigs on the floor and started to make up a bonnet for herself. She cut out paper shapes and made little suns along the cornices of the room. She left him lovingly misspelt notes: *My Anders is so distingwished.*

She excused herself afterwards. 'I've never had enough learning. It never does any harm to know more, though my mother maintained the opposite. Most of what I know, I've taught myself, and I don't think it need have a negative effect on feelings.'

They sometimes treated themselves to boiled beef with horse-radish sauce, weak beer, an orange liqueur. When times were good: marinated ox tongue and milk pudding. Other days would end with boiled lambs' tongues with rosemary, liver sausage and pickled gherkin, a smoked shoulder of mutton. Lotta would magically produce filled doughnuts she had bought from the stalls outside Jakob's Church, and almond biscuits from the baker in Yxsmedsgränd. And there were evenings of carp and crucian, spareribs and suckling pig, as well as herring and anchovies, waffles and soured milk.

From the harbour came the dull thwack of hemp ropes against masts. Cleaners and wood-carriers clattered down from Skomakargatan, and violent disputes could be heard from the barber's shop opposite. A hunter came by with snared grouse and capercaillie on his back, and a peasant, somewhat unsteady on his feet, was offering eggs and chickens for sale, even though such street-trading was prohibited.

'When you bury your head in a book, I can't see your eyes,' Lotta said, 'and then I wonder who you are, so serious and determined, and yet so sprightly when you swing me round. I have a spark of life in me, too. You fan it into flame and my soul is lightened of its burdens, and I rush into your arms. I had learned to accept my miserable fate and had become hardened by it. I was an ant that couldn't find its way out of the anthill. Being subjected to the most dishonourable of men, and exploited in so base a manner, made me yearn for a pauper's grave. I should never have been born, the world didn't want me. But your love finally understood me, and I didn't have to force a smile any more, when all I wanted was to weep.'

'Don't try to suppress your pain!' said Anders. 'If you do, it will spring out at you like a wildcat when you least expect it. But I will lift you out of the dark river. I have doubted my abilities, the gold buttons on my Academy waistcoat are gone, but I shall give you a new and happy life.

'Now we make our own rules. I bend the knee to no-one, and will not take any words at face value, unless I have proof that even a government knows what it's doing. You may have observed that I have remained cool and rational, even when I have been seething within. I'm nobody's fool, and I'm not looking for miracles where there are none.'

Having made that speech he turned to her with unusual passion. He had the distinct impression that they had long been in mysterious equilibrium. And when he lay still, beside her, inside her, it was not like the threatening calm of the Equator, but an almost imperceptible mutual and unified encircling of one another, where no time was squandered and neither of them weighed more in the balance than the other.

Was this affection, liberation or an elation that was not really part of his nature? There were no words to roll around the tongue for this freedom of feeling. They remained in limbo in the far more extensive domain of the unexpressed.

6

He would observe Lotta with the expertise of the natural scientist. He stole glances at her elbows and knees, angular in a rather appealing way, the line of her jaw so pronounced that he felt the urge to run his little finger along it. She was wearing a lock of hair behind her ear in the latest fashion. One of her finest belongings was a silver-backed hairbrush engraved with runes. He saw in her a good and simple person who reminded him of Daniel Immelman's sister Anna.

One day she asked him out of the blue, 'They say that in Paris you can see dogs, with their paws bound, mating with beautiful women in the dog position. And you can see a donkey being aroused by a woman's hand and having its pizzle sucked in public view. Is that the sort of thing they do in other countries?'

'Anyone who has sailed around the world knows that everything human beings are capable of imagining does actually take place, at some time and somewhere,' Anders replied.

Desire stirred in his body, shy and undemanding. With a delicate movement as soft as an earlobe, he opened her up and went into her with the cry of a newborn babe. She had a voice that became slightly hoarse whenever she whispered. She breathed as the sea breathes, and her nipples were like pebbles that he licked into life.

With his lips in her groin he mumbled her name, repeated it

quietly – as if to bring her back to herself. He looked up over her navel and breasts, and she gasped in that surprised way he was beginning to recognize, in recurrent waves of pleasure.

A hailstorm was passing over Stockholm. She stood in the doorway like a frightened bird, watching out for him to come walking home with his doctor's bag. She didn't want him to see her concern. She was struggling against a self-contempt that kept her locked in a room of her own to which Anders had no access, because there she was the person she had been before she met him, and before her own disintegration had been reassembled in him. She used to curse life for keeping her pressed so hard up against the wall that she could feel her bones being crushed to powder. Never bargain with predators, she had exhorted herself. She should have been more crafty and cunning.

Lotta had mentioned all this to Anders, in her eyes a man who combined a joy in life and a contempt for life into a badge of heroism. But this was a type of courage he could not make use of in Stockholm. She realized he wanted to go out into the unknown again, he wanted to ride once more through South Africa, and study the simple and mysterious aspects of foreigners who would never fully understand him.

But more and more frequently now she felt proud of the land he had taken possession of. He lived in her and she was where she thought he was. It was to her he had sailed, and through her he had found a passage to the uttermost limits.

She didn't want his freedom for herself. Her wings kept her aloft anyway, when she was in his care. Anders had given her novels to read: one about a poisoner in Brittany, another about a Scottish trumpeter who fell in love with the lady of a castle married to an elderly husband. They gave her a headache. What was she to make of events which she either found uninteresting or which affected her too powerfully?

She soothed herself by making chive soup with hardboiled eggs. Their food was often simple: roast potatoes, rye bread, dripping.

She cooked a pike-perch with parsley, she rubbed mint, red onion and pine nuts into a side of pork and poured a ladleful of hoppy beer over it.

He saw her as strong, even authoritative, or sometimes rather the opposite: slim and graceful, with big childlike eyes. She could change from hour to hour. When she drew her finger quickly across the nape of her neck, he knew something had made her feel vulnerable and exposed. When a dark shadow flitted over her eyes, he held her shoulders and wrists in a firm grasp of unity.

'I am living myself into your life,' she said, 'into all that I have not experienced myself. And I'm not bothered about what you've done in your long life. With women, I mean.'

'The problem is that I've done a lot less than I dreamed of doing.'

Having roamed so far afield in Cape Province, in Stockholm he felt like a cockchafer fastened by a pin in its box, never to flex its wings again. When he toyed with the idea of making another speech to the Anti-Slavery Society in London, Lotta said, 'Go! I'll wait for you, however long you're away.' But it never came about.

She stroked his hair anxiously. 'You have a tormented look. I can feel a cloud hovering over us. If you want to leave I would never hold you back. I dreamed that I left you, because you had taken an interest in another woman. I dreamed that you left me to be on your own. They were dreams of very different colours.'

At the same time she laughed at his childish stories, at his facial and verbal expressions when he imitated people he had met in African villages, and at his attempts to horrify her with the delights of Hottentot cuisine. His own thoughts ranged over all the regions of Africa he had never had time to visit. Now his place was with Lotta, and he hoped that no-one and nothing in the world would steal her from him.

Because love was the real journey. It picked up all the other stories of his life and rendered them less significant, less clearly memorable. But rather as an extended preface. What a time it had taken him to find the right track!

'I have blown on the wings of butterflies, lifted the legs of gall-wasps and run beneath the rainbow. But it was only when I slowed down that I caught up with you.'

'You are learned and playful. Yesterday, when you swallowed a fly, you just shrugged your shoulders. And you don't really believe in your expeditions. You want to write about them, but you never get to the end. Yet you still keep on talking about the Southern Ocean.'

7

Anders had strolled past a rowing boat, carelessly left moored beside Nya Kungsholm Bridge. Seeing no-one around, he turned back and climbed down into it and put out the oars. But he had forgotten to untie the rope. He sat for a while in a state of tranquillity, his mind empty, then shipped the oars and looked out across the grey water of Klara Reach, which seemed in the mist to stretch to the horizon. This gave him the feeling of having achieved something. He had given himself to Nature and the heavens and offered no resistance.

Before the mist entered his bones, he jumped ashore to resume his life. He made his way home, totally unaware of his surroundings. The city opened up before him, its solid earth under his feet. The street where he lived was empty and glistening, like a wide-open eye, and seemed to want to see him for what he was.

So dusk merged into night. Thunder rumbled in a leaden sky, lightning struck at roof timbers and birds took to the air in silent fear. But his fever had passed, his legacy from Africa. He woke up refreshed, beneath a more congenial firmament. It was still dark.

But Lotta had weariness etched under her eyes, feeling ineffectual and abandoned. 'Don't desert me! I've had such ill fortune in my life. Only with you have things turned out well, Anders.'

'First I employed you. Now you are my treasure, my nearest and dearest.'

She recovered herself, and said, 'I shall help you just as you saved me and had the courage to see me as I am, and not be affrighted. But I've already given you all I had to give.'

She noticed that he would frequently withdraw into himself, or not be fully there. She listened to his stories and waited to see him in them, as in murky water. She touched him, inquisitively but cautiously, not wanting to steer him.

Her embrace was bitter-sweet. His remaining life was now so short. Which made him say, 'I want you to know everything about me before our lives lie like burnt-out wicks on the floorboards, waiting to be swept up. Sometimes I'm incapable of talking about myself. We've invented a lot, we human beings, but not love – that seems to have its own laws, not governed by us. It imbues us with all our strength, and robs us of all our stability.'

'You are full of beautiful words that no-one has ever spoken to me before,' Lotta replied. 'They open up a landscape where I come to meet you and we walk hand in hand, through my heart and loins and out into the vast open spaces that I've been so afraid of.'

They lay together in the brown-blue shadows of the late afternoon. The power of writers is great, he thought. They pinpoint sunken islands. But you and I are stepping into a story where no-one will find us, though the words will remain, visible through time's layers of dust.

'I know you, dear Anders. There is so much in you that others barely suspect. But I can read you, even when your eyes seem unfathomable. I can see when you are troubled and tormented. I can see everything in you, because I love you. Others find you hard to penetrate, but you yourself are perceptive, nothing seems hidden from you. You seek out the genuine; appearances and ostentation have no influence on you.'

She watched him with eyes as bright as the sea, his soul opened up in absolute trust, trembling at her beauty. He felt a reverent attachment to her very being as well as a secret anxiety. His lips were like a divining rod as he felt his way down her body, discovering and moving on at the same time, kissing the inside of her thighs and the tendon in her groin, brushing her heels. Their uninhibited caresses invigorated them, they were in a garden of delight and she blossomed under his fingers, following them closely as if they were revealing something she had kept to herself.

'We could so easily never have met,' she said. 'I can hear you coming up the stairs. Your footsteps are lighter and quicker than they used to be. You know so much and have held such high office. Now you are physician to the poor . . . It's so strange! And we love one another, which is also strange! I had no idea such a love existed.'

He noticed her hands were chapped from washing. He rubbed some beeswax on them. 'You know, in outward appearance you sometimes remind me of others, but the rest of you never ceases to astonish me.'

'I'm more calm and composed than you. You see guile, conspiracies, manoeuvring behind the scenes, where I just see ordinary people taking advantage of your goodness and patience.'

Anders explained that he had never been interested in ingenious diversions or dissolute living. He had never been in thrall to gaming and gambling. Languages like the Hottentots' – regarded by others as gibberish – he had recorded in his notebooks and found as enjoyable a challenge as naming flora and fauna. He was stimulated by the intractable, just as Captain Cook had been.

He put his arms around her and said he thought it might be their childishness that bound their souls so intimately. 'We shall love each other as wildly as the quivering leaves in the trees, as exquisitely as the dragonflies dance over moss and grass. You shine as bright as ytterbium, that basic element Afzelius discovered. You are as effervescent as Nordenskjöld's flasks and retorts.'

'What high-flown notions you have,' said Lotta. 'I'll go and get the coffee. I don't want you to make me cry.'

On other occasions she was the one who seemed at ease with elevated concepts.

'People are intrusive, inconsiderate and calculating. You have been the exception in my life. So there is no sickness, no danger and no dishonour I'm not willing to share with you, my beloved doctor. When the fire has gone out and the birds have fallen silent, you will see that passions diminish and desire abates. Although maybe it's the other way round: there is a flame so hot that the wind cannot extinguish it, and it doesn't turn to ashes. A love so strong that we dare not face it. We try to go around it, but it's still waiting for us at the end of the road.'

'You are afraid of the secrets within you,' Anders said. 'You dare not bring them into the open. My knowledge is my love for you. I hope to be able to see you as you really are, and sometimes I think I have, sometimes that there is more to come. But eventually I shall see as much in you as you see in yourself, and even more, since I love you more than you love yourself.'

'Now you've heard many things I'd been afraid to talk about,' Lotta replied. 'You know everything about me that I know myself, and you've understood more than I have. I wouldn't have thought that possible. Until we met I put off my questions and my anger and my cares, because everything seemed so hopeless; someone had pawned my life, I no longer owned it. But everything that nearly happened to me, never happened – thanks to you.'

The Third Volume

1

No tailor has got the measure of my life. I have slid from one rocky ledge to another. No planned course, but a vague map drawn by the erratic pencil of chance, or steered from below by a magnet. My travels have been shared with others, though the words to capture them have been my own. It was only Lotta I met by myself, on my solitary path.

Freedom has been more important to me than influence; mobility more than the yoke of discipline. I've seen the greedy and ignorant clothe themselves in lies. I've indulged in few of the excesses of youth. Linnaeus advised me to observe and listen. The joys of sex that confirmed the beauty of life reached me late, and then in a love that had only one object.

Vociferous protest was not for me. Yet on the other hand, I had no desire to follow instructions issued by mummified officials. My defiance of the legions of functionaries has cost me both position and comforts. The result: no worldly goods to speak of, no personal power, no circle of close friends.

The evidence for animal magnetism is as elusive as that of reason in explaining what is valuable and durable in a person's life. Without Lotta's hands on my body, without the oft-repeated caresses of love, I would have been staring vacantly out of spirit and formalin like many of my captive creatures.

My peccadillos have certainly been fewer than for most men. I used to talk to George Forster – who was possessed of a virility that demanded daily release – about my more subdued nature, which could tolerate both hot and cold conditions. That was before I was in the grip of the recklessness engendered by love, the only state of mind that can bridge those giddy moments.

I've recorded much from my happy years of study. Nothing will be written about the remainder of my life, least of all by me, having no wish to explain it or even understand it. I've had something to tell, but little to confess. My story need not be related.

And what would be the point of opening a door on to something which would still remain dark and attenuated, even if in later years very beautiful? To try to reproduce happiness with the precision of science would be as misleading as to describe a basic element with the florid vocabulary of sentiment.

I wanted to be both passionate and factual at one and the same time. We cannot be blinded by tears under water. But I seem to get no further than drafts, and I've no hope of being read – though, equally, no fear of not being read.

So, have I unburdened myself of my travels? Have I let the geography of memory rewrite that of reality? Have I changed shape, or am I not able to lead my senses forty years back in time, when they are fixed by love in the here and now? My expeditions formed me. Now I am formed by something else. I have a subterranean life, but the infinite skies above.

2

Sitting by a flickering lamp, he lifted a heavy tome, a leather-bound book he had oiled until it gleamed like a horse chestnut. The butterfly net he had brought back from the South Seas stood in one corner.

He was trying to retrieve an unrecorded memory from Africa, pushing through vegetation that rippled and curled like Lotta's frizzy bush. He could make out the marshes south-east of Cape Town, the white women's long skirts and the black women's sturdy legs; he sensed that something was being offered him that he'd never been able to accept. That was where his aquifer was, where he craved to be again, but he could not make the leap across the ravine.

His voyages were encapsulated in the past. He wanted to make his way back there to recreate himself as the man he had been among icebergs that groaned and roared, and the man he had been among those who had perished in their youth. But he came to a halt on a desolate watch duty at his notebook, his pen scraping as if in sand. The lamp was faltering and smoking and his verbal pyrotechnics had fizzled out. The East India Company disbelieved his reports. Cook and both the Forsters, Daniel Solander and Joseph Banks were all gone. But it was not death that was the great mystery, it was life. He knew all about death.

His third volume ... he was scarcely bothered about it any more. Others had reported on the voyage round the world with Captain Cook, not least the Captain himself. But everything he had to say about South Africa had been new. So many thousands of facts he had discovered in the Cape, so many insects and mammals, plants, fossils and minerals, and peoples, white and black, their customs and ways of life. Then everything had seemed worthy of recording. Now it mostly seemed to consist of insubstantial fragments.

He had delved deep into prehistoric caves, traced the intestinal flow of the hippopotamus, listened to the Boers' malicious prayers, examined the sex organs of Hottentot women, travelled regions of land and sea that only subsequently found a place in mankind's atlas. He remembered all of this as if someone else were remembering it for him.

But who said a long-distance adventure could be narrated with a click of the fingers? To regard those expeditions as frivolous would have been tantamount to erasing them from the history books. So he went on copying out his notes. The shadows moved patiently around him, listening without understanding. His hand shook. He rinsed some of his quills, leafed through his notebooks, found blank spots in the atlas, extra pages untouched by blotting-sand, as white as bedsheets still awaiting their monograms.

He wrote the way Lotta wound skeins of yarn. In the evenings, when he returned from his visits to the poor, he would take out his old drafts, delete repetitions, but avoid adding artificial colour. An ink blot of silence spread over the paper and the pages looked burnt, or singed, though he didn't know by what.

'You must get on with your final volume.'

'I'm biding my time. But I don't know whether anything will come. There's a stone growing inside me.'

'Is it heavy?' she asked.

'Like a sounding lead, heavy when it reaches the surface. If it doesn't get caught in the rocks, as once occurred in the surf at Cape Agulhas, when the line snapped.'

The snowfall in the night had covered the horse droppings on the street. The cold was setting in and Lotta was nagging him as they put up the winter glazing. When his mind was about to wander off into the unknown, she put a hand on his arm and held him back with a question.

'What are you thinking about?'

The look she gave him was both watchful and artless.

'Others have undertaken even more hazardous voyages since, and have had the skill to garnish their accounts with horrors that make their readers' hair stand on end. Samuel Ödman is composing the most authentic journeys from his bed in Uppsala. I can't do that. I've chewed more leaves, berries and roots than anyone else in the country, but has it been of any use to our agriculture? I doubt it.'

She urged him not to let this melancholy go to his head, and not to concern himself too much with the precise locations or the vegetal distribution he was muttering about.

'You needn't disown one jot of your old life. You've never written better than now, never loved more fiercely. Don't look for unnecessary obstacles – and leave the Academy's ghosts to their threadbare tailcoats!'

He had seldom heard Lotta so eloquently decisive. She was defending him, and she wouldn't give in. And even to him his early expeditions and his belated love stood out as his least average achievements. It was in these that he had with the greatest ardour broken through the membrane between his own body and the universe.

'I wish we could always share the same orbit. We entered it from different directions. There was a space between us which we filled in, and our fates merged; we grew into one another, with no other foundation than the unguarded expanses of the emotions.'

Never would that be repeated: his journey to his beloved house-keeper. What had arisen between them and emerged from the inexplicable was a love so inexpedient that it had no contract or conditions, and no division of labour or rest. It simply existed.

'Thoughts come to me at night,' said Lotta. 'Your belief that nothing lasts is not easy to cope with. Is it only from sorrow and loss that we can draw strength? That surely can't be what you mean. What if your feelings for me evaporate, and I don't bring a smile to your face when I touch you? What if your interest turns into aversion, and I have no refuge, out in the wilderness where my brother drowned?'

On the table lay the illustrated volume of his *Museum Carlsonianum* and a map of South Africa in a leather pouch; on the wall a copperplate engraving of Captain Cook. The tea-caddy and a tin of coffee beans were a reminder of Immelman.

'I wonder if he's still alive, with all his children? And the Resident's spoilt daughter? Ah, well, one gets used to not know-ing anything. People disappear. The postal service could be better.'

He kept his journals in his grandfather's chest, their indeci-pherable abbreviated script faded, as if from exposure to a strong sun. The lid had split under its heavy iron mountings, and what he was searching for seemed to have gone missing. He never man-aged to create system and order. But the oak planks from Biskopskulla still gave off an aroma of sunlit tree roots, tobacco and Chinese ginger.

He heard the rasping of the coachmaker's saw down in the courtyard on Prästgatan. He watched the children playing bandits and soldiers, and burying their dead canaries. A carthorse laden with bundles of wood was making its way slowly towards Stortorget, and a stallion stamped impatiently, its member dis-tending, black and knobbly.

Anders' pension as an Advisory Board member and the income from Lotta's needlework were adequate for their daily bread. His desire to involve himself with the world had diminished, he was turning more inwards and seldom let anyone get close to him except Lotta, who helped him live and would help him die. She was his long-standing point of contact, his nourishment, so that he had no need to seek elsewhere.

But there were days when his brain felt full of nothing but echoes of what they had already said, and he no longer had a view from his lectern. His eyes narrowing like a cat's, he waited to catch a glimpse of something.

His hands, so dextrous when caressing Lotta's body, became weak and helpless when confronted by the pages on which he wanted to transcribe his arid travel journals into a more luxuriant form. When he looked back and tried to focus on the events he had once witnessed at such close quarters, he couldn't single out what it was he wanted to put into words.

He had always abhorred any slave-driving and coercion in life. He needed to be a wanderer who set his own targets. And now he was heading for very different limits from those he had over-stepped when the *Resolution* turned back with Antarctica in sight. He was staring out towards a horizon where his thoughts could not follow him.

Lotta was wearing her hair in two plaits again. She picked up a pile of papers inquisitively from the narrow writing desk Anders regarded as his own and had brought with him from the Cabinet of Natural History.

'Your handwriting is so difficult. I can't understand what this is about.'

'I can't understand it all myself.'

'Are you really a hypnotist? Can one person transpose his will on to another?'

'That's what you've done to me,' he said.

His own will had less power over him. He complained to Lotta that he was like an untidy hovel inside. He had never been a true man of science, as his rival Quensel's shameless nose had rightly sniffed out. Lotta told him to concentrate on life's positive dispensations – for instance, how lucky they were that Providence had brought them together. He admitted immediately that there was a splendour in this which had never dimmed, and a mystery inviolate.

So he said, 'I love you now, and in all the years gone by and yet to come. You must know and feel that this is true. I'd do anything for you, anything.'

'Yes, I can feel it. Only time can separate us. That, too, is inviolate.'

3

More than two decades had elapsed since Sparrman had returned from South Africa. To prove that he still existed he published *Findings and Collections*: essays on the sixth sense of the bat, spontaneous combustion, painful menstruation, adulterating wine, curing rattlesnake bites and making lingonberry-water. His report to the government on the possible Swedish colonization of part of the coast of Africa had by this time been rejected and was omitted from his book.

He was a man of multiple interests who undertook numerous projects following on from his observations of Nature. He crushed wood-anemone leaves and flowers to control the flow of the menses, and even applied these floral poultices to the forehead for headaches and between the shoulderblades for shortness of breath. He belonged to a generation that invented and discovered. But in medicine the wheels of change ground slowly.

Carl Peter Thunberg remained one of his few friends, and as late as 1815 he tried to persuade him to apply for the Chair of Economics at Uppsala. Anders refused, maintaining that he could be of greater use to humanity in his medical practice, and he was still nimble enough on his feet to negotiate all the streets and steps, was trusted, and enjoyed benefits in kind from tailors, bakers and butchers. Thunberg had had luck on his side, whereas he himself had been unlucky in everything except love, and that had never been in his contract. Goddess Fortuna, he wrote, 'is seated on a ball, not on a plinth, and she can easily slide off'.

That same year, under the pseudonym 'Lover of Science and Truth', Anders Sparrman published *Letters on Spiritual Healing and Animal Magnetism*. He disclosed nothing of his own experience as a mesmerist, but took as his starting point a parliamentary debate on training priests to combine theology and medicine, since medical knowledge cast light on psychological and spiritual processes.

His work was coolly received. In the periodical *Allmänna Journalen* he was described as 'an ageing hypnotist, sleepwalking in a sort of chiaroscura, with no real idea of what he is saying or where it is taking him'. The reviewer contended that hypnotism caused unrestrained sexual urges, convulsions and fits of rage, and misled students into closing their minds to reason and seeing what they imagined to be miracle cures. In the same publication Per Adam Wallmark went on the attack against Swedenborg's and Schelling's theories of dreams, and portrayed hypnotism as leading young women into dangerous temptation.

A scientific committee was set up to investigate hypnotism, at that time called animal magnetism. Sparrman was offered a seat on it, but declined. The committee never met: it was realized that hypnotism did not lend itself to empirical study.

Sparrman persisted in maintaining, however, that there were two magnetic poles not just on the Earth but also in the human soul: one situated in the intellect, the other in the emotions. Day and night alternated, even in humans. And he had learned on his travels that all phenomena should be carefully examined before being rejected. After all, he was among the first to have sailed across the southern Polar Circle and seen the fiery southern lights sweep the heavens with electromagnetic particles, and heard the icebergs roar as they calved. People in Stockholm forgot that he had seen events which no other human being had ever witnessed.

He expressed his discontent to Lotta. 'I have put up suggestions for soap-works, starch manufactories and sugar refineries that would have flourished not just under Alströmer. They were equally deaf to my views on the use of the iron-water of the bogs, and the decreasing sea levels in the Baltic. Yet I am no unrealistic dreamer. At breakfast I'm a man of reason and critical observation. In the evening, on the other hand, I walk with you in realms unknown to surveyors.'

These were hectic years. The mood had lightened after the loss of Finland and the expulsion from the throne of the incompetent king. The elected Crown Prince from the south of France was regarded as doing his best, and had already displayed a magic touch with many things that had stagnated in the country. According to one report, more than half of the women in Stockholm were widows or unmarried. They were permitted to sell haberdashery, trinkets and tobacco, and to run bakeries and inns. Many women declined to marry, because they would lose control over their own assets.

On Sundays Djurgården Park resembled nothing less than a complete re-enactment of street life of the Gustavian era. Cavalrymen recreated Napoleonic campaigns on the newly laid-out paths, rowing boats in the bay provided amusement for youth. Ladies in pink muslin gowns were escorted by officers of the nobility, insufferable and immoral in the eyes of the young women of the bourgeois dwellings on Skeppsbron. Higher-ranking civil servants partied with their subordinates in tavern gardens, clergymen waltzed in the ballroom of the Exchange, Chancellery staff appeared in broad daylight on Norrbro dressed up ready for a masquerade. Unemployed ex-soldiers from the armies of the Finnish War wandered the streets as pedlars, beggars and thieves.

Here and there on the open land of Ladugårdsgärdet and Djurgården the developer Fredrik Blom had erected his houses, impermanent and regimented, making the whole area look like an army encampment. Anders and Lotta disappeared into the crowd.

They ordered a glass of punch in Kumlander's Cellar at the Blue Gate, where the hard biscuits reminded Anders of past years of need. Smoke was rising from the hazel-bush slopes, chickens pecked for worms among the stones and the sky was as milky blue as a blind man's eyes. The public had given up waiting for Sparrman's third volume.

His career had come to an end long ago, but it was no privation for him to sacrifice power, honours and worldly goods in order to devote his energy and vitality to the semi-destitute in their decrepit houses. He moved among them cautiously, as if slowing down his blood circulation, so as not to arouse false hope. In bare and shabby rooms as dark as caves he encountered the grey and emaciated, who brought him their most fervent desires. He felt stressed and benumbed by the experience of what he saw, but found peace and solace with Lotta, who helped him wash away the smells and sorrows of others.

His work in Klara had enabled him to achieve a tiny fraction of what he would have liked to do for the slaves in the Cape and Senegal. It was a sort of labour of love, unaffected and practical. It threatened his equilibrium to see the mistreatment of others. In his exploration of life he had posed questions to which he had never received answers – insofar as Lotta had not, in her own way, answered them. In optimistic moments he considered he had striven against injustice in the world and for a freer order of things, without compromising his integrity.

He was still a member of various learned societies in Lund and Gothenburg, London, Paris and Philadelphia. But despite these titles he had ended up outside the Linnaean circle, which had expanded to include new generations of scholars. His famous map of the Western and Eastern Cape was now forty years old and no longer really worth having, though it had laid the foundation for all subsequent maps.

Sparrman was faithful to his early experiences while they continued to have a sensual presence. He thus regarded himself as steadfast in feelings, even when they brought disappointment. But his inner enthusiasm had waned, for better or worse, silently dissipated, and he had entered a new climate. He had, as it were, lured himself away from the oceans, and even from Mälby after von Carlson's death, and from the exotic cases in the Cabinet of Natural History. And he could blame everything on one single creature, who filled him with both exaltation and serenity.

He had no objection to this state of affairs, but it never ceased to amaze him. He didn't have the energy to reflect on how one phase of life simply replaced another instead of going through a gradual transition. And he didn't find it entirely easy to decide what had happened. Instinctively, his thoughts racing round in his head, he groped for an explanation that was not simply Lotta.

When, eventually, the third volume was published, two hundred and thirty-four pages in length (it continued where the second had left off, with chapter twelve) Sparrman was nearing seventy. It aroused less attention than his book on spiritual healing and was accorded brief notices rather than full reviews in the press. Opinion was that the pedagogical urge had ousted the narrative flair, or that didacticism tended to obscure the imaginative spark that people had come to expect, but which Sparrman had come increasingly to distrust.

In the very same month that his book reached the shops, Samuel Owen, from his boatyard on Kungsholmen, launched the steamboat *Amphitrite*, described as the first steam-powered vessel. She sent up reverent black puffs of smoke over Riddarfjärden, and on this maiden voyage carried passengers to Västerås and Uppsala, for a substantial fee. Who – asked Anders Sparrman – would henceforth remember Captain Cook's Whitby barques *Endeavour*, *Adventure* and *Resolution*?

Death

1

The icebergs of Antarctica, which I was the first man to catch sight of, came back to haunt me as a visitation without spirit or soul. They were naked and desolate, beyond fear and beyond grace. My lead-line broke. Human emotion sailed away on foreign seas. That is how it seems to me decades later.

When my voyages were over, I became detached from the world. And in my arrogance I didn't let the world encroach on me, which may perhaps have been the reason for my lack of inclination to write. I'm trying to distil a raw material, to squeeze the juice out of ever-drier matter. I refuse to offer games and dissimulation, masquerades and diversions. So the public that was kind enough to subscribe to my first volume, on Africa, has turned its attention elsewhere.

Slavery still exists, and will continue to do so under other names. I was witness to some of it, but was unable to reform any of it, just as efforts to prevent incurable diseases have been no more successful than transforming unrequited into requited love.

No-one summons me now except the febrile and suffering in Klara, or Lotta, whom I cannot capture in formulae and images from my zoology. The animals will survive me and continue to exist – the quagga and the wildebeest. I no longer classify plants – I let their scents have free rein in my nostrils: the spotted orchid follows the late lily of the valley, and the bog myrtle as heavily fragranced as ever.

If my life's work has remained uncompleted, it's because I have never been sure of its purpose. My grand schemes have been rejected by others, until even I lost interest. Thanks to love I have not had to stare my life in the face.

Yet I have seen more than I need. Detours are necessary, but I've strayed from the path too often. The past is swallowed by the present, just as oxygen is consumed by fire. It's time to bring things to a close, and let this last unpublished journey disappear without trace.

If I happen to meet my Maker, we will ask each other the same question: Why did you not do your utmost?

In Cape Town I remember raving to Thunberg in a sort of poetic delirium: 'Life is a difficult piece of music to play, a score carelessly composed.'

To which he replied, 'Beneath the burning skies we hear Him whose voice lacks intonation and whose countenance defies description.'

As Professor Linnaeus, my rigorous master, taught me: 'Finding is different from retrieving. When reality steps forward the colours are denser. There are no diluting agents! That's why our journey never ceases.'

But the traveller himself stops travelling.

After our bodies have frolicked upon its surface the Earth takes us unto itself. It has its own breath, and we twirl in and out of its mouth as long as we live. And when, at last, we have to lie for ever in the soil to rot, we ourselves become the Earth's lungs.

There is no subterranean Arcadia awaiting us. But an invisible lake lies dark beneath the surface of memory. Let the contents sink to the bottom until the water clears again. We are vessels for those we love. They are souls inside our glass. That's where they breathe.

I dreamed about the *Resolution*. I was shut in my cabin, as if tucked into an opaque pouch, a container that, like the ribcage enclosing the heart, produced both warmth and pressure. When I awoke I felt as if I'd been on a voyage through my own anatomy. Is death this pouch slowly tightening around us, or is it a stone deep inside the body, growing outwards?

The understanding that prologue is followed by epilogue is unique to human beings as we wing our way through life, even if we like to confuse the issue in games of hide-and-seek, with fine words about meeting again elsewhere. But let us not be denied this sophistry.

Time does not do what we ask of it. The time we have had, Lotta my dearest, has been one long embrace, and perhaps it will continue in unknown form – like a splash of colour in a weave whose overall pattern we cannot discern, like a carriage lamp that passes in the night, too fleeting to reveal its direction.

2

Anders hunched his shoulders and thrust his hands inside his jacket. It was cold, and he had lost the resilience he once had. He realized he would soon end up where countless numbers of his patients had gone before him. Insects would suck his congealed blood and leave him like an ink blot surrounded by the white bones of birds.

He knew from Torbern Bergman, and more recently from Jacob Berzelius, his colleague in the Karolinska Institute, about organic decay as a controlled reversion to simpler constituents. He took leave of his hands, of pen and paper, and of time, over which he no longer had any control.

'Don't depart this Earth without taking me with you!' Lotta had begged him one afternoon on the darkest of Klara's streets. They had met by chance on his doctor's round, had hugged each other, with no-one to see them, and then she had uttered this plea. He embraced her, so that they stood motionless. He didn't want to spill a single drop of their love.

An ebbing tide exposed the dominion of transience, and revealed the sound of sombre waters retreating, albeit reluctantly, even further. A blackness was seeping into him. It was some incomprehensible misconception that had prostrated him like this. He closed his eyes: a dream provided the missing element – he was travelling over the thinnest ice, but made it safely back to terra firma.

He could have said: I'm going aboard the *Resolution* again – but not without you, Lotta. He would much prefer to disappear in an open boat out on the sea, one rainy day at dusk, when the heavens had no more light to soak up and little was visible. But what he actually said was: 'Let no storm render you unstable. Let sorrow stroke your sweet soul with the gentlest hand. Think of our daughter, and don't trouble Death unnecessarily. Let something of me live and breathe within you. Then you will hear my laughter when you least expect it.'

It went without saying that Lotta would watch over him when he died. She would lean over him in a long farewell. Her hands would be thinner then, with sinuous veins. Her eyes, steady in their love, would follow him into an internal landscape.

With a voice that was barely audible, she reiterated, 'My dearest and best, we have given one another a great deal of love. We can never have too much. Come to me and I will hold you tight, have no fear. We have had a life together, brief perhaps, but it was ours. And one day I shall fetch you, my travelling companion, and we shall go down to the sea and out on the tide, you and I, together.'

He was incapable of satisfying Lotta's thirst for education – or, for that matter, any other thirst. Diderot was dead and the *Encyclopaedia*'s thousands of pages had contracted to a few indispensable ones. Anders withdrew to his dictionaries and reference books. He wanted to stay on this Earth, this defaced, unnaturally beautiful planet, over whose lands and oceans he had travelled further than any other Swede. He had sometimes seen himself as a semaphore telegraph on the outskirts of humanity. But all he had been able to do was to suspend a few birds in mid-flight with his pen.

A faint tremor in the head when he awoke from his slumbers betrayed his age. He shrank back and stretched again to make way for the unfamiliar. Nature was playing with him in its shameless, all-too-physical way – just as he had disapprovingly observed it harrying his patients in Klara.

In the thin air of late winter, beneath the idle stars, even language arranged itself in black and white. Weightlessness beckoned. Everywhere except Sweden was at war.

His possessions were few. He had purchased an English carriage clock. The maker was one John Ellicott, and it only showed the right time when hanging on a spring from a hook in a carriage and swaying in unison with the seconds. On a firm base the hands moved with a peculiar waywardness.

His expedition, comprising four distinct stages, was over. Life was contracting to a staging-post, a harbour. Some power whose authority he did not recognize was ordering him to vacate his abode, the only home he had had for more than half a century, in order to dispatch him to shores more monotonous than ever Easter Island's had been. Because he had mostly carried his dwelling with him. The tutor's bunk, the claustrophobic cabin, the flimsy tent, the underside of an ox-wagon, the bedroom in the Cabinet of Natural History had all been temporary accommodation, as if in preparation for an imminent departure from this Earth.

Anders felt he had become thin and scrawny, gangly-legged, with sunken and flecked cheeks. He breathed in the ineluctable, like bone dust at the butcher's. A sponge soaked in ice-cold water on his brow kept his fantasies at bay, those confused eruptions of a tropical fever, that made even such an obstinate character as his feel highly intoxicated and devoid of any sense of time and context.

He was transported back through geometrically precise days as pale as egg white, and crumbled into his own remains. Half-flayed rats were fleeing along cellar tunnels. Leeches sucked the hours out of his blood, and he was freezing cold. They lit the stove, shut the damper to increase the heat and opened it again before they dozed off, he and the woman he regarded as proof of his existence. She whose love was still for a while longer preventing Death from taking command of his heart, and towards whose embrace he was still constantly bound.

Summer came round again. Lotta saw herons landing on Riddar-holmen, whatever they might portend; perhaps a new royal infant. He mentioned Hagastranden and Bellevue, places that were theirs alone, where they had strolled under shady branches and fancied the trees were groping for one another, as if to make love.

She leaned over him, her skin as soft as a mangling-sheet, and she seemed to waft away his sight. Though a glimmer of light remained. He was where he had never been before. On a sea without waves. In a forest without voices.

'Wait! Not yet!' she whispered, as once she had done in other circumstances.

Thunder in early August, as so often. Swifts circled the spire of the German Church. It was said they had no resting place on Earth. Time made itself felt in fits of ague, taking hold, stumbling on, unable to resist playing its selfish tricks.

He could hear military music in the distance. The band was outside the Palace to mark the king's return from his summer sojourn at Rosendal Palace, Lotta told him. There had been crowds of people: stevedores and customs men, tradesmen, freemasons, heavy-footed boatwomen.

Sugar crackled in the butter in the frying pan, where Lotta was cooking potato pancakes. She stopped what she was doing. 'You must be thirsty, I'll make some tea.' He drank three cups while she darned his socks. He felt so hot that when she bent over him she thought he must be feverish. He saw her lips move as if behind glass. She sat down and put her head in her hands. He couldn't understand why.

Then they had a visitor. He heard Lotta answer, 'He's not here. Did he send for you?'

The stranger had the voice of an old man. 'No. So he's not here any more?'

'No,' Lotta replied in her calmest voice.

'Goodbye then, Mrs Sparrman.'

It was a sailor from the *Stockholm Castle* who had served under Captain Ekeberg. He and Anders had trodden the same decks half a century earlier. Anders heard his steps going off into the distance, a door closed, the sound faded away.

He moved his head as if to shake something out or throw something off. Then a pain struck him in the chest and his legs buckled under him. A fly on the wall was magnified to his wide-open eyes. He called for Lotta and said he didn't feel well. He reminded her there was a pile of unsawn birchwood in the courtyard, which she should see to before autumn.

She was ever-watchful, stooped over him, anxious and pensive, as if peering at a map, looking for a parish boundary or a place omitted in error.

In a very low voice Anders said, 'Something ominous is happening. I can't hold on.'

She thought she saw a half-smile of apology, before he covered his face with his arm. He was struggling to find words, to find a voice in his dry throat.

'Don't grieve, keep in good spirits, tread lightly on this Earth! Don't worry if there's something you don't understand. Don't allow yourself to be enslaved! Don't let this strange, insignificant little country take anything from you!'

He tried to reach for an inkwell to write an instruction, a sort of testament, before every exit was closed. A slice of sausage that Lotta had put on his bread fell to the floor. Nothing would stay in its place. A glass of brandy was raised to his lips. A child's voice shouted, but he had no idea where from.

Leaves know when it's time to say goodbye to one another. They sail off on their own courses and land without finding each other again. But Creation goes on, it has no seventh day of rest, and every new work of Nature brings with it a mirror image of what has preceded it.

His last words were: 'I am dying . . . not now.'

It was the 9th of August 1820. Even then no-one had been further south on the globe than Anders Sparrman. He had lived with Charlotta Hedvig Fries for more than two decades. He was seventy-two-and-a-half years old.

4

Anders Sparrman died a bankrupt. His estate did not cover his debts. His library, curios and natural history specimens fetched one hundred and thirty-three *daler*, and furniture and household goods amounted to almost the same. Among these last were an oak chest, a rattan chair, a Dalecarlian wall clock, a tea-strainer, a preserving pan, two jelly moulds, a pair of opera glasses and four pairs of curtains.

Sparrman's zoological collection was purchased at the auction of his effects by the Academy, which printed a laconic biography in memoriam. He had been as far removed from the elevated realms of honours and as indifferent to the temptations of vanity as it was possible to imagine. His correspondence, journals and field notes – everything that had not found its way into print, apart from a few letters written in his official capacity – vanished, and have never been found.

He was a botanist and zoologist who was also something of a poet, a man who combined sober precision with pregnant feeling in his observation of the unknown and exotic. He was a Romantic before his time, but the man himself and his achievements were swept aside as antiquated and naive by the currents of contemporary ideas.

In the same week that Sparrman was buried, Gustaf von Paykull's natural history collection, which included objects from

Sparrman's expeditions, was transferred to the Academy of Sciences from Vallox-Säby on biers and ox-carts on board the paddle steamer *Amphitrite*, which made three round trips to transport eighty mammals, thirteen hundred birds and nine thousand insects. King Karl XIV Johan himself received them, and the collection was squeezed into the Academy's premises on Stora Nygatan.

Coffins were normally purchased from the Public Coffin Store, and were sometimes referred to comfortingly as 'sleeping chambers'. The dead were laid out on view, with myrtle leaves on the bedcover and twigs of boxwood round the pillow. Saffron buns were eaten at the wake, their shape signifying eternal life. Anders had forbidden all this. He had stipulated that any suggestion of worldly pomp be avoided.

His wish was more than fulfilled. No-one was told when and where the funeral was to be held. He shared the fate of nameless beggars, and we don't know why Lotta didn't object. He was brushed away like horse dung and the weeds in the street. It was over so quickly that no-one noticed he had even existed. He had long been erased from public consciousness.

In all probability his burial was left to the discretion of a grave-digger who worked at night so as not to disturb everyday life and trade around Stortorget; a callous individual who could just drop the circumnavigator into the anonymity of the Common Grave without even uttering his name. No-one knows in whose presence it was done. Nowadays a passageway runs there between the church and the former stock exchange. An invoice was raised for seven *riksdaler* for the shroud, a single toll of the bell and the opening of the grave.

Just over ten years later the Common Grave was closed down for ever. The anonymous bones were conveyed to the still fairly new Northern Cemetery in Solna Forest out at Haga. They were re-interred in the Southern Pit, together with skeletons from the pre-Reformation period, which came to light during building work on Riddarholmen, as well as many of the three thousand seven hundred victims of the 1834 cholera epidemic.

The Southern Pit was near the boundary fence of the Karolinska Hospital. It was covered almost immediately by the huge Wetterstedt Chapel and the gravestones of Ulrik Winberg and Jeuns Peter Hemberg, tradesmen from Ystad, both cholera victims.

A private member's bill put before parliament in 1843 proposing a monument to the nameless dead was never adopted.

POSTSCRIPT

The Author's Path to Sparrman

The following two affidavits are in my possession:

Miss Jeanette Sparrman, living in Stockholm in 1886, informed me, George Valdau, that her father's uncle, Professor Anders Sparrman, who participated in Cook's expedition of 1772–5, took this oak chest with him on all his travels. She was angry with Olof Ljungstedt for selling this memento of her ancestor. According to the Register of Deaths of the city of Stockholm for 1820 this chest was listed among the goods and chattels left by Professor A. Sparrman.

The undersigned declares herewith that the oak chest purchased in February 1886 by Mr Knut Knutson in Mbanga on Cameroon Mountain from Mr O. Ljungstedt was stated to have been the property of Professor A. Sparrman and to have accompanied him on his travels, and to have been acquired by Mr Ljungstedt from his paternal aunt Mrs Carolina Sparrman, née Ljungstedt. The said chest, which has decorative metalwork and hinges with two oblong slots, is still today in the possession of Mr Knutson, as is attested herewith.

Stockholm, 2nd July 1907
Georg Valdau (resident in Mbanga, Cameroon)
Mr Valdau's signature witnessed by B. Eriksson,
H. Andersson.

How I, Knut Knutson, became the owner of the chest: In 1886 a young Swede, Olof Ljungstedt, arrived in Cameroon on the west coast of Africa, where I was living in Mbanga as a collector and trader with the natives . . . [*page missing*] . . . Professor Anders Sparrman took the chest with him on Cook's voyage of 1772–5. He joined the expedition in Cape Town and went on board the ship *Resolution* with Cook on 22.11.1772. His nephew, the surgeon Nils G. Sparrman of Gävle (1776–1829), was survived by his wife from his second marriage, Christina Sparrman (1782–1864), and her son Johan A. Sparrman (1810–81), who spent his last years in Gävle. His wife, Carolina Sparrman, née Ljungstedt (1825–85), gave the chest to her nephew Olof Ljungstedt, who sold it in February 1886 to the undersigned Knut Knutson, born 1857, merchant, of Stockholm.

The chest is thought to have served earlier as a parish chest for the collection of silver and copper coins. I believe Professor Sparrman's grandfather, a clergyman, to have been one of its first owners and probably to have bought the chest from the church of which he was vicar. It would seem to date from *c.* 1570–1610.

Knut W. Knutson.

My own story begins and ends with Anders Sparrman's seaman's chest. Its solid oak planks have withstood both termites and tempest. It probably stood in Biskopskulla Church in the county of Roslagen, where Anders Sparrman's grandfather was rector. When his grandson was about to go to China, he was given the chest to keep his finds in, and it accompanied him to South Africa and around the world with Captain Cook. Sparrman may have lined it with oiled cloth, of which there appear to be traces. It housed waxwings and birds of paradise, sloths and flying squirrels, elephants' tusks and whales' teeth.

Anders Sparrman has been part of my life for a very long time. On my wall I have drawings from South Africa, which have come loose from his travel journals. A great black woodpecker from his *Ornithology of Sweden* hangs in my dining room. Of Linnaeus' more notable disciples, Sparrman is the one surrounded by the most question marks. He is outside the frame for both travellers and scientists.

Captain Cook has been with me even longer. As a ten-year-old I ordered O. H. Dumrath's *Jordens erövring* (Conquest of the Earth) by mail order at five *kronor* a volume. Then I read an abridged edition of Cook's logbooks, after which I went to the library for the account of the whole voyage, translated into Swedish by Samuel Ödmann.

In the very first novel I wrote, *Ett gammalt skuggspel* (An Old Shadow Play), Cook's voyages gave me my basic structure. The young protagonist seeks peace and quiet one summer to concentrate on writing his notes about Captain Cook. The mariner was an exemplary model: upright, objective, incorruptible. Compared to Stanley, Speke, Burton – those commercial travellers in racism and brutal servants of social Darwinism – he was unprejudiced and represented no master race. But his arrival had meant the beginning of the end for the culture of the South Seas, as he knew and lamented.

Other sailors of the South Seas have become more popular – from Stevenson and Gauguin to Thor Heyerdahl – because they dreamed of happy islands where old age is not a burden, desire does not fade and where Nature rewards man not for his labour but merely for his existence. It is a dream in which the alienated creatures of the industrial age probe for their roots deep in the Bronze Age of the soul. Captain Cook never set out on that particular voyage of discovery. His compass was more securely fastened than that.

In the background were fleeting glimpses of Cook's botanist and zoologist, Anders Sparrman. I had come across him in the house of Bertil Knutson at 29 Norrtullsgatan in Stockholm, and had been shown the chest and the two affidavits. In 1977 I followed in the tracks of Bertil's much adored father Knut Wilhelm Knutson from village to village on Cameroon Mountain and reported back to Bertil, who, childless himself, adopted me as his father's African heir. Knut Knutson came to provide the documentary basis for my novel on Cameroon, *Bergets källa* (The Mountain Spring). I had also hunted for traces of Anders Sparrman in Cape Province, and of Johan Fredrik Victorin, a consumptive zoologist, who traversed the same region eighty years later.

Bertil Knutson had constructed a series of prefabricated houses on Lidingö in Stockholm, and in his spare time was a magician, much in demand, which was hard to believe of such a dapper elderly man. He kept his magic wand within reach, but had no need to wave it; there was enough magic for me at Norrtullsgatan in any case.

I remember evenings when Bertil Knutson read aloud from his father's manuscript about the German Governor of Cameroon, Jesko von Puttkamer. Sparrman's chest stood in one corner of the dining room. Bertil lifted the lid, and there lay the works of the Linnaeus apostles: Thunberg, Hasselquist, Kalm, and the Germans Schweinfurth and Nachtigal.

That chest was for me a real person, who had not yet started to talk. It represented both cruel imperialist projects and romantic boyhood notions of a different life. It contained notebooks, sections of journals, business contracts, most of it in disorder and its yellowing ink not easy to read. The magazine *Kolonie und Heimat*, published in Berlin before the First World War, was also there. And with a photograph of Knut Wilhelm Knutson in boots and unstarched linen shirt was this bill of sale:

We the undersigned acknowledge that in accordance with the wishes of the inhabitants of Mbanga we have sold the entire

Mbanga district to Mr Knutson and Mr Valdau, who from today are the legal owners and masters of the said land. The full payment was as stated here: six pieces of cloth of 245 fathoms; three tablecloths; three umbrellas; five pairs of boots.

The chieftains' marks were witnessed by John Gustafsson. The title applied to untilled land; cultivated soil belonged to the villages as before. It was the largest Swedish possession in Africa.

On the Calabar coast Knut Wilhelm Knutson discovered one of Sparrman's descendants, Olof Ljungstedt, a trader, whom he found weak and impoverished – he had sold or bartered all his merchandise and had been unable to dispose of the useless items he had received in exchange. In the equatorial heat of Africa he was shivering with a bout of malaria, and spoke in a low voice, which Knutson thought seemed to indicate his disbelief that anyone would want to listen to him. He had lugged the chest from Dakar in Senegal to Port Harcourt and Victoria, past Sierra Leone and Liberia, a hundred years after Sparrman; a hundred years before me. He now wished to part with it, and Knutson bought it.

I remember at Norrtullsgatan a sharp-toothed pine marten on the sideboard in the dining room, a shelf of Baedecker's chunky red travel guides, a photograph of the steamship *Alice Woermann* from Hamburg on the wall. An expanded clothes cupboard was reminiscent of a century-old left-luggage office. The cast-iron grate of the fireplace wheezed as we sat drinking tea and cherry brandy over a tablecloth that Bertil's mother had hemmed with swirls of runes and dragon ships; its creases from the mangle threatened to tip over our glasses. The light indoors had a faded sepia tint, like an antique map.

That apartment was a keyhole through to an Africa which no longer existed. Within its high double doors with their moiré glass I felt I was re-experiencing something of my childhood as it had been at my grandfather's. It still had a slightly uncanny exoticism alien to Stockholm. And the objects there were so numerous that they could well have been stowed on board a ship to meet every need for a lengthy voyage.

Bertil Knutson told me how his father used to gather a little amateur natural history society together to discuss some object, preferably African. After entertainment by a flautist, and herrings au gratin with beer and Norrland aquavit, they would open the chest and ponder Sparrman's fate, while their host described how this historic storage box had come into his hands.

There was a respectful understanding between Bertil and me. He went off to bed, but told me to stay as long as I wanted. He put out some soda water. I sat in a straight-backed armchair covered with wavy green upholstery. Outside, the street lamps were lit, as were a couple of windows opposite. The dusk was flinching back, as if to avoid the light. The walls creaked like a house in the country, sounding like footsteps and voices in the distance, and there was a smell of African spices, sharp and heavy.

With an almost reluctant feeling of veneration I peered down into the chest, inhaling the smell of dry paper and dust, and was launched on a journey which might very well last a lifetime. So much that was unexpressed hovered around that chest. I was holding sheets of Lessebo paper covered in an old-fashioned elegant ink script. They merged together for me: Bertil, who was about eighty-five, and his idolized father Knut Wilhelm, who had died in this very apartment almost half a century before. And everything his father had left – furniture, china, books and letters – was untouched, as if he had just popped out for a moment to the shop round the corner.

Shortly before Bertil Knutson died, I inherited Sparrman's chest, with all its maps, photographs, manuscripts, documents on the German administration of Cameroon, complaints that Knutson's collections were not being properly cared for by museums in Vänersborg and Gothenburg – just as hundreds of the items Sparrman had brought back were still in their boxes in the cellars of the Ethnographical Museum in Stockholm until well into the

1960s. During his years in the village of Mbanga, Knutson had locked away in the chest title deeds, court proceedings and survey maps as well as the drafts of memoirs he had written on Cameroon Mountain, only excerpts of which were ever published. Captain Cook must have looked down into that very same chest.

When I brought the oak chest home in the late 1980s and emptied out all the documents, frayed pocket diaries and almost indecipherable pencil notes, it still didn't seem totally empty. Over the years I felt it was signalling an appeal or squeaking out a challenge from its lock: Break Sparrman's silence and shed some light on his obscure life! Decode the messages he wove into his matter-of-fact accounts!

Where did his sympathy for the oppressed come from, so unusual among his contemporary natural scientists and possibly a reason for the scientific world turning its back on him? Older Linnaeans sneered at this most philosophical and least robust of the disciples, and thought his imprecise words and personal feelings were affectations, but such was the new, more sentimental, era to which Sparrman belonged. His narrative is free of formality, it is boyish and playful, with an existential undertone of why and wherefore.

And although for a century to come Sparrman depicted South Africa's animal kingdom more comprehensively than anyone else, there are only two portraits of him, one full-face, one in profile.

F. Hubert's copperplate engraving after M. Mollard's painting is in a splendid illustrated volume of living persons of distinction printed in Paris in 1787. He is wearing a plain coat with a small stand-up collar, a shirt with a frill or kerchief tucked into a partially unbuttoned waistcoat, a thin tie-wig which does not cover his high forehead. He has heavy eyelids, a prominent nose and unusually full lips. His jutting chin is divided by a tiny cleft.

Niclas Lafrensen the Younger's miniature was done for Sparrman's friend Erik Edholm around 1800. It is held in the Academy of Sciences and shows Sparrman in profile. He is wear-

ing a velvet coat with high turned-down collar and revers, match-
ing buttons and again a scholar's tie-wig.

Since my narrative encompasses everything that can be docu-
mented in Anders Sparrman's life, another event should be
mentioned which, like the existence of Lotta, does not appear in
reference works or other accounts.

Anders was quite advanced in years by the standards of the time
when Lotta, almost thirty years his junior, gave birth at the
General Maternity Hospital to a daughter who was at first named
Fries, since her parents were not married. But after Anders
acknowledged her in writing as his daughter and his only child, she
was called Carolina Charlotta Sparrman.

Little is known of her life. What I have been able to ascertain is
what was registered after Anders' death. When Lotta died in 1825,
the daughter inherited the estate 'after a decent burial had been
provided for'. She was married in the Cathedral on the 7th
December 1826 to a goldsmith's apprentice, Sven Granander, who
was subsequently admitted to the guild as a goldsmith. He was
born in Lidköping, had an excellent knowledge of the scriptures,
was honest and decent – that much can be gleaned from the banns.
He died in 1850 in the parish of Adolf Fredrik's Church. His heirs
were his widow and Anders Granander, Anders Sparrman's only
grandchild. Carolina continued to live at 38 Holländergatan, without any pension, and moved in 1864 to a widows' home, where she
died in 1872.

I could have invented something of her life. She may have been
luminously beautiful, the child Anders had never expected to
have. He may not have been the best person to have charge of the
little girl's upbringing. Perhaps she even spent lengthy periods
breathing the country air at the house of her uncle Nils, rector at
Skånela, with his children and two unmarried sisters.

Such things must remain more speculative than everything else
that has been narrated here of Anders Sparrman's career. So I have
left her, still very young, at the end of Anders' life. But of course

she too has a story that can be teased out of the imagination and may perhaps find a pen in its own time.

Anders Sparrman's life is full of lacunae, unreliable witnesses and overgrown inscriptions as hard to interpret as old gravestones. I visited the churches in Tensta and Lena to look for traces of his childhood in the rectory. I went to the municipal archives in Stockholm and the Academy of Sciences, and tried to find the paupers' grave where he was interred.

No-one seems to have known anything about his many years with his housekeeper, their daughter, or the end of his life. The new facts I found in the archives are the source of my assumptions, which – I like to think – have fitted like a shell around a kernel of truth.

I have picked up shards and fragments and joined them together with various kinds of glue. Faces have emerged from the mist, none of them complete, none wholly visible. I thought I heard Anders Sparrman in the next room: I put my ear to the wall and heard voices. But I didn't dare check whether the door between the rooms, Knutson's and Sparrman's, was locked.